I'll Never Go Away
Vol. 2

Edited by

Lyle Perez-Tinics &
Charlotte Emma Gledson

Rainstorm Press
PO BOX 391038
Anza, Ca 92539
www.RainstormPress.com

ISBN 10 – 1-937758-389
ISBN 13 – 978-1-937758-38-7

Interior book design by –
The Mad Formatter
www.TheMadFormatter.com

Cover Design by Eloise J. Knapp

Table of Contents

I'LL NEVER GO AWAY VOL. 2

DEAD MEMORIES
WILLIAM COOK

1

I had a dream on the anniversary of her death. In the dream, I heard her unmistakeable voice calling me, then I saw her and she was so real I could almost touch her again. Everything about her hit me deep in the chest, I sat bolt upright in our big empty bed. My breath gasped, sweat beaded itself on my cold skin. Awake now, I could still hear her voice in the dark. I rationalised there were only two possible reasons why I could hear such a thing. I was either hallucinating, or what I heard and saw was her ghost, whispering in my ear. Then silence returned and she was gone again.

I lay down and listened, my breath held in my chest, afraid to break the silence. The dawn light bled through the cracks in the blind as I strained my ears, listening. Listening for her sweet voice, playing her words over repeatedly in my weary mind—

'There's no turning back.

There's no turning back now.'

I longed for her touch, the feel of her soft cold skin, her beautiful words carried on her sweet breath. The memories came flooding back—projections of my need. As I began to drift back into sleep, I thought of the way she played me with her brown eyes, teasing me, imparting so much desire ...

The radio-alarm went off, waking me violently. I checked the time and acknowledged the precious two hours of sleep I just had, turned the screeching alarm off and got out of bed. I passed her photo in the hall on the way to the bathroom. It was the only photo I had on display: an enlarged black and white shot of her sitting on a beach in a lotus position, gazing mystically into the sun, long black hair out behind her in the breeze, framed by a silver expanse of ocean in the background. All the other photographs were in the bottom of a bedroom drawer. Some memories were just too painful to look at in such quantity.

I went to work, exhausted. Throughout the day, I thought about the morning's events. Waking up with her pristine voice whispering in my ear from behind, thinking she was beside me in bed—it was so real. *Must be stress*, I reasoned with myself. *Loneliness does strange things to a man's mind.*

Ghosts don't exist. Do they?

The day finished quickly and I gladly closed the office door and loosened my tie with a yawn. Outside, the day had turned to night. On the way home I heard a song she used to love on the car radio. I passed the streetlight down the side road where we kissed beneath for the first time. I stopped at the liquor store before turning into my street and our empty house.

2

The voice came again, the same words. Her voice seemed closer than before; I could

7

almost feel the skin of her soft lips against my ear. I woke with expectation but she wasn't there, just the dim light cast across the sheets and a hangover from hell, twisting its evil blade between my tired eyes.

As the days fell into each other, her disembodied voice permeated my senses, seeming to talk louder until her whispers became shouts. The same words—*'There's no turning back now.'* *There's no turning back* adding emphasized vignettes that began to take on an ominous air—*'There's no turning back ... NOW. There's no turning back, for YOU.'*

My nerves dissolved. My mind began tumbling over itself, trying to bridge the gap between reason and a slow-turning madness.

The voice remained unmistakeably hers, the intonation painfully real. Her name was, *is*, Alicia. We had been together for seven years before she left. We had a passionate relationship to say the least. A veritable love and hate fest, with more making up and breaking up than we both needed. We had met at the office and soon fell for each other. A drunken bout of knee-trembling sex, against a photocopier in the stationary room after a work party, heralded the official beginning of our tumultuous relationship.

I didn't want to think about the inevitable disintegration of our passionate affair, but it eventually happened and that was that. As Alicia said, there was no turning back now. We were young and had aged well together. Into our fifth year, we even started talking about marriage and children and then she got a new office manager. I heard the talk amongst my colleagues. At first, I thought it was mere gossip, as office talk usually is. Then I saw his eyes undress her as he sauntered past her desk. A coy look as she pretended to shuffle papers, her eyes caught in his swagger.

Alicia started working late. I asked around discreetly and no one else knew of any overtime available. Then she 'transferred' to another floor, "promoted" as she put it. The evenings became a waiting game. I tried to impress with the usual chattels of love—the flowers, gourmet meals, expensive perfume. In short, I tried to purchase her affection as I had exhausted all other means of reconciliation. When Alicia did arrive home, she was always freshly showered and well mannered, courteous almost. A peck on the cheek that made Grandmother's kisses seem like incestuous advances. Her back turned toward me perpetually. A 'not tonight' was the standard response to my romantic overtures, every night.

Good old Mr Forgiving tried to get on with things, forget her indiscretion and lies and pretend that she still loved me. I knew she didn't love me at all—not even a fraction of desire was left in her cold heart. I started to think things—what could I do, how could I get her back? The migraines kicked in and I started to drink heavily. It seemed to block reality out, for a while, and then Alicia didn't come home one night. But that was over a year ago; that was then, this is now.

3

Things started slipping. I called in sick three times in one week. When she spoke in my ear now, it was nearly a scream. In those frenetic waking hours, I started 'feeling' the words. After two goddamn weeks of visual and auditory apparitions, I started feeling *her*. I felt her tucked against me at night, relishing each second, stuck between the ecstasy of the moment and agony of the inevitable realization that Alicia wasn't actually there. Her full tanned breasts against my back, soft lips brushing my shoulder, soft hands so soft like silk caressing, supplicating my disbelief. Then I noticed her photo—I can't explain it, but she seemed to move within, animated, changing pose each morning. One day Alicia would be staring at the sun, black and white. Next, a different tilt of the head, her hand rested on her leg just so ... and then she left the picture, leaving behind an empty landscape.

I began to find dark coils of her hair on the pillow next to me, a fleeting glimpse of a smooth-brown shoulder out of the corner of my eye. I would see a shadow of a person standing by the bed or in the living room and I knew Alicia was here with me at that time. Then she'd fade away again until the anticipation drove me delirious. I lost my mind, my heart pumped desire and love to every cell. Whatever she was, ghost or hallucination, I hungered for each second—a panacea for the sad soul. If her memory was just an indentation in the bed where she slept, I could've lived with her this way if it weren't my own words—*'There is no turning back for her NOW'* screaming in my brain, almost painfully so.

I tried to shut it all out, to no avail. The migraines increased, nausea, bursts of white spots before my black-ringed eyes. I couldn't shave; the sound of the razor sent blasts of pain ripping through my skin and shattered nerves to my brain. I took a month's leave from the office—they gladly gave it to me—"You need a break, Harry. You've been working too hard lately. Rest up. Take a break. Come back when you're better, okay?"

I'd like to kill those patronizing bastards, just walk in one day in Gucci suit and tie, axe in hand. Walk into the office—"Good morning Miss Secretary, Mr Boss ... I've come to kill you!" Chop chop chop chop chop ...

"*My love, my love. There's no turning back for us now*" Alicia whispered, standing next to me completely naked in the cold bathroom, caught midstream as I emptied my bladder. Her burning eyes glowing hypnotically. Her hair coiling like twisting black snakes, framing her beautiful deathly countenance. I tried to touch her. She reached into me, cupping my pulsing heart in her frigid hand. I could feel it. She withdrew and walked into the bedroom. I followed. She wasn't there ...

I couldn't eat anymore, my appetite was non-existent. I looked in the mirror: my gaunt pale unshaven face stared back at me forlornly—eyes blackened, pupils dilated, trembling ... my heart quivered delicately under my ribcage, then missed ... a beat. It felt like my heart was frozen. I felt sick to my stomach. Where was Alicia? I decided that it was the sleeping that did it, conjured her from the dark. Maybe I was reciting a spell in my dreams, lodged deep in my subconscious mind, calling her forth every morning. Invoking the muse at every breath, so to speak. I was fucked, my mind had finally imploded.

4

It had taken exactly one year and twenty-one days after our break-up, or should I say her 'disappearance,' before I realized I could not go on without her any longer. I mean Alicia was back with me all the time, all day and night now— naked, following me around the house, hovering above me on the ceiling—whispering to me indescribable things, obscenities of the vilest nature. Alicia started to taunt me relentlessly, yet my love grew stronger as if with a will of its own. Then she started to slap me—ferocious backhanders that rattled my teeth and left droplets of nose blood on the white walls. Half of me wanted to leave, just run as far away as I could. Pack the car and put a match to the godforsaken house as I escaped, but the other half—the stronger half, wanted to stay—couldn't leave. Besides I knew if I tried to escape, I'd look into that rear-view mirror and those dead black eyes would be boring into my soul, her white forearm draped around my neck, her blue lips mouthing the words, rotten tongue lolling from her mouth— *"There's no turning back now ..."*

That day I ordered in two litre bottles of gin— I'd discovered booze could block her out for a while. I began to drink sitting with my back against the bedroom wall, watching as she undulated like a snake on the yellow duvet on the bed. Her once tanned now white body arched, her full breasts swelling with her movements, her hand pressed deep between her thighs—pink tongue darting across her full lips. Moaning, I gulped the gin— ten quick mouthfuls, my jaw clenched and then it was easy. Half a bottle, Alicia began to fade out like bad TV reception. Each drink twitched, erased another part of her lithe form—I couldn't take any more. I knew I had to rid myself of her finally. *Get rid of everything,* I thought, as I emptied the minimal contents of my gut onto the bedroom carpet, before collapsing in a drunken stupor next to the puddle of rancid bile.

5

I stumbled to my drunken feet, pulling drawers out, cupboards open, throwing photographs, letters, clothes, newspaper clippings, onto the floor. I looked over my shoulder. Her now bloodied head and torso moved on the bed. Her arms, legs, pelvis— gone. I stared at what was left of her, tears involuntarily spilling down my face. Her eyes were glazed, wispy hair matted, writhing across her face like black worms, her skin was peeling—she was visibly putrefying. Alicia mouthed her silent words again—*"There's no turning back."* My head spun. I threw everything in the bathtub, all the photographs, letters, clothes, newspaper clippings, all the detritus from our defunct relationship. I set the fire and watched the flames dance, black smoke filling the small bathroom. I opened the window and watched the dark plumes of smoke get sucked out into the atmosphere.

I shuffled down the hallway past her photo, now completely metamorphosed from the original. Alicia had returned to the picture and was now staring out at me from the frame, arms outstretched like Christ. Her blank eyes, pleading. The sun behind her a ball of blazing fire. Her wild hair danced blackly around her gaunt white face. I took the photo and threw it through the bathroom door into the fire with the other memories. I'm sure I heard her scream then, but it wasn't a scream of pain—rather a triumphant yell of defiance. I sat down on the toilet next to the burning bathtub and put my head in my hands as the fire started climbing from the bathtub.

Flames ran up the plastic shower curtain, dropping molten lumps of fire like napalm on the linoleum. Flames licked the walls as black smoke billowed and swirled as I saw her shape solidify and morph from the tendrils of smoke. I looked up and the smoke had melded together, transforming the ghostly mass into the unmistakeable shape of Alicia. Snake-like coils of hair twisted and swirled in the smoke, reaching for my gasping throat. Long black fingers danced in my eyes, in my ears, forcing my mouth open in wrenching breaths, reaching deep into my burning lungs. My heart felt like cracking ice trapped between my heaving ribcage. I collapsed to the floor as the flames licked my clothes. The fire burned red and blue but no heat now—just intense cold—so cold. I shivered, inhaling my last breath of her love—the dark swaying shape of Alicia stood over me. I could hear her words still hissing in the black smoke, echoing in my dying thoughts—*"There's no turning back now. There's no turning back …"*

BREAKING IN TWO
TRACY L. LYALL

The night crashes in—solemn, pervasive, bearing fruit; hovering clouds and a quivering moon. Valentine's candy melts in its heart box on the dashboard of the car, fuzzy steering wheel cover and baby zombie dangling from a noose down the rear view mirror; crinkled tan seats cracking from the blazing heat.

These horrid summer days. Darkness begins to wander down dirty bayous, while left over broken toys float in the kiddy pool to the side of the duplex. The sun slips down easy, no respect, no regard—the pavement still steaming, burning the soles of bare feet. Toads croak in puddled back alleys. It's time for the water sprinklers, the slip-n-slides, water guns, ice tea, and depression. Sex and death. What do you do when it's too hot to move, 100 degree summer, and so hot that Prophylactics melt in your pockets? They just screw around here. Complain and moan. Give up, drink, shoot animals, get high and have sex. Every creature on the face of the planet can do it—every mammal, rodent, insect and slippery slimy thing crumpled up beneath tug boats on the river.

She still loves Reed even though he broke up with her on Valentine's Day. Now, the engine of the vehicle is cooling down, dripping oil and water into tiny pools on the driveway. A crack in the headlight. The busy city streets grow quiet, hour by hour; one by one they drift off the highway and into their garages, their one way street parking spaces. Empty bellies waiting to microwave their TV dinner or awaiting their wives home cooked meal. Maybe their children greet them at the door or maybe they crack the metal top of a beer can and mourn the death of the unborn child their ex-cokehead girlfriend refused to have. Or their kids are far away from their urges to continue crimes and diseases which plagued their lineage for decades. No. No. Not her. Not tonight, or ever. The red shades are slightly drawn; the TV mute and glowing along the walls. Dogs begin to bark behind their chain-link cages as the nocturnal birds and bats begin to flutter beneath the streetlamps. She leans back on the couch, kicking her feet up on the coffee table, yanking open a bag of popcorn. It crunches, buttery melt in her mouth, she stares out the front window.

A young woman in black, strolls through the side alley alongside her tattooed and ruggedly-handsome boyfriend. They carry coffee mugs, their keys jingle and clank against the cups; holding hands while staring into each other's eyes. A neighborhood kid throws a rock at them, bouncing off of her window and hitting him in the back of the neck.

She gets up, dropping popcorn to the floor, and unlocks the window. Then, she unlocks the one next to it and both in the dining room. The mantle of the ash-ridden fireplace, now dead, harbors the weight of a multitude of melting candles. This faux alter she resurrects in honor of the spirits. Some spirits. Some are sicker than others. She tunes them out: people riding by on their bikes, scooters, skateboards, in museums, on the train—she'd given up headphones years ago.

On occasion, she allows people in, scheduled, appointment only, specific times on specific days. She checks her book. Today, she's scheduled to interact with the grocery clerk as she goes for her weekly food supply, and Dan, the gas station attendant.

Her cat knocks a metal can of cat food off the kitchen counter. Its black fur blends with the marble floor. The doorbell rings and she hears someone cleaning their feet on her door-mat. Blinds up; green glass bubble lamps illuminating the dense area. The darkness floods in like a fog as she opens the door to this stranger peering into her mailbox. Always peering into something, her windows, her car, gawking from down the street.

"Can I help you?"

"I live a few apartments down ... I know this is a bit odd but can I borrow a cup of sugar?" The muscles beneath his T-shirt and on his forearm bulge. His slender and aged face melts into a tightly formed body; the skin clean with an olive complexion.

"How much sugar do you need?" She stares into his dark eyes, secretive and disturbing.

"Just a cup...thank you so much." He hands her the cup, stepping back to light a cigarette.

The rank smell of tobacco smoke permeates the living room. Her heart races as she returns, wishing she could throw the cup at him. He notices her edginess, steps back, into the chewy grass.

Maybe he's the internet porn type, the cheat on your girlfriend with the bar whore type.

She should be a bar whore, the last-call call girl, the one left when the lights go down, run out to the curb; still hoping the drunkest one would choose her. *Evil jerk.* He's one of those men who could leave with more than one Rainbow Brite. Flash some bicep on the table, clink his glass about, wink, throw down a couple of twenties as the women watch him; the suave finance broker type. *The love.*

"Thanks again." He nods to her, walking back into the void, along the sidewalk.

She wishes it was college fundraiser night and there was a beat up old car waiting to be smashed with a sledgehammer for $2. Smash in a window, a rear-view, side fender; stand on the hood in a mini-skirt with her pale white girl legs, pounding away. He hadn't come over for the sugar anyway. Creep. Maybe she should unlock the doors. She peers out into the night, down the sidewalk, the rustle of leaves, crispy, and silent. Everyone's tucking themselves in, locking doors, turning down lamps, whispering to children and wives beneath sheets. She knew the family type were setting alarm clocks while the single and lonely were dressing to impress at nightclubs or coffee-shops.

Her windows unlocked, doors unlocked, candles glowing on the mantle, cats purring on the sofa, soda fizzing in the cup at her side. Dark. Quiet. She knows, and waits; pretends to fall asleep on the sofa, nightgown ruffling up on her thighs. She fumbles beneath the cushions, making sure ... yes, everything secure, in place.

An hour of daydreaming and waiting. After some time she could hear the doorknob click, an inaudible rattle as someone opens her back door. The rubber soles of the shoes squish on the linoleum, one, two, three seconds before they touch the carpet. His breath is raspy, heaving, and she is certain that he has come for her. Closer, his shoes pad along the carpet, closer. He is soon by her side, his hand before her mouth. He covers it as she pretends to startle. Those drama classes in high school have paid off; she's the victim, cast in the role by her own directing fate, her wishes to ...

He hovers over, his dark green eyes boil with anticipation, and he is lifting her skirt, his hand along her thigh. Play along, she reminds the victim, just a few seconds longer, trust me. A struggle attempt, a fake groan and scream; damn she is good, best supporting actress of the year. His hands fumble with her smooth breasts; he somehow manages to suppress her, hold his hand over her mouth, grope, and assume an awkward yet sexual stance upon her body. He is aroused and anxious, the more she struggles, the more excited he becomes. Yes, she has found this strange man's weakness and wonders how much time she should give him.

She closes her eyes, clock ticking—now. Now. She manages to wriggle her hand beneath the cushion, pulls out the gun and places it on his forehead. Frozen. Her little deer caught in the headlights, what a shame. How amazing he is, doing exactly what she expected him to do. Creep. Same body type, same eye color, same style, only Reed would have blown it as he always did. Ruining Valentine's, Christmas, her birthday—always forgetting until the last minute and then picking up a gift or card on the way home. She'd thought about poisoning his food, finding out where he lived now and getting revenge. But, hell, this creep will do. God, he even *smelt* like Reed. She licks the sweat off her lip that drips from his brow; tastes like Reed, grinds his body into hers like Reed. He probably even made love selfishly like him, rolls over when he's done, saying "good night sweetie" as if she is the only one in the world to endure his obnoxious manhandling and in some sadistic way, enjoys it.

She reaches beneath the cushion, yanks out a stun-gun and paralyzes him long enough to tie him to a chair and gag him with a dirty sock from the floor. "Well, Reed, I got you a birthday present." She electrocutes him again with the stun-gun. After locking the house again, she returns to the living room where she flicks on the TV to play Mister Rogers' Neighborhood—one hundred and sixty-eight hours' worth. He would be here awhile. 'It's a beautiful day in the neighborhood, a beautiful day for a neighbor.'

Creeps.

DANNY IN THE DARK
TIM REYNOLDS

Danny Angles kept tight to the wall, tucked in behind the dumpster, out of sight of the man he hunted. Milton Wayne Tennyson's killing spree was in its third week and this was the closest Danny had been to putting a stop to the psycho's madness. Ten victims in twenty-one days, each and every one with their throats cut and their entrails pooled in their laps. Each and every one a middle-aged, middle-management, white male just shy of six feet in height—the spitting image of Tennyson's own abusive father.

Two nights ago, Danny got a text tip that Tennyson was on the roof of the Metropolitan Museum. He wasted five minutes trying to reach his wife, Lucy, but ended up having to drop Kayley and Travis at his mother's place and speed downtown to the museum. He arrived three minutes late, finding accountant Scooter Dymbroski staring into the night, his life-blood soaking his cheap suit. Tennyson had once again vanished into the night.

Tonight, Danny was in the lead, waiting for Tennyson at the only place he could be, based both on Danny's profile of Tennyson as well as on the computer-printed note tucked neatly in Scooter's breast pocket daring the authorities to 'observe' Tennyson's 'Twofer Tuesday Special Serial Surprise'. Dressed in black from head to toe, Danny waited in the shadows behind the University Observatory on the main campus. He gripped his loaded, night-scope-equipped crossbow tightly, and waited. The weapon was deadly up to thirty yards and nearly silent. For hunting a hunter, it was perfect.

A nearby boot-scuff froze Danny in place. He held his breath, heard a second scrape on gravel and flicked off the crossbow's safety. He let the breath out slowly and watched as the shadow at the end of the alley shifted. Milton Wayne Tennyson, 26, stepped into the pale light cast by the dusty street lamp. Danny raised the crossbow to his shoulder and regarded his prey through the scope, confirming his target. The visual ID would have been enough for the ex-cop to act on, but then butcher spoke and dispelled any lingering doubts Danny may have had.

"Hi. Good evening, folks. Milton Wayne Tennyson here with the latest—".

Danny shot Tennyson in the throat and the alley behind the observatory was suddenly silent again, or nearly so. Tennyson gurgled and thrashed about while his executioner expertly dismantled the crossbow, hung it under his long coat and slipped off into the cool night.

Four miles away, in the SW-ABS broadcast studios, pandemonium broke out.

* * *

"Go to commercial, NOW!! What the hell just happened, people?! One second I've got Tennyson live, giving us the lead-in to tonight's double killing and the next I'm at ground level, looking down at the observatory's Emergency Exit and no audio from the nutball! I've got three-hundred-million fat, ugly, and stupid viewers hanging on the edge of their damned Barcaloungers, waiting for tonight's twofer!" Ralph Weinberg threw his headset at his feet and jumped on it.

"Ralph! Check out 3. I've captured the alley security cam." Franco pointed up at the third monitor from the left.

All six sets of eyes in the control room locked onto Monitor 3 where a wide, overhead shot showed Tennyson's body on its back, in a spreading pool of blood.

"You must be kidding me! Please tell me his Kill-Cam recorded this!"

"Rewinding now!" Franco had Tennyson's footage playing in reverse on Monitor 2. Monitor 1 still showed the live net-feed of the Emergency Exit from the Kill-Cam, while Monitor 4 was playing the string of dead-air-covering commercials for rolling papers, the new Chevy Cyanide, and Sony's new Watch-Em InvisiCam digital camera. "Got it!"

The image on Monitor 2 froze, and then started forward again. Ralph and his team stared with rabid interest as Tennyson approached the back entrance of the Observatory. He walked with purpose and confidence, but he still took the time to look around at all the shadows, to check over his shoulder before stepping into the light at the end of the alley. Tennyson unclipped the miniature camera from his glasses and pointed it back at his own face. "It's Showtime!"

"Why do they all do that? It's such a goddamned cliché." He complained, but Ralph didn't take his eyes off of 2. Tennyson clipped the camera back onto his glasses and stepped fully into the light. The joy in his voice was obvious as he revelled in the attention he was getting from his personal little reality show. Then there was a soft, meaty, thud, and Tennyson went down, face up. He didn't die immediately and his gagging, gurgling, bubbling expiration seemed to go on forever. His death rattle shook the control room and when he finally sagged into death, his position shifted slightly and the SW-ABS crew could now plainly see the feathered end of an arrow of some type. Ralph shattered the silence.

"Get Connie out of make-up and behind her desk on set, now!" He couldn't help but stare at Monitor 2 and the wreckage that had been the best ratings machine *ever*. A door slammed behind him as someone rushed off to find Connie and get her ready to do her colour commentary half an hour early. "Franco, you've got ten minutes to get me a highlight reel of Tennyson's ten kills. I want slow-mo gore *everywhere*. I want sound effects at double-volume and canned applause overlaying each kill. I want this sick bastard to be made out as a hero." He finally tore himself away from the monitors and searched the room to see who was left. He settled on Raj, over in the corner.

"Raj-man! Get me the name of that freak in Northlake that said he could double Tennyson's kills in half the time and would do it all to an 1980s pop soundtrack. I want him ready to roll tomorrow night. I'll drive the broadcast gear out to him myself if I have to."

"Yes sir!" Raj grabbed his tablet and started scrolling through his messages.

Ralph spun around and fixed his glare on a broad-shouldered, fiery redhead still staring at the monitors. "Annie!" She turned slowly, her eyes taking a moment to focus. "Annie, where are we with 'Cheater, Cheater'?"

"It's almost over. The cheating spouse lasted four weeks without getting caught by her husband and the finale is tomorrow night. If she can keep him in the dark until 8pm tomorrow she gets the whole five million. I've got her in here for an interview tomorrow at noon. Like her affair, it'll be live, unedited, and Rotoscoped to alter the image and keep her identity a secret until the reveal tomorrow night."

"Perfect! Now cut me a new best-of-Cheater-Cheater-moments for the end of Connie's Tennyson wrap-up and go heavy on the sex. Even drop in a hint that after tomorrow the un-altered screwing segments will be online for the Gold Level network subscribers. Have Lupo do the voice-over for this one." Movement on the studio floor caught Ralph's attention and he turned to see stunning, nearly naked in her see-thru power-suit, Connie Nakamura drop into her chair behind her commentator's desk. Connie slipped on the earpiece someone handed her and licked her lips.

"Ready any time you are, Ralphy-baby."

"Fantastic, Conn! Now, this is how we're going to spin it..."

* * *

Danny let himself into his mother's house and curled up on the couch. He'd sent a quick text from the car to let her know he was on his way over but would let the kids sleep. He also sent Lucy a message to let her know where they were and that he'd have Kayley and Travis home in the morning in time to log-on and start school. He added a promise that he'd make sure they wore their masks and helmets the whole trip home and wouldn't eat anything at Grandma's until it had been checked and cleared by *his* new bug-meter, not the uncalibrated, three-year-old model his mother had stuffed in a kitchen drawer. No one would ever accuse Danny Angles of not protecting his children, even if it seemed a whole lot of over-the-top to him. You could slander or libel someone with impunity but if anyone, qualified or not, deemed his children unprotected, he was going to jail. As he said to Lucy just that morning, the world was seriously messed up.

Wrapped up in his grandmother's old quilt, he shivered as the last of the night's adrenalin sloughed off and drifted away into the dark. His mother's eight-foot-wide screen glowed softly on the wall, the fish tank screen-saver lulling him. It was a beautiful screen, Panasonic's best at the time, but he wasn't even tempted to turn it on and catch up on the crap that passed for entertainment these days. It was another bone of contention between him and Lucy. She wanted him to pay the extra three hundred a month for the full Voyeur Viewer Package with seven hundred live net-feeds, and he wanted to cancel everything but the kids' shows. He'd cancel those, too, but the Child Welfare Act made the 24/7 Kartoonz net-feed a constitutional right for the over-protected Generation Snowflake. At least technology prevented his children from being exposed to the crap their mother watched. If the screen's sensors detected a Child Chip-identified minor, it automatically blocked all commercials and changed the channel to Kidlette Kartoonz.

Danny was sure that the downward slide started with Big Brother and Survivor in the 1990s and kept going straight to hell until now the glassy-eyed masses got their kicks watching shit like Botched Medical Procedures, Most Creative Suicides, cartoonized cheating spouses, and, up until an hour ago, Milton Wayne Tennyson and his slaughter spree. It disgusted Danny, and he was in no way ashamed of his actions tonight. That psycho, Tennyson, had needed to be put down like the animal he was. Who cared that fifty percent of the advertising revenue from the show went to the victims' families? It was obscene and inhuman. He was proud that he was able to rid the world of a killer scum. It was like being a cop again, back before the layoffs. He fell asleep with a small smile creeping on to his usually grim face.

DANNY IN THE DARK

* * *

"So, Travis, are you going to log on and learn something neat-o today?"

"No thanks, Momasita. Today's Math Day and you know numbers make me itchy." Travis scratched the back of his neck to make his point.

"Hives, again? Oh my poor baby." Lucy moved a dirty plate so her ten-year-old son could put his feet up on the coffee table. "Do you want lotion? Or maybe some dessert? Whatever you want, Honey-bunch." A scream from the other room startled Lucy, though Travis didn't even flinch, as though he'd been expecting it.

"MOM! Travis tore the arms off all my dolls!" Six-year-old Kayley charged into the living room with an armless doll in each hand, furious. She held one out as evidence to her mother and threw the other at her brother's head. Her aim was good but his reflexes were better and the doll instead hit the table lamp behind Travis. The lamp teetered for a moment and then toppled over and crashed to the floor.

"Well, that's not good, kids. Travis, did you dismember your sister's dolls?"

"Yah. So?"

"Is there anything you want to say to Kayley, like an apology?"

"No."

"Okay. No problemo." Lucy turned to Kayley. "You broke my favourite lamp. It was a wedding present from Grandma. I think you should go to your room. What do you think?"

Kayley leaned around her mother to look at the wreckage of the lamp. "I think it's broken."

"Yes. Yes it is. Would you please get the broom and dustpan and we'll clean it up, before I go to my doctor's appointment."

"No, I want to watch Kidlette Kartoonz." She walked over to the couch and sat down, giving Travis a dirty look before turning her attention to the wall screen.

"Okay, Honey-bunch. I'll clean it up." Kayley went to find the broom but her head was elsewhere, thinking about the exciting day she had ahead of her. Half way to the kitchen she changed her mind and started upstairs to get changed. Danny met her on the stairs, rubbing the sleep out from his eyes.

"The kids up already, Luce?"

Lucy continued up the stairs past him. "In the living room. It's Math Day, so don't let Trav work with numbers or his hives will get worse. I have a doctor's appointment myself at twelve o'clock so they're all yours."

"Sounds good."

Lucy turned back around at the top of the stairs. "And don't forget that we've got that my Sales Champions Dinner tonight at the Airport Marriott."

Danny stopped and looked back at his wife. "Tonight? Couldn't we just stay in and do something family-oriented? Play some games, maybe?"

"No, Danny, we can't." She folded her arms, shutting out any opposition. Danny noted to himself that she'd been doing that a lot lately. "This dinner is important. It could change our lives. Besides, the kids are too young for games. Competing means that there'll be a loser and that's not proper childcare."

"That's bull, Luce. I don't care what the so-called stuck-up, childless professionals say, if the kids don't learn to compete and win or lose gracefully in childhood, they'll be screwed when they hit sixteen, when their Child Chips come out and they're forced to be instant grown-ups."

"What do you want to do, Danny? Move to one of those free-range family communes, take the chips out, and turn off the net-feed?"

"That'd be better than having them turn out like your sister's kid. Larue hasn't been able to sit through a single job interview without weeping. He's such an emotional cripple than he even posted a weeping montage online and asked for sympathy 'Likes'. If that's what Travis and Kayley have to look forward to, then a commune is the way we'll go."

She lowered her voice and leaned forward to make sure he and only he heard her next comment. "You're an idiot. Maybe if you spent more time at home and less time out pretending to still be a cop, you'd see the reality of child-rearing first hand."

"I'm trying to make the world safe for our children, *Lucy.*"

Another scream punctuated Danny's comment, but this time it was Travis. "MOM! DAD! Kayley gave me the finger! I'm feeling traumatization or something!"

Lucy laughed cruelly. "Yah, well good luck with that, Danny. Since you can't save everyone, maybe a free-range commune is exactly what all three of you need. I'm going to be late." She spun around and stormed off to the bedroom.

"Da-a-a-d!"

Danny shook off the anger Lucy brought out in him and turned his attention to Travis and Kayley.

"Travis, suck it up. She gave you a hand-gesture; she didn't force you to watch a Tarantino film. That's what your Grampa did to toughen me up. Just deal with it and move on."

"I'm calling Child Services as soon as this episode is over."

Danny looked at the screen with the perfectly round, bright green, cartoon characters bouncing around a meadow. "What episode? It's all the same, Trav. The characters are all the same colour and the same shape. There're no squares, no triangles, not even a rhomboid, and all so no one is made to feel different. The only differences between them are the numbers on their chests!"

A clear tone sounded from the screen and a neutral female voice—The Monitor—interrupted the show. "Please lower your voice, Mr. Angles. A raised adult voice is not conducive to childhood safety. Children, do you need assistance? Shall I send a police officer to save you?"

Danny threw his hands up in frustrated surrender. "No, everything is fine, thank you."

"I was addressing Travis and Kayley, Mr. Angles."

"I know you were, but don't you think making a decision like that could traumatize them even more?"

There was a pause, and then the Monitor came back on. "You are quite correct, Mr. Angles. Kayley's heart rate increased eighteen percent when the police were mentioned, but it seems to have gone back down. In the future, please refrain from raising your voice. Undue stress is harmful to children. Have a neat-o day."

The sound of the Kidlette Kartoonz came back on and Danny wandered off to the kitchen, muttering under his breath.

DANNY IN THE DARK

* * *

Young Danny stood high on a stump, clutching the thick rope that hung from the elm over the creek. He moved his grip a little higher, pulling the huge knot on the end of the rope closer to him. He knew he could swing two or three times across and back just holding on with his arms, but if he could get the knot between his legs and sit on it, then he could keep going back and forth until the swing energy wound down and he had to pull the rope back up the hill for the next wannabe Tarzan.

"Danny! What the hell are you doing?!"

What was his mother doing here in the ravine?

"Get your ass out of bed and get dressed! The taxi'll be here in fifteen minutes to take us to the dinner!"

It wasn't his mother; it was Lucy. Danny pried his eyes open. "Yah. Okay. The dinner. Are you sure I need to go? I'm exhausted."

"You're going, if it's the last thing you do. Get your ass up. Now."

Danny dragged himself out of bed and managed to shave and climb into the suit in ten minutes. He needed a shower but since he was just the plus-one at some stupid Sales Celebration dinner, no one would give him a second thought. By the time Lucy ushered him into the waiting taxi he was fully awake and thinking that a nice dinner paid for by someone else was just what he needed.

* * *

"Ladies and gentlemen, it's the time you've all been waiting for." The evening's Master of Ceremonies clinked his spoon on his wine glass right in front of his microphone, getting their attention immediately.

Danny looked up at the man, thinking he'd seen him somewhere before, but he couldn't place the face. He shrugged it off and speared the last piece of steak with his fork, popping it into his mouth before the waiter at his shoulder grabbed his plate and scurried off. Everyone else in the hotel's massive ballroom had finished eating five minutes ago and many were staring at him and giving him odd looks. He didn't care. With two kids in the house, he never got to have red meat anymore and he was going to savour every morsel.

The MC continued. "Before we go any further, I have to ask someone a simple question." A scantily dressed young woman appeared at Danny's elbow and smiled down at him. He could have sworn there was sympathy in her eyes but he had no idea what she was doing there.

"I'd like to ask Danny Angles a quick question before we go on. Daniel…"

Danny looked up at the stage and a microphone suddenly appeared in front of him, held by the woman. "Uh, yah?"

"Danny, do you know why you're here tonight?"

"Sure. Lucy is getting some kind of sales award."

There was laughter around the hall, and some of it none too kind. Someone in the back shouted out "Loser!" and someone else answered "MASSIVE loser!" and the laughter ramped up a notch. Danny was confused as hell. He looked at the pretty young woman with the microphone but her sad half-smile didn't help. He looked over at Lucy

20

for guidance and was shocked to see her smiling so big she was almost in tears. As a matter of fact she *was* in tears, and she was trying hard not to laugh. But he saw cruelty in her eyes and had a feeling that the shit was about to hit the fan. The MC came to his rescue, though. Sort of.

"Danny, you're here because of Lucy, alright. But tonight's also about *you*." The MC pointed at a television camera on the end of a crane Danny hadn't noticed before. The crane was sweeping slowly over the heads of the celebrants, right at Danny. "Look into the camera for me, Daniel, and give a big smile." Danny managed maybe a quarter smile, at most. "Good enough, my friend. Thank you. Now, Daniel, what would you say if I told you that I'm going to give your lovely wife, Lucy, a certified cheque for five million dollars?"

"Um… okay? Sure?" What the hell was going on?

"Now, what would you say, Daniel, if I told you that I'm going to give Lucy a cheque for five million dollars because… for the last four weeks she's been screwing another man on world-wide live net-feed and *you* have been totally oblivious? Welcome to 'Cheater, Cheater', Daniel!"

The entire assembly erupted in boisterous applause and laughter, including Lucy, who laughed the hardest and meanest. Danny could see in her eyes that the MC was telling the truth and this was no prank. He stood, looked coldly at the MC, then at the embarrassed young woman with the microphone, and finally back at Lucy. He took a deep breath, gazed straight into the camera and finally answered the MC's question.

"At least she's good at something, because as a wife and mother she was an utter failure. Hopefully her next john won't want a used-goods discount." Then Danny turned, kissed the now-smiling microphone girl on the cheek, and walked out of the Airport Marriott ballroom. As he pushed open the fire doors leading into the lobby he remembered that he'd last seen the MC hosting the One Hundredth Academy Awards. The guy was even more of an idiot in person.

* * *

Danny gave the cabby an extra hundred bucks to lose the paparazzi on the way to his mother's house to get the kids; but a block from Mrs. Angles' cul-de-sac Danny changed his mind and had the man take him home. While they drove, Danny slipped his earpiece in and called his mother.

"Hi Mom."

"Oh, Danny-boy. I'm so proud of you!"

"You saw?"

"Seven hundred million people saw, Honey. Are you on your way over?"

"I don't think so. Do you mind watching the kids for a few days? I don't think Child Services would be impressed if I let Trav and Kayley be traumatized by seeing me box up their mother's crap and put it out on the front lawn for the whole world to pick at."

"Good thinking, Honey. I'm happy to watch them for as long as you need."

Danny sighed. "I guess the world'll be laughing at me for a long time."

"Probably not, Honey. The network is already advertising a replacement for Milton Wayne Tennyson. This new sicko is supposed to start a live net-feed tomorrow evening. He's promised at least two kills a night, every night. They hinted that he lives right here in the Pacific Northwest, so you lock your doors tight and I'll do the same."

"Another one? Goddammit! We live in a sick, sick world, Mom."

"We sure do, Honey. You get a good night sleep and I'll try to get the kids to call you when they wake up, some time after noon."

"Sounds good, Mom. Love you."

"Love you, too, Danny-boy."

* * *

Danny's mother was right. By the time Peter Thomas Rockney broadcast his fifth and sixth live-feed shotgun-and-dismemberment murders, the street outside Danny's house was empty of reporters. He did an online search of his own name and the most recent article was two days old. They'd already dismissed him as old news and he was more than fine with that.

While he was online he spent an entire morning reaching out to his police and private investigation contacts, trying to find out everything he could about Peter Thomas Rockney. By time his growling stomach forced him to take a break, Danny was pretty damned sure he knew where the two-a-night serial killing bastard was going to find victims seven and eight, and the ex-cop was determined to get there first.

* * *

The crossbow seemed lighter in Danny's gloved hands than it had been when he was stalking Tennyson and he took that as a sign that he was doing the right thing. Danny's research had revealed that Rockney seemed to have a thing for public parks, beautiful couples, and the Greek alphabet, so Danny sat, hidden in the shrubs of Omega Park on the outskirts of the city. He popped another stick of gum in his mouth, leaned back against the tree at the centre of the thick shrubbery, and thought about the chat he'd had with his mother after the kids got bored talking to him and went back to watching Kidlette Kartoonz.

When he'd suggested to his mother that maybe a free-range commune might be the best place to raise the kids, she'd brightened right up. She loved the idea and even offered to round up information for him about the various communes throughout the Pacific Northwest. The more Danny thought about it, the better the idea sounded. If Kayley and Travis were to ever have a chance at a real life, it had to be away from the city and the Child Welfare tyrants.

A woman's giggle pulled him out of his daydream and Danny moved up onto one knee so he could lean forward and see the pathway. A couple strolled along, hand-in-hand, laughing and chatting without a care in the world. Danny was almost envious; and then they stepped into the dim light cast by a mock gas lamp and he recognized Lucy. He didn't recognize the man, but it didn't take a genius to figure out that he was the son of a bitch who'd screwed Danny's wife all the way to the bank. Wouldn't that just screw with their heads if he stepped out of the bushes just as they passed and shouted "Boo!" He nearly laughed out loud at the thought, but bit it back.

Nearby, a twig snapped. It sounded like it was in the bushes on the other side of the wide path. Probably just a squirrel, Danny thought. Then the squirrel pumped a shotgun and Danny knew with utmost certainty that Peter James Rockney was broadcasting live from only a few yards away, waiting for his prey to move within range of his sawed-off ratings-maker. Danny slowly, silently placed the crossbow on the ground, lay facedown beside it, and then covered his head with his hands. What difference would it make if he waited a couple minutes before stopping Rockney? Like Lucy said, he couldn't save everyone.

JULIE
JOSHUA SKYE

A derivative noise played on the radio, something puerile and pathetic by some unjustly popular celebrity that called himself Eminem. Oh, she knew who Eminem was, the blond little gutter snipe that likened himself a streetwise badass when in reality he was little more than Vanilla Ice on crack. The music was plagiarized from some 80s pop song she couldn't quite remember the name of and the lyrics were just laughably ignorant. She was often amused by the lack of sophistication in America. There simply was no reason for it except pervasive bad taste. Vulgar and insipid, the state of America's music scene was just so outlandish. And not in a good way! How she hated it with every fiber of her being.

Still, she turned the shit up.

Julie simply had to do whatever it took to stay awake and suffering through auditory pollution was as good a torment as any other. She rolled the window down inviting the chilled night breeze to slap against her face and arms. Her eyes burned with sleepiness. What an asshole the sandman was. She drew in a deep breath of the cold air and then sighed it away. The moon was a crooked beam in the sky above surrounded by millions of little star friends. It was a beautiful sight, one that city dwellers couldn't afford even if they had all the money one could possibly earn, well considering that they would even want to buy the view.

Her ass hurt. The drive had been a lengthy and tremendously tedious one. New York City was a long way behind, Jamestown was coming up and, if she was really honest with herself, she really wasn't looking forward to it. Her hometown held no pleasant memories, certainly nothing that she was particularly nostalgic for. Her childhood had been rather bereft of affection and wonder. She didn't dream about sweet returns or fairytale reunions. If her father hadn't died she would not be going back at all. Jamestown was dead and drying up fast just like the towns that surrounded it. They were all falling prey to the corporate world and its eternal mission of downsizing. Her father had worked for the Phillips plant just across the Pennsylvania border in Warren for over two decades when they decided to fire everyone and move their operations to Mexico. Julie, since then, had openly preached her anti-Phillips gospel, a task that wasn't too difficult considering that the quality of their products had gone severely downhill since their cold and calculated move.

She yawned and wished that some other driver in the opposite lane would be rude and not dim his high beams just so she could have something to bitch about. No one came. The road was dark and unlit and deserted except for her. She cursed her father for dying at such an inopportune time when she was in between boyfriends and otherwise had no other friends to come with her. Ah, dear old dad, she didn't like to think of him. Memories of growing up weren't all roses and ponies.

The song about drug use, mother fucking and gay bashing was over and something else began. It was something by some bratty little kid named Justin Bieber. It was sickeningly sweet and so not what she was in the mood for. The Eminem trash was at least loud and sufficiently obnoxious enough to keep her on the opposite side of sleep. Fuck it. To hell with music anyway, it wasn't helping. She flipped the radio off.

The road before her loomed in a flat stretch of off-highway that no one really used any more. The pavement was cracking and allowing things to grow up through it. The signs along the sides were in long need of replacement. There were shadowy, unkempt woods on both sides that didn't appear as quite the kind of bedtime story forest that anyone would want to wander around in. Julie smiled to herself at the thought of children lost among the crooked trees like step-kids tossed out by new mothers, intentionally misplaced by fathers oh so enamored by new pussy that he was willing to sacrifice his own for just one more little taste.

A glimmer!

Suddenly pulled from her macabre thoughts by the glint, Julie sat up erect in her seat and peered out into the yawning darkness ahead. There was something up there along the side of the road. She was instantly curious as only the utterly bored could be of something as slight as a faraway gleam in the night. Perhaps it was the lost hope in the eye of something that had been hit by a car long ago, a deer dying perhaps, mangled and lying in a pool of its own blood on the side of the road.

Again the shine!

She lifted her foot and the car began to slow. Her high beams pierced the dark and sluggishly revealed what was causing the attention getting shine. Not some broken thing. It was strange, she felt oddly sad that it wasn't. It was a naked little boy, standing there blue and shivering. He was hugging a silver framed mirror to his skinny body. Was she really seeing that? How could that be? It was so surreal, unexpected, and even perverse. She watched him watch her in wide-eyed fascination as she pulled over. Her car came to a quiet stop beside him.

Julie hurriedly got out of the car and walked around to the boy. Faraway sounds came from the deep, dark woods, the sounds of animals and other things. What were those *other things*? She knelt down beside the shivering child. His skin was a most unhealthy blue-green flush. His fingertips were bleeding; tiny streams of red oozing down the glass. She looked into his big, pleading eyes and immediately an overwhelming sense of concern washed over her. She might have called it maternal if she'd ever once entertained the notion of having children. But she hated kids. They were cruel, rude, spiteful and dirty. No, she didn't like them at all.

A growl, close!

She moved her gaze passed him to peer into the blackness of the woods. Yes, there was something there. She could hear it, a rumbling growl, a twig snapping under foot. She imagined something most hideous out there. Something terrible was coming. Was he being pursued by a monster?

The underbrush moved!

Gripping images of insidious creatures pulsated through her fatigued mind. Trolls had surely been chasing this boy and they were right there. Right there! She almost smiled at the storybook superlative but there it was again the undergrowth moving and not because of the cold wind! It *was* a monster.

In a flashing movement, she scooped the child up into her arms and ran around the car practically throwing him into the passenger's seat. She rushed back around to the driver's side and jumped in herself, slamming the door. *Behind, behind*, leave the *evil thing* behind. She sped along the road, breathing heavily as her mind raced with dreamy thoughts. Was that the arrow from some hellishly forged bow that had just hit the bumper? She glared into the rearview mirror and scrutinized the dark, everything falling away there. She could see no movement, no hopping horrors enraged over the loss of their prey. Maybe *they* were invisible?

Julie drove on in silence for some time as she allowed her mind to swirl with fantasy images and fantastical explanations. They were, after all, more preferable to the possible real world horrors that certain kinds of sick adults visited upon poor, innocent children. She shook away the invading thoughts of reality, swallowed hard and asked, "Who are you?"

The boy's purple lips quivered uncontrollably, his tiny pink tongue peeked out and licked them. His large, round eyes glared at her with an almost forced virtuousness. He responded in a sickly sweet voice, "Who are *you?*"

"Of course," she replied. Yes, of course he would want to know who she was, and he certainly had every right to know who this towering giant was that had plucked him from along the concrete path. She swallowed again; there was a damn lump in her throat that would not go away. "I'm Julie."

"I'm Julie," the boy said.

"What?" She frowned. His response might have been some bizarre childish joke had it not been for the strange, deep tone of his voice. There was seriousness there, a chilling honesty. "That's my name. I'm Julie."

"I'm Julie," he insisted with a furrowed brow.

She was bemused and even a little bit alarmed. Was the kid crazy? "What's wrong with you? *My* name is Julie." She tried to rationalize with him in a childlike way. "You can't be Julie because you are a boy!"

His eyes no longer looked quite so innocent. His fingers wrapped tightly around his mirror. His body tensed, toes curling under, lips pressing into a thin white line before he suddenly screamed at the top of his lungs, "*I'm Julie!*"

Troubled and incensed by the boy's sudden, inexplicable outburst, she leaned over to glare down at him. "What's wrong with you? Are you crazy?"

The child flinched and moved away from her. As innocence flooded back over his tiny features then he started to weep, his small bony shoulders heaving and twitching. His crying was loud and peculiar, garish and disingenuous. He seemed as though he was outlandishly pretending the emotion. There was deceit there. Julie thought him ridiculous, humorous even. His performance was pretentiously glib, counterfeit emotions akin to every insipid and tired Tom Cruise routine.

For just a second the car swerved, just a moment out of her control. She took a deep breath to calm herself and straightened back up. She turned her vehicle back into her own lane and reminded herself to keep her eyes on the damn road. Just because it was straight didn't mean it wasn't dangerous. She glanced over to him, just a fleeting little glimpse, and wondered where he was from, what he was doing out in the cold night alongside a rarely used road.

Who was he?

His hair was dirty blonde and his facial features that of any typical little white boys. He had a slender, slightly upturned nose, large puppy eyes, nice full lips that would most definitely thin with age. At the same time, however, he had features that would never be attributed to someone of his age. His cheeks were curved inward in a waifish appearance; there were dark circular bags under his eyes and a stern, masculine jaw line.

And then there was the color of his skin that wasn't getting any better in the car. Julie realized that the window was down. She hurriedly rolled it up.

His sobbing, at a snail's pace, ceased. The blood on his fingertips, and the smears across the glass were drying into that crisp, flaky black cherry crust. She was ten miles from the next town. There she would drop the kid off at the police station and they could deal with him. After that the crazy little creature was no longer her problem. And she didn't need another problem. Daddy dying was problem enough.

Out of the corner of her eye she saw him staring intently at her. She chanced another quick glimpse his way and said, "You through?" She realized that she wasn't being very patient with him. She told herself it was because she was so tired but of course she knew it was because she really didn't like kids, especially weird ones.

He nodded. His brow was lowered, he was clearly angry. *He better not be angry at me,* she thought. *Little shit! I just saved his scrawny little ass.* His breathing was loud; there was a rattling in his chest. He was most likely sick. *Probably has pneumonia! Who knows how long he'd been out in this?* She asked, "Why were you in the woods?"

He looked away from her to the world outside the windshield. His thin arms gripped the mirror in a tight embrace. There was a slight rocking, as though he were trying to comfort himself.

"Don't talk to me then. This isn't a concern for me. It will, however, be a concern to the police because that is where I'm taking you."

His head snapped to the side and he glared at her with a new facial feature, one of fright and dread. He seemed to panic. He shook his head 'no' violently.

"Oh yes," she said. "I have to."

Gritting and grinding his teeth, the sound of it like twisting metal, he pinched his face, squeezed his eyes shut and let out an earnestly yet eerily frustrated howl. Then he burst into a fit of fierce hysterics, violently kicked the dashboard while throwing himself ferociously about. The shrieks that spilled from him slowly distorted to something animalistic, inhuman even. The little fucker was throwing a temper tantrum!

Little bastard!

Without even a moment's hesitation, Julie backhanded the little brat. It caught him completely off guard. It caught her off guard! She suddenly felt like her father. Yes, that was definitely something her father would have done. The blow struck the kid across the lips, splitting them open and allowing fresh blood to dribble. His screams immediately halted and he took in a quick, desperate influx of air.

"Let's get one thing straight," she stated hearing her father's voice inside of her own. "I'm not going to put up with shit like that. I don't give a rat's ass what you've been through tonight! Got it?"

He didn't look at her, didn't make a sound. He nodded.

She secretly winced; she'd hit him purely out of instinct and hadn't controlled it at all. She'd hit him hard, it had to have hurt him quite badly because it had unquestionably hurt her hand. Her skin had even split open, the blood was warm as it oozed down her wrist. She secretly took a peek at the back of it. She must have cut herself on his teeth, there were several small gashes. *Shit!*

He spoke in a weak little kid voice, "I'm gonna tell."

"Excuse me?" she asked as she looked at him fiercely. Her heart leapt into her throat joining the lump that was still there.

27

"I said," he stated as he turned to look at her with a queer little smile, one of impish delight, "if you take me to the police, I'm gonna tell them that you hit me."

She thought a moment and knew that what she had done was a goddamn crime. The fucking cops would lock her up. She took a deep breath and told herself not to show fear, not to show the kid anything. She had to put up a front.

Through a cracking voice she said, "So fucking what? I'll just tell them that I slapped you to calm you down. After all, I found you alongside the road in the middle of the night buck-ass naked. I don't think they will care."

"I'll tell that you stole me. I'll tell that you took off my clothes and that you touched me in private places."

What the fuck? "What are you talking about?" Julie was shocked by what the kid was spouting. What the hell was he trying to do? *I'm only trying to help the little fuck.*

"I'm talking about the way you *kissed me.*"

"I did *not* kiss you!"

"If I say you did, that won't matter."

Infuriated, Julie slammed on the brakes! The car screeched to a halt, sliding to the right. The boy was momentarily thrown off balance. He braced himself with one hand, not letting go of the mirror with the other. She turned to him with a baleful look upon her face. "Get out. Get out. *Get out!*"

He got wide eyed, the innocent kid was back. He asked with a quivering, trembling, pitiable voice, "What?"

Julie put a finger in his face. "I said, get the fuck out! Now!"

"You can't make me get out."

"Like hell I can't. Now, I know why people don't help anymore, even the goddamn victims are fucking crazy. As far as I know, this is just some crazy hillbilly scam. Out! Now!"

In one nearly elegant movement, one that seemed almost in slow motion to Julie, the boy twirled elegantly around. In a second Julie saw his crotch, his bare and hairless ass crack, his red rosebud anus, his sagging scrotum, his fully engorged penis, and tiny swirls of blonde pubic hair. This was not a child!

Jesus-fucking-Christ! *Not a child.*

What the hell was this? *Not a child!*

He began kicking her. His feet moved in a wild frenzied attack. He was strong, too fucking strong! She screamed out and put her hands up to shield herself. She was hit several times in the face before covering it with her arms. Her chest and belly were then receiving the entirety of the vicious beating. His kicking was relentless. It was a blur, a furious grease smear of peddling feet striking her again and again and again. He was screaming out a war cry, a terrible rumbling roar, animalistic, irate!

She tasted blood and there was a rivulet of warmth on her left cheek. Several kicks to her breast knocked the wind from her. A searing pain spread across her chest. The attack was relentless, merciless. He showed no signs of weakening or slowing down. She had to do something. She had to! Amidst the turbulent flailing, Julie was able to turn herself around and mindlessly return the violent gesture. With hard-soled sneakers she began kicking back. She delivered several powerful blows before he ceased his assault.

"Stop!" he screamed.

Julie did. She slowly put her feet back on the floor. She touched the gash on her cheek and flinched. Her tongue darted out to poke at the bloody gap there, again she flinched. Sucking back snot she growled, "What you do to me, I'm going to do to you." It was blunt, it was matter-of-fact. She meant it. She was breathing heavily and tried to calm herself. Blood seeped down her chin and she wiped it away.

He laid there in the passenger's seat motionless except for the up and down heaving of his chest. He still clung to that damn mirror. Julie looked back down in the direction of the boy's crotch, but it was covered by the looking glass. She wondered if she had really seen what she thought she had. She doubted it. How could she have? He couldn't be over ten years old even with that distinctively masculine jaw. What she imagined she'd seen was impossible for that age. She pulled her eyes away from him, embarrassed, self-conscious.

"I still want you out!" she hissed.

He was silent for several seconds and then responded, "Please, don't make me get out. Please, don't."

As tears uncontrollably trickled from her eyes she touched the wound on her cheek again anticipating the pain. It wasn't as stinging as it had been before. She murmured, "Look what you've done to me. Why should I help you?"

"I'm lost." The proficient phony innocence had returned, deeper and even more incongruous. There was even a shudder in his cadence.

"That doesn't answer my question."

"Because I'm only a kid."

Julie closed her eyes and laughed out loud. "Really? How old are you?"

"I don't know."

Okay. She chuckled again. "What's your name?"

"I don't remember." The innocence and shudder were draining away again.

Bullshit! "Bullshit. Tell me your name or get the fuck out."

"I told you, I don't know."

Liar. "Tell me your name."

"I don't know."

Her eyes shot open and she glared at him furiously. "Get out!"

"No! Please." The innocent routine.

"What's your god-damn name?"

"I'm, ah I mean my name is …" he stuttered and took a deep breath, "Julie."

And yet another incontrollable chuckle came out of her. She couldn't believe any of this. She shouted, "What kind of sick fucking game are you playing?"

"I'm not. *I'm not.*"

"What's your god-damn name, or so help me I'm gonna …" Even as she said it she remembered her father saying the exact same thing to her once. *So help me I'm gonna…*

"I don't have one, okay! I've never been given a name."

"What?"

"There! Are you happy now?"

Julie looked away from him. There were small splashes on the windshield; it was starting to sprinkle. The cold dark world was about to get wet and it would only get colder. God, she hated the cold and the wet. She asked, "What do you mean you were never given a name?"

He was crying and there was an authenticity to it this time. There were even tears, tears spilling down his little blue cheeks. He murmured, "They never gave me one. They never cared enough to give me one."

"Who are they?"

"My benefactors," he said.

She shook her head and asked, "What does that even mean your *benefactors?*"

"The people who kept me, the people who tied me up, the people who brought me food, the people who said they loved me."

Oh shit! This is so fucking weird. She tried to clam herself down again, tried to will away the anger that filled her, the anger she had toward this, this little brat. "Look, we have to go to the police. I don't know what you have yourself mixed up in, but I don't think I can help you. The police can."

"No they can't. One of them was a policeman."

And another chuckle, she couldn't believe what she was hearing. What was going on here? What was she going to do? She wished none of it had ever happened, that her father hadn't died and that she hadn't felt obligated to come back to this god forsaken place. She wished she'd never stopped to help a child on the side of the road. And then she laughed yet again at the heartlessness of that thought. How could she have been so callous not to have stopped to help?

Julie drove. The nameless boy crawled into the backseat and just for a moment when his ass was right there nearly touching her shoulder she could have sworn that his legs were crooked, disjointed, and that his feet weren't really feet anymore. She hissed at herself for thinking it, refused to take a second glance to vainly verify that she'd just seen goddamn hooves. It was stupid. It was ridiculous. It was just a strange little boy that was mixed up in some strange affair. She heard him curl up into a ball on the leather seat and she was certain that he was still holding onto that damned mirror for dear life. Before long he fell asleep.

Julie's mouth stung, her left eye was throbbing and puffy, surely blackened. She had several bruises over her, she could feel them welting. Her dull night had become something akin to a nightmare, a fairytale dream so bizarre and wild. She was confused, in pain, and at a loss for what she should do. And she was fucking hungry. Her empty stomach grumbled out its annoyance. The only good thing she could think of at that point was that she was no longer tired.

A shallow snoring crept up from the back seat.

For some strange reason the memory of how she found out about her father's death came to her. She had been late getting home from work, her affair with the married boss keeping her just long enough for him to ejaculate. But it was long enough to miss the nearly inaudible phone call from her mother. Her answering machine was the one to break the news in a most insincere and cold fashion. *'Julie, sweetie, your daddy passed away tonight.'*

"No," she'd whispered out loud, not because she wanted the old bastard alive or that she hadn't expected it, it was just news she didn't want to hear.

'Please, Julie, come home. I need you. Your brother can't get away until Saturday. I need to make the funeral arrangements and I can't do it alone. Please, Julie, please ...'

The barely understandable words trailed into a slow and mournful sobbing. It was excruciating to listen to. Her poor mother crying over the man she'd been with for forty-five years. The recording had gone on for nearly six minutes until finally going silent. And the silence seemed worse. The silence made it all real.

To her, ten miles was like driving hundreds. The memory, the knowledge of what awaited her and the situation with the naked little creature in her backseat were taxing her sanity to a monstrous extent. She took the exit. She stopped at the only open gas station and asked for directions to the police station. She drove there in silent confusion. She parked and waited. She felt like some sort of automation. She did not know what she was waiting for. What was she waiting for? A sign? Someone to come out and notice her, greet her, ask if she needed help? She let her thoughts to go blank. There was comfort in not thinking about anything.

She watched several policemen escort cuffed individuals into the station, watched a few of them come out. A couple of cops even looked at her, but no one came to her car window to inquire whether or not she needed assistance. She sat there listening to the sounds of the boy sleeping and watching the sparse activity going on in front of the station. It was all so terrible ordinary out there.

She forced herself to think again, to think of the blue skinned boy and what needed to be done. She had to go inside and tell someone. He surely had hypothermia and need to go to the hospital. So she had to go in there and have a strong and handsome young rookie come out to her car and take the sleeping boy in his arms and then take him inside and then take him to a doctor. She opened the car door and forced herself to get out. She took great care to close the door without making too much noise. What noise was made did not seem to disturb the sleeping child.

Her legs and feet were horribly heavy. Her body was telling her not to go inside. *But I have to, I have to! This is the only way to help him, to really help him.*

The stairs to the front doors were insanely difficult to climb. They didn't want her to, she was sure of it. They were enchanted. They were cursed! She reached the top as a portly old uniformed cuss brushed passed her and went inside not bothering to hold the door open for her. *Asshole! Fucking troll.*

She went inside. It was warm and smelled of greasy things. She looked around. There was about as much activity going on inside as there was outside. The only difference was that it was brighter and warmer, of course. Warmth, nice. So very nice. She looked down at her feet and there on the tile floor was a trail of bread crumbs. She could hardly believe it. Fresh tears stung her eyes as she followed it to a large desk behind which sat a dark skinned uniformed woman with asymmetrical cornrows. The woman did not look up from some trashy romance novel she was reading.

"Excuse me," Julie said.

The cop raised a rude finger to indicate she'd be with her in a moment.

Julie sighed and looked to the Wanted-Sign-plastered wall behind the policewoman. There were so many, so many mean and evil bad guys. The mug shots were of the typical motley crew, beaters, abusers, drug dealers, murderers and rapists. Most of them were men with scars and bald heads in their mid to late forties. Most of them were white and some had tusks and horns and big bushy beards with things peeking out, things with little red eyes, things with sharp needle teeth.

'*... one of them was a policeman.*'

Julie inhaled hard. Her lungs protested in agony. *Do I really want to be here?*

The policewoman practically read the final words of the paragraph out loud before she marked her place and closed the book. The novel was put aside on top of a stack of even more Wanted Signs. Frowning, she looked up and said, "Help ya?"

But there was no one there. She looked toward the door just in time to see a white female exit the building. *Not very tall,* she thought to herself. *She walks like a thing, like some strange otherworldly thing.* The policewoman sneered. The door closed with an all too familiar rush of cold air. She shrugged and went back to her book.

Julie no longer found it difficult to walk. She hurried back to the car and got inside. She smiled to herself, not quite sure of what the hell she was going to do. One of those wanted men had been a police officer; one of the kid's benefactors had been a police officer. Was there any logic at all to what she had done? Should she just march her stupid ass right back in there? She looked in the back to check on the nameless boy. He was gone! Her jaw went slack and once again her mind went blank. The mirror, however, was there lying face down and covered in bloody fingerprints.

Shit. Shit. Shit.

After telling her tale and getting some cop out to her car this would have looked real good, real incriminating. No child, only a mirror covered in a child's bloody fingerprints, only a mirror and much evidence of a struggle, only a mirror and the tale of a naked and bloody child alongside an old road in the middle of the fucking night. It was the stuff of homicidal pedophilic fantasy. Sick. Sick. *Sick!*

She turned around, started the car, and drove away. She kept the windows down; the night air had gotten much cooler. She switched the radio on and was disappointed by the selection playing. Then again, who gave a shit? It was only a fucking song. She left the tuner alone. She thought for a moment of the mirror. With her left hand on the steering wheel, she reached into the back seat with her right. She felt along the chilled seat for the looking glass. She imagined for a split second that the boy was still back there, somehow hidden in the dark and waiting to bite.

There!

She had it and brought it around into her frame of view. It was damn heavy and ornately hideous. It was an antique surely, old most certainly. She glanced into the dried blood streaked glass; her reflection was just as shrouded in darkness as she felt. Her eyes shifted back and forth from the mirror to the road and back again. *Why was he clinging to this thing for dear life? Why? Why? Why?* The questions were fast and furious and none of them had any reasonable answers. *God-damn it! What a fucking night.*

An explosion! The car swerved uncontrollably. Julie screamed and dropped the mirror so that she could use both hands to control the car. It crossed over into the other lane and then shifted back again. The trunk flew open! She tried to turn into the direction it wanted to go, *turn into it, turn into it,* that was what she'd always been told but that only made it worse. She slammed on the brakes and the car shrieked to a stop.

Fuck! She got out of the car and immediately saw that the left front tire had blown out. She kicked the car and screamed out in frustration. Then she heard a moaning. She turned her face in the direction of the pitiful sound. It was coming from the back of the car. Gingerly she walked to the open trunk and peered inside. Her shit was a mess and he was there, too.

He was lying among her clothes and open packs the tire iron had penetrated his right leg. There was an enormous amount of blood and it spilled out from the wound in a deep red gush. There was a gash on his forehead and it seeped its own red mess. He looked up at her with tears in his puppy dog eyes.

Instinctively she put fingertips to her quivering lips. *What the fuck am I supposed to do? What the hell am I going to do?*

She reached in and took hold of him under his arms. She lifted him out into the night air, held him at arms length and carried him away from the car. She laid him down on the side of the road. *Gotta go away. Gotta get help. Gotta just go!*

"Mommy," he said in a low voice before closing his eyes and allowing the dark to take him. His breathing was shallow, but rhythmic.

He'd only passed out from the pain.

Julie looked back toward the police station; it was quite a way away. No one had seen her. Then she looked in the opposite direction into the woods on the other side of the road. *There!*

She reached down and took hold of the tire iron, leveraged with her other hand and pulled it out of the little blue boy's crooked little leg. It made a horrible sucking sound and then the wound spat out a stream of red. She wiped the tool off in the grass and then threw it over near the blown tire. The air was getting extremely cold. Julie went back to the boy, leaned over and grabbed his ankles.

She dragged him into the woods and left him just inside among the trees. God, she was a terrible person! She cursed herself even as she left him there even though she could hear that he was snoring lightly. She looked back at him. Oh God, he was bleeding so badly! His little body was twitching, his blue lips wavering. She looked over his pale body, a body that nearly glowed in the moonlight that filtered down through the treetops and she nearly screamed …

He wasn't a little boy!

She wept uncontrollably. Indeed, as she had glimpsed before in the car, he had pubic hair, tight, short blonde tufts of it. And his legs were crooked, twisted at perverse angles. What was he, a deformed dwarf, a misshapen midget? He did not have the distinctive features of either. And yes, *dear Jesus*, He had hooves! His head moved ever so slightly, turned to the side and there just peeking out of his hair was the tip of a markedly pointed ear!

Julie screamed. What the hell was that thing? What had she found on the side of the road? What had she invited into her car? The moonlight glinted, she flinched. Was that a fang just there caressing his bottom lip? She screamed again before realizing that would draw unwanted attention. The fucking cops were right over there after all.

She ran back to the car. She peered into the trunk and could see splashes of blood on her clothes. *Gotta get going. Gotta get out of here.* She took a deep breath and emptied the trunk. The spare tire was heavy, but she managed to get it out and roll it over to where she needed it. The task was a long and tedious one. She kept looking back over her shoulder to the forest, to the place she'd left it. And she kept checking the goings on at the police station. She wondered how long she'd have before they took notice of her. She had to hurry; she had to get out of there! She was exhausted when she was finished. She put the flat tire in the trunk and reloaded her things. The trunk slammed shut with a mighty sound that echoed into the woods. Movement in the underbrush! Animal sounds. *Other sounds!* There were monsters out there.

She got in behind the driver's seat and stared the engine. She took a peek in the rearview mirror and saw him. The blue skinned thing was stumbling out of the woods holding the wound in his leg. There was a painfully severe and desperate look on his face. He called to her and reached out. He was coming toward the car.

Julie closed her door and promptly drove away. She turned the radio up really loud and was pleased to hear that one of her favorite songs was on. She sang along and smiled slightly to herself. She couldn't bring herself to think of the boy, and in fact did not want to. It wasn't long before she could no longer see him or the police station in the rearview mirror. And thank God for that. He was someone else's problem now; someone else would have to deal with whatever he was. She was free of it and so she sang louder, screaming out the wrong lyrics and enjoying it until …

A low sweet little giggle came from the backseat and a high-pitched voice that whispered, "I am Julie."

HER LAUGH
CLINT SMITH

1

Clay Cooper wasn't crazy. But Chicago fixed him. The screaming fixed him.

In summer of 2000—after several failed attempts in acquiring the identity of a serious college student, each half-hearted foray concluding in his lapsing back into status of a drop-out—Clay Cooper had made the casual statement that he should move away to go to school, that he should get out of Sycamore Mill and, as he phrased it, "just start over." On more than one occasion, he made this suggestion to his drinking buddies and his mom.

His martyr's gamble backfired. Clay's mother—who had become a sort of indulgent and doting landlord—actually supported the idea, even going so far as to fund a down payment on an apartment. Clay's mom, evidently, wanted her twenty-one-year-old son to "start over" too.

Concerned his reputation might be damaged if he backed away from this bluff, Clay made the leap to leave town. Clay conceptualized his impending endeavor as having its own loner soundtrack, something in the vein of an AC/DC album—leaving with a sneer to the tune of "Highway to Hell," and making a prodigal return to the blues-groovy conclusion of "Night Prowler." These were the things Clay imagined. He'd read parts of Orwell's *Down and Out in Paris and London* for one of his classes, and he considered his self-imposed expulsion from Sycamore Mill as being a sort of romantic exile, a Byronic exodus. In the end, Clay would discover that Chicago wasn't London or Paris or even New York, for that matter. It wasn't romantic. But it did *fix* Clay.

* * *

The apartment complex was located north of the city in a neighborhood district that maintained a bygone air of esteem—one-way streets lined with remodeled carriage houses and French renaissance brownstones. That's not to say the neighborhood was without mediocrity, buildings whose renovated, regal-looking façade belied the shadow-drab shabbiness from within. That was Clay's apartment.

As opposed to the rent, tuition (even with the generous monthly check his mom had promised to send) wasn't cheap. Clay found a job as a dishwasher at an unassuming bistro around the corner from his apartment. The work, for Clay, was nobly menial, appropriately lending itself to his loner's sojourn.

In the mornings, he'd taken to buying a newspaper before catching the bus, skimming the pages as a means of avoiding potential contact or conversation. For Clay, this apparent cooperative disregard for politeness and conviviality was one of the more appealing aspects of living in the big city. He hadn't been good at being affable or gregarious in Sycamore Mill anyway, so the funny game of acting indifferent suited Clay just fine; and, initially at least, he adopted this daily disinterest to all his neighbors.

All his neighbors except one.

HER LAUGH

In November, winter grew teeth and began devouring what was left of autumn. Clay had narrowly passed his classes for the fall semester, and went home for two weeks during Christmas break.

Clay returned to Chicago on a slate-colored, snow-swirled Sunday afternoon. Stomping slush from his boots, Clay walked into the lobby of his apartment complex and saw a girl, who he'd never seen before, over by the bank of mailboxes. She was bundled up, but Clay could see the profile of her small, elfish face under a thick wool cap, a few strands of black hair fraying out on the sides of her cheeks. Clay guessed she was close to his age. He went to his mailbox, acting as if she were just another neighbor to be dismissed.

Clay pressed the UP arrow on the elevator, stepping inside and taking a jab at the button for the fifth floor. She turned then, as if cued by the sound of the elevator's sliding doors. Clay leaned forward and caught the door. The girl offered a quick smile as she slipped into the elevator. "Thanks," she said, raising her eyebrows, her nose and cheeks pink and she was sniffing a bit from the cold. Moving to press the already dim-glowing button for the fifth floor, she hesitated, apparently understanding that Clay had already hit the button and simply said, "Oh," before returning to leaf through her mail. The lights overhead flickered as the doors closed and the compartment rattled to ascension. She was standing close to the doors, and despite himself, Clay ventured a few curious glances over her shoulder, at the bills she was leafing through, wondering what her story was. But after a few moments, Clay's attention was drawn to the unpolished panels on the elevator doors, where he could see the girl's reflection—her chin tilted down, her face obscured in shadow under the thick wool cap. He thought she was unusually attractive, even in the funhouse-mirror distortion of the tarnished door.

The elevator lurched to a stop, the doors opened and the girl, still flipping through her mail, stepped off, steering to the left into the corridor. Clay followed and began fishing in his pocket for his door key. The girl—who Clay now heard humming to herself—had rounded the corner. As he stepped up to his door, he could hear that her humming was now joined by the jangling of keys at the end of the hallway near the stairwell. *She lives on my floor?* He'd never seen her before. And he would have remembered *this* girl. He unlocked the ancient-looking deadbolt and entered his apartment, closing the door and abandoning any personal sense of restraint as he swiftly leaned up against the peep-hole and squinted. From Clay's angle, and through the bulging scope of the convex eye-hole, he merely glimpsed a shape making a mouse-quick slip into the apartment, and the sliver-nictation of the door winking closed behind her. *Lucky me.*

During the day, returning from school or heading out to work, Clay frequently ran into a neighbor or two. Most of the people on his floor were elderly, and in the winter months he'd seen very little of them. *Maybe it's cheap for them to live here*, he often wondered. *Maybe they've lived here since it was built.* There was a garbage chute around the corner on his floor, down at the end of the hallway. From time to time, Clay would walk by someone taking out a small bag of garbage. Sometimes he'd say hello.

More often than not, he'd remain silent.

There was an old black woman who lived on his floor, just down the hall in the direction of the elevators. She lived alone, as far as Clay could tell. Because of her observable independence, and because Clay had acquired a healthy sense of anonymity, he never asked if there was anything she needed, or if there was anything he could do to help.

4

The girl down the hall was some sort of art student. Or a musician, maybe. Or part of some avant-garde acting troupe. She dressed with trendy eccentricity, and her bohemian demeanor—when he'd see her in the lobby or on the sidewalk—seemed to fluctuate between fussy hostility and friendly contentment. On the weekends Clay could hear her playing her stereo down the hall—usually some sort of techno-melancholy that he found agitating. She played it loud, but none of his elderly neighbors appeared to notice or complain. They, in fact, kept their televisions up near distracting levels, particularly for game shows or the local news.

During those first, late-winter weeks, Clay never saw another person enter or leave the girl's apartment, and guessed she was living alone.

So much about her was intriguingly strange—and that strangeness, for Clay, translated into exoticism, and exoticism into something like tepid obsession.

During the day, Clay began toying with ways to introduce himself. He'd walk down the snow-slushed sidewalk, wondering if she'd be in the lobby getting her mail. Of course the climax of these daydreams was the indulgent fantasy of the girl—for whatever contrivance—inviting Clay into her apartment, and with movie-script convenience, consent to sessions of consensually unobligated sex.

Ordinarily, the lobby was empty when he returned in the late afternoon, and he'd taken to habitually peering in the small glass slit of her mailbox to see if she'd picked up any envelopes for the day. In the elevator, propelled by the possibility of seeing her in the hallway or taking out the trash, Clay often dreamed-up possibilities for what the name on those envelopes might be, what *her* name might be—tumbling Ls and Ms over his tongue, aroused by the hiss-syllabic quality of her imaginary appellations. During the day, Clay created seductive vignettes in which he whispered her name. But at night, lying alone in bed, he imagined the girl whispering his.

5

One Saturday night in March, Clay was stretched out on his couch—half-dozing, half-watching a movie, his face paled by the anemic, mercury-flicker of television light—when he thought he heard some muffled giggling in the hallway.

Earlier that night, after clocking out from his dishwashing shift at the restaurant, Clay had decided to unwind at a popular pub around the corner from his apartment. He'd sauntered in, slid onto a barstool and ordered a beer, scanning the smoke-filled tavern, glancing at the clusters of good-looking, loud-laughing twenty-somethings— *mostly college kids*, he thought. *Just like me.* No. *Not like me.* Clay drank his lukewarm beer, alternating between trying to affect a loner's air of mysteriousness and hoping to make eye contact with one of the well-tanned coeds. This little social experiment lasted five beers. Clay finally decided he was tired—tired from work and of not being noticed.

The security attendant in the lobby of his apartment, an old man—who, to Clay, seemed too old to work security and too happy to work a Saturday night—greeted him as he tottered to the elevators, and, as usual, Clay did his best to tolerate the old man's attempts at small talk.

Now, laid out across his couch, Clay's cheap-beer drowse dissipated as he heard the voices coming from the hallway. His blinked a few times, shaking some clarity into his head. He thought he heard *her* voice.

Springing off the couch, Clay bumped his shin on the coffee table—grunting a curse and clenching his teeth—before weaving through the darkness and stumbling into the corridor leading to the door and the peephole. Clay approached on tiptoe—a useless movement that he'd grown accustomed to when peering through his tiny spyglass.

Two people were at the end of the hallway, down by the girl's apartment door: The girl—back was against the wall—and a guy, standing in front of her, looking as if he were whispering in her ear. In the wide-angle distortion of the peephole, the pair looked like one groping tangle. The girl intermittently gave up a tinny string of stifled shrieks.

The guy was tall and lanky, a slim body type that Clay associated not with tough-ness—not like the bigger guys at the bar earlier that night—but with a sort of harmless ghoulishness. Dark, mod-looking bangs—which he continually shrugged off his fore-head—fell over his brow, obscuring his face. Clay caught only fleeting flashes of pale-ness between the hanging bangs of the guy's stylishly disheveled hair. The girl contin-ued giggling, swaying against the wall. The guy occasionally buried his pale face be-tween her shoulder and her ear, eliciting vampirish images to Clay; although this victim sounded as if she were enjoying the attack and appeared to be putting up a pretty weak fight.

During all this pawing, the girl's laughter gave way to a series of elated exhala-tions—the pre-ecstasy sounds of foreplay; or at least a sort of corridor foreplay. Clay held his breath, intently imagining the girl's face changing. With erotic clarity he pic-tured her expression morphing from mischievous contentment, to lip-biting bliss, to brow-furrowing euphoria—eyes closed, jaw unhinged—as she inched toward the deep-end of orgasm. Clay began to feel the images as a dull twinge in his pelvis.

Clay's legs were getting stiff as he stood in front of the peephole, and as he shifted his weight from one foot to the other, he bumped his forehead against the door, produc-ing a soft, but tangible, thud. Clay winced. When he opened his eyes the couple was still there, the girl still pressed against the wall. But after a few seconds she gave the guy what looked like a playful shove, to which he reacted by straightening up and giving her some space. Clay listened to the brief chiming of keys, and heard the girl hiss something as she dropped them on the floor. Retrieving them, the girl finally brought the jangling tangle to the lock, and the couple shuffled into the apartment.

Everything, save for the whispery background sound of his own television, was quiet now.

Clay, still aroused by images of the girl, pushed himself away from the peephole and began walking back to the living room. He passed the darkened kitchen, catching a glimpse of the trashcan in there. He quickly conjured the pretext to take the trash to the garbage chute down the hall; and while he distantly recognized a lingering compulsion to want to see and hear her, his beer-imbued logic was that maybe taking out the trash—taking one final stroll past her apartment—might shake free this urge for *more* of her.

He slipped on a pair of sandals, covered his lunatic hair with a ball cap, and knotted the half-full bag of garbage. He opened the door and squinted at the bright, fluorescent light in the hallway—the corridor's normal symmetry seeming almost alien after having viewed it for so long through the marble-sized bulge of the peephole.

Although he gave the girl's bronze doorplate and peephole a quick glimpse, he didn't slow as he passed by, rather continuing his casual gait to the back hallway, turning left around a crook of wall. The garbage chute was halfway down the hall. Clay opened the lower lip of the thing and dropped his garbage, listening as it skidded against the inside of the shaft before making a glass-clinking landing.

Quiet again.

Clay slipped his hands into his jeans and headed back. As he rounded the corner wall, he slowed as he walked by her apartment. The door was almost out of his field of vision when he heard something that made him hesitate—something he first took for a muffled scream but now realized was a low, throaty murmur. Coming to a full stop, Clay turned toward the door, staring at it, straining to hear. The sound came again, as if from the inner recesses of the apartment. Giving a cursory glance at the bronze number plate, he took a couple sly steps toward the door, holding his breath and leaning in, the side of his face and ear nearly touching door.

Clay listened to his pulsing heart for several seconds before a voice suddenly spoke. "*I seeeee youuu,*" a male's voice sang from the other side of the door, just inches of wood dividing Clay's face and the speaker. Clay reeled back as if he'd dipped his face into a thickly spun spider web.

And now there was the eruption of laughter on the other side of the door—a guy's laugh and a girl's laugh, h*er* laugh—and the unrestrained chuckles echoed into the corridor. Clay stared dumbly at the peephole for a moment before retreating, walking swiftly toward the sanctuary of his apartment, his flip-flops making an absurd suck-pop sound as he strode down the hallway.

The crow-caw laughter began to diminish as Clay neared his door. He went for his keys, sliding a hand into the pocket of his jeans. The empty pockets of his jeans. He could picture the keys now, laying on the coffee table in front of the TV, along with his wallet and a spill of loose coins.

Clay tried the doorknob only once. Locked, of course. The laughter had died down now, but there was still the intermittent titter of something—*whispers.* Clay turned and walked over to the elevator, pressing the down arrow. He listened as the yawning cables and gears lifting the compartment to the fifth floor. The doors dinged opened and Clay stepped in, clenching his teeth and stabbing the button for the lobby. He'd have to request an escort from the security guard to unlock his apartment. He could already imagine the old security guard beaming at the prospect of late-night company.

On the ride down, Clay inspected his own distorted reflection in the warped and tarnished panels of the elevator door. He closed his eyes, trying to chase away the echoic laughter that seemed to have followed him into the small space.

6

HER LAUGH

Spring—or at least spring-like weather—overtook Chicago almost overnight.

In the weeks following his mortifying eavesdropping experience, Clay had done his best to avoid the girl, as he was beyond certain she'd designated him a four-star creep. Now, he used his peephole *before* leaving his apartment, to make sure she *wasn't* out there. If he happened to pass her in the hall, he'd avert the possibility of eye contact by keeping his gaze trained on yellowed, peeling wallpaper and the antiquated stains in the burgundy carpet. If, coming home from work or returning from school, he'd see her through the foyer windows getting her mail in the lobby, he'd take a short walk around the block. And she was usually gone on his second pass.

One spring evening, Clay entered the lobby, tucking his newspaper under his arm and steering toward the bank of mailboxes.

The girl silently appeared from the stairwell. Out of the tail of his eye, Clay registered her presence, and quickly shut his mailbox, giving her a wide berth as he flipped through his mail, reading nothing, briskly walking toward the poorly-lit stairwell. But as he pivoted, doing his best to avoid her face, his attention snagged on something, his eyes doing a touch-and-go on her subtly curved abdomen, at the gentle distention of her belly. *Pregnant*, he thought, sorting through an admixture of reverence, disbelief, curiosity, all laced with traces of jealousy and carnal covetousness. "Pregnant," he whispered as he clomped up to the fifth floor.

7

Months passed. And as the weeks accumulated and days folded over on themselves, Clay did a reasonable job of ostensibly disregarding the girl as he circulated through the pleasantly monotonous cycles of work and school. He was approaching the end of his spring term, and for the first time felt a foreign sense of confidence at having coped with college.

The girl being pregnant, for Clay, somehow affirmed that she had her own life to worry about, and therefore couldn't be concerned with some lonely guy down the hall with a questionable preoccupation. Pregnancy somehow indicated that her life was moving. And Clay took this as a cue that he should do the same with his own. And no matter her opinion of Clay, he felt as if he (*the peephole creep*) were off the hook.

She seemed as flightily independent as ever—more so, in a way. When Clay'd pass her in the lobby, sometimes she'd be humming to herself, her tiny belly plumping by degrees. But, as far as Clay could discern, she was still alone. And aside from the one night he'd been caught by the mystery man at the peephole, Clay had never seen anyone else go in or out of her apartment. And while he wouldn't allow his eye to linger too long, Clay, out of his periphery, thought that maybe—*maybe*—she was trying to make eye contact with him. And in that fuzzy sort of instant-replay, Clay was sure she was grinning at him, gently trying to reel his attention toward her.

8

The summer of 2001 was particularly miserable in the apartment complex, and not for any reason that had to do with the girl or school or his friendlessness. It was hot—in the apartment, on the bus, in the subway. Clay, lying in bed at night with the windows open, listened to car alarms and horn-honk rhythm of taxis; he listened to the voices inside the apartment, imagining the old building as being a stifling beehive producing only an ambient buzz and sauna-haze streams of steam. Sometimes he coaxed himself to sleep by placing himself on the night-cool sand of the waterfront, gazing out at Lake Michigan, drifting away to the metronomic lapping of black waves curving over the lake shore.

One sweltering afternoon in July, Clay was sitting in the laundry room, waiting for the dryer to finish and reading a newspaper. He was frowning at an article, fumbling with the word "epizootic," when the girl walked in, toting a laundry basket on her hip. She was wearing gray sweatpants, pink flip-flops, and a hooded sweatshirt—the thick material stretching over her breasts and the pregnant hump of her stomach; her raven-black hair—which had dyed streamers of purple in it—was pulled back in a ponytail. *A hooded sweatshirt in July?* he wondered distantly. His heart thudded in sync with the rhythmic tumble of the dryer. As if through cotton, he heard her say, "Hell-o," drawing out the two sing-song syllables as she passed behind him.

In the reflection of the dryer window, Clay watched her plucking panties and bras and pajamas from her laundry basket. His eyes eventually returned to his paper, concentrating on the columns of small words until the tumbling stopped.

A few weeks later, Clay was on his way to work and waiting in the hallway for the elevator. When the bell gave a flimsy ding and the doors slid open, Clay stepped forward, nearly colliding with the girl as she exited the elevator. They both reacted simultaneously, skidding just short of bumping into each other. She was carrying some sort of wicker crate filled with pink tissue paper and what looked like baby-shower gifts; and in that torturously awkward instant, Clay noted a plastic baby doll sticking out of the crate.

"Sorry ... excuse me," she said.

Clay, eyes aiming at the floor, made a face that was his version of an apology. But as he stepped on the elevator he paused—his mind lurched as if trying to stop his mouth from wandering into a busy intersection. It was too late. "My, um..." he said over his shoulder. "My dad ..."

The girl stopped and turned. "Pardon me?" she said.

Clay cleared his throat and made himself look at her. Her face was soft, pretty and puckish and confident; the way her eyebrows were raised implied sincere curiosity instead of haughty impatience. *Was she being an actress?* The crate was propped up in front of her, on her belly. *Is that hump ... is her stomach smaller?* Clay's eyes flicked down at the crate, alternating back and forth between her eyes and the eyes of the baby doll—the sort of ubiquitously nondescript toy that was a staple of garage sales and donation centers.

He started again, hoping to sound casual, "My dad used to tell me not to rush onto an elevator, that people should give other people enough space to get off"—*what the hell am I talking about?*—"... so that was my fault." He offered a clench-thin smile. "Sorry."

An easy, no-big-deal smirk appeared, her lips arcing up. It was a smile that, in Clay's perception, suggested both his tepid attempt to interact, as well as his pointless anecdote, were both acceptable gestures of simply acting decent. "Sure, no problem. See ya'." She turned and disappeared around the corner.

9

September.

Clay was several weeks into his second fall semester at the university. On Tuesdays and Thursdays his classes started early, and for the first time since he'd moved to Chicago—even more than that, for the first time in years—Clay was growing confident with the work he was doing in Chicago, with the job he'd moved here to do.

It was a Tuesday morning, Clay's alarm beginning its staccato bleating at the accustomed time, and he began eliminating items on his daily itinerary: coffee, shower, check weather, get dressed, load-up backpack, shut down and lock up the apartment.

One of the morning rituals to which Clay had remained faithful was buying a newspaper to read on the bus. While those inky pages still served as a device with which to disengage and tune-out other passengers, Clay now found solace in the comfort of catching up with the city and the world.

As usual, he boarded the bus at the same spot with most of the same people, and as he shuffled on to the normally crowded bus he was surprised to find an open spot on a bench seat along the window. He sat, flipped through his newspaper, occasionally glancing out at the passing strips of blue sky between the slate- and sandstone-colored buildings. Blocks passed, and the bus slowly filled with passengers. Clay looked up again. The sky between the buildings was growing narrower as the bus neared downtown.

After creasing his paper, Clay gripped a bench pole and began to stand, but as he did a passenger strode by him, bumping into Clay's shoulder and knocking him off balance, almost back down into his seat. Without glancing back, the guy simply continued on, joining others in the short line near the front of the bus. Clay was still leaning over from the jolt. A girl sitting directly across from Clay snickered. She had stringy blond hair and was wearing a pair of headphones—her smile appeared as a sneer to Clay. He scanned a few other faces. No one else seemed to notice. He yanked himself the rest of the way up, adjusted his backpack and began shuffling toward the front of the bus.

The guy was now a few heads in front of him, his face pointed straight ahead. Clay's pulse began to percolate, to throb along his throat in his ears. The bus slowed and lurched to a stop, the doors folded open and the people poured out. The guy stepped down to the sidewalk and turned south. Clay stepped off the bus, balling his fists as he steered in the same direction.

His plan was simple—*Catch up with this prick on the crosswalk ... return the favor.* But the guy was moving fast, and keeping up quickly became a task. Clay was only several paces behind the stranger as they neared an intersection where a cluster of people were waiting for the light to turn. Clay judged that this guy was roughly his own age. But now as he glowered at the back of the guy's skull, Clay grew nervous, considering what sort of possible retaliation might occur. *Would the guy ignore me too if I just kept walking?* And that was what infuriated Clay the most—it wasn't the physical contact so much as it was not being acknowledged. The guy had just kept moving as if Clay hadn't—*didn't*—exist.

The light turned green and the crowd stepped forward. Clay made a halfhearted attempt to pass the guy, but the stranger was moving fast again, pulling away. Clenching his teeth, Clay allowed himself to fall back. He was now a block or two out of his way and heading in the wrong direction. *Fuck it*, Clay thought, abandoning his pursuit, watching the guy blend in and disappear with the bustling multitude.

No longer in the mood for school, Clay caught a northbound bus to take him back to his apartment. He'd take the day off. *It's a gorgeous day and people are ugly.* He was thinking of the girl on the bus with the headphones. In the eye of his imagination, her tiny teeth were filed down to haphazard fangs—cannibal's teeth. And when he imagined his own version of the stranger's face, he saw the guy turning slowly on the crosswalk, gleefully revealing a broad, piranha-mouth smile.

It took Clay a long time to get back to his neighborhood.

Walking into the lobby of his apartment, Clay could already sense a different atmosphere about the place. Being a weekday morning, and even with the significant number of elderly people in this his complex, the place seemed—looked, felt, sounded—more subdued than usual. There was a drowsy-feline sort of languor about the place. Clay checked his mailbox. Nothing. He stepped to the elevator and stabbed the UP arrow. After waiting for what seemed too long, Clay gave a to-hell-with-this exhale and walked toward the stairwell.

Clay emerged through the fifth floor door, strode past the garbage chute, rounded the elbow of wall, and passed the girl's apartment, giving her door—number plate and peephole—a glance before aiming straight ahead toward his own apartment. He noted the TV sounds coming from his elderly neighbors' rooms, a sound he'd grown used to. But even their hard-of-hearing volume seemed more suppressed this morning.

As Clay pulled the key from his pocket he heard something else—a scuttling sound, like a mouse scrabbling along coving. He turned, fidgeting a few glances here and there, he looked and listened. *Whispers?*

Clay swept it away, jamming the key into the lock and twisting. He pocketed the key, slipped off his backpack and sauntered into the living room, where he crossed to the window, yanked up the shades and cracked the sill. A warm breeze—a unique mingling of the best qualities of summer and autumn—sighed into Clay's apartment. He took a deep breath and flipped on the television. It'd be the network news at this time in the morning.

He was about to head into the kitchen when the sound of a reporter's voice—something unusually unrefined—seized his attention. The reporter was saying something about airplanes. "… the plane struck the building …"

Standing directly in front of the screen, Clay instantly recognized the dark pair of skyscrapers, one of them hemorrhaging a thick trail of grim-tinted smoke. Over the summer, the newspapers had had several stories about private planes crashing in strange places, or recreational pilots making emergency landings; and in a presumptive flash, that's precisely what Clay believed he was watching now.

He increased the volume, the flustered-sounding reporter was saying something about a possible hijacking "… *and then the airplane struck the north tower …*"

Even as he listened to the piecemeal details of what was happening—and even if it was a hijacker—Clay had almost automatically assumed that hijackers had stolen a private plane—a small Cessna, or something like that—and had executed the crash among themselves, among a scant number of terrorists. But slowly, Clay began to comprehend the certainty that the airplanes had been larger aircraft—passenger planes. *Full of peo-*

ple. Probably some kids. The reporter was suggesting similar things now.

It wasn't just a few people who were now dead in New York. It was hundreds.

Clay absently took a seat on the coffee table, staring at the dark building with its ugly, smoky tail curling into the blue sky. Prefaced by terms like "alleged" and "uncertain," the reporter continued to repeat the words "hijackers" and "terrorists." The news anchor in the studio was dispensing information about the airplane, confirming that the 767 had been part of a commercial flight from Boston to Los Angeles, and that the hijackers had targeted this particular flight because it had been fueled for a long-distance trip. *They used the fuel for the explosion.* There was no sign of the airplane, having imbedded itself deep within the building—the source of the black smoke metastasizing from a smoldering, high-octane core.

Clay licked his lips, which felt numb. He was suddenly aware of the sound of other televisions. Glancing across the room, out the window, Clay could hear the dissonant chatter of overlapping broadcasts coming from his neighbors' apartments. He could still feel the delicate breeze drifting in through the window; the sky was wide and painfully blue.

The aerial shots of the Trade Center continued. And suddenly—just as Clay rose to pick up the phone—another airplane violated the screen, momentarily disappearing behind the other skyscraper. A second later came the explosion, an almost gelatinous, slow-motion swell rupturing horizontally along the side of the building. Glittering shards of glass and steel spilled from the building. Clay thought he heard a collective gasp issue from the neighboring apartments, as if united in the horror of witnessing was happening in New York. Clay's stomach began to wring itself in his midsection as his eyes scoured the screen, acknowledging what he was seeing but not really comprehending it.

Several minutes passed. Both buildings were smoking in earnest now and the city skyline was streaked with billowing charcoal smoke. And Clay reluctantly imagined the scene inside the buildings—the panic, tramplings, the suffocation, the furnace-blackened bodies. The reporter now mentioned that people had been seen jumping from the buildings. And that repulsive notion was nearly too much for Clay—the nauseating gratuity of bodies, of pieces of bodies, littering the debris-filled streets. Clay thought about the kids who'd likely been on the plane, the kids in the building. Moms and dads. "Christ," he muttered—a weak sound that simply reaffirmed his being anchored here: breathing, safe, sitting on a coffee table, staring at the TV like some helpless, friendless, useless … boy. He thought about the people in his apartment, the city strangers he'd made his tacit adversaries over that past year—even if only inwardly, privately. Clay thought about the guy on the bus. Compunction, and something that was almost shame, began to needle him. He quickly dismissed it.

On wobbling legs Clay stood and took several steps toward the phone, but stopped when he heard a scream.

He punched the mute button on the remote and waited. Again, an echo-softened scream sounding as if it'd come from the hallway. He made a few strides for the door, giving a cautioned check through the peephole to discover the hallway empty; even so, Clay opened the door and stuck his head into the corridor. Frowning in concentration, he was prepared to close the door when he heard it again.

Clay heard another scream, and knew it was coming from her apartment. And in that last wall-cushioned call for help, he thought he heard his name, *Clay*—maybe even *Clay … help*. He rushed forward, down the hall.

Distantly aware of the layered discordance of televisions and radios filling the hallway, Clay slowed as he approached her apartment door, his eyes moving from the bronze number plate to the peephole. He swallowed, extending a loosely clenched fist to knock then stopped, noticing the vertical, black slit of the door jamb. The door was cracked open slightly, almost imperceptibly. *Had it been open when I passed by earlier?* Clay shoved the question aside as another sob-laced wail escaped the inside of the apartment.

He pushed through the door, which opened into a narrow entryway. The apartment was dark inside, and that darkness swallowed Clay as the door creaked shut behind him. He squinted, his eyes adjusting to the darkness in the corridor; he noticed dim light coming from the room in front of him. The air was stifling and held the perfume of patchouli and something like the stagnant incense of decaying plants.

"Hello," Clay called out, instantly hating the frailty in his voice, "is everything okay?"

"Please," came the girl's voice, sounding as if she were panting. "Please … come help me."

Clay, still squinting against darkness, strode forward. He emerged in a living room area. The windows on the opposite side of the room had been covered with some sort of purple, tie-died wall hanging, which tinted everything a dark shade of lavender. There was an old stereo cabinet, some pieces of furniture, a patchwork couch.

Clay glanced left, toward the kitchen and beyond to the shadow-darkened rectangle of the hallway which—as the layout was evidently identical to Clay's apartment—surely led to her bedroom. Still frowning, Clay called out again. "Where are you?"

Suddenly part of the girl's face sprang up from over the top of the couch. Her skin was pale, almost gray in the purple-dim light of the room; her eyes were shaded beneath with dark scallops. Her thin eyebrows were arched in an expression of pain and expectation.

"Please, Clay," she said in short bursts, "it's … the baby."

Although his mind twitched at the peculiarity of her *knowing* his name, Clay rounded the side of the patchwork couch.

She was lying on the floor between the couch and a coffee table, her bare legs splayed in a sit-up position—one slender hand fanned on the couch cushions, the other braced on the coffee table which was cluttered with what looked like spools of yarn and sewing paraphernalia; threads of her dark hair clung to her fever-damp forehead in stringy clumps. She was wearing a long, white nightshirt, the hem of which was pulled taut across her knees, canopying her inner thighs in shadow. Wanting to act and react with the same momentum that propelled him in to her apartment, Clay crouched on one knee.

"You have to help me … I'm going to have the baby."

He thought he could see dark smears along the inside of her thighs, and his eyes darted back up to her deathbed face. "Listen, I…" He licked his lips. The room was so dim. He gave a panicked glance around the apartment, as if uselessly seeking for help. *How does she know my name?* "I don't know what I'm doing … I don't want to fuck this up. Let me call for a doctor or someone—"

45

"No," she hissed. An expression, as if she were going to laugh, skittered across her face and disappeared. "No ... it'd be too late. You have to help me, Clay. It has to be *you.*"

And again, with the uttering of his name, Clay was moving. Leaning forward, squinting, willing his eyes to adjust to the purple gloom, he now saw something under the hem of her nightshirt, in the shadowy fork between her legs. Something pale. Clay's eyes bounced back and forth between the dark smears on her thighs to the pale shape between her legs. He had been frowning; but now, pausing on her face, his expression went slack.

She was smiling, her tiny teeth glittering in the purple half-light. Still whey-faced, her eyes—still feverish, still nested in bruise-colored sockets—had gone from being filled with desperation to almost dancing with feral delight. And behind her tiny teeth, a cackle began to swell.

Clay recoiled, falling back on his palms.

With lurid smoothness, the girl slid her hand off the couch and down between her legs, withdrawing a plastic baby doll. A mock umbilical cord had been knotted around the baby doll's midsection.

Clay—on his ass, his knee-bent position looking as if he himself were giving birth—watched the girl's pale hand crawl across the coffee table, and from the loose-spooled clutter of yarn she withdrew a pair of scissors. She was still cackling softly, her unblinking eyes still locked on Clay, as she opened the blades with a clean sounding *shink*, and moved the silvery knives to the baby's fake umbilical cord, severing the fleshy material. The plastic baby doll clomped to the floor.

The girl's giggling stopped suddenly. Clay had been inching back on his palms and heels, but the unexpected silence forced him to stop. The girl was no longer smiling and she seemed to be measuring the space between she and Clay. Both, sitting in the same position, simply stared at each other for a moment—their chests rising and falling with labored breathing. The girl's lower lip was glistening with saliva.

She began blinking rapidly, eyebrows twitching, as if intently listening to telepathic instructions from some unseen stage manager. And then, as abruptly as the silence had settled, the girl's face quivered and contorted as she raised the scissors over her head.

In one galvanic move, Clay twisted up and was on his feet, scrambling for the shadow-boxed corridor. In the darkness he groped for the doorknob, at the same time he heard the sound of feet pounding the hardwood floor.

Stumbling into the hallway, Clay bolted straightforward, nearly tripping once and only slowing as he neared his door. Clay whirled, giving an over-the-shoulder glance as he began fishing through his pocket for his key. For a moment everything was silent. He began walking backwards, and stopped, the pounding of his heart giving the drumming suggestion that he start moving his ass again. But Clay stood still, absently stalled on the elusive notion that he'd missed something—*this can't be right*, he began repeating silently. *This can't be right. This can't be real.*

A queasy ripcord tugged his midsection, as he watched the girl—slowly, almost sleepily—emerge from her apartment doorway. Her stare was empty, an unblinking expression resembling someone in a critical stage of shock. With her long, loose-hanging nightshirt looking like a hospital gown, she was a vision of delivery room misery. But all at once, here, in the fluorescent sterility of the hallway, Clay could see the girl clearly. The dark scallops under her unblinking eyes seemed overdone, and her bloodless complexion seemed grossly vaudevillian—horrifyingly burlesque. He briefly considered how skinny she was—that her belly held no sign of having ever been pregnant.

Her arms hung loosely at her sides. Dangling in one hand was the plastic baby doll. Clay paused on the object before the light caught the silvery glint in her other hand. The scissors. The girl slumped one shoulder against the wall and began sliding, almost gliding, toward Clay.

Clay was still fishing for his key, frantically sifting through loose change, pens, his bus card … then it was there, in his fingers.

He pulled the key from his pocket, jittering it around the lock before quieting his mind long enough to slip the jagged teeth into the deadbolt's keyhole. In the instant it took for Clay to push through and slam the door, he had the flashbulb glimpse of the girl raising the scissors, her slender arm hooking over her head in an almost celebratory gesture, her mouth arced up into a rictus. She sneered and rushed forward.

Clay braced his shoulder against the door just as the girl slammed into it. He could hear her, growling, making hissing sounds as through clenched teeth. But this dissipated, and the short-lived silence was replaced by a scratching sound—the sound of wood being gashed and gouged. *The scissors*, he thought, *she's carving up the door with the scissors*. This sound, too, subsided after a minute.

Slowly, gently spreading both palms to either side of the peephole, Clay moved his face, his eye, to the peephole.

She was out there, but was walking backwards now, arms at her sides, in a sort of tip-toe retreat. Her body language—slumped shoulders, under-hung chin, scissor blades aimed toward the floor—suggested adolescent defeat or child-like disappointment. Then she stopped moving.

Clay swallowed, held his breath and listened as the silence was lacerated with a single tormented scream, and watched her arm recoil and fling the plastic baby doll, causing Clay to flinch back from the peephole as the toy hit the door. A few seconds later he heard a door slam shut, and when he returned to the marble-sized peephole, the hallway was empty.

Gripping the knob, Clay opened the door open a sliver. He was again aware of the faint sound of news coverage on televisions and radios. He glanced over at his mutilated door, scanning the damage. There were long slashes and zigzag scars in the paint-flecked wood. He took one tentative step into the hall, and his sneaker squashed something. Clay took his foot off the plastic baby doll. Reaching down, almost tenderly, he picked up the doll—the toy's long-lashed eyelids bobbing open and bobbing closed.

A door swung open down the corridor. The elderly black woman, his tough-old-bird neighbor, leaned out into the hallway. With her door open, Clay could hear a TV droning loudly from within her apartment. "You screaming?" she asked, grimacing. "Who's screaming out here?"

Clay slipped the baby doll down and behind him, out of sight. "Yeah," he said, clearing his throat to affect confidence. "I thought I heard that too." For a moment, both craned their necks up and down the hall, as if searching for the source of the scream.

"You been watching this news?" she asked, her wrinkled face scrunching up.

"Yeah … it's unbelievable." Clay then heard himself ask, "Are you okay?"

Raising a withered hand to her cheek, she said, "All those *people*."

Clay glanced askance down the hall, toward the girl's apartment. "Hey," he hated how thin his voice sounded through the thrumming pulse in his ears. "Let me know if you need anything."

The woman said, "What's that?"

Clay spoke up. "Let me know if there's anything you need." He felt the plastic coldness of the baby doll. "I'll be right here."

A weak smile fluttered over her face. "That's kind of you, young man. That's kind," she said, shuffling back into her apartment and closing the door.

Clay shot another anxious look down the hall, hearing the sound of televisions and radios from other apartments—breaking-news noises. The occasional gasp.

Edging the door closed and locking it, Clay looked through the peephole one last time before returning to his living room, to his own television and to the chaos unfolding before him. He inspected the baby, eventually dropping it to the floor as he watched the skyscrapers collapse.

10

Clay stayed in school, and in Chicago, until Christmas. And in those three months before breaking his lease and moving back home to Sycamore Mill, he never saw the girl again, only hearing what he thought might be an occasional laugh.

He never told the landlord about what happened. Or the police. Clay never told anyone the truth. It did occur to him that he had entered the girl's apartment without permission, no matter how frantic, or how sincere, she'd sounded that day. He did see and speak to his neighbors frequently, particularly in the days following the historic cataclysm in New York City. He had arranged for his deposit money to repair the apartment door.

Sometimes, the thing that happened in the girl's apartment seems like an elaborate piece of performance art, and that Clay hadn't properly played along with some game. But in the moments after jarring himself awake from the dreams—awakening in his new apartment in the most silent and darkest part of the night—Clay's memory strains, and he struggles to maintain crystallized accuracy in his mind's eye. Sometimes Clay recalls something else: In her apartment—in those moments of hesitation when the girl was on the floor, cackling, clutching the scissors as he readied himself to run—Clay believes he sees something over in the hallway on the far side of her apartment, someone in the darkened corridor further off toward her bedroom: a tall, slim silhouette, as if cleanly cut from black paper, standing within the corridor—a distinctly darker shadow mingled with other shadows. Sometimes his mind accents this voyeuristic entity with eyes, a ribald grin. Most times, Clay convinces himself that this is just his memory playing tricks on him. Most times.

Clay keeps the baby doll in a shoebox, and has cushioned it with crunched-up newspaper clippings from September, 2001. Once in a while Clay will pull that box from his closet, sit on the edge of his bed and inspect the toy, turning it in his hands, examining it for any peculiar clues about where it came from. He watches the dolls eyelids wink open and wink closed, and wonders what she is doing now.

DAUGHTER'S PREY
DALE ELDON

One

I haven't killed in twenty years... I'm gagging for it. It's time little Tracy gets to meet her mother's killer. Lance Carlson sharpened his knife.

It wasn't difficult for him to kill. But the target has been in his sights longer than any other. This one was extra special. He loved her mother, Holly. Despite his better senses, he fell in love with his prey, and the insuppressible urge to kill won out. Tracy was his game since she was an infant. He watched her grow. She wasn't ready for his knife as a child. Even a serial killer has standards, well this killer anyways. Lance wanted this one to be ripe. Twenty-one was a good age. His target had no clue he even existed. Watching her from various places throughout her day, always in a different disguise, as paranoid as she was, she was oblivious.

My sweet, sweet Tracy. I can't wait to lick your blood from my knife.

Lance sat in front of his lit-up mirror, bulb-framed-mirror. He combed his thin brown hair over the bald spot. Usually he wore a wig or a hat, but he did the comb over for the bus ride. He added a fake mustache for additional anonymity. Out of his five favorite disguises, this was the simplest. He was practically going as himself. It took very little prep for the bus ride. He dressed in a nerdy white button down shirt, with blue-stripe-plaid design. Followed up with gray slacks, and dark brown wing-tipped shoes. The last touch, his thick rimmed glasses. In every other guise, he used contacts. He looked so different with the specs, and as nerdy as it made him, he liked it. She never noticed him, he might as well walked around with a cloaking device shoved in his pocket.

Finally he threw on a brown dressy sports jacket, with padded elbows. Every time he went out, though he didn't plan his strike, he carried the kit. Small piece of rope for strangulation, bottle of chloroform, a rag, and a four-inch lock blade folding knife. A pretty standard kit, but the knife was his favorite. It opened with one fluid flick of his thumb without the pivot point being too loose. A nice jagged edge that turned into a smooth curved blade. It was a custom blue steel metal. It held the sharp edge well.

He had it designed with a seat belt cutter in the shape of an upside down check mark on the butt end, along with a pyramid point on the very end for shattering car windows. Just in the chance he ever had to take out the prey in a moving vehicle and went over a bridge into a lake. Seemed a little much, but in his line of work, one must prepare for everything. He liked his prey to be feisty, and put up a good fight, but it was their place to lose. Lance didn't spend ungodly amounts time watching a woman just to receive a blow to the nuts, and pair of handcuffs, or worst, he ends up the prey.

Most of the time, killers like Lance get caught for doing something stupid. They rarely die by the hands of their own prey. Sometimes it does happen. But not to him.

* * *

It took twice as long for Tracy to sit in front of him compared to a normal day. The bus

49

got held up with two wheel chairs, and the lift almost stopped working altogether. There she was, standing outside of the movie theater where she worked. She sat right in front of him like she always does. Her berry scented perfume and her light wavy dark brown hair. Skin perpetually tanned, and those light brown thin rimmed glasses, so adorable.

Her clothes matched her complexion. Her bangs which met her eyes was Lance's favorite detail. He wanted to reach out and cut a lock of her hair. She was such an innocent girl. Not like most her age. And Lance took credit for that. If he hadn't killed her mother, Tracy would be like every other twenty-one-year-old that he watched. Tracy had become so phobic about men that she didn't date. Paranoia was her soul mate.

Some of her hair fell over the back of the handle bar head rest. It killed Lance not to touch. He didn't allow himself that luxury. When the kill comes, he would touch plenty.

His attention drifted as the bus turned down the street that ran parallel to the old Killjordan Trailer Court. What a name for a place. Pity it had been bulldozed, and smothered in grass ridden gravel. He couldn't remember which spot his old trailer had been. That was when he lived with Holly. Tracy had no clue.

Not being able to resist, with a pair of fingernail clippers that Lance had sharpened, he snipped a couple of strands. He quickly stashed the hairs in a tissue from his pocket. The bus stopped in a small housing community. The houses looked like glorified double-wide trailers. Tracy got off, and Lance slowly, causally followed behind. For the first time, Tracy looked back. Lance never made eye contact with her in public; he didn't even look directly at her from behind. He continued his nonchalant walk with his hands stuffed in his pockets, as wind tossed his bangs. Tracy didn't seem alarmed. She only looked back for a moment then went on looking towards her path home. Lance turned down his ally. He lived only a couple of houses down, but his front door aligned with the ally that separated the block. He could still see her through a row of trees, only her lower legs. But enough that he could visually follow her into her home. Lance went into his "cave" as he coined it.

If she saw him enough times, his cover would be blown.

Two

Today Lance Carlson has a long haired blond wig, tied into a pony tail. He has contacts that make his brown eyes look green. For extra effect he added a blond soul-patch. His eyebrows are fake and blond. He keeps his natural brows shaved, so that he can change any combination at will.

The persistent beep of bar-codes swept across the register scanner as Lance peeked from the corner of his eye. It was shopping day for Tracy. Every Tuesday at 2pm, she picks up her weekly groceries. So far, after five years working at this very market, Tracy has never come through Lance's line. Until today.

Every day at this very moment, Lance always has the longest line. Today was the first time his line was the shortest. He avoids eye contact. She seemed unaware that Lance was the same guy she saw from the bus. Tracy piled her products onto the conveyor belt. Lance swept them across the scanner, and followed up by placing them into plastic bags.

Without making eye contact Tracy slid her card through the key-pad slot. As

Lance handed Tracy her bags, she looked at him puzzled.

"Is everything okay, miss?"

"Y-yes. You just, look familiar."

"Oh?"

"Sorry. I'm just not myself lately."

"No problem. Have a great day."

"Thank you. You too."

Damn close. Too close. Apparently I don't control how we interact anymore. I don't like this.

* * *

Lance hid in his bedroom, staring at the shrine of Tracy, made from her pictures and schedules. Thumb tacks with bright colored yarn strung in a chaotic pattern. He stood, studying, with his right elbow resting in the palm of his left hand, rubbing his chin with his right thumb. Oddly enough he couldn't focus on Tracy. His thoughts centered on her mother. Her death to be exact. Lance loved that woman. More than he has ever loved a woman.

He was twenty-one at the time; Lance had kept a close eye on Holly. It was "her" that made Lance a better stalker. He took his time with her. When he was ready, he asked her out on a date. So charming, how could she resist? After a couple of months, Lance forgot all about wanting to kill her. The one woman who could change him, make him a husband. Oh, but bad habits die hard.

He lured her out to a state park in the middle of the night. She thought he was being spontaneous. The next morning her body was found with a blow to the head from a hammer, a T-shirt wrapped around her neck, and her burnt face on top of a cold fire-pit. He was good. Lance never took unnecessary risks. As much as he hated himself for what he did, the greatest gratification overcame him.

He didn't spend all of these years watching Holly's daughter grow into a ripe candidate just to throw everything away. He killed the woman he loved for the lust of the kill. And did so with relish. It was too late to walk away from his latest target. Tracy may have no clue what he was up to, but what if she found out? His face was becoming recognizable to her. By now he knew everything she did throughout the day. The time to strike was at hand. But it was like it was, with Holly he began to grow attached to his victim. Also, just like it was with Holly, he wouldn't let his "typical emotions" get in the way. The urge drove him. It was him. He was the devil, and he was here to do the devil's work. And Lance loved it.

Three

Is that guy following me? Tracy never avoided to admit the fact she was paranoid. Maybe even beyond rationality. But she did have a funny feeling that her neighbor was following her. Would someone follow her everywhere, change their appearance just to stalk her? Sure she was gorgeous, but she kept a low profile. She didn't even have a social life. Always afraid of the shadows. Afraid they would take her; the same way they took her mother.

Tracy thought long and hard about shedding the introvert life-style. She liked people, well at least good people. The world may have had an abundance of stupid, mean, and predatory types, but there were people Tracy would love to get to know. Maybe go wild and have a movie night with a couple of "friends." She chuckled at the thought.

Tracy watched from her living room window at the man who always came home the same time that she did. Today, the middle-aged, balding, nerdy looking man was cleaning his backyard. He seemed harmless enough. But isn't that how predators always seem? At least that's what the old America's Most Wanted show had taught her. That was her favorite show; she even had John Walsh run a segment on her mother in the hopes of catching the killer. Which came with zero luck. She spent all of her non-sleeping/work hours poring through the case files of her mother's death. She made a profile of the killer, but it was vague. Tracy wasn't a criminologist, and had very little to go on. The man she sought was causal, normal looking. Just like her neighbor. *God, I am paranoid.*

Feeling stupid, Tracy forced herself to walk away from the blinds. This guy was just some everyday-Joe, with no real ambitions, who probably was a super-market manager. Then again, he did remind her of the guy who bagged her groceries. But still, this guy was just some schmuck. *Maybe it would be a good idea to befriend him. What if I do end up with a stalker down the road? I could use some support. Maybe this guy might even be fun.* Oh the lonely ramblings of one's mind.

It wouldn't hurt to have a male friend close by, and one who could know her past without judgment. A knight in shining armor. Not that she needed a knight, but she wouldn't mind having the back up.

* * *

Tracy made sure she looked her best. She always dressed nice. She threw on some Angel Violet perfume, combed her hair, making it perfectly straight. Her bangs curled just above her eyes. *I should look pretty damn good. I hope.*

Tracy picked up her purse and stopped short of leaving the house. *Oh crap, my pepper-spray. I forgot I left it by the bed.* She decided to leave it home, and left the house without it. The first time ever. She needed to get past her trust issues. Though it was a good idea to keep the pepper-spray on her at all times, but she needed to toss the security blanket aside.

She jogged to the house which sat catty-corner to hers. She choked back the fear, and knocked two-times followed by a gulp in her throat. She waited about five minutes, but the guy didn't answer. Lifting her hand in a fist to knock once more, she froze. *Should I knock again? What if he is more of an introvert than me? I should just go.*

The lock clicked, the door opened, and there stood the middle-aged, balding, nerdy man. He seemed a little confused.

"May ... I help you?"

"Y-yeah. Um. I was wondering, since I just noticed that you live next-door to me, if you would like, um, to—"

"Are you asking me out?"

"What?" A pause. "No, no. I... I'm not good at social settings, and I thought it was time for a change. You seem nice, so, I figured, I could use a friend. Like I said, I'm not very good at this." She ended with a nervous giggle.

"Well, I have to say that this is a first, I don't usually have nice young ladies knocking on my door looking to hang out. But sure, maybe we could go for a cup of coffee sometime and you could tell me whatever is on your mind. I'm not too accustomed to the social setting myself."

"That's great." A wave of relief washed over her. "My name is Tracy." She held out her hand, and the man shook it. "And I live right behind you. So when you want to get that coffee just stop by and let me know." Another nervous giggle.

"Alright sounds great. I'm Lance, by the way. I'll see you around."

The door shut, and Tracy felt damn proud of herself.

* * *

Lance watched Tracy through the blinds as she happily jogged home. *What the hell was she doing here? This is really getting out of hand. Now she's at my house. I need to fucking kill her already. Hmm, though, I might be able to use this to my advantage. The prey, in my cave, my home. The lion's den. How's that for a blockbuster movie? Or hell, at least a Lifetime movie special. I always saw myself as a Stanley Tucci look-a-like. He's even played a stalker-killer before. I can think of no other actor I would want to be me on the screen.*

When Tracy disappeared into her house, Lance walked away from the window. He took his pipe, stuffed a portion of tobacco into the bowl, and lit it. He took a long puff, and held his pipe, cocking his left eyebrow. *Movie deals aside, this would be a great chance to have her at last. I wanted to take her in her house, but this, well this is perfect. I could never get her without a chance of someone seeing me. Even if I drugged her. Too many nosey-bodies. But, if she comes here, maybe during the night... As long as she is quiet, yes, I could kill her in the basement, hide her body in the floor, pour concrete over the grave, and poof, no one will ever suspect me. Yeah baby, mmmmmmmm, I have been so ready for this. Come to me... come to daddy little girl.*

Four

The next day, Tracy woke up feeling better than she had her whole life. Leaving the house to make a new friend, turned out to be exactly what she needed. She jumped out of bed in her pearl white, flannel pajamas, and threw open the blinds. Like a vampire to the sun, she winced, but it didn't stop her. She stood, basking in the sun, the liberation made her float. Slowly she opened her eyes, and surprise, no one was watching her.

She kept the pepper-spray by the bed, but didn't bother to put it back into her purse.

After a long, hot shower, she dried off and put on her clothes. Granted she didn't have a huge selection in her wardrobe, but she always looked nice. In a couple hours she would be at the movie theater, with a real smile on her face, and in her voice. Who knows, this guy just might end up more than a friend. Not that he was much of a Brad Pitt, but he didn't look bad. And his eyes were pretty damn sexy. His voice wasn't bad either. Though his voice did remind her of that cashier at the grocery store, but anyways. He looked like he might even be strong. Nice strong arms to hold her. Sure he was twice her age, but she didn't care for guys her age. They were all knuckle-heads. Drinking themselves stupid, chasing ass, especially if it was easy-ass. None of the men she had seen around town seemed like they wanted anything more than a booty-call. Of course most men only cared about sex anyways, and she wanted it so bad that she was gagging for it, but damn, she needed a man who would want her, for her. Sex, was just a byproduct.

Tracy's thoughts still wouldn't leave her alone. She knew that she gave this Lance a lot of credit. *Too much credit.* She didn't know spit about this guy. He just looks like the type who would make a great friend, a good provider, even. Maybe a good lover. Whatever that would be. Being a virgin wasn't making things any easier. Spending her nights falling asleep with various erotic books in hand, made her want to feel what the authors wrote about. Lance didn't look anything like the male protagonists from those tales, but he surely could fill the shoes with the personality, assuming that she didn't give him more credit than he deserved. His biceps didn't need to ripple, just be strong enough to make her feel safe. Tracy was a woman who could kick ass, but she never liked the idea of being her only warrior. In a world that was fueled by the mentally-deficient, the criminally insane, she could use some old-school romance in her life.

Time for work.

* * *

Matinee time was the slowest part of the day. The doors were open, and so far no one had come in to purchase a ticket. Tracy had the popcorn already popped, and now she waited.

Almost starting time for the first movie, there he was, Lance. She leaned on the counter, watching him buy his ticket. Then he turned, and smiled in surprise.

"Well, well, well, looky who I found. I didn't know you worked here."

"Yeah, I've been working here for about four years now."

"I'll take a medium size popcorn, with extra butter, and a large cola. So, given any thought where you would like to get that coffee?"

"I was hoping you would stop by my place with an idea."

"Seeing that I ran into you here, and I have no idea of your schedule, how would stopping by at my place, say around eight tonight, sound?"

She smiled and hesitantly responded. "I'm not really used to going to people's houses for coffee. I don't know."

"I understand. No biggie." She slid his drink to him across the counter and scooped his popcorn. "Tell you what, when you feel more comfortable with joining me for a cup at my place, you know where to find me." Lance turned with his food and drink and headed towards the movie.

"Wait, Lance." He turned around. "Okay, tonight would be great." She smiled.

"Awesome, doll, see you then."

What the fuck, girl? Are you serious? You know him enough to go over to his house. It was stupid enough the first time, but now you will have to set foot inside. You know better. Shut up! I'm tired of living my life inside of a cage. It's time I lived my life.

* * *

Two minutes until eight o'clock, Lance just finished cleaning his place. He never in his life dusted, which became clear during his reformation of the humble-abode. He threw together a tossed-chicken salad just in case Tracy might be hungry. Just because he planned to kill her was no reason to be rude. After all, it was her idea to enter his cave. She wanted to meet the man who watched her every move, who planned her death from the moment she was born. The least he could do was to offer her a last meal. She didn't eat a whole lot, but from what he could read from her trash, she ate a lot salad. Never an empty bottle of dressing, though. He never knew a woman who didn't put dressing on a salad. So, now, Lance likes salad with no dressing. Diced carrots, tomatoes, red onions, almonds, three different kinds of lettuce, shredded cheddar-jack cheese and minced chicken. Actually he could see why she liked it so much, it did taste good.

The coffee sat on the burner of his brewer, the smell intoxicated the air. *Coffee and salad, hmmm, not really the combination that inspires hot dates, but not over the top 'romantic' for a first time meal either. Not that there would be another date. But Tracy doesn't know that.*

The rap at the door yanked Lance out of his anticipating thoughts. *Mmm, she's here.*

She looked her best, wearing the perfume, which after his years of snooping through her trash was always, and had to be, Angel Violet.

"Hi, wow, I can smell the coffee clear out here."

"Ah yes, it's ready and I prepared a salad for us."

She stepped inside as Lance shut and locked the door behind her.

"Wow, I love salad. But I hate salad dressing. Please tell me you didn't add any?"

"No, my dear. I absolutely appall salad dressing. I fixed my favorite, a tossed chicken salad. Pretty average fixings, I hope you like."

Tracy looked at the glass bowl that sat in front of one of the chairs. "Looks perfect. You're good."

"Not so much good, as lucky. Well lucky that we have similar taste."

"More like, exact."

Lance pulled out the chair for her, and scooted her in.

"I don't get many occasions where I can treat a guest, or a friend for that matter. So I thought for a simple night, and to honor this occasion, I would treat you to a salad. Nothing too terribly complicated, but delish none-the-less. And here's your cup of premium, roasted, coffee. Do you take sugar or cream in that?"

"No. Black is perfect." *Of course, my dear. But I wouldn't want to come across like I know everything.*

"Okay, so, what is it that made you come to my door, exactly?" *A curiosity that will drive me nuts for the rest of my life, if I don't get the answer before I kill you.*

"It's ... kinda, kind of a long story." She took a mouthful of salad. "Mmm, ish-o-ood."

Lance let out a small chuckle. "I'm sorry, what?"

"Oh, no, I'm sorry, what I said was this is so good."

"All fresh produce from a local farmer's market."

"I can tell. That's where I get my vegetables too."

"Great minds."

"Okay, the reason I came here yesterday, well, this isn't easy to talk about, but the reason I'm here is so I can talk about it. I have an issue with people. Especially men."

"Oh really?"

"Not you, but men in general. My mother was killed by a man when I was a baby. And ever since I have been paranoid that I am being watched by a man, who would kill me. I know, it's silly. But I always worry because it happened to her, it can always happen to me. Not to mention when I am out there are always pervs making comments, on occasion playing with themselves in public, for me to notice. So, it's difficult for me to make friends. And people don't always understand where I'm coming from."

"I do."

"Really? I mean I'm glad to a point you can understand, but—"

"No, I understand. About being paranoid. There are nasty people everywhere. In small towns, big cities, even in the country, nowhere is safe anymore. Hell not even our own homes. And assholes who make their comments to you, and play with themselves, they're a dime a dozen. Sick people, violent people, they are everywhere. They can look the part, or they can look like some sweet grandfather, all the while having a thing for raping kids. A lot of times we don't know until long after, and when the person in question can't be held accountable. So yes, I do understand."

"Thank you. The biggest problem that people don't understand, is me losing my mother at a young age, and how I lost her. Not everyone loses a parent to a killer. Not like I did."

"That makes sense. I mean the fact that few people, especially around here, would understand that. It is something I would think a person would have to go through to fully comprehend."

"Exactly. Though you seem you understand pretty well. You know what's funny? It just hit me, we both drink coffee in the evening. I thought I was the only nut in town that did."

"I drink it so often that the caffeine doesn't keep me awake."

"Yeah, it keeps me awake, but I have problems sleeping anyways, my whole life in fact, that I figure what the hell?" She finished her cup. "May I have more, please?" she said in a cute tone.

"Coming right up." Lance took her cup and headed for the kitchen.

This was it. Where he would add the liquid X. He poured the coffee into the cup, and started to reach into the cabinet for the unmarked, clear bottle. Two arms from behind wrapped around his stomach.

"Thank you for being so sweet. I was afraid of meeting you, but I can see that it was a good choice."

What the fuck? I never figured you for a hugger. Damn, that perfume smells even better up close.

"Um ... I-I ..."

"I'm sorry." She pulled back releasing Lance.

"No, it's okay, you just, took me by surprise." *As I have stated before, that's not allowed.*

"I know, and I like you. I do. But a lot of it comes from me wanting to be with someone. I'm lonely and this isn't right. I want to get to know you, and for you to get to know me, but, as a friend, and that's hard right now. This is why I was nervous about coming over here. Wasn't about you, as it was me. I would rather just talk here and there in passing for a while, and slowly get to know each other as friends. Maybe even make some new friends, have a group night out. I don't know, I'm new to having a life. I should go."

"What? No. Don't go. I promise you have nothing to worry about. No funny moves from me, we can keep the hugs down to just hands shakes, and a nod, and finish our meal."

"As I said, this is more about me. You are fine. You really are a nice guy. And I do like you. I just don't want to throw myself at you out of being lonely. I will see you around." And then Tracy left.

DAMNIT! I almost had her. This girl is problematic. I should give up now on this one, but that's too many years to throw away. Damn you.

Five

"Oh my God, I'm such an idiot. Why did I have to hug him?" Tracy slammed the door and slid along her back down to the floor in a squatting position. "It felt good. Damn good. But fuck, I knew it was stupid the moment I opened my mouth. He's going to think I'm a freak now."

She held her eyes with cupped palms, and cried.

Her chest ached, and finally the tears dried up. She sat completely down, leaned back onto the door, and stared into a vacant gaze.

* * *

Mornings always made Tracy feel anew. A second chance to get things right. But not this morning. She left for work and this time Lance wasn't there at the bus stop. *Dammit, I made him walk.*

Turning around, Tracy went back home.

A brief moment of paranoia returned. It felt like someone was watching her. She forgot to push away her old feelings, and now they were having their way with her. Before sliding the key into the lock, Tracy turned and looked towards Lance's house. The backside tree shrouded house seemed non-threatening enough. The blinds were closed, no one standing in the yard staring. She shook it off and went inside.

She locked the door and at that very moment there was a thud in the other room. *Did it come from my bedroom?*

Tightening her fingers around the ceramic handle of a coffee cup she forgot to take out to the kitchen, she walked towards where the noise originated. *My door is closed. I never leave it closed.*

She twisted the knob, pushing the door open slowly as she held up the cup.

The window was open and the wind rushed in. The pepper-spray had blown over onto the bare floor.

Another thing she never did, was leave her windows open, or unlocked. In a panic she checked the room, under the bed, in the closet, as if she was a parent securing the room from monsters for a terrified child. *Safe! For now.*

She peeked out the window, and no one was around. She slammed it shut, and again locked it. *How did someone unlock it from the outside?*

57

DAUGHTER'S PREY

***

Back in his cave, Lance slid the soaking wet face mask off of his head. Wiping the sweat from his forehead, he grabbed the binoculars that sat on a nearby stand, close to the window. With two fingers, he slightly pried the blind-slats and watched Tracy's house. *Too bad I can't see her bedroom from here.*

Then, the blinds from her living room moved. She was peeking back at Lance's house. *The game's a foot. So my dear, you want to spy on me?*

Lance let out a snicker. She was becoming paranoid again. Something Lance knew all about, and he was okay with that. At least she was consistent. The rules were going back as he planned. Still, he had to move quickly, she was starting to piece things together, but for now she was unaware. But for how long would that last?

Lance put the binoculars back on the stand and rubbed her house key with his thumb. *I will be using you more, my little friend.*

Six

Tracy got off with a verbal warning over the phone when she called into work five minutes after she was supposed to be on the clock. She was lucky, most employees would have been slapped with a write-up, and one more time would be a termination. Though her boss didn't make very many exceptions, he was aware of her past. She could feel in his words the pity, the sympathy. It annoyed the piss out of her, but today she was using it to her advantage.

Lance probably didn't have anything to do with this. He was such a sweetie. But *someone* broke into her home. Nothing was missing, but she never left the window unlocked.

Tracy threw together her overnight pack. More like a week away bag. Today was a trip to the country side. A nice little house out in the middle of nowhere. It was her grandparents, and since her mother was gone, the house went to her. They had the land paid off, and the taxes taken care of for the next five years. Considering her lack of substantial income, that was for the best. She had considered selling the place, but the idea of having an escape plan changed her mind.

The best part about not having any friends, was that no one knew of her exit strategy. With three outfits, basic hygiene supplies, and extra food, she was packed. The pepper-spray went into her pocket. In the other pocket a folding knife that opened with a flourish of the thumb.

She bundled the bag into the old Pontiac Sunbird GT. A car she hadn't driven in two years. Her idea to save on gas. The car fought to start, but after the fourth time it came to life.

Hopefully after a few days away, she would have a clear mind and figure out what the hell to do.

***

In the darkness of the woods, raccoons screamed as they tore each other a part. A nice cover for Lance as he snuck up to Tracy's hiding place. *Such a naïve little girl.* Twenty years of watching her every move, looking through her most precious belongings, there wasn't anything that he didn't know about Tracy, which was why it freaked him out when she came to his cave.

Lance knew the time was near to pounce on his prey, but now that the prey had toyed with its unbeknown predator, his hand was forced. He admired Tracy for so, so many reasons. Just like her mother, Tracy was beautiful, brilliant, and strong. She had no idea just how strong she had been. Lance thought about being her friend for real, and actually caring about her like a normal person would, maybe even help her come out of her shell. He could have been the very miracle Tracy desired. Lance wasn't the man she thought him to be. The killer of her mother among so many other victims, he could be the greatest thing for Tracy, but if he came clean about his dark side, she would run.

Lance for the second time in his life felt a longing for companionship, and it was the blood of the first time that had done it to him. *Damn women, they will always take your soul, and tear it apart.* Just like with Holly, Lance knew what he had to do. This insatiable hunger to stalk, to kill, it was beyond his ability to control. He was meant to be a predator, meant to watch from afar, up close, but never to engage until that moment came. Lance studied police work in regards to his kind. They were always asked, "Why, why are you like this? Why are you the way you are?" Normal people always have answers. Their unsatisfiable appetite for the truth for what makes the world go round. Lance would never be able to give such a black and white answer. It's like asking someone who is gay, "Why do you like other men?". Silly questions asked by the ignorant. You can't understand something that you don't feel. You can't feel the same as the abnormal. Lance knew he was different from the world, sure there are many with his need to hunt, but most people don't understand because most people are nothing like him.

Just another monster for headlines. People love to hold wild and dangerous animals above the wellbeing of humans; protect wolves and bears when these very animals will tear a human being to pieces just out of pure natural instinct. Did it ever occur to these people that Lance was such an animal? Why doesn't his kind have a protection act? Wolves, bears, cougars, they all have their ways of stalking, killing, and people come to their rescue. The food, their savior. Would anyone other than a money hungry defense attorney do the same for Lance? Probably not. Only the sick and twisted would go to bat for Lance, and not the average person. It's okay for animals to be predatory killers, but once a human does it, *let 'em die.* This thought made Lance love what he did even more.

It didn't matter if the whole damn world were to string him up by his own innards, and prance around his mounted body in Time's Square, he was what he was, an animal, stalking its prey, and going for the kill. Fuck the world, fuck their hypocritical views; nothing could stop Lance being what God made him to be.

The gorgeous old farmhouse stood before him. The old fields over grown by weeds were taller than him. So much cover. Tracy's sanctuary nestled in greenery. A nice fantasy, but she wasn't capable of creating her dreams, like Lance. He could live out his fantasies, and he was about to it again.

* * *

Every time Tracy tried to sleep, Lance invaded her dreams. He was everywhere. Different hair and clothes, but it was him. She made herself wake up each time the dream came back, so sleep become lacking. The paranoia feasted on her nerves like a heavenly smorgasbord. She could almost hear the nomming of her phobia. *Seriously?* Even in the quiet house, away from the world, she couldn't escape herself. *Might as well go back to the city.* It did strike her as odd that even before befriending Lance that he seemed familiar. Tracy suspected him then changed her mind because she wanted to believe that not all people are bad. She needed him to be a white knight, and so turned him into one. *So fucking naïve.*

What if the man she liked, was the monster she feared? There it was again, the stupid paranoia. This was why she needed professional help. There was no one out there to get her. The odds of it happening to her after her mother, was zilch. But how could she get herself to see this? Maybe she could still make things right with Lance, and at least have a decent friendship. But she couldn't do that until she could tell herself to get over it, and move on. Saying it and believing it were two different things.

Tracy headed out to the kitchen for a sandwich. If she wasn't going to sleep, then stress induced gorging it was. A flick of the light switch revealed the back door ajar. Without the need to entertain her paranoia, she knew that the door was locked when went to bed. Again, someone knew where she was and found a way around the lock. *SHIT!*

She hurried towards the counter for a knife, but magically they were all gone. Tracy left everything in the house the way it was when her grandparents passed, and she did use some of the kitchen utensils before going to bed. Tracy had knives in this house. Had. But whoever it was that took the knives missed the pots and pans. She reached for the skillet but then someone grabbed her from behind. A gloved-hand placed a rag over her mouth, chloroform from her guess.

She drove down her barefoot heal onto the intruder's foot, then slammed her head back into his chest.

He stumbled a little but kept his grip. She grabbed the skillet handle swung it almost striking the man.

He sliced her arm forcing Tracy to drop her weapon.

"Nice try, kitten."

The voice, so familiar. *Lance?* Why was it his name kept coming back to her? Why did she have to keep making him the bad guy? But it was his voice. It was him. *Dirty bastard.*

An arm locked around Tracy's throat like a Python. She couldn't breathe.

He held her for several minutes before her vision went dark.

* * *

Her sight begrudgingly returned, the bedroom ceiling appeared. Her head woozy, but the memories, mostly physical recollection, made her fear moving. Suffocation. Powerless. The tightening of her throat, the constriction of her body... *LANCE!*

She slightly twitched her wrist expecting it to be duct taped to something, but oddly she wasn't constrained. *Asshole already knows I'm not a threat. He knows everything after all. He's a real fucking Santa Clause.*

"There's no point in playing dead, my dear." The came from the far corner of the room, where a small cushioned chair sat. "Just as there's no point in concealing my identity. You know who I am; you were starting to figure it out before I could have my way with you. Smart. Little. Bitch."

"Look, asshole." She sprang up with her arms supporting her posture. "If you want to, 'have your way with me' then get it over with."

"Silly girl, I'm not like that. I don't want to fuck, please. I want to kill you. Slowly." Lance slid a six-inch, full tang knife from a sheath on his belt. "I'm going to kill you, not quite like I killed your mother—" Her face enraged. "I was a little sloppy, since I loved her. Don't worry, I'm not going all Darth Vader on you, I'm not your father."

"Piece of shit." she said in a growling whisper.

"I've watched you all of your life, and you were now discovering me. Of course I didn't think you would. I have been doing this for a very long time. Oh well. I have people to kill, and new targets to check out."

Lance moved towards Tracy. She swung her legs in a semi-circle, slamming her left ankle into his jaw. He reached for her leg and grabbed air. She yanked open the drawer of her nightstand but the pepper spray was gone.

"Oops, yeah, I tossed, sorry. I think it expired." He swung the knife at her.

Tracy ran crouching.

Lance charged as Tracy slipped into the bathroom. Tracy slammed the door shut, stopping Lance's momentum. The concussion from his body nearly forced Tracy down to the floor, she held onto the doorknob, and slid the lock into place.

* * *

He thought about copying the Scream movies, and stabbing the knife into the wooden door. But the door was solid, good quality unlike the more modern crap most new houses are made with. He really didn't want to snap his favorite blade. Instead, Lance kicked at the base of the door with his steel-toe boots, not really doing much damage so much, as scaring the shit out of poor, little, Tracy.

"Herrreeee, little kitty ... get your obnoxious ass out here." A pound thudded from the other side, ringing Lance's ear. "Oooo, got some fight in you. Guess what? I know everything about you. You were paranoid before, just think about how paranoid you will be if you get away. I am a master of disguise; there is no where you can go that I can't find you. Think about it, Tracy. I stalked your mom, dated her, even fucked her, then killed her. And then I watched little ol' you grow up just so I can kill you! Mmmm, I love to kill twenty-year-olds. I don't know why. I've tried to come up with some decent answer, you know, in case I'm caught, and some FBI analyst asks me the 'why's' on Primetime Television, but I got nothing. It's like asking why a bird flies. It just does. You know what I mean?" Lance brushed his hair with his fingers over his balding spot.

No sound.

"I swear, *WOMEN!*"

Lance slammed his body repeatedly against the door until the lock gave way. He almost stumbled into the tub. The window next to the tub was open with the white see-through curtain whipping in a breeze.

Damn her.

DAUGHTER'S PREY

Lance peeked his head out half expecting something blunt to smack him in the head, but to his surprise she wasn't anywhere to be seen. He looked around the second story roof, and there was no way she had jumped. Not as dainty as she is. The roof though sloped was manageable enough to climb. *Great. She sneaked to a different room.*

Lance pulled back and checked the other rooms. Now that he had reason to cloak his presence, the creaking floorboards betrayed him. Even with his stealth-slippers, there was no concealing his approach.

He peeked into the bedroom and the window was open. It was shut when he left. Slowly he peered around the corner with knife ready. No one. Then a floor board creaked from behind. He turned and the flat end of a wood closet rod rammed him in the eye.

Dropping the knife he cradled his face. His vision blacked out. Then the sharp stab into his stomach. *The bitch got my knife.*

"You fucking prick, that one's for my mother." *Oh fuck.* "This one's for me."

The next several stabs tore into his crotch, and then into his chest. After that, there was nothing to feel.

* * *

Lance was butchered on Tracy's bed in the old farmhouse. The bed would have to go, but more importantly, so would the body. She didn't just kill him in self-defense, she carved him up. These days you can be well within your right for killing out of self-defense, and still face prison time. Not for this shit-bag. Her mother's murder was avenged. And she protected herself. To Tracy, this was a clean kill. But the burden of burying Lance in the woods was on her now.

She rolled him up in the bed spread, then in plastic, and used five rolls of Gorilla duct tape to make sure he was good and wrapped. Then she rolled him over to the window, and hoisted him over the window sill and onto the sloped roof where gravity fished the decent.

Now the hard part. Digging, and dragging. But the best part, no more paranoia.

THE PERPETUAL PILL
TOM BARLOW

Years before, Fletcher's brother Burton, showing off his knowledge of the arcane to some distant cousins at a family reunion, had explained perpetual pills.

"Antimony is a metal, but it acts like a laxative," he'd said, voice burred by malt liquor. "Families used to pass a ball of antimony down from generation to generation. When one of them was constipated, he'd swallow the ball, then recover it the next day when it came back out, still as good as new."

The camera pill was still warm to the touch as Fletcher rinsed it off. Most of the accounting staff was still upstairs yawning through sexual harassment training, so he had the men's room to himself.

He dried the cold-capsule-sized pill in the breeze of the hand dryer and examined it closely for damage. Even after 15 laps through his digestive system, the tiny medical device showed no sign of wear. He pulled the iPhone from his holster and confirmed that the device was still transmitting camera images via Bluetooth.

He popped the camera pill in his pocket, looking forward to a big lunch. He hated fasting every Tuesday, purging his system to provide a clear view for his weekly Wednesday photo shoot.

Fletcher continued to worry about his duodenum, though, as he took the elevator to the ground floor and walked outside. Although the pill camera theoretically spun as it passed in order to provide 360 degrees of image, every time it passed through his duodenum, the video feed missed the same inside bend. He was convinced that something dreadful was lurking there. Colon cancer had killed his father, his mother, and both of his grandmothers, and he was determined that it wasn't going to get him.

As was his custom, he broke his fast with a tempura lunch box at the neighborhood Japanese restaurant, and arrived back at the office logy from two pots of tea. His mouse finger would be jittery from the caffeine for most of the afternoon, making it difficult to place lines on the blueprint he was updating.

To his surprise, the cubicle next to his was occupied. It had been vacant since Li Keqiang, a young draftsperson with an annoying fondness for body sprays, had decided to quit six months before to grow lettuce for farmer's markets.

In his place sat a woman around Fletcher's age, mid-30s. In profile, she reminded him of one of his high school crushes; high hairline, arching eyebrows over widely-spaced eyes, delicate jaw. Her shoulder-length hair was a lovely sienna with streaks of brick red, iridescent under the fluorescent lamps. Not a knockout, but Fletcher was self-aware enough to know that he wasn't an Adonis himself.

She was scrolling through the assembly drawing her predecessor had left incomplete, oblivious to Fletcher's presence. Veins protruding like maple roots from the back of her mouse hand, and her fingernails showed very faint lunulae. Fletcher watched her work for a couple of minutes before clearing his throat.

She started, then swiveled to face him.

"Hi," he said. "I'm Fletcher. In the next cubicle." He tapped the half-wall dividing them.

She smiled, rolled her chair a couple of feet toward him to extend a hand up without rising. "Alice. The temp. Pleased to meet you."

Ah, a temp. He'd heard a rumor that the company planned to trim expenses by using temps. He worried that they'd be screwing with the health insurance next.

"Ben has you working on the stamping press drawings?" He pointed to the screen. "You might want to double-check the work Li did just before he quit. He was stoned most of the time."

"Ah," she replied, nodding. "That explains the four dimensions in the girder assembly directions."

"Did Ben give you any idea how long you'd be here?" He liked her smile and her outfit, pressed slacks the color of lemon cream and a vanilla blouse with a scoop neck, a flat gold chain and gold hoop earrings. Dignified, not like the women in the sales department, who usually dressed as though the place was a bowling alley.

"A few weeks, maybe more. But companies always lie, then dump you without warning. That way people don't slack off."

"Must be hard, just getting to know the job and the people, then, poof." He made an explosion gesture with his fingers.

"Sometimes. When the problem is the boss, though, leaving can be a relief."

"That's not a problem here. We rarely see Ben. We rarely see much of anybody, really." He glanced beyond her workstation to the dozens of empty cubicles, each still containing an old drafting table. The sales office beyond was separated from them by a glass wall at the far end of the room, which allowed him to watch the bustle inside any time he felt lonely.

"Ben said I should come to you if I had any questions. They didn't tell you to expect me?"

"Nope. I'll probably get a memo about it the day after you leave."

"Let's hope that's not for a while. I can use the money."

"They measure us by the number of drawings we finish each month. Anything over 30 is pretty good."

"Then I'd better get busy." She shoved off with her feet to roll back to her drawing board.

"Me, too," Fletcher said with touch of regret. He returned to his own cubicle and spent the afternoon working though updates to an electrical schematic he'd been procrastinating over for a week. The presence of another human being nearby made it difficult for him to concentrate.

*　*　*

That evening, as he hung his dry cleaning in the closet, he wondered if he should update his wardrobe. His button-down shirts ranged in color from royal blue to Dodger blue, his ties from black through charcoal to slate gray, and his pants and shoes black, black, black. His thick sepia hair was beginning to lighten around the temples and thin out on top, and he was tweezing more and more gray hairs from his meticulously-trimmed moustache. Perhaps some flamboyance would relieve the tedium of his days. A mint green shirt, perhaps, or tan chinos.

Burton phoned just as Fletcher was settling in to watch college basketball, UConn and Georgetown, on his new high-definition television. His half-brother was half-drunk, as usual.

"Some dude here is selling his tickets for the Bulls game," Burton said. "Versus the Knicks. Thirty each, almost courtside. What do you say?"

Fletcher muted the television. "Where is here?"

"I'm at Mike's. You should come over. We can play some darts. There's a table of school bus driver women here, too; a couple aren't bad-looking."

Fletcher unconsciously rubbed the dart scar on the outside of his left elbow. "Not tonight. I'm beat."

"You can't get laid sitting at home."

"I also can't spend my pay check sitting at home." Burton only phoned from Mike's when he was broke, and Fletcher was trying to wean him.

"Mom worried about you. Before she passed, she said to me, Burton, she says, you make sure your brother finds a wife before his starts developing a gut. Don't let him turn into a recluse like his daddy."

"Recluse? She used the word recluse?"

"And a hypochondriac. When's the last time you had a date?" Burton's words were punctuated with the snap of his Zippo lighter.

August 22nd, 2009, he thought. "You have a good night. Don't drive drunk." He hung up the phone, turned the TV sound back on and picked up his laptop. He uploaded the latest colon scan and ran it side by side with that of the previous week. There was a new patch of angry pink at the ligament of Treitz, where the duodenum and the jejunum met. He tagged the clearest frame. He also confirmed his earlier observation that the camera had, once again, failed to capture the same bend in his large intestine. On the bright side, he remained free of polyps, so no worries about familial adenomatous polyposis.

Yet.

* * *

Fletcher stopped at Krispy Kreme on the way to work the next morning and bought a half-dozen glazed for the office. Alice was already at her computer when he arrived.

He held up the bag. "I brought breakfast." She was blond today, sunny against the cardinal red pants-suit that looked two sizes too big for her.

She smiled wanly. "That's so nice! But I'm not eating this week."

He draped his sport coat over its usual hanger and placed it on the otherwise empty rack in the hallway outside his cubicle. "Like, you're not eating much? Or you're fasting?"

"Clear liquids only. I had colon cancer last year, so I try to flush the pipes every month or so." Although she was blushing, Fletcher detected no hint of embarrassment in her voice.

Which was good, because he couldn't stop himself from prying.

"You had a colectomy? I mean, they caught it in time?"

"So far, so good. Only time will tell for sure, though."

"That why you're temping?"

"Yeah. When human relations hears the "C" word, all they can think about is the "I" word. Nobody wants to add that kind of risk to their insurance pool."

"That sucks." Fletcher's Dad had died first, leaving his mom without insurance. With it, she might have lived years longer. "Let me know if I can do anything to help."

"That's sweet, but I've moved on from cancer. I just wish my hair would catch up. At least my sister owns a wig shop."

He looked more carefully at her face. What he'd taken for eyebrows were painted on. He'd never have figured her hair for a wig, though. The air in the cubicle, for so long stale and papery, was scented with something like lavender.

"I need to get back to this," she finally said, nodding toward her drawing board.

"Me, too," he said, with a hint of chagrin as he realized he'd been staring.

Just before lunch, Fletcher reviewed his morning's work, and was appalled at the number of mistakes he'd made.

* * *

Over the next couple of days, he and Alice fell into a routine of taking their breaks together. He learned about the many accomplishments of her only child, Cyan, apparently a world-class cheerleader and high school politician. She told him about her marriage, which lasted less than two years, her truncated career in car design, but nothing about her illness, although he fed her several segues.

He told her about his career at the company from the time he started as a rookie draftsman through the great recession contraction, his aspiration to visit Rome and Athens to see the architecture, his love of fruit pies, and his parent's cancer. He also made up a long-lasting but now ended love affair.

* * *

Thursday, on returning home from work, Fletcher found his brother asleep on the couch. Burton's black T-shirt had ridden up his stomach, revealing a paunch the color of cheap vanilla ice cream.

He turned on the television, keeping the volume low, and watched ESPN. Burton woke halfway through a discussion about the West Coast offense; was it passé? He rubbed his face like palming a basketball, pried a cigarette out of his breast pocket, and lit it.

Fletcher didn't complain, knowing his brother would just ignore him anyway. He stepped into the kitchen, snapped on the oven hood fan, and took a seat at the table until the smoke cleared in the living room.

However, Burton followed him.

"You're a cliché for boorishness," Fletcher said.

"That's the testosterone talking," Burton said. "You got to take your dog out for a walk before you blow to pieces."

"At least I don't let mine run loose."

"No, that's the last thing I'd expect of you. Seriously, man, you know any women? Any at all?"

Feeling that his libido was being impugned, Fletcher replied, "There is a woman at work. Very pretty. We've been taking breaks together."

"Tell me about her." Burton ran water from the tap over his cigarette butt and tossed it toward the trash in the corner.

"She's my age," Fletcher said, realizing how little he really knew about Alice. So he embellished; after all, it was only Burton. "Blonde, stacked, reminds me of Nicole Kidman a little bit. She's divorced, one kid. Graduated from Purdue in engineering. She's planning to open her own design company, which is why she's temping—so she can meet some people she might want to recruit."

"Sounds promising," Burton said. "Maybe you should introduce me."

"She's not the kind to show her tits for some Mardi Gras beads."

"I could teach her."

"God forbid."

"So you going to ask her out?"

"I'm thinking about it."

"Thinking don't cut it. Just ask her out. It won't kill you. Sex doesn't cause cancer."

* * *

Fletcher thought about his brother's exhortation all that evening.

The next morning, Alice couldn't have been more fetching, hair the color of tangerine Kool-Aid, a sophisticated black pinstriped pants suit set off with a huge honey citrine in a short pendent that rested in the hollow where her neck met her breastbone. She wore a wide golden band on each wrist, reminding him a little of Wonder Woman. He'd had a crush on Wonder Woman when he was young.

As drawn as he was to her, however, there was fear that held him back. After his experience with his parents, he couldn't stand to watch another loved one die before their time.

"Penny for your thoughts." She had come around the corner unawares, catching him with his mouse pen poised to drop on a new section of the blueprint. It had been poised for who knew how long while he mulled over his dilemma.

He slid the pen to the edge of the page. As he laid it down, he had an inspiration.

"I was wondering," he said, "about your nutrition. Fasting, that is. How do you control your electrolytes?"

"I drink Gatorade," she said. "The clear kind."

"Are you sure you're getting all the nutrients you need? I use this supplement, one pill, that packs everything— amino acids, bee pollen, bromelain, lycopene, MSM, glucosamine ... you name it, you got it."

"Thanks, but I'm pretty happy with my routine." She gave him a smile that he read as forbearance.

"I'll bring one in tomorrow," he insisted. "Just try it one time, see if it helps."

"I guess," she said. "In the interest of a harmonious workplace."

"There you go," he said.

* * *

On the way home, Fletcher stopped in at the electronics store where he'd spent way too much money over the years; he loved gizmos. There he picked up a new toy—a battery-operated, cigarette-pack-sized repeater that captured and retransmitted Bluetooth signals, extending the range up to a couple of miles.

With the repeater, if he could get her to swallow the pill camera, he could inspect her colon, assure himself that there were no pressing problems. Only then would he be able to commit to a relationship. It didn't please him to realize he was that timid, but after 35 years perhaps it was time for him to accept and live within his shortcomings.

He pawed through his vitamin collection until he found a supplement in a large enough capsule. He took one apart, blew out the remaining powder, and carefully inserted the colon camera, which fit perfectly. Putting the halves of the capsule together, it looked so very ordinary he was sure Alice would never suspect. The capsule would dissolve in her stomach, allowing the camera to take a tour of her colon so he could see for himself that she was cured.

* * *

He didn't confront Alice with the pill first thing in the morning, which proved to be a mistake. In the two hours between starting time and their morning break he was unable to work for worry, and by 10 a.m. he was damp with sweat.

"Time for a break?" Alice was standing in his doorway. Today she wore a silky tiger-print top with three-quarter sleeves and white toreador pants. Her hair was black, her jewelry silver and chunky, including rings on both thumbs. The effect was stunning.

"You bet," Fletcher said. "Let's get some coffee."

As they walked across the drafting room toward the cafeteria, he said, "How many days left on your fast?"

"Today's the last day," she said. "And boy, am I tired of eating nothing."

Fletcher bit the end of his tongue to quell his nervousness before saying, "Good, because I brought you one of those super supplements I told you about. Taking it on an empty stomach will make it easy for you to judge if it helps or not."

They reached the cafeteria, almost empty, since most of the few employees left went outside to smoke. The company provided free coffee, brewed cup by cup by a vending machine. Knowing Alice's preferences, he punched up hers, black, one sugar, before his, two creams, two sugars.

He carried them back to their usual table, dead center in the room.

"Thanks," she said, accepting the cup.

He took a seat and pulled the envelope containing the capsule from his pocket. He laid it on the table and slid it to her. "Here's the supplement."

She took the envelope, opened it, and picked up the capsule between her thumbnail and index finger.

"What's in this?" she said, holding it up.

Fletcher listed every nutrient he could think of, including a couple that may have only existed in the minds of the persons writing supplement ad copy.

She raised her faux eyebrows. "There's nothing in here that's going to hurt me, is there?"

"It's all good," Fletcher assured her. "I take one every morning, and I'm as healthy as a horse." He tapped on his chest as he said so, and had to restrain a cough.

"What the hell," she said, and placed the capsule in her mouth. "No risk, no gain."

Fletcher couldn't wait to return to their cubes so he could test the camera. Sure enough, as they sat in their cubes divided by a fabric wall, the signal strength from the camera was strong, although there was nothing to see; the capsule had not yet dissolved.

Within an hour, though, the capsule was gone and the camera began to show pictures of her stomach wall. Fletcher was delighted with the quality of the transmission as the camera slid through the pyloric valve into the small intestine.

Half an hour later Alice, who drank water diligently, took a trip to the restroom. The signal cut out once she left her desk. Like most buildings, though, the men's and women's restrooms shared a common wall. As soon as Alice was out of sight, Fletcher hustled after her. In the men's room stall, by leaning against the wall, he was able to pick up the transmission, as the camera dropped a few more inches to expose a new section of colon.

Fletcher got almost nothing done that day except watch his iPhone. It was like watching the world's most boring documentary, the trip through the human digestive tract, except his longing for companionship made it a compelling drama.

At 4 p.m. the camera finally reached the surgery spot, high up in the large colon. He could see a scar, where a section had been removed, but it was totally healed, and other than the scar tissue he couldn't tell that it had even been repaired. His heart was lightened.

But he was also anxious, so much so he got a case of the hiccups that it took twenty minutes and a sharp couple of raps on the back from Alice to stop.

* * *

By quitting time, the camera was well along the colon, and Fletcher was enraptured. He walked Alice to her car, as had become their custom. Along the way he casually asked her how she was going to spend the evening, and was relieved when she told him she was going to work out at the gym before going home.

Fortunately for Fletcher, the sun set early in February, and Alice's upscale neighborhood featured old-fashioned cast-iron streetlights that looked lovely but illuminated very little.

He circled her block twice to assure himself that the lawn separating her apartment building from the next was dark enough that no-one would likely see him there. He parked on the street in front of her building and walked up to the front door as though he had come visiting. Once he reached the slab porch, though, he slid to the right and around the corner of the building.

He crept down the side of the building to the dining room window, center of the apartment. He placed the repeater on the outside ledge.

Back in his car, he tested the repeater. The signal was very strong. When Alice returned home, he would be able to download the video that had been recorded since he'd last seen her at work to review, and he'd be able to monitor her overnight in real time from his house.

Once home, he plugged in his iPhone to recharge it and set it on his kitchen table. Alice returned home shortly thereafter, and the image transmitted was as sharp as if he were standing next to her.

Fletcher ate his supper in the company of Alice's large intestine, which he found remarkably clean and healthy-looking. After dinner, he carried his phone into his living room and set it on the arm of his chair, watching it and an Illinois basketball game side by side. He found the former more exciting.

* * *

At halftime, Burton stopped by to ask his help moving a refrigerator over the weekend.

His brother glanced at the iPhone as he passed the chair on the way to the fridge for a beer. "You're still fixating on your colon?" he asked from the kitchen. "Does your girlfriend know about your obsession?"

"It's not an obsession," Fletcher said, "if the risk is real. Remember Mom and Dad. You might as well accuse a snorkeler of having a shark obsession."

Burton returned to the living room and took a seat on the couch. "Trust me, brother," he said. "Any woman that sees you watching a tape of your own intestine is going to walk away. Or maybe even run."

Fletcher turned his iPhone screen-down. "This is the last time," he said. "So get off my case."

"The last trip for your little camera?"

"Right. It's history."

Burton raised his beer bottle in a toast. "Here's to you for showing some sense for a change."

Fletcher didn't share with his brother just why or how he'd sacrificed his camera.

* * *

Fletcher found something incredibly intimate about watching Alice's colon as she slept. The camera moved only slightly, probably jarred along its track as she tossed and turned.

Around 3 p.m. he nodded off; when he woke at 7 a.m., the camera was back in motion. He wondered if, were he more experienced, he could determine what she was doing by the motion of the camera. Was that rotation caused by steps across the kitchen, making coffee? Did it flow smoothly as she raised her hands to scrub her scalp in the shower? Did it jump slightly as she bent to put on her shoes?

He wanted to view the stored video from the time he was asleep, but he couldn't tear himself away from the live feed. And to his relief, the tissue looked clean. No polyps, no seams or twists or mottled marks. In fact, her colon looked better than his did.

By the time he reached the office, he was convinced that she was recovered, that her prospects were all positive. Now he just had to work up the nerve to ask her out.

He tried to get it out during the morning break, but was so distracted by her eating for the first time since he'd known her, yogurt and a banana, that time got away from him.

Finally, that afternoon, after she'd been cross-eyed rapturous at the taste of the Reese's Cup that they shared, he managed to find his voice.

"So," he said, reaching for a casual tone, hoping his voice didn't squeak on him, "would you be interested in going out this weekend? There are a couple of good movies on at the Midtown 12."

She carefully folded the empty candy wrapping rather than looking him in the eyes. "I'm so sorry, Fletcher. That's really a nice offer. I'm very flattered. But I don't sense that we have enough in common to date."

Fletcher was so disappointed he felt light-headed. "But we do. I mean, we do the same work, so there's at least that."

She pursed her lips for a moment. "Well, the thing is—you're so fixated on your health? Believe me, after you've been through what I've been through, you want to move on. Been there, done that, and moved on."

"But ..." Fletcher started, but could find no real response, except disappointment; not in her, though, but in himself. A furtive pain kicked up in his abdomen.

* * *

The next few weeks were difficult, fighting off the urge to buy a new pill camera. By the time the last Wednesday of the month came, though, he was pleased to find that he didn't really miss his weekly examination as much as he thought he would.

And when he felt lonely, he could always watch Alice's colon videos.

SHE'S THE ONE FOR ME
VINCENZO BILOF

Lena's brown hair half-covered her face. Her knees were nearly drawn up to her chest as if she lay curled in fetal relaxation. On a sunny day, the bright, illuminating peace could make her hair seem to glow with a red crown atop her head. The back of her skull had been caved in by a blunt instrument, so I didn't see any blood. When I tried to move her, to talk to her, her head stuck to the floor because she'd been dead for almost a day, according to the coroner's report. In memory, she's forever locked in that serene pose.

No matter how hard I try to picture the sunlight upon her hair or listen closely through the corridors of memory for the sound of her laughter, there's nothing. The photos in our home show a woman whose smile had been the product of laughter and delight. That's not how I remember her.

Pills and therapists. Unpaid bills and suicidal ruminations. Sleepless evenings. Numerous phone calls from family and friends who receive nothing more than hollow responses from my throat. There are days I wish Lena never existed. She remains a ghost that haunts the shades of bleak darkness that have invaded my life.

Everything reminded me of Lena; she composed half of my existence for nearly twelve years. She meant everything to me. We loved each other selfishly and couldn't share our lives with a child. After she was murdered, I didn't succumb to alcohol or drugs. I wanted the world to end, and my life with it. Anger and sorrow create a toxic rage that cannot be satisfied.

Of course, I was a suspect. I was in New York to show off four of my paintings in an exhibition, and when I returned home, Lena lay on the floor with the shades drawn over the windows. I could hear the birds chirping outside. I remember thinking about the lawn mower that started up while a passing car's subwoofer rattled doors and windows. Everything was slow. I'd said her name only once, and stared for a long time.

Her skin was pale, I think, but I can't quite remember. Her innocent posture and the hair across her face; these I can recall. The kitchen was relatively undisturbed, as if she'd invited her killer inside our home as a gesture of kindness. There were two empty cans of caffeine-free Coca-Cola on the counter, which was her favorite drink. Flies incessantly buzzed near the window, desperate to escape.

My paintings had been featured in several exhibitions across the country, and we'd argued more than once about the time I devoted to my career. She wanted more from me. Naturally, I blamed myself for her death. I should have been home with her. But I was the breadwinner and I needed to sell and promote my paintings.

A primary suspect emerged, and I sought vindication in the court room during the brief trial. Day and night, my thoughts were ruined by the concept of justice. I didn't know what I wanted; what could possibly please my thirst for vengeance?

The cold, dispassionate face. The clear, ocean-blue eyes. A family man in his late fifties, a grandfather, a retired cop. A head of wavy gray hair and a hairless face. The square jaw. Each eyelid blinking slowly over piercing eyes that seemed to be looking at something only he could see.

Brendan McNeil. The bane of my existence.

It was a short trial because there was little evidence. He was apparently the only person anyone had witnessed her talking to while I was away; they'd spoken briefly at a coffee shop. Why did you want to speak to a complete stranger, Lena?

With the sinking, deflating dread pressing into my stomach, I knew what the trial's outcome would be. The trial was nothing more than a show.

When McNeil was cleared of the charges, I rose to my feet and declared the death of justice. My tongue lashed out against the depravity of a system that couldn't produce my wife's killer, no matter how many episodes of "CSI" we've all watched, where the good guys have all the technology and know-how in the world to catch the bad guys.

During my moment of hysteria, McNeil turned and looked into my face for the first time. As the police dragged me across the court, I stopped kicking and shouting. I was still as I met McNeil's calm gaze, and we spoke to each other without words. I'd looked into the face of horror, the stone visage that had taken not only Lena's life, but mine as well.

I killed her, his eyes seemed to say. *There's nothing you can do about it. She died in front of me. You weren't there to help her.*

The police didn't have enough evidence to convict him, so I would find it.

I would have to follow him and catch him in the act of taking another life.

* * *

What if I followed the man for years and he wasn't the real killer? How long would it take for me to decide he wasn't the one? What would I do if I caught him? Would I have the courage to step in and save a life?

I spent several hours on the internet learning everything I could about McNeil. I found his address on the web, and I learned about his prolific police career.

No more therapy visits. No more phone calls from friends and relatives. They'd given up, or they considered their "obligation" to extend their sympathies or help fulfilled. There was enough money to continue to pay for the mortgage and the rare meals I ate, but I remained under cover of darkness. The shades were drawn. The lawn sprouted weeds and manufactured insects, and I received several notices and fines for failing to maintain my home. It was falling apart around my head, but I paid for my home and my internet bill.

Lena's corpse in the kitchen. The cold blue eyes of Brendan McNeil. I never forget either image. In the sobering silence of a sweaty morning, these are the images that greet me, and they are my constant companions throughout my long, tedious days.

My own home was a haunted house, and I became its ghost. More than once, I thought about selling it, but I couldn't muster the energy to initiate the process, nor could I pick up my phone and call anyone for help. My broken mind became a prison where I languished without nourishment; I suffered from self-inflicted poverty and physical disintegration. When my thoughts finally turned from McNeil to reality, I envisioned myself becoming a pile of dust in my computer chair with images of Lena's killer frozen for all time on the laptop's monitor.

On a clear Saturday morning, I drove to his home.

Parked across the street from his neat little ranch-style property with its colorful garden and green, manicured lawn, I stared at the palace of a killer. I wondered what kind of dreams plagued the mind of a man who could take an innocent woman's life while her husband was away at an art exhibition. On that first day in his neighborhood, I sat with my knuckles whitening along the grip of my steering wheel, wondering what I was going to do next.

More than anything, I needed him to appear.

And that was how I started to watch McNeil.

* * *

Painting was the only way I could raise money to fund my new habit. It should go without saying that my latest works were the product of a different style. My work became frenzied and chaotic. I would blindfold myself and paint the murder scenes I imagined lingering in the realm of nightmare behind McNeil's bright blue eyes, eyes that had witnessed a productive career as a decorated homicide detective. I began to depict shattered faces and women whose profiles were a mess of hair and ice. Variations of red and gray were my favorite colors.

My renewed fervor for painting allowed me to purchase equipment that was illegal or extremely expensive. You can buy anything over the internet.

I was able to bug McNeil's home. I hid a camera in a tree in his backyard while everyone in the neighborhood was asleep. In the empty hours of a dark morning, there's a lot a man can do without anyone noticing. I bought an audio device and sound amplifier, and hooked it up to a recorder. Over the course of six months, I managed to create a system where I could sit in my car at the corner store and listen to arguments between husband and wife.

McNeil.

He lived a normal, boorish life. He ate breakfast. He went to the store in the morning and bought coffee and a newspaper. There were paperback thrillers near his armchair and trashy romances near his wife's. He and his wife, Selma, who seemed to look exactly like him, received calls on a land-line.. It wasn't until I invested in more expensive gear that I was able to determine that the calls were from his kids. He had a son who was away at college, and a thirty-year-old daughter who was married with a two-year old boy.

During his career, he'd assisted in the apprehension and conviction of seventeen killers. Some of them were jealous husbands, while others had been crippled by the gross economic monster that chewed on the financial dreams of families until they met ruin and disappointment. The killers were victims of frustration and unrequited love. McNeil never chased a serial killer, though he'd given counsel on several occasions for more prolific manhunts. He avoided headlines and high-profile cases. The spotlight wasn't for him, because he seemed to loathe the pressure it placed on his family over the years. He was a quiet, taciturn man who enjoyed his newspaper and coffee in the morning. He looked forward to phone calls from his kids, and every once in a while, he stopped pretending to be "technologically ignorant" and spent time on the internet on social networking sites. His wife, Selma, was of course sleeping at the late hour when he would rise from his bed and plant himself in front of the computer.

I took notes and listened through my headphones to the sound of his television, the toilet flushing, the phone ringing. Meat frying in a pan. Long stretches of silence. I was inside the house with them, living their mundane lives. In the beginning, I would take a picture of Lena from my pocket and stare at it for a while, my hand shaking uncontrollably. It was a picture of her lying dead on the kitchen floor; I found it on the internet from a press junkie who'd released their fair share of crime scene photos without consent. Lena's corpse could be seen by anybody, anytime. A picture in a seemingly endless sea of anonymous images.

Nothing out of the ordinary happened in McNeil's home, yet I was infatuated with the concept of his life. The normal, boring marriage, something Lena and I could never experience together. Why did I keep up my surveillance? I was painting again, and in a way, I owed it to this man. I could live without him.

McNeil was supposed to be a killer. If he'd killed one person so casually, he would do it again. I reasoned that I wouldn't learn anything during the day, so I spent more time in the evenings parked in his street; I didn't want to be noticed in an empty parking lot, but under cover of night I could hide in the street inside the car. I normally painted in the evenings, and because I still needed to pay for my habit, I couldn't always visit McNeil during the late hours.

I became more curious about his propensity to dust off the computer and turn it on while Selma slept. Dating websites. Old files about crimes he'd worked on. Photographs of murdered victims. He was obsessed with his past, but he was searching for something along memory lane. For an older man, he was very adept at the computer, playing old audio files through a pair of headphones while opening several different windows on his screen at once. Nude pictures of overweight, middle-aged mothers. Women in the mad throes of loneliness.

And every evening, before shutting his computer down, he ran several maintenance programs that wiped away every trace of his footsteps across cyberspace.

One day, his routine changed. McNeil explained to Selma that he was going to see an old friend for coffee, and she allowed it grudgingly. Even though he'd been a homicide detective for more than twenty years, retirement made him complacent; he didn't see me tailing him all the way to his rendezvous.

He met a woman named Mary at the local Starbucks. With a long-range receiver and a pair of binoculars, I listened and watched McNeil make uninteresting jokes to ease her into casual conversation. Chatter around the diner made it difficult to pinpoint their voices. Her shoulder-length brown hair was cut with neat bangs that covered her forehead. McNeil continued to disarm her with several jests; he was charismatic, but why would this younger woman want to talk to him at all?

They left after a while and she agreed to go with him to a local bar. The audio signal was even worse, and after three hours in the bar, they got into their separate cars and parted ways. Her laughter had been reduced to giggles, and McNeil smiled awkwardly at her drunken pleasure.

I imagined scenarios in which I would catch him hurting her and I would intervene.

In the evenings, I pored over his old cases and began to find several similarities. The victims were all middle-aged women. Only one of them was unmarried. Each woman was either face-down or was turned sideways with hair encapsulating the profile. The method of execution varied slightly between victims. They were either bludgeoned or choked with a household item like a phone cord. None of them were sexually molested.

These similarities seemed obvious to me, but why didn't anyone else pick up on it?

SHE'S THE ONE FOR ME

Because McNeil always got his man.

To assuage my own loneliness, lest I descend into a pit of madness, I pretended to have conversations with McNeil. The interviews always included questions about his motive, or if he thought he would do it again. I asked if he could ever stop himself. How did it feel? His responses were textbook, stoical replies. McNeil would remain emotionless and detached through the process, his blue eyes never leaving me.

McNeil dated Mary again, and on the third date, the inevitable conclusion was a return to her home sometime during the mid-afternoon. Then, he didn't see her again for a long time. It was business as usual in the McNeil household, with the phone calls, newspaper, and arguments about the lawn or the bills. It was as if Mary was an event that never occurred.

Did McNeil charm my Lena while I was away on my exhibitions? The very thought infuriated me. She'd loved me so completely, but this bastard had somehow entered her life. There was no doubt in my mind that McNeil was a killer. The results of my research were convincing enough, and if he never attacked another woman, I would be disappointed; I spent months devoted to my crusade against the man who killed my wife.

My paintings continued to depict the terrible images of dead women, victims claimed by the strange lusts of a man who was ruled by his iron-fisted, scowling wife at home. In my dreams I sat across from McNeil at my dinette, and we talked amiably while Lena brought us coffee and cookies. The window was open in the kitchen, and I could hear a car driving through the silent neighborhood. Someone fired up a lawn mower.

In the real world, McNeil began to stalk Mary.

* * *

I watched him watch her. He was very good at it, though he was hardly alert to my own presence. He knew where she worked; he waited for her outside of Walgreens where she worked as a pharmacist. He followed her home. A sly smile often crept across his face while he watched. Sometimes, he brought a newspaper with him. Other times, a magazine. A hat. Sunglasses.

We both watched and waited outside of her home. She enjoyed reality television shows and whole-wheat crackers. She was a Facebook addict who used several different dating websites to find her perfect match. Her workaholic lifestyle had prevented her from meeting men. She enjoyed working out on her elliptical machine and taking long, steamy showers. She didn't have any eccentricities, but McNeil watched because she was alone. There wasn't anyone to protect her.

She was different in every way from the other women McNeil had killed; she wasn't married, nor did she have a boyfriend. I began to second-guess myself. Was he in love with Mary? Did he really want to kill her? Did he actually kill anyone before?

Would she change her habits if she knew we were watching? Would she perform for us?

Mary was a fairly attractive woman, and I couldn't help but think I could save her life if I simply told her that she was being stalked. Would she even believe me? I could help her understand, but I wanted to see it all play out. I needed McNeil to assault her so I could bring him to justice.

Mary had no idea she was being hunted. Her life amused and thrilled McNeil. A smile would linger on his face for long moments when she met another gentleman at the same Starbucks where they'd first met.

I knew McNeil's game. He needed her to meet another man to remove himself from suspicion. If the police asked any of her coworkers or family if Mary was seeing anybody, they wouldn't exactly remember McNeil. Mary wasn't exceptionally close to anybody, and the people she spoke to on the phone would hardly remember every detail about the woman's life unless she bragged about McNeil.

Among my cache of spy accessories was a pair of night-vision goggles. I brought them with me the evening McNeil left his home at a late hour and drove over to Mary's house.

At least a month had passed since the last time they saw each other. What terrible engine drove this man to the deed he was about to commit? I was excited and anxious: I was convinced the moment was at hand. How would I step in, once he began to abuse her?

I admired his attention to detail. He borrowed his son's car. Black clothing. A hand-held vacuum cleaner was packed into a small canvas bag. A long telephone cord. Gloves. Ski mask and goggles. Not a single piece of flesh would be exposed. Not an eyelash. Not a single hair.

McNeil was allowed a head start because I knew he would be hyper-alert. When he stepped into his car, I knew where he was going. I also knew how he would get into her home; we both knew she often forgot to lock her patio door.

It was the perfect nocturnal visit. On my way to Mary's, I envisioned his tactics: he would park across the street where there wasn't a street light and close the door softly behind him. With ease, he would slink through the shadows and around the back of her house.

When I arrived on Mary's street, I parked my car with fiery, jangling nerves. I took deep breaths and tried to think about Lena, but all I could remember was her body lying on our kitchen's wood laminate floor.

McNeil's car was across the street. The night-vision goggles seemed to leap into my hands.

I could see through her bedroom window, but I was already too late.

He'd crept into her room while she slept. Consider the horrifying moment when you awaken and there's a shape in your room, a shape that wasn't there before. You think you're still sleeping, or you're not quite awake. Your heart races as you realize the shape isn't going away while your eyes adjust to the dark.

McNeil sprayed her face, eyes, and hair with something that was in a can. He then reared back and punched her in the jaw with a massive fist. She had no idea what was happening, and I puzzled over his method. What was in the can? He quickly wrapped the telephone cord around her throat and dragged her from the bed.

The killer was incredibly powerful because no matter how much she kicked, he wasn't moving an inch. She seemed to hang in his grasp, her feet unable to touch the floor.

I made no effort to move. I was used to watching.

When her kicking finally stopped, her fingers rested against the cord, and McNeil held her there as if she were still alive. Finally, he eased her onto the bed very gently as if any sudden movement might shatter her body into shards of glass. He looked at her for a while, and then methodically adjusted her body. McNeil decorated the bed with a broken doll of a woman, covering a lifeless profile with strands of her hair.

After he played with her corpse, he hunted through the house for her computer. McNeil turned it on and inserted a flash drive with software that wiped out her entire system.

I remembered something the police had said about Lena after they'd gone through her laptop: it was as if she never used it.

I'd just witnessed my first homicide.

* * *

McNeil went about his days as if nothing happened. He protested whenever the roving dictator, Selma, nagged him about chores that needed to be done. They fought about their kids.

The evenings were uneventful. He stayed away from his computer and slept soundly through the night. The police never showed up at his house to question him. Mary's murder disappeared from news headlines after only a few days, buried beneath the endless body count that could produce the faces of killers for the public to deride.

Mary's face and hair had been spray-painted in the steel-gray likeness of Selma McNeil, and her jaw had been shattered. They never mentioned that her face had been turned sideways and had been covered with her hair.

My own life didn't change, either. I attended Mary's funeral and signed the guest-book. I told her friends and family that I'd met her once at the pharmacy and had be-friended her. Nobody seemed to care. Her lips were drawn tightly as if she were disap-pointed with life. Somehow, her corpse didn't look right. Her face was too ... exposed.

I began to paint pictures of lovely, innocent Mary.

The hallucinatory conversations with McNeil continued, and he always asked me why I didn't have nightmares about Mary's murder.

MCNEIL: Why didn't you feel anything? Why didn't you report it to the police? Did you enjoy watching me kill Mary?

ME: McNeil, you son of a bitch, how long did you watch Lena before you decided to kill her? Did you know that I loved her, that she wasn't lonely? Did you break down her defenses with a smile? How many times did you meet her at Starbucks?

Thus, I raged. Until McNeil's life became interesting again.

McNeil approached his next victim with different tactics.

He packed his bags and begged his wife for a chance to stay at a cabin by himself for a "few days away". Selma decided that it needed upkeep, anyway, though her furious battle with Mr. McNeil involved newspaper flying through the house and some broken dishes.

The seasons turned. I'd started my observations in the spring time and I tracked my old friend to his cabin along roads that were blanketed in two feet of snow. I realized it would be far more difficult to watch him, considering there weren't many cars on the road. I found a local motel in town that had a Wi-Fi connection and studied the inter-net. I drove down several roads until I found the McNeil family ranch, which, according to the arguments between the McNeils, was usually used by their kids. Most of the ranches in the wooded community had little signs sitting outside of dirt driveways with family names painted on them.

Where would he find the next woman?

I visited the town's local watering hole, and after one night, I decided it was far too risky for McNeil. Wouldn't they know him? Even if he only visited his cabin once or twice a year, these people likely knew his kids. I could recall an argument he had with Selma about retiring to their cabin permanently, though of course she decided it was there for the kids to use.

The next town over, then? McNeil would surely change his methods. He wasn't going to use the internet, but instead find a lonely widow who had nothing to do and nobody to do it with. But everything seemed off, somehow. Would he try to make it look like an accident? A death in a much smaller setting would garner more attention; he would have to watch from a distance before making his move. He would need to act quickly, too, because Selma wouldn't permit him to stay away too long.

I became anxious. I didn't sleep. On the third night, I spent the majority of my time in some dusty bar called *McGrady's Tavern,* where I sat in a corner by myself for the first hour until my entire world turned upside-down.

She looked just like Lena.

Behind the bar, wiping it down. A quick smile and long, brown hair. A youthful face with smooth cheeks. A quick glance over her shoulder with a smile full of white teeth.

My heart stopped. I watched and watched, and watched.

She was just as beautiful as I remembered. I hadn't looked at a picture of my wife in some time. Even the portrait of her corpse, which I used to carry around with me in my pocket, had been lost.

I would do anything to hear her laughter, and I did. I hadn't realized how much I missed my wife until I was in the presence of her clone. Had I really been so infatuated with McNeil that I forgot everything he'd taken from me? My obsession defined my life for the better part of a year, and all along, I was supposed to prevent him from killing again. I'd already failed once. This Lena look-alike was similar to a McNeil victim, and if I didn't watch her closely, then her life would be in danger. Who else would protect her?

Her name was Sarah James. I learned her name by listening closely and by asking another resident what her last name was because she looked "awfully familiar" to me, though I was clearly mistaken. I'd asked about her, and I could acknowledge that it was a mistake. McNeil would have never done that. He was too careful.

After closing time, I returned to my car and waited for her to leave. I was well-versed in tracking and following another car, although the deserted streets in the town with only one traffic light and one church made me easy to spot. It was still quite easy to learn which dirt road she lived on, though I didn't follow her all the way. Not yet.

I needed her last name so that I could find her address on the internet. I needed to see the sign outside of the driveway.

After conducting my research, I wiped my computer was wiped clean, just like McNeil would have done.

I drove by her house twice during the day. Sarah was married, but I was ignorant about everything else. So far, she fit the profile as a McNeil victim, though she was in her mid-twenties, a bit younger than he preferred.

At *McGrady's,* Sarah continued to light up the dusty, tiny bar with her smile. Greasy, grilled food was served along with baskets of popcorn and pretzels, while the patrons indulged in domestic beer. The balls for the pool table were kept behind the bar and there were only two crooked sticks. Sarah never stopped smiling. The jukebox played classic, recycled rock music over and over again, and still, she smiled.

Sarah James was incredibly beautiful, and was just like Lena. The resemblance was so close it became painful to look at her, but if I didn't help her, then McNeil would surely find her.

How did her breathing sound when she slept? Did she chew her nails like Lena did? Did Sarah enjoy surrealist art and caffeine-free Coca-Cola?

There was only one way to find out.

* * *

Camouflage gear and a knapsack full of black clothing. Binoculars, night-vision goggles, audio receiver. Beef jerky, bottled water, Saltine crackers. A day in the woods, lying in the brush, waiting, listening, and watching.

A couple hundred dollars were spent on camouflage gear that could help me blend into the gray, snow-laden wasteland around her house. The trees kept most of the wind from scouring my face. I managed to remain relatively dry, and my attention was always riveted upon Sarah; the cold couldn't keep me from her.

Most of my time was spent in the early morning hours listening through the static on the receiver to Sarah and her husband, Brian, arguing about how much time they weren't spending together. He worked long shifts at a post office during the day, while she worked at the bar in the evenings. They couldn't see one another.

But I could see her, through the windows. Brushing hair away from her face. Drinking her coffee. Lying on the couch amid the world of dreams while reruns of MTV, reality shows played on the flat screen TV. I admired their simple, warm décor, with candles, earth-tone furniture, and pictures of family in wood picture frames.

I watched her chest rise and fall with slow, relaxed breaths. Once in a while, Lena, I mean Sarah, would shift her body on the couch. When she awoke after two hours, she went to the restroom with strands of hair sticking to her face. There seemed to be long stretches of silence that the television couldn't conquer. She was so alone. Her husband was away at work, laboring to pay his share of the bills to keep their nice little home in the woods.

She danced around her house in a purple bra and white panties while listening to country music play from her laptop speakers. Sarah showered and sang while she washed herself. Afterward, she started to apply makeup while she prepared for work, once again wearing undergarments that didn't match. I felt like she was doing it all for me. She was lonely, and she saw me outside and wanted to put on a show. I knew her and I believed we could be close friends if she let me in.

Sarah needed to be warned. On any day, at any time, McNeil would come for her.

Courage wasn't required to knock on her door, because I knew that it was unlocked. What were the chances that she would open her home to a complete stranger? Townies were notorious for leaving their homes and cars unlocked, because they lived by the idea that "I live out in the middle of nowhere, so who's going to want my stuff?"

Sarah was quite surprised to see me. I put my hand up in the universal gesture which is supposed to indicate that I don't mean any harm.

The country music was incredibly loud, and she seemed vulnerable with wet hair draped over her shoulder blades. I could see her rib cage and the dangling jewel that hung from her pierced belly button.

"What are you doing here?" she demanded. "Who are you?"

Of course, those questions were predictable.

"I just want to warn you …" I began before she cut me off.

"Get out before I call the police!"

She was truly afraid, and I didn't know why. Her hands clenched and unclenched repeatedly, and her head whipped around the room several times to look for her phone or maybe a weapon to defend herself against the intruder. I would do anything to see her smile.

I tried to reason with her. "Listen, I've seen you. Don't you recognize me? At *McGrady's!* We have a lot in common. I just came here to talk to you. There's something you should know. Please, just let me talk."

"I've never seen you. Just get out!"

"But there's a man, a retired detective, and he's got these bright blue eyes …"

I kept taking small steps toward her, and she backed away from me. Her eyes were incredibly wide as we kept up the exchange. My last rational thought was a question: *Why are you so afraid, Sarah?* After all, I was there to save her life. Why couldn't she just listen to me?

Some murderers claimed they blacked out right before they killed, as if another type of consciousness takes over, or another personality. It's more like swimming underwater, and all of your movements are slow and preordained. You move as if each muscle knows what it's supposed to do, and everything falls into place. You become an observer rather than a participant; I was still watching Sarah, and there was so much I wanted to say: *I'm an artist, I can provide a nice home for you. Don't hate me. Don't be angry. Listen to me, just listen.*

She was already against the wall by the time my fingers latched upon her throat. She tried to bat my hands away, but fear had weakened her, while unreal strength possessed me. Sarah's face became a mess of tears and snot while she choked. I was amazed at how easy it was. Maybe if she lost just enough oxygen to her brain, she would fall asleep and then awaken to find herself full of reason and understanding. She might listen to me.

I stood well apart from her so that when her final, desperate attempts to break herself free resulted in kicks that found nothing but air, she was at my mercy. It was as if she finally realized that her life was in danger. There was something I wanted to say, but I can't remember what it was.

My hands became magnets on her throat, and when she slid downward against the wall, I followed her down, until both of us were sitting across from one another on the floor. She'd stopped moving altogether, and still I couldn't take my hands from her. I slammed her limp, unresponsive head against the wall several times.

At some point, I realized that Sarah was dead.

With my hands withdrawn, I stood and looked down upon her. She looked peaceful.

SHE'S THE ONE FOR ME

I discovered a dark spot along her crotch and could smell the urine.

McNeil wouldn't have done it that way. He would have worn gloves. He would have vacuumed the room.

But her face. All along, she was the one for me. My dearest Lena. So dead, and so lovely.

I gently brushed strands of wet hair across the side of her face. Why did she have to leave me?

* * *

I wanted to paint but could not. McNeil hadn't been staying at his cabin for as long as I was in town, which was nearly a full week.

When I returned home, I thought about my next move. Sarah's murder would make headlines, for sure. I tried to imagine what they would say. I wasn't very concerned with self-preservation.

When I turned on my computer, the first thing I did was look for dating websites. I needed someone to talk to. My conversations with McNeil weren't cutting it anymore. If I could share my long, uncounted hours with another woman, life might be so much easier for me. Sarah could have filled that void for me, if only she'd listened.

But I would do things differently next time. I'd wanted to warn Sarah, to save her life. We could have been friends, maybe even secret lovers behind her husband's back, if only she'd given me a chance. Watching McNeil had deluded me. I needed his presence to fill my own time, but more than anything, I needed a companion. That's what Lena had provided me, and that's really what I wanted from Sarah. It's too bad things didn't turn out better for her.

It only took two days for McNeil to knock on my door.

He wore a suit and tie, and his face seemed a picture of a stone slab rather than a composition of flesh and blood. I opened the door and simply let him inside as if we were old friends. We sat in the kitchen amid the cobwebs and dust, where spiders nested inside of Lena's old caffeine-free Coca-Cola cans and flies danced around the window. He sat down at the table and I apologized for the mess.

"I haven't cleaned since you killed Lena," I said.

McNeil pursed his lips and folded his hands together on the table. "You followed me for a long time," he said simply.

"Admit that you're a murderer, and that you should be locked away," I demanded.

"We know you're a killer, Mr. Jenkins. We've collected evidence from the home of Mrs. Sarah James, who is now deceased. Did you know her?"

"You're retired," I pointed out.

"You live a very boring life," he said. "You've wasted away in this prison cell you call a home. Did you enjoy sitting outside of my house? You must have known that I wanted you to follow me to the cabin. You were very predictable."

I wasn't surprised by his words.

"What do you mean?" I asked.

"Every killer is predictable."

"You're a mass murderer. You killed several people and pretended to catch the killers to cover up your own trail. You've been doing it for years."

He produced a photograph of Sarah James, lying dead against a wall, her chin resting on her shoulder, hair across her face. At first, I thought it was a picture of Lena.

"Some men lie awake at night, thinking about what they've accomplished." McNeil leaned back. "I thought about blood. My entire life was soaked in it. If your accusations were true, then I am very likely insane. I have a damaged mind, my soul has withered. But I'm a detective, and you're not the least bit upset to find me here, in your home. If you thought I killed your wife, then here we are, at last. You can have your revenge. Lash out at me. Become angry."

I stared at the picture. "I loved her," I said.

"Who did you love? Your wife? Sarah James?"

All of the questions I'd asked in our interviews evaporated from my mind. I was helpless against his power. His detached voice seemed an echo, or like words spoken underwater. McNeil confused me, and while I stood in the room where he murdered my wife, I seemed to forget who I was.

"You did this to me," I accused him. "Your profession made you, and you made me."

This was the moment where I was supposed to cry or become afraid of the future. McNeil wanted my confession, or at least, he wanted to gloat over me. My fate was already sealed, but all I could think about was Sarah, or Lena. Hair splayed across a dead face. Words never spoken. I really was at fault for Lena's murder, and more than anything, I wanted a chance to make it up to someone. To spend time with a woman and make her feel loved. To talk instead of argue.

"You've admired me," he said. "I'm your hero. It's too bad you slipped up. I thought you would have learned something ..."

The front door crashed open, and the police swarmed into my home. They shouted and pointed guns, but I didn't hear or see them. I couldn't take my eyes away from McNeil.

Frozen in time, on my computer screen, was the profile of a married woman who was looking for a "part-time" lover. She had shoulder-length brown hair, and perfectly round, smooth cheeks.

And then I couldn't stop laughing.

She looked just like Lena.

SECOND WIFE
ROB BLISS

I started with the basics. Spent a month digging a pit in my basement. I bought the house to treat myself after a small family tragedy, which is best left in the past, like most of life's moments. A gorgeous Victorian dating from 1870 or so, with the basement as a small unfinished labyrinth of wooden doors and rooms with stone walls and dirt floors.

Was going to line the pit with shards of broken bottles, but the quarry – when I caught her – could use them against me. Or against herself, which would've been worse for my purposes. Instead, I got sheets of Plexiglas to wall the pit with a slippery surface so she couldn't climb. Hammered them into the earth with three-foot long spikes. If she tried, she could eventually pull out each one, remove the Plexiglas sheets, then dig herself some footholds in the earth to make a ladder. But I would keep her under my watchful eye, and punish her for the slightest attempt at escape.

It would take a little longer to build the bedroom. I had another basement room prepared with all, or most, of the wood and nails and paint already purchased. Didn't want to have to leave the house on errands for too long.

Naturally, I needed the quarry soon, before I began construction on the bedroom. The drive is there, of course – it's always there, strong and with purpose. Grew stronger as I dug the pit, thinking about its eventual inhabitant. Wondering what kind I wanted. Pretty would be nice, but not some vain cheerleader type. A pretty geek. That old cliché. Take off her glasses, let down her pinned-up hair, and her face is as stunning as her body. Preferably, she had been picked on in high school, didn't fit in, called a freak and a loser, never got invited to the parties, drank her daddy's liquor cabinet at midnight in the basement when the parents were asleep. Likes older guys, thinks they're more mature, will treat her with respect and not just see her as some punk-ass kid to be ignored. She needs a daddy to love her.

That's the one I wanted. Hell, she might even get a touch of Stockholm Syndrome, and make it easier for both of us. All those thoughts rushing through as I dug. So I couldn't wait for the bedroom to be built. I needed her in my pit.

Drove the main roads and the country roads looking. Headed to the small towns where people are more trusting. Watched a few high schools, inspecting the potential merchandise, followed a few lone walkers home. Too many lived on main streets, their houses surrounded by other houses or stores, gas stations, libraries, government buildings. Too many eyes in too many windows and doorways.

But it was the library of this small town I won't name that gave me my opportunity.

Followed a girl, dark hair, almost black with two pink butterfly clips jutting up from her hair like devil horns. Glasses too big for her face. Her clothing likely bought from a thrift store. She walked through the snow in man's boots. She was all hand-me-down, a gypsy wearing whatever rags she could piece together. Walked with a heavy knapsack, eyes on her path ahead. And if she headed to the library, what does that tell you? She has no life. Her life is borrowed from books. She dreams of bigger things beyond a small town. Perhaps even her home life is lousy – a divorced alcoholic mom, dad ran away years ago, killed her self-esteem thinking no one wanted her. Left a vacuum to be filled.

Perfect.

Over a week, I waited for the school bell, saw her make the same snow trek to the library every day, watched her leave, followed her home. She lived above a fish and chips restaurant, went through a side door. Three tenants listed on the small aluminum mail boxes, on only the top floor above the restaurant. So if the apartment was small, she likely lived with only one parent, probably had no siblings. I felt I was right.

I ignored her school and watched the restaurant. Sat all day from six in the morning. An old man with a walker came out of the side door. Came back with shopping bags hung over the walker, made his slow way back through the door, and somehow got himself up the flight of stairs. Thought of playing the Good Samaritan to get inside with him, recon the interior. Decided against it – no witnesses.

A toothpick of a woman, possibly in her high forties, but looked older, long feathered hair from her youth in the 1980s, chain-smoking, exited in track pants, a light spring jacket, and the man's winter boots that the girl had worn. Mommy. Went to a variety store, probably bought cigarettes and lottery tickets. Mama was desperate for a better life, too.

No third tenant ever exited that I saw. Probably a vacant apartment, with the last tenant's name never removed from the mailbox.

I admit: my method was sloppy. I couldn't help it. I was desperate. My hands shook, I shivered sitting in the van with the heat full blast, couldn't keep my feet still. Every time I saw the girl, I wanted her more and more. And my libido was making associations. If I saw the restaurant, I got an erection. If I saw her mother, my pants expanded. Hell, even the sight of the old man made my cock start to swell.

I sweated with the window rolled down, snow swirling inside. I had it bad. I needed her. The desperation makes you sloppy, but so be it. I had a good feeling about my girl.

A blizzard hit halfway into the school day, so they let the kids out early, and would probably cancel classes for the next day or two if the blizzard kept up. Which it was supposed to, according to the weather girl with the huge tits and black stockings under her business skirt. Whores told you the weather, opened up your opportunities, escorted you into the beginning of a beautiful life. Thank you, whore.

She trudged down the sidewalk, head down as the snow whipped her. Halfway to the library, she looked up. Breath smoking from her mouth, cheeks flushed, a thin toque too big for her head slipping down over her eyes.

A change of heart, she turned away from her library trek and headed toward home. No kids packed the sidewalks, loitered in front of stores. All sped home to their toys and toboggans and instant messaging. Fewer witnesses.

She cut through a dentist's parking lot. I drove in, wheels spinning, slipped into a spot, rolled down my window.

"Hey – wanna ride?"

She stopped, peered up while trying to keep her chin tucked into the collar of her coat.

I was nervous, took deep breaths, kept the smile on my face to appear relaxed and friendly. This was the first good close-up look I got of her. "Come on, hop in, I'll take you home." I smiled. "Pretty girls shouldn't be walking around in blizzards."

SECOND WIFE

She scanned the van, couldn't see the plates from where she stood. Just a normal mini-van, like the one my wife used to own, but a different colour at least.

Her boots – girl boots now, pink with white laces – slipped through tire ruts in the snow as she passed across the front of the van. Didn't glance down at the plate. My heart was a ramrod in my chest. Thought it would punch through my ribcage when I saw her raise her hand to grab the passenger-side door handle.

She was in, bringing the snow and arctic wind with her. She lifted her chin over her jacket collar, slipped off her toque. Strands of her long hair like Medusa snakes, alive with static electricity. Red cheeks made her even more beautiful. Eyes like blue pinwheels. Her stare at my smile was hard, determined, a little suspicious, but with a soft touch in the folds of her eyelids.

"I don't want to go home," she said, looking at the snow piling up on the windshield.

I played coy and confused, my eyes smiling. "Where'd you wanna go?"

"Your place," she stated, eyes forward. She pulled the seat belt across her thin body. She wore tiny pink cotton gloves with bunny faces on each, folded her fingers in her lap as she waited to go.

I said nothing, pulled out of the dentist's parking lot, and she and I headed for my place.

A slow ride in the slashing snow, salt and sand not yet spread on the main roads. And the country roads were worse, wouldn't be ploughed for hours, maybe a couple days.

I kept the radio off to listen to her breathe, glanced over at her lips, slightly parted. She didn't return my gaze.

"What's your name?" I asked to fill the silence.

"Does it matter?" she asked the windshield, the white landscape. "What do you want to call me?"

I chuckled from surprise, kept my eyes on the road as I thought about the girl beside me. Just whom had I picked up? What was going through her head? She knew more than she let on. I had to play her game and crack her brain.

"How old are you?"

"Eighteen," she said quickly. Then she looked at me, hard. "Sorry. You probably thought I was younger. I had to skip a few grades, my dad died and my mom was sick for a while. I might look younger, but I'm legal. Mind if I smoke?"

My eyes widened. I couldn't stop looking at her, fascinated, reading her every movement and minute facial gesture.

She took a pack of cigarettes and a plastic lighter from inside her jacket. The lighter had a naked girl on an ace of spades on each side. She lit her cigarette and shot smoke from her cold lips to the windshield.

"Can you crack a window?" I asked politely.

She kept her eyes on the road, looking for landmarks in the uniform whiteness, smoked compulsively, nervously. "No, it's cold out."

I resigned, let her fog up the van. Drove in silence a little more, turned off the highway onto a country road.

"Don't get us killed before we get there," she said. "Keep your eyes on the road, not on me. You'll have plenty of time to stare at me when we arrive."

I cracked my window, sucked fresh air into my lungs. Kept my eyes on the snow road. I started hating the silence, thought of anything to ask her. Even if she didn't like to talk.

"You got a boyfriend?"

"Again, does it matter? You want to fuck me, right? That's why you've abducted me."

I stuttered, "I didn't … I – no, no, that's not –"

"Watch the road – fuck!" She braced her feet and arms, sat back hard in her seat.

The van slipped. I took my foot off the gas, spun the steering wheel, gained control. Didn't lose a heartbeat.

"Don't worry – I know this road," I assured her.

"Then keep your fucking eyes on it!" she yelled. Dragged a few puffs off her cigarette, cracked her window, flicked out the stub, rolled the window up again. Lit another smoke.

My mind was spinning. What did she think about me, what should I say next, should I deny or agree with her accusation?

"What makes you say I abducted you?"

"You've been following me for a couple weeks. You know where I live. You've seen my mother and Mr. Chadwell who lives in our building. You know I go to the library after school." She looked at me with a straight smile on her lips, nothing vicious, just a smile of understanding. "And I know you know all these things about me."

I watched the road, felt my breath grow solid in my lungs, paid more attention to the snow scenery surrounding us. Tried to imagine what was going through her mind. My leg started twitching. It had never done that before.

We made it home. She flicked her cigarette out onto my driveway. This wasn't going as expected. I thought I would have to drag her kicking and screaming, my hand smothering her mouth – she takes a bite, I smack her face and threaten her with death – she promises to be a good girl and not tell anyone if I just let her go. Instead, she walked from the van to my porch, and was waiting at the door while I fumbled with my keys.

I opened the door for her. She wandered in, kicked off her shoes, dropped her jacket on the floor, started looking at my stuff, touching things, picking them up, putting them down in the wrong place.

"You got anything to eat?" her voice asked from a different room. I caught up to her after hanging up our jackets and putting my Goosey Goose figurine back beside Froggy Frog. "Or how about a drink?" Her head was in my refrigerator. I forgot to look at her ass as she was bending over.

This was not right. I had to assert my will against her. Managed to get her to follow me to the basement after making her a bourbon and soda – even though she wanted something with lime in it; I don't have lime, why would I need it, who the goddamn hell needs lime in their daily diet? Showed her the pit. That would change things – she would know she was the victim.

"So what do you want me to do?" she asked with a hand on her hip, sipping her drink. "Am I supposed to get down in there?" She put her drink down on a piece of stone that had fallen from the wall, lit herself a cigarette.

"You know, cigarettes are very bad for your health."

She peered down into the pit, taking up her glass and sipping as she smoked. "So is rape. So how am I supposed to get down there? Got a ladder?"

She was a Miss Smarty Pants. Smugly, I took the ladder off its wall hooks and slid it into the pit. (Of course I had a ladder, Miss So-and-So. I prepare for everything at all times.) Without a word — the cigarette held between her lips, drink in hand — she climbed down the ladder, didn't fall or slip once.

She glanced around her new surroundings, poked a finger at the Plexiglas, kicked it.

"Hey!" I said. "You know how much that costs?"

She dragged off the cigarette as she looked up at me. "So? You got money. Don't you? Can't imagine a lot of abductors have steady jobs — your victims could escape while you're out flipping burgers." She spat a stream of smoke up at me. "So what am I supposed to do down here? Scream and beg for mercy? I've seen movies. Horror movies are boring — I'm not following their rules. Real life is the real terror. You got a book I can read? And which way to the bathroom? Unless you like watching me piss and shit. You one of those?" She gulped the rest of her drink and tossed it against the Plexiglas. Joke's on her — the glass didn't break.

I was stunned. Hands on the ladder, I peered down at her. She peered up. The muscles in my forehead were tight and they hurt. My nose started running.

"Come back up," I said curtly, then turned away from the pit.

"You sure?" she echoed up from her depths. "Might be kinda fun to fuck in a pit."

The ladder's rungs creaked as she climbed. Flicked the cigarette over her shoulder into the pit. Thankfully, Plexiglas doesn't catch fire very well. I planned for that. She smoked way too much.

She followed me as I led the way into the bedroom. I had the bed, of course, the first necessity. And I bought a nice comforter with cartoon characters, fluffy pillows, and small stuffed animals I got from a bargain bin, outgrown toys. But the walls were still stone, the floor still packed earth. I wanted something nice for the victim. A place she could enjoy staying in. A room of her own, much better than her room in that small upstairs apartment.

"Cute," she said, slipping beside me, her shoulder touching mine. I moved away an inch. "A little ghetto, but that can be fun."

She entered the bedroom and sat on the bed. Bounced to test the springs. I could've assured her that I bought nothing but the best of mattresses, but I said nothing. Didn't feel like talking anymore.

Then — dear God — she slipped her shirt over her head, peeled off her socks with a finger, flicked them across the room.

"Okay — stop!" I yelled. My face was burning. Wiped sweat off my upper lip with a swipe of my sleeve. My chest felt tight. I just couldn't pull in any air. "You gotta listen, okay, you gotta ... this isn't ... it's not ... you just walked right in, and now ... this —"

She tilted her head to one side as she gazed up at me. I think she had pretty feet, wasn't sure. She patted the mattress. "Sit down before you fall down."

I sat. Hunched over, holding a cool palm against my burning forehead. "This isn't how it was supposed to go." I couldn't look her in the eye, couldn't even raise my head to speak to the stone wall. "You're the victim. I torture you — you scream and cry — you're helpless. I fuck you anytime I want. You're my sex slave. I'm going to put a baby in you. My wife and daughter died in the car wreck – I got a van like hers, different colour, for some change. I need a little change in my life, who doesn't? You're going to be my new wife and daughter all rolled into one. I will breed babies from your womb against your will. Incest is legal in Japan, Israel, Brazil and Portugal – we could move to one of those places. There are no good laws here."

I was rambling, but those last words merely croaked out of my throat. My chest heaved and nose ran as though I had run a marathon. I was sincerely exhausted. Didn't even notice that her arm was around my shoulders.

"Okay," she whispered. "Now it all makes sense." She took out her cigarette pack again, but I told her no. It would be bad for the baby. It felt good to say no. My chest released some breath.

She pulled my chin up with a finger, made me look her in the eyes. "Wanna know a secret?" she whispered in a little girl voice. She knew me so well so quickly. "I want a baby. I want a family. I've been looking for the right guy to knock me up. I had an abortion when I was sixteen because I hated the guy. He was too nice. A pussy. He did the honourable thing and said he would marry me and help raise the child." She took out a cigarette, I let it go. "I'm smoking – get used to it." Slipped her arm back around my shoulders. Was nice enough to blow smoke away from me. "I ditched the baby and the daddy. But I knew it was something I wanted, just a little later in life." She leaned her head in, brushed her lips across my ear. "I like older guys. I like sick psycho fucks. I read serial killer novels and my pussy gets wet." She held my face in her hands, the cigarette burning so close to my hair. "I want you to get me pregnant. And stay with me forever, in the pit or outside it, here or in another country." She inhaled deeply, looked into my eyes through wisps of smoke rising from between her lips. "I'll never tell on you. Hell, maybe you and I could grab some pretty little girls together ... raise them as our own. In case your sperm doesn't work. Or my eggs." She kissed me softly. Both of our eyes were open as we kissed.

That was important. I could see both calm and a swirling vortex of violence in the black depths of her eyes. Love makes bad poets of us all.

I felt calm. Mostly. Still slightly nervous, but for a different reason now. I was excited to be with her. For there to be an 'us'. We tried to make love on my pretty bed surrounded by stone and earth and abandoned toys. She was very willing and exciting and excited, but, for some reason, I couldn't get an erection. She soothed me with her words and caresses, said we had our whole lives to try again and again.

A baby would come, somehow.

PROTECTOR
RASMENIA MASSOUD

The neighbors were asking too many questions about the boy's arm. Dennis looked at the four boys seated at the kitchen table, busy having a serious discussion about wrestling while they smacked their lips and stuffed their faces with Beefaroni.

"Steve Austin is the best," David said.

"Nah," his twin brother Kevin, said. "The Undertaker is cooler. He does the Tombstone Piledriver and that's more awesome than anything Steve Austin does."

"You guys are dumb," Scott said. "Hulk Hogan is still the best ever."

"Whatever," said David. "You just think you're smart because you're in middle school."

Charlie never looked up at his brothers. Nothing on his face indicated that he even heard their voices. His left arm, wrapped in a plaster cast up to his shoulder, sat propped up next to his bowl at the table. His eyes were looking somewhere far away, past his spoon, past his bowl, somewhere miles beyond the dinner table. Dennis found it unsettling the way his youngest son spent so much time daydreaming and spacing out instead of acting like a normal kid. His other sons, they were normal. That was because they were his sons, not the bastard larvae of some cracked-out, cheating bitch.

The neighbors around the apartment building had been eyeing him and whispering more than usual since he brought Charlie home from the hospital the other day. He knew what they chattered about behind his back; they thought he was a child abuser and a tyrant.

Every night when he came home with the boys, they would trudge up the steps to their apartment on the fourth floor, smiling, nodding and waving at the other tenants.

The neighbors always smiled and waved back. They were nice to his face, but he knew they judged him, whispering to one another about what an ogre he was. Dennis knew they were afraid of him. When they saw his thick frame moving toward them, he could see his menace reflected on them as they made small talk and stammered for an excuse to get away before they scurried to their own apartment. He had a head full of thick chestnut hair, but kept it shaved clean and always wore big, heavy boots to appear taller.

Dennis liked people to be afraid. It kept them in line—especially his boys. But, not Charlie. That kid just wouldn't learn, no matter how much Dennis tried to discipline him. It was obviously a genetic defect. Probably from the boy's real father.

Dennis gazed out the window, focusing on the front door of the third floor apartment in the southeast corner. He couldn't see any of Rita's windows from here, which annoyed him, but he had a perfect view of the front door so he could keep an eye on the comings and goings of her place.

"What do you think, Dad?" Kevin asked.

"What do I think about what?" Dennis lowered the blind, but stayed at the window.

"Who's the best wrestler?"

"Jerry Lawler."

The three boys looked to one another to see if one of them knew what their father was talking about.

"Who?" Scott asked.

"Never mind." Dennis laughed. "Your dad's old." He looked down at Charlie, still lost in another world.

"Charlie."

Nothing.

"Charlie!"

The boy looked up, blond waves of hair going in random directions, a smear of Bee-faroni on his babyish mouth.

"Go see if Rita needs any help."

"I'll go," Scott said, his green eyes lighting up through a shag of dark hair.

David laughed. "Scott has a crush on Rita."

"Do not," Scott said. "She's old. But, she's nice."

"She's not old," David corrected. "She's way younger than Dad."

Scott looked over at his baby brother. He looked at the cast on his arm and wished he could help him.

"Enough," Dennis said. "Charlie, go."

Saying nothing, Charlie stepped down from his chair and began walking toward the door.

Dennis stopped him and held out a napkin. "Wipe your face."

Scott watched his little half-brother go out the door. He wished he was burly and intimidating like his dad, then he could do a better job of protecting Charlie.

* * *

Rita opened the door and looked down to find Charlie grinning up at her, his spindly arm wrapped in plaster and bent like a tiny chicken wing. Rita smiled and crouched down to his level.

"Hey, Charlie," she said. "What can I do for you?"

"Um … my dad wanted me to ask if I can do any chores for you."

"Oh," she said. "He did, did he?" Rita looked up at their apartment on the fourth floor. Dennis stood in the doorway, his burly frame silhouetted by the light coming from the living room. He waved at her. She waved back, trying to ignore the sensation of her skin crawling.

"Yes, ma'am," Charlie said.

"Charlie, I told you … you don't have to call me that. We're friends." She tousled his hair.

"Okay. It smells weird in there." He looked past her, into her apartment, where a half-finished painting sat upon an easel.

"It's probably the paint," she said, following his gaze. "Or the turpentine. Would you like to come in and see?"

"Um … my dad …" Charlie looked over his shoulder, up toward his apartment.

"It's okay. I'll tell him you were doing a little job for me."

Charlie nodded and stepped inside, fixated on the painting: an image of a girl, kneeling in a bright, sunny meadow. The wind blew through her hair and the long grass all around her as she held her face in her hands.

"Is she sad?" Charlie looked up at Rita, his eyes wide with concern.

"Yeah," Rita said, smiling. "I guess she is."

"She looks so lonely," he said. "She makes me feel sad."

Rita looked down at the cast on Charlie's arm. It was still clean, without a single mark or signature.

"Hey," she said, picking up a Sharpie. "What say I sign your cast?"

Charlie nodded and finally smiled big enough for Rita to see his teeth and held up his skinny little chicken wing. He watched intently as Rita drew one curved line after another. After a minute or so, his cast was decorated with a funny-faced cartoon dog telling him "Get well soon!"

"There. That's better, eh?"

Charlie inspected the drawing and let out a tiny laugh. He nodded.

"Right, then. Your dad wanted you to help me out, so maybe you can help me clean some of these brushes before you go back up to your place."

"Okay."

The two of them sat on the kitchen floor of Rita's apartment, cleaning out the brushes while Rita asked Charlie about school, his brothers and anything else she could think of to get the boy to talk.

What she didn't ask about—what she really wanted to ask him, but knew she couldn't without making him nervous —was his arm. The small, broken limb wrapped up in plaster.

She asked Dennis what happened last week when she ran into them returning home from the hospital.

"You know kids," he'd told her. "They're clumsy. They fall down all the time. It's no big deal. But, I noticed your car making a knocking noise when you pulled up. I can take a look at it if you want."

The boys had scurried upstairs to the apartment without looking at her or saying hello that day.

Rita had already turned Dennis down twice. He asked her to dinner just a few days after she and Evan broke up. That's when she realized that Dennis had been watching her.

"I couldn't help but notice you've been spending a lot more time hanging out alone," he'd said when he asked her to dinner.

She tried to be polite. They were neighbors. No reason to tarnish a neighborly relationship. "I'm afraid it just isn't a good time. I really need some time to myself right now."

He seemed sincere enough the first time he offered to help her with her car. He was a mechanic, after all. If he said that he wanted to help a neighbor, she didn't see any reason to doubt it.

It was just an oil change. No harm in an oil change.

I noticed your spark plugs need changing while I was changing your oil. I can help with that.

Couldn't help noticing a vacuum tube needs replacing.

Did you know you've got a busted headlight?

Now, Rita's car had one problem after another and Dennis was sending little Charlie down to her apartment almost every night, knowing she had a soft spot for the boy.

Looking down at Charlie, sitting on her kitchen floor, cleaning paintbrushes and talking about the second grade, Rita stares at the tiny cast on his tiny arm. She nods and smiles even though she feels her cheeks flush with anger.

Rita said goodbye to little Charlie and watched him go up the stairs and walk around to the other side of the U-shaped apartment building. She waved at him once more just before he turned the knob and entered the cramped, two-bedroom apartment he shared with his father and three brothers.

She sat down on the steps in front of her own apartment and lit a cigarette. She didn't look back up at Dennis' place. She could feel his eyes on her, knowing that he peeked out at her through the blinds whenever she came outside to smoke.

Rita didn't even notice when Lennie came staggering home from the bar across the street, or when Juan turned up his stereo downstairs. The sound of Dire Straits usually got on her nerves, but this time, she couldn't even hear it. The only thing she could hear was the voice of the new mechanic she had taken her car to this morning. The mechanic's face twisted in confusion as he held up a piece of her engine and said, "I've never seen anything like this. Who ever did this had no idea what they were doing ... it almost looks like someone got in there and smashed it with a hammer."

No, Rita said to herself. *He knew exactly what he was doing.*

* * *

Dennis sat at the kitchen window, smoking cigarettes while he waited for the boys to fall asleep. He'd turned the lights and television off so that the only sounds he heard aside from the soft crackling of burning tobacco were of someone outside having a loud argument.

He knew that Rita stayed up late, so usually an hour or so after he put the kids to bed, he would go for a little walk out by the empty swimming pool at the east side of the building. There were a couple of cottonwood trees on the other side of the pool that he liked to sit under while smoking and having a beer.

He appreciated being able to look up from there and see almost every window in Rita's apartment; her living room, bedroom and kitchen. Everything except the bathroom, which he didn't want to see, anyway. It's not like he was some kind of pervert, or a creep. He had no doubt regarding his character. He knew he was a good man, even though the whispers of his neighbors claimed otherwise. Dennis understood why people talked behind his back. Because they were hateful cowards who always wanted to think the worst of him. They preferred to look at him as a child abuser instead of a good disciplinarian; as a stalker rather than a watchful friend and protector. He knew what they said about him. He never heard them talking, but he knew. And he knew they were wrong.

He watched Rita in her kitchen, leaning against the counter and talking to someone on the phone. Every few minutes, she laughed and took a sip from a brown bottle. Probably one of those microbrews, Dennis thought, looking down at his can of Busch. He liked Rita, but she was too much of a beer snob. With time, he could probably convince her that beer from a can is just as good. She had mentioned once that she wasn't much of a kid person, too, but since he started sending Charlie over to her place, she'd been coming around.

He considered explaining to her that if his kids just had a mother, he'd be able to make more money. If only he had someone to take care of them, he'd have the time to drive long haul again and wouldn't have to work as a mechanic.

Then she could drink all the fucking microbrews she wanted to.

He thought about explaining this to her, but thought it might be best to wait until after the first time he made love to her.

Or, at least until their first date.

Dennis wondered who might be on the other end of the phone. Most likely a girl-friend, but it could be a man. She'd said she wasn't interested in dating at the moment, but maybe she lied.

He shrugged to himself and emptied his can of beer, knowing he wouldn't have a problem chasing off any asshole who came around looking to mess with something that didn't belong to them.

He finished his beer as he watched Rita set the phone down and disappear from his view. He smashed the empty can in his hands and dropped it in the dry grass. He popped open the second can he'd brought down with him and looked up at Rita's windows, waiting to get another look at her.

* * *

Rita stepped outside and lit up a smoke. The building was unusually quiet. It was normal to hear her neighbors even this late at night, as they fought, fucked, partied or just watched TV. But tonight, it was calm. She snuggled herself deeper into her sweater as she listened to the dry leaves falling to the ground, dead and blown loose by the October breeze.

It was on a night like this, a year ago, that she and Evan popped open a bottle of Merlot and ran outside naked, wrapped in blankets to look up at the stars. But, that was last year. Before they had moved into this place, before they became the two sad strangers that they were today. Now, Evan was gone and she was looking up at the stars alone, trying to figure out if she missed him more than she enjoyed being on her own. Until she heard a faint crunching sound, followed by the familiar pop and hiss of a can being opened. She looked around but didn't see anyone. All the doors to the other apartments were closed. Leaning forward toward the railing, she peered down to see if someone might be quietly boozing at the picnic table below.

For some reason that she couldn't understand, Rita stepped out from her doorway and gazed into the darkness beyond the swimming pool. She couldn't see much besides the sagging chicken-wire fence and cottonwood trees.

Then something moved. Something big.

* * *

Dennis never heard Rita's door. She caught him off guard when he saw her at the top of the stairs in front of her apartment on the third floor. He watched her as she looked down, then around.

For a brief moment, he thought she might be able to see him, so he leaned down, almost lying in the dead grass, trying to sink deeper into the shadows. After a few seconds, Rita disappeared from his sight and he heard her door close.

Well, it's getting late anyway, he thought to himself. He got to his feet and began heading back toward the building.

* * *

She couldn't see what or who was out there, but Rita suddenly became aware of her heartbeat. Fragments of pictures and voices whooshed around in her head: a little boy with a broken arm, the mechanic's befuddled expression as he showed her a cracked engine piece.

It's Dennis, she thought. *Dennis is out there and he's spying on me.* Her first thought was to get back inside, lock the deadbolt and call Evan. No. Evan's gone. No calling Evan for help. She considered going back inside just to get her keys, her purse and then go spend the night somewhere else. Yes, that's what she'd do. Leave. Get out of here. Now.

She turned and opened the door to her apartment. Her eyes went directly to the keys and cell phone just a few steps away on the kitchen counter. Then the fragments spun around in her head again. She took a step backward, back outside. She slammed the door closed. Feeling the little hairs on her arms standing up, Rita leaned back against the door, out of the light and waited.

* * *

It only took a couple of minutes before Dennis came out of his hiding place. Rita heard the crunch of dead crispy leaves being smashed by his heavy boots. Then she saw him, a can of beer in his hand as he started up the stairs at the other side of the U, just across from hers. She took a deep breath and stepped out under the light. "What were you doing out there?"

Dennis turned around, startled. "Oh, hey Rita. What're you still doing up?"

"I asked you a question." She hoped she didn't sound as nervous as she felt.

"I was just out for a walk. I couldn't sleep." He walked up another flight of stairs.

"A walk?"

"Yeah." Dennis shrugged and took a drink from his beer. "I walk around out here sometimes when I can't sleep."

"Were you spying on me?"

"Was I ... what? No!" He walked quickly up another flight of stairs and stopped when he was on the third floor, directly across from her. "You can't be ... nah, don't think that ... I wasn't ... no, I wasn't spying on you!"

"You were. I know you were. Look, my mistake. My blinds will be closed after dark from now on ... and if you would be kind enough to please, just leave me alone—"

She didn't get the chance to finish her sentence before Dennis threw his half-full beer down to the ground. She flinched and took a step toward her door.

"Listen to me, you fucking bitch. I've been nothing but kind to you." He started walking away, but not to the next flight of stairs. Dennis was quickly making his way around the U-shaped building, approaching Rita's apartment.

Dennis continued shouting and ranting as he walked, but Rita didn't hear any of his words. She ran back inside her apartment and slammed the door. She turned the deadbolt, and the tiny, almost useless lock on the doorknob. Rita grabbed her cell phone as Dennis shouted on the other side of the door.

"C'mon, Rita … open the door. I just want to talk. This has all been a misunderstanding." He pounded on the door with his fists. "Rita! Open the fucking door!"

Just as Rita began to dial 911, she noticed how much the door shook when he kicked and pounded on it. She briefly wondered if it would be enough to keep him out.

Before she could finish making the call, she found out.

* * *

"Charlie, you'd better get back into bed before Dad comes home."

Charlie looked away from the kitchen window and saw his oldest brother Scott standing there.

"Dad's down at Rita's," Charlie said.

"Okay. Well, I'm sure he'll come back up soon and when he does, you'd better be in bed. You know how he gets."

"Yeah. Okay." Charlie slid down from the tall chair next to the window and walked past his brother, back into their bedroom where the twins were asleep.

Scott walked over to the window and peeked through the blinds, down at Rita's apartment. The door was open. A piece of the doorframe stuck out from the wall and just inside, a table lay on its side. Keeping his eyes on the open door, he reached for the cordless phone on the wall.

After Scott finished his call, he returned the phone to its place on the wall. He went to the bedroom and stepped up the ladder where Charlie lay in the top bunk, just above his own. Charlie opened his eyes.

"Is Dad home?"

"No." Scott pulled the blanket up around his little brother's chin and lightly patted the plaster wrapped around his arm. "I think he's going to be gone a while, but don't worry. I'll be right here."

DANCE WITH ME
ROCKY ALEXANDER

"I love you, Zoe." The words were spoken in a whisper surely meant to sound ominous, but the effect was spoiled by the noise of the mall crowd and poor cell phone reception; instead it was just annoying as hell. "I don't know how much longer I can take not being with you."

"Fuck you, Robert." Zoe hung up and shoved the phone back into her purse.

"Ex-boyfriend again?" Rachel asked with a sympathetic pout.

"Why can't he just get over it already? I mean, it was fun for a while, but high school is over now and I'm ready to get on with my life. Did he honestly expect that we were just gonna run away and get married or something? We were together less than a year, for chrissake."

"Maybe he thought you'd take him off to college with you and smuggle him into the sorority house," Molly giggled. "Oh gee, no, House Mother, I had no idea my boyfriend has been hiding under my bed this whole time."

"Well, you can't really blame him for being such a cry baby," Rachel said. "He'll never have another girl as good as you, and he knows it. I mean, the guy is a fucking loser."

"Hey, watch it," Zoe warned. "I had sex with that loser."

"Don't get me wrong, he's cute and everything, but he totally kissed your ass twenty-four-seven. He was like a little puppy lapping at your boot heel everywhere you went. He gave you no space whatsoever. If he isn't a loser, then why did you break up with him?"

"I wouldn't say he's a loser. I mean, he's a little OCD, but ..." Zoe smiled at the exaggerated scowls on her friends' faces. "Okay, fuck it. He's a loser."

The three of them laughed together like they had so many times throughout the lengthy history of their friendship, but Zoe felt a tightness in her throat as she considered how much everything was going to change when she went away to Penn State in the fall. For as long as she could remember, Rachel and Molly had been like sisters to her. Everything that comes along with growing up in the world, all the triumphs and all the pain, had always been shared between the three of them. What one felt, the other two felt as well.

When Zoe was thirteen, her father had succumbed to the cancer which he had so exhaustively battled for nearly three years. She and her daddy were as close as any father and daughter could be, even though she had known deep inside that his life was to be cut short, and had tried desperately to prepare herself for that inevitability. When the day came, she was more devastated than she ever imagined she could be. But she wasn't alone. Rachel and Molly had cried right along with her. They'd grieved just as she had grieved. They had given their strength to help carry the burden of her suffering, lest she be crushed beneath the weight of it. They loved her. She loved them. She was both saddened and frightened by the thought of being so far away from them.

"So, Zoe," Molly said, "is your mom still taking that trip to Denver next weekend?"

"She is if everything goes according to plan. I can't believe we're going to have the house all to ourselves for two whole days."

"And *three* whole nights." Rachel did an excited little ballerina twirl. "*Paaar-tay!*"

Zoe rolled her eyes and chuckled. "Look, we've already talked about this: No parties. My mom would kill me, and you can bet your life that my uncle Mike will be checking up on us. It's going to be a good opportunity for some quality *girl* time."

"You have no sense of adventure."

"Oh, come on," Zoe laughed. "It'll be fun, just the three of us. I'll be leaving town after the summer, ya know?"

Rachel smiled. "I'm only kidding. Of course it'll be fun. One last hurrah."

"That's right," Molly said. "One last hurrah."

Zoe's cell phone rang in her purse. She fished it out and saw BLOCKED CALL on the display screen. She didn't answer it.

* * *

After leaving the mall, Zoe went home to have dinner with her mother. They ate baked pesto chicken with angel hair pasta and French bread. Later the two of them sat on the living room sofa together and shared a pint of Ben and Jerry's while watching an old science-fiction movie about a guy with two brains.

At eleven o'clock, Zoe showered, dressed in fresh underwear and a T-shirt, removed her laptop from its case on the dresser, and lay on her belly atop the thick, blue comforter that covered her queen-sized bed to begin her usual nightly ritual of email checking and Facebooking.

At exactly midnight, her cell phone rang. BLOCKED CALL. *That fucker, Robert.* She rejected the call and slammed the phone down on the edge of the bed. Just who the hell did he think he was, calling her at this hour? The nerve, calling her at *all.* He was out of his fucking mind.

There was a time when Zoe thought she loved him. Those first few months, when everything was magical. When she lay awake until late at night—every night—thinking of him. When all that mattered to her was his touch on her skin. His lips—his body against hers. The way he smiled as she ran her fingers through his thick, blonde hair.

She had met him when he changed a flat tire for her one summer evening just after the start of senior year. It was pouring with rain, and he had insisted she wait inside the comfort of her car while he switched out the tire. He was dripping wet by the time he had finished. She had offered him a ride home, but he had refused because there was no room in the car for his bicycle, and because he didn't want to get her seats wet. The next day, she had seen him in the hallway at school, and thanked him again for his assistance. It had turned out that they shared a couple of classes together, and she felt bad for having never noticed him before. From then on, she had started paying more attention. He was shy, reserved, and a little bit socially awkward, but the more Zoe had gotten to know him, the more she was enamored with his intelligence and humor and boyish charm. And yeah, he was cute. It wasn't long before she had decided to take the initiative to ask him out, and it had only taken one date for her to realize she wanted to be his girlfriend. And for those first few months, she couldn't stand being apart from him.

But then, as often happens in a relationship, the magic began to wear off. Robert became obsessive and clingy, expressing no pleasure in life independent of Zoe. No joy but through her. He seemed to be happy only in her presence, or while talking with her on the phone, or chatting online. And after a while, Zoe began to feel less like a girl-friend and more like his emotional support system. She couldn't be there for him every waking moment, and this created a substantial amount of guilt, and subsequently, re-sentment. By the end of the school year, she found herself feeding him one elaborate excuse after another in order to establish some breathing room. Finally, with tremen-dous support from Rachel and Molly, she dumped him on the morning of the day of high school graduation ceremonies. That was three weeks ago. She had been revelling in her freedom ever since. "No looking back," Rachel had encouraged.

Zoe had no intention of looking back.

The phone rang again. *Don't answer it, Zoe*, she willed herself. If she ignored him long enough, he would go away.

But he wasn't. Not tonight. He called three more times, and then Zoe's phone noti-fied her that she had a new voicemail. Against her better judgement, she listened to the recording. But there was nothing but dead air.

Again, the phone rang, but this time it was the land line. Now he was really push-ing it. The cordless house phone was on the nightstand next to Zoe's bed, but there was one in her mother's room as well. If Zoe let it continue to ring, her mom would wake up, and then Zoe would have to listen to a twenty-minute lecture on why she didn't choose better boyfriends. She snatched the handheld from its charger cradle and hit the talk button. "Okay, fuckhead, what do you want?"

"I love you, Zoe." It was the same obnoxious whisper as before, but it seemed a little creepier in the late-night silence of her bedroom. "It's hard for me to live knowing you're out there in the world and I can't have you."

"Why don't you just go ahead and *die* then? Fucking psycho."

"That isn't very nice, Zoe. It's not the way to treat someone who loves you as much as I do."

"Look, you *freak*, I have nothing to say to you. *Nothing*. Got that?" Zoe felt her skin grow hot with rage. There was a tremor in her voice. "Listen to me, and listen closely: I. DON'T. LOVE. YOU. Understand? It's *over* between us, so just stop this."

She waited for a response, but the line was quiet for several seconds. Good. Maybe he was finally getting the point. He was probably going to start crying now, but Zoe didn't give a shit. Not anymore.

Then, "Zoe, how can you say it's over? It hasn't even *begun* for us."

A cold chill gripped the back of her neck. She shuddered. Okay, enough of this. "I'm going to say this once, you *fuck*. If you call me one more time, I swear to God I'll call the police. You know my uncle Mike is a cop. He *will* arrest you. You and me are over, and that's that. Deal with it and get on with your life. If you keep fucking with me, you'll go to jail. I mean it. Do *not* call me again."

She hung up, closed her eyes, and took in a deep breath, let it out slowly. Robert was obsessive, but surely he wasn't so obsessive that he would risk being locked up in a jail cell with a bunch of criminals who would, more than likely, defile him in ways she couldn't conceive. Then again, how well does one really know someone?

Just as she lay back down on her bed, there was another ring from her cell phone. She clenched her teeth. *Alright, you bastard, if you want to play hardball, let's play.* She picked up the phone. "You blew it, punk. Now I'm calling the cops."

"I only wanted to tell you something," he said.

"I have zero interest in anything you have to say."

"I wanted to tell you that you look sexy in those pink panties."

Zoe reflexively looked down at her underwear. Pink cotton. She grew so cold that she thought she might be able to see the white vapor of her breath in the air.

"Pink panties?" she asked, her voice wavering.

"Yes. The pink panties you're wearing right now."

She struggled to hold back the spiny tendrils of panic that tickled at the edge of her mind, threatening to corrupt her senses. He was toying with her, trying to manipulate her through fear. She wasn't going to fall for it.

"Nice try, asshole," she said, "but I'm not wearing pink panties."

"Yes you are. Pink panties and a T-shirt with the high school team logo on the front."

The first thing she imagined was that he was somehow spying on her through the webcam on her laptop. She impulsively closed the display lid and sat bolt upright on her bed. That's when she noticed the three-inch gap between the curtains draped over her bedroom window.

"I've been watching you, Zoe."

He's bluffing, she thought, as she stood up onto the floor. *He's not out there. It's Robert, for chrissake. He doesn't have the balls.*

But what if it wasn't Robert?

Her legs suddenly felt too weak to support her own weight. *Get a grip, Zoe. Of course it's Robert. He's messing with your head. There's nobody outside.*

"Robert?" she asked into the phone.

No response.

"Okay, if you're watching me, what am I doing right now?"

No response.

She felt her strength slowly creeping back into her shaky limbs. Her breathing began to slow. "If you were watching me, then you would know."

"You're lying on your bed," the voice eventually replied.

Wrong, fucker. Zoe smiled devilishly as her trepidation gave way to audacious self-assurance. Robert had made a lucky guess about her clothing. Their relationship had been a very intimate one after all; no doubt he'd seen her numerous times dressed exactly the same as she was now. Hell, he was probably whacking off to a photo of her in this very T-shirt and panties as they spoke. Yuck.

With renewed confidence and a spark of mischief, she moved closer to the window and seductively peeled off her shirt. "What am I doing now?" she asked, rocking her shoulders to make her breasts jiggle.

No response.

"That's what I thought, you worthless piece of—"

A sick groan emanated from the phone, and now the voice was more than a whisper. Thick. Gravelly. Guttural. "Sublime ..."

Before Zoe's courage could escape her, she lurched forward and threw open the curtains.

And there he was. His masked face only inches from the glass. His head cloaked beneath a dark hood. His right hand held a cell phone against his ear.

100

Zoe had flung open her bedroom door with such force as to nearly rip it from its hinges, and was running through the hallway toward her mother's room before she realized she was screaming at the top of her lungs. Her mom was already up out of bed and wrapping herself in a terry robe when Zoe burst into the room.

"Zoe, what is it? What's *wrong?*"

Zoe could barely breathe. Her hands flailed at her sides as she tried to force the words from her throat. "There's somebody ... somebody ..." She gasped for air, her head swimming with adrenaline.

"Zoe, please calm down and tell me what's wrong."

"Mom ... there's somebody outside my window."

"What? Who?" Her mother glanced toward her own bedroom window and moved instinctively toward the opposite wall.

"I don't know. I think it's my ex-boyfriend."

"Who? Robert? Why would Robert be outside your window? What's going on, Zoe? Why are you naked?"

Zoe looked down at herself through the blur of her tears, and immediately threw her arms up to cover herself. In her hysterics, she'd forgotten she was completely nude from the waist up.

"Here, put this on." Her mother removed a turquoise blouse from a hanger in the closet and passed it to Zoe. She then took a flashlight from the bottom drawer of her nightstand and cautiously went to the window to shine the light into the back yard. Zoe admired her mother's bravery, and felt more than a little ashamed at the lack of her own.

"There's nobody out there, Zoe," her mother assured after a few long, grueling seconds.

Zoe felt her muscles loosen. She considered going to the window to look for herself, but she had seen too many horror movies for that.

"So," her mother said, "are you going to tell me what's going on?"

Zoe wiped her tears with the palm of her hand and nodded somberly.

* * *

"Are you okay, sweetie?" Zoe's uncle Mike asked as he entered the kitchen area, where Zoe sat at the table sipping from a cup of hot chamomile tea.

"Hi, Mike. Yeah, I'm okay. Thanks for coming. Mike gave her hair a couple of gentle strokes, and kissed her lovingly on her forehead before taking a seat next to her. "I came as fast as I could. Your mom sounded pretty concerned over the phone."

"Everything's fine now." She forced a smile. "My ex-boyfriend messing with me is all."

"Listen, honey, if this guy has been stalking you, that's illegal. We can arrest him."

Zoe was instantly comforted by the calm authority of Mike's voice. She relished having a cop for an uncle, even if it wasn't always easy. Growing up, there was little she had found more thrilling than the occasional ride in his patrol car, complete with flashing lights and wailing siren. Or the time, when she was fifteen, when he had convinced her mother to allow him to take her to the firing range to teach her how to shoot a handgun. "Hopefully you'll never have to use one of these," he'd said, "but if you should ever need to, at least you'll know how."

As a little girl, her schoolmates thought it was cool that she had a policeman in her family, but that changed in the tenth grade, when she was seldom invited to parties due to fear of her being a snitch. It made matters worse when Mike arrested the high school football quarterback for drunk driving. That incident had wrecked Zoe's social status to the extent that she had briefly entertained the idea of home-schooling. But people forgot, and life went on, and it had given her a chance to prioritize the things that were important to her, such as her family. Mike was her father's brother. After her daddy died, Mike stepped in to fill the void as best he could. He provided for her a father's love, and guidance, and protection. For that, Zoe would be forever grateful.

"I'm not a hundred percent positive that I saw someone outside my window," she said. "It could have been a reflection. I was pretty creeped out by the phone call; my mind could have been playing tricks on me."

"Couldn't we charge him for harassment or something?" her mother asked, taking a place at the table.

"Well, if you can't be sure he was actually trespassing on your property, there isn't much that can be done from a legal standpoint, I'm afraid. Tell me about the phone call, Zoe. Did he threaten you at all?"

"No. He just keeps telling me he loves me. He said he has been watching me though. He knew exactly what clothes I was wearing."

"He knew what *clothes* you were wearing?"

"Well, yeah ... but he could have guessed."

"The thing about phone calls," Mike said, "is that there's a certain expectation within the legal community that a person can simply hang up at any point, or choose not to answer a call in the first place if it's a number the person isn't familiar with. Now, that being said, if he keeps it up, or threatens you in any way, then it would be easier to charge him with stalking or harassment. Keep in mind we have to actually prove that it's him calling. We usually do that with a call trace or some type of recording. Honestly, the best advice I can give is to just not answer the phone if you don't recognize the number. That should put an end to it."

"Well, I'm cancelling my trip to Denver next weekend," Zoe's mother said. "I can't leave with this kind of stuff going on."

"You can't do that, Mom. They're paying you a lot of money to speak at that seminar."

"Oh please. I'm a college professor, not a rock star. They aren't paying me that much."

"I'm sure it'll be fine, Mother. Rachel and Molly will be here, and Mike will be keeping an eye on things as well."

Mike nodded in agreement. "I don't think there's much to worry about, Janine. It sounds like a simple case of teenage heartbreak. Kids do silly things sometimes."

"But you didn't see how upset she was, Mike ... the way she was screaming. She practically gave me a heart attack."

"Mom, I told you, I just got freaked out."

"And suppose he *was* outside," Janine said, "*peeping* on you."

Zoe lowered her eyes and said nothing. The more she thought about it, the more convinced she became that there *had* been someone outside the window. But if she was wrong, and it had only been a matter of her imagination getting the better of her, then it could result in a whole lot of needless trouble for which she wasn't willing to take responsibility.

"I'd be happy to hang around 'till morning," Mike said, "if it'll make you both feel better."

"I don't think that's necessary," said Janine. "Zoe can sleep with me tonight. We'll be fine."

"Well, if you're sure. I'll take a look around before I go. Just keep your doors and windows locked, and if you have any more problems, please don't hesitate to call."

Zoe and her mother thanked Mike as he stood up to leave. Janine offered to walk him out, and after Zoe hugged him goodbye he looked her in the eyes and said, with stone cold seriousness, "Listen, if this guy scares you again, you let me know. I'll take care of it. I'm not telling you this as a cop; I'm telling you this as your uncle. Do you understand?"

"Yes, Mike. I do."

"Good."

* * *

After the next four days passed without further incident, Zoe was able to convince her mother that it was safe to go forward with her trip to Colorado. On Friday afternoon, Zoe drove her mom to the airport, then met Rachel and Molly for lunch at the Denny's on 23rd. When they were finished, the three of them headed to the mall for some shopping and to catch the latest summer blockbuster at the mall cinema. Zoe drove herself, with Rachel and Molly following in Rachel's Mini Cooper.

Three hundred dollars later, with eight full bags of newly-purchased merchandise stored inside their locked vehicles, the girls loaded their arms with popcorn, Twizzlers, and diet soda, made their way into the crowded theater and took some seats in the fifth row. After getting settled, Zoe took her cell phone out of her purse and switched off the ringer. It vibrated in her hand before she could put it away. She winced when she saw what was on the display screen. Not a blocked call this time. Not an unfamiliar number. The display read ROBERT.

She dropped the phone back into her purse without answering. Anger flared in her chest, but she willed herself to maintain her composure. No way was she going to let him ruin her weekend. No way. But twenty minutes into the movie, Molly nudged her with her elbow. "Guess who's sitting four rows behind us."

Zoe straightened and twisted her head around to scan the moviegoers in the seats further back. She spotted him immediately. He raised a hand and wiggled his fingers at her. His face was expressionless. On his left was his best friend, Ryan, who flashed a smile, then looked away uncomfortably when she didn't reciprocate. Robert only continued to stare at her with eyes that, in the darkness, looked like polished black stones.

"We don't have to stay here, Zoe," Molly said. "We can get a refund for the movie ... watch it some other time."

Zoe shifted her attention back to the film screen and shook her head defiantly. "I'm not going anywhere."

But she already knew in the back of her mind that she was only kidding herself. She could feel him watching her, and it made her skin crawl. When she could bear it no longer, she pulled out her phone and dialed Robert's number. She recognized his ringtone at once. "Dance With Me" by The Leftovers. The asshole didn't even have the common courtesy to turn off his ringer in the theater. When he answered, she said, "Just so you know, I hate your fucking guts." Then she hung up. "Okay," she said to Rachel and Molly, "let's get the hell out of here."

They left the mall without bothering to get their movie tickets refunded, and agreed to meet up at Zoe's house. As Zoe was backing out of her parking space, she nearly hit Robert, who had walked up behind her car. She saw him in her rear -view mirror and slammed on the brakes. A moment later his face was in her window. *Deja friggin' vu.* He was so close that his breath fogged the glass. "I need to talk to you, Zoe."

She hit the door lock button and stepped on the gas pedal. He made no physical attempt to stop her, only stood in the parking lot, shouting her name as she sped away.

A couple of miles from the mall, Zoe realized she had forgotten to turn her phone ringer back on. Worried that her mom might try to reach her and be unable to get through, she dug the phone from her purse and immediately noticed she had three missed calls. One was from Molly. The other two were from Robert. She pounded her fist on the steering wheel and whined in frustration, "Why won't you leave me *alone?*"

At the next red light, she brought up Molly's number and pressed her finger against the screen to dial, but stopped. Instead, she dialed the number for her uncle Mike.

"Zoe?" he answered.

"Mike, remember when you told me to call you if my ex-boyfriend scared me again?"

"What happened? Are you okay?"

"I'm okay, but he's been following me. I can't take this anymore."

Without hesitation, Mike said, "Don't worry about a thing. I'll deal with this guy."

"Are you going to arrest him?"

"I'm going to do whatever it takes, sweetie. Whatever it takes."

* * *

That night, Zoe, Rachel, and Molly watched movies and ate pizza and played drinking games with raspberry-flavored wine coolers. They talked and laughed and gossiped until early morning, then the three of them slept in Zoe's room.

They woke late, and had lunch at a Greek restaurant downtown. In the afternoon, they returned to Zoe's to primp for an outdoor rock concert they planned to attend later that evening. The show started at seven, but after a couple of hours it began to rain heavily, forcing an abrupt end to the festivities before the headlining act had a chance to perform.

At ten, as the girls sat in a little Italian bistro on Dove Street, drowning their disappointment in Fettuccine Alla Romana and Zucchini Ripieni, Zoe received a phone call from Mike.

"I took care of that problem for you," he said. "I don't think he'll be bothering you anymore."

"What did you do, Mike?"

"Don't worry about it. What I did isn't important. What matters is your safety and well-being."

"Mike, what did you *do?*"

"I just put a little scare into him. That's all. I don't think you'll hear from him again."

"Did you hurt him?"

Mike was slow to answer. "I just put a scare into him."

"Okay. Whatever you did ... thank you."

"You're welcome, Zoe."

The girls finished their dinner and drove back to Zoe's place through the pouring rain. Once they were inside the house, Zoe called her mother to check in. They talked for about ten minutes, then Zoe wanted to get a shower and change into some comfortable pajamas.

As she stood in the tub, her head hung low, letting the warm water wash over her neck and shoulders, the bathroom lights flickered. "Oh, great," she said aloud. "Don't you dare go out on me." She wondered how long it had been since her mom had changed the bulbs. She felt a knot form in her stomach at the thought of being thrown into complete blackness while standing naked and vulnerable in the confined space of the bathtub, and promptly decided it was best if she didn't spend another second pondering such a horrifying possibility.

A moment later, she sensed movement through the shower curtain. A dark shape near the bathroom door. A shadowy silhouette of what might have been a person. *Stop it. You're being ridiculous. Creeping yourself out. Nobody there. Nobody—*

The shape shifted, moved. It came toward her and she could clearly see the outline of a head, shoulders, limbs. She froze in place, unsure even of the beating of her heart. In a second or two the shower curtain would be yanked open to reveal a wig-wearing, butcher knife-wielding psycho who would stab her repeatedly as she helplessly watched her own blood spiral down the drain. And then the damned lights would go out. Forever.

"Zoe?"

She lost her footing and fell against the shower wall. A piercing cry escaped from her throat, and then the curtain did open, and she saw the face.

"Zoe. *What the fuck?*"

It was Molly.

Reality came flooding back as quickly as it had been torn away.

"I'm sorry if I scared you," Molly said, "but I saw some lightning in the distance and I wanted to give you a heads-up. I don't think it's safe to be in the shower during a lightning storm."

"Oh." Zoe hardly recognized her own voice, high-pitched and stridulous. "Okay. Thanks. I'll go ahead and finish up."

"Mm-hmm. Are you alright?"

"I'm fine. You just startled me."

"Sorry."

"It's okay. I'll be out in a few minutes."

After Molly left the bathroom, Zoe leaned against the shower wall and tried to laugh, but realized she was sobbing instead. *Christ, I need a Xanax.*

She soaped her hair and skin until she was covered in a thick, frothy lather. As she began to rinse, she heard a deep, distant thumping noise, like heavy furniture tumbling down a flight of stairs. A series of vibrations rose through her feet. And there was another sound, a shrill howl, muffled by the walls and running water. A scream. From the hallway.

She quickly shut off the water and pushed open the shower curtain. The lights flickered again, and then there was a deafening *crash-boom* which caused her to shriek involuntarily. The storm. Thunder and lightning and wind ... *Oh my*. Just the storm.

She toweled the remaining soap suds from her body and dressed in a loose T-shirt and flannel pajama pants. She then wiped a broad circle in the condensation on the mirror above the sink, and ran a brush through her hair. Her cell phone rang on the shelf above the toilet, to the right of the mirror. She picked it up and saw ROBERT on the display. Whatever method Mike had employed to discourage this asshole from hassling her had obviously not worked. She tapped the REJECT CALL button on the screen, and did it again when he called right back. She twisted her hair into a dry towel, slid her feet into a pair of furry, blue house slippers, and stepped toward the door when the voicemail alert tone chimed on her phone. She listened to the message as she opened the door and crossed the threshold into the carpeted hallway. For a few seconds there was nothing on the recording, but then came the familiar, disquieting whisper: "I love you, Zoe." She resisted the urge to throw the phone against the wall. "If I can't be with you, no one will."

She hung up and dialed Mike's number while she stomped down the hallway to her bedroom. When she pushed open the bedroom door, she was seized by terror and revulsion. The room was painted in splashes and sprays of glistening, liquid crimson. The floor, furniture, even the ceiling dripped with red. Rivulets ran from wide streaks on the walls, like a massive wound had been opened in the house itself.

Oh God ... Molly.

Her body lay sprawled prone on the carpet in a widening, uneven, dark circle. On the bed, tucked among the blood-soaked pillows, was Molly's head. Her hair hung in limp ringlets over her unseeing eyes. Her mouth, locked open in a silent, eternal scream.

Zoe willed herself to run. She bolted for the front door, choking on hot, acidic vomit. She stopped in the living room when she saw Rachel laying face up on the floor near the sofa. She had been cleaved open from her crotch to her throat. The contents of her lower abdomen had spilled out into clumps around her. On her arms were deep gashes, and two fingers were missing from her right hand. A vile stench hung thickly in the air; an amalgam of wet copper and feces and Amarige perfume. Rachel turned her head toward Zoe, her eyes pleading. She coughed, and blood erupted from her mouth. Zoe's whole body shuddered uncontrollably. *No. How can that be? How can she still be alive?*

Through the whole of their friendship, what one had felt, the others had felt. But Rachel's suffering was beyond anything Zoe could even begin to comprehend. When Rachel reached out to her and mouthed the words "help me"—*or was it "kill me?*—Zoe brought her trembling hands up to her face and felt her very sanity being carried away on the resonance of her scream.

Then the lights went out.

Zoe reached the door in three strides. She jerked it open and hurled herself into the night. She didn't see him standing there on the front step until she slammed into him so violently that it knocked the wind out of her and sent her tumbling backward into the doorway.

Rain trickled from the tufts of blonde hair which stuck out from beneath the hood of his black, fleece sweatshirt. His arms hung at his sides, his hands balled into fists at his waist. In his eyes, Zoe saw rage. Robert bent down and grasped her forearm. She kicked at him until he let go, then she scrambled to her feet and rushed back into the darkness of the house. She ran into the hall, took a left, intending to go out through the window of her bedroom, until she remembered that the room contained Molly's dead, mutilated body, and instead opted for the bathroom. She locked herself in, cursing her mother for buying a house that had no back door. She could hear Robert's footsteps in the living room, and crashing sounds as he blindly knocked over unfamiliar objects in the path of his pursuit. She felt her pockets for her cell phone. It was gone. She remembered having it her hand just before she had found Molly.

When she had been calling Mike.

A spark of hope. Maybe her uncle had been on the phone listening to her screams. He could be on his way there right now. Maybe, but she couldn't count on it.

There was a window in the bathroom, but it was narrow, perhaps too narrow to accommodate her, despite her slender physique. Nonetheless, she raised the sash up on its track, punched out the screen, and hoisted herself into the opening. She blew all the air out of her lungs, twisted and compressed her body and ground her flesh against the metal window frame. *Please God please God please God.* She pressed her hands against the exterior wall and pulled with every ounce of strength she possessed. It wasn't enough. Robert was calling her name now, searching for her, getting closer. She made one last vigorous effort to squeeze through, and realizing the futility of it, she reversed herself and collapsed, weeping, onto the cold tile floor. Then Robert was there, pounding on the door and rattling the brass handle.

"Go AWAY," Zoe begged.

"I only want to talk to you. Come out."

"Fuck you!"

Robert struck the door harder, and Zoe heard wood crack. "Fuck me?" he yelled. "Fuck *you*. Do you know what your uncle did to me? He handcuffed me and took me into the woods outside of town. Then he beat me in the head with a thick phone book for ten minutes. Do you know why he did that to me, Zoe? Do you know why he pointed his gun at my face and said he was going to kill me?"

"No."

"Yes you do, you bitch. He did it because you *told* him too."

"Robert, I swear to you, I never asked him to do anything like that."

"Open this fucking door."

"I'm calling the police."

"You're calling the police, are you? Calling them on your cell phone?"

"That's right."

"You're such a liar, Zoe. You dropped your phone when you fell outside. I picked it up. Open the door and I'll give it back to you."

Zoe stood up and thrust her head through the open window. "*Help me! Somebody, please help!*" She screamed until her vocal cords were raw, but her voice couldn't compete against the thrashing of the storm. She soon gave up and sat down on the edge of the bathtub and tried to calm herself. Robert had stopped beating on the door, but she knew he was still out there, trying to fool her into believing he had gone.

A shine of light below the door. Bright, artificial, the incandescent beam of a flashlight. Then a voice different from Robert's. Strange, yet familiar, suppressed by the cacophony of the thunderstorm and her racing heart.

"Zoe?"

Mike?

She wanted to believe it—would have given her soul for it to be true, but her shattered mind resisted. Only when he called to her directly from the other side of the door did Zoe realize she had been saved.

She opened the door and flew into his muscled arms and let her tears wash away the world. Mike held her tightly against his chest and told her everything was going to be okay, and then she heard footsteps rushing toward them. She raised her eyes to look down the hallway and in a dazzle of lightning she saw Robert almost upon them, holding something over his head. There was a smacking sound, and Mike cried out and fell forward onto the floor with Zoe beneath him. The flashlight clattered across the bathroom tile and blinked out. Zoe felt Mike push himself off her, then she heard him struggling with Robert. Another smacking sound. Someone moaning in pain. Then only the hammering of rain drops on the roof.

When lightning lit up the hallway again, Zoe caught a glimpse of the handgun on the carpet only three feet away. She picked it up and ran her fingers inquisitively over the metal. She guessed it was Mike's personal revolver, different from the semi-automatic he carried while he was on duty. Simpler to operate; no slides or safety switches to fumble with in the dark. All she had to do was aim and shoot.

From the blackness, Robert spoke. "He tortured me, Zoe. He beat me until I was barely conscious, then he took my shoes and my phone and left me out there in the woods. I was out there all night, suffering. This morning I started walking. I walked all the way home, barefoot. Ten miles, Zoe; ten miles with my head hurting so bad I thought I might die." He let out a sound that was half chuckle and half sob. "Do you hate me so much, Zoe? Do you hate me so much that you would send your sadistic cop uncle to rough me up? He told me he did it for you. He told me other things too. You want to know what else he told me?"

Zoe didn't say anything. She could hear him moving, could hear his voice coming closer to where she was hidden, on her knees, in the dark. Her mind swirled with images of Rachel and Molly, and the understanding that she was never going to see them again. She forced herself to imagine what they must have been feeling as Robert butchered them; it made it easier for her to do what needed to be done. She raised the gun, and when the next flash of lightning came, she pulled the trigger.

The muzzle blast was like a bomb exploding in front of her, and an intense, painful ringing instantly flooded her ears. Deaf, blind, and disoriented, she could only cower in wait for Robert to reach out from the nothingness and grab her. But when he didn't, she rose to her feet and slowly felt her way down the hall toward her mother's room, where there would be a phone and a flashlight and a window wide enough to afford her an escape. After a few steps, her foot brushed against a body on the floor. She didn't know whether it was Robert or Mike, but she didn't waste any time thinking about it. She broke into a sprint, tripped over the next body, and scampered the remaining ten feet on her hands and knees.

She located the phone on her mother's nightstand, and her heart sank when she remembered it needed electricity to operate. But there was still the flashlight in the bottom drawer. She was nearly overcome with relief when she switched it on and the walls blossomed with white light. She guardedly crossed the room and stood in the doorway with both the gun and the flashlight pointed into the hallway. Robert sat with his legs outstretched on the floor, his back against the wall. His right hand clutched his chest, and Zoe saw smears of blood on his fingers. Lying next to him was a twelve-inch trophy that Zoe had earned when she was on the high school swim team. The figure had broken off the top of the column, probably when Robert had used the award to bludgeon Mike in the head. Robert raised his left hand to shield his eyes from the glare of the flashlight beam. He said something, but Zoe could hear only the ringing in her ears.

A few feet further in the hallway, Mike was on all fours, weakly trying to stand. Zoe moved to help him, keeping the gun trained on Robert as she did. "Mike. Oh, God, Mike, are you okay?" Her voice sounded far away, and she wondered if she had suffered permanent hearing loss. She placed the flashlight on the floor as she draped Mike's left arm over her shoulders and guided him into a sitting position. He gestured toward the gun and she gave it to him. "I need your phone, Mike." She shouted to hear herself. "I need to call for help."

Mike pulled her close to him and said, "I already called it in when I found the dead girls. Help is on the way."

Then Zoe heard Robert's voice behind her. It sounded as if he was speaking from inside a deep hole. She couldn't make out his words at first, but as she strained to listen, and watched the movement of his lips in the glow of the flashlight, she understood what he was saying. "I only wanted to talk, Zoe. Only wanted ... to talk."

"You *killed* Rachel and Molly. You took away the two best friends I will ever have."

He shook his head and mumbled something Zoe couldn't understand.

"I can't hear you, Robert."

"I said I didn't kill *anyone.*"

Zoe stared at the wound in Robert's chest. Even through the black fabric of his hoodie she could see he was soaked in blood. "You're probably dying right now," she said. "You still want to play this game?"

More muttering of words that Zoe couldn't make sense of.

"For chrissake, *speak up*, Robert."

"Your uncle ... as he was torturing me in the woods…he told me ... he told me he is in love with you."

Before she had even a chance to contemplate what Robert was saying, there was a burst of flame over her right shoulder, and a sound like an inflated paper bag popping next to her ear. She saw Robert's head snap back hard against the wall before he slumped over. Agony mushroomed through the right side of her skull and she collapsed onto the floor. She lay writhing in pain, then Mike bent and clenched her and sat her up with her back on the wall. He knelt before her and caressed her cheek with the back of his fingers. In the shadows, he looked like her father.

From what seemed like a thousand miles away, Zoe thought she heard music. A melody she had heard many times before, perhaps in another life. Mike reached into the

109

pocket of his windbreaker and pulled out a cell phone. When he did, the clarity of the song improved, and Zoe remembered.

"Dance With Me" by The Leftovers. It was Robert's cell phone. Mike smiled and clicked it off.

He beat me until I was barely conscious, then he took my shoes and my phone and left me out there in the woods. Robert had told her that, only minutes ago. She felt numbness wash over her. The phone call she had received just before she discovered Molly slaughtered and headless in her bedroom; it had come from Robert's phone.

He told me he is in love with you.

Zoe saw the knife in Mike's hand, then she felt it enter her below her breastbone. She gasped as seething fire filled her chest. She gripped his wrists and tried to force the blade out again, but her muscles gave up their strength and the fire rose and disgorged from her mouth in a spew of salty blood.

Mike spoke. The words were undiscerned by her ears, but she watched them form distinctly on his lips: "I love you, Zoe."

THE ART OF ANGLING
REBECCA JONES-HOWE

She walks into the store like every other woman, paying me no attention. She sidles through the tight aisles of antique furniture and I catch sight of her reflection as she passes the Danish teak mirror on the wall. The refracted sunlight touches her face. She's silver and exact. She matches the poem in my book.

My fingers shake over the page. I lean over the counter, picturing her face made up porcelain pretty. Instead of straight locks, her hair's done up with gentle blonde curls. Her pearl earrings dangle when she turns her head. I set the book down and step away from the till. The store warms as I approach.

"Nice piece, isn't it?" I ask.

She nods. I smooth my hand over my shirt pocket, right where my heart's pounding. Her gaze meets mine in the mirror's reflection. My palms sweat and I tighten them into fists at my sides.

"How much is it?" she asks.

I reach for the price tag. "Six hundred."

She sighs.

"I can give you a discount," I say.

"My husband would hate it. He thinks mid-century is all trend." She runs her hand along the frame. Her nails are pink, with speckles. "The wood is beautiful, though."

"I can let you have it for three-fifty," I say.

"Are you even going to make a profit from that?"

"Let me worry about it," I say.

"I don't know." She looks back at the mirror and bites her lip. The glass reflects her pale face, her lashes dark, curled. She opens her purse and reaches for her wallet. "I won't be able to take it in my car," she says.

"We do delivery," I say. "I can set it up for you." I walk behind the till and grab a sold tag from the drawer. "Can I get your name?"

My fingers shake around the pen as I write it down.

* * *

Her house is old, Victorian, with blue siding, white trim and a wraparound veranda.

She answers the door in sweatpants and a navy T-shirt.

She'd look so much better if it were a pink dress from the fifties, the fabric fitted around her waist. She'd look so much better if her hair was curled, meticulous.

"I had the day off," I say. "I figured I could do the delivery myself."

"Oh," she says. "That's nice of you, I guess." She steps back from the door.

Inside, antique mahogany furniture matches the mahogany floors. The wallpaper is deep red with damask smears. The darkness ruins her complexion, makes her skin look sallow.

"Where did you want this?" I ask.

She nods up the stairwell. Pictures line the walls of her with another man. He's tall and dark-haired, stern-faced.

THE ART OF ANGLING

"His name's Ted," she says. "He's an antiques dealer. He's out of town a lot."

The picture at the top of the stairs is of them at a park, running mid-stride. He's grabbing her, his hands around her waist, his tendons tight. In the picture they're both smiling, but she's the one trying to get away.

She leads me into the master bedroom. There's a massive Georgian bed, its thick hardwood posts like giant columns, dominant fists thrust in the air.

"I thought about hanging it here," she says, pointing to the empty space above her vanity. Her jewelry's laid out on top, strings of delicate pearls and gold chains with heart-shaped lockets. She steps closer and everything is calm, just like her voice, poetry in my head.

Faces and darkness separate us over and over.

She gets her husband's tool box and I help her hang the mirror. We both step back, reflected in the middle of its four-cornered eye. "It brightens the room, doesn't it?" she asks, her smile a flicker that warms the tightness in my chest. "I'm not sure what Ted will think, though."

I picture myself taking her hand, pulling her out of the dark-infected house.

"How much do I owe you?" she asks.

"Owe? No, I just, I came to help. That's all."

Her cheeks blush in her reflection, but it doesn't hide her apprehension. It's easy to see, the pretty girl she should be.

* * *

My brother's high, just like always. He swirls a homemade fish stick in a bowl of tartar sauce. The deep fryer is still on, crackling. The whole apartment smells like a lake.

"Don't be such a fucking sissy, man," he says, biting into the fish stick. Flakes of batter land on his shirt. "Seriously, just grow some facial hair and get laid by somebody you actually have a chance with."

My gaze drops.

"I'll show you the kind of girl you can take a dip in," he says, laughing. "She'll be a fucking angler fish, man."

I pick up my book from the counter: *The Collected Works of Sylvia Plath*, all her secrets compiled. I know more about women than he ever will.

"Seriously, dude, if you can fuck her, I'll worship you for the rest of my life, but chicks like that don't trade down for losers who read poetry all day."

The book feels like a weight in my grasp.

"Take it from your big bro," he says. "There are plenty of other twats in the sea."

* * *

She goes to the gym in the morning and she comes out looking pretty and pristine. She drives to the grocery store and she buys eggs and milk. She's in a pink dress and she buys vodka from the liquor depot. She puts the bottle in the passenger seat and she adjusts her hair in the mirror, rolled blonde waves pinned back in an ivory clip.

She goes home and parks her Volvo in the driveway. She climbs up the front steps in pink sling- back shoes. I watch her from the antique store delivery van, my gaze tracing up her pale calves.

When she's inside, I slip a Thank You card in her mail box. Included is a half-price coupon I designed using the logo from the antique store. There's an expiry date on the bottom, so I can save her before it's too late.

* * *

She buys a yellow glass vase with her coupon and I lay out newspaper on the counter to wrap it, protect it.

"Do you even make any money, giving away discounts like this?" she asks.

"Don't worry about it," I say. "It's a gift."

Her gaze drops to the vase. "Ted never gives discounts. The antique business is so competitive, you know?" She looks up and her smile widens. "Ted usually deals with English pieces. He's fond of Georgian and Chippendale styles. He likes the detail, the craftsmanship. He's very particular."

"Well, we're a small store," I say. "We appreciate our customers. We want you to keep coming back."

Her gaze meets mine and her smile fades. She looks back at the vase, at my shaking hands. Her lip twitches but she says nothing.

I picture her words in my head, lingering with beats, syllables, the throbbing in my chest.

I am important to her.

I look down and finish wrapping the vase, the newspaper marking fingers with black. The dark ink makes me think of rotting fish. I shake my head and try to smile, even as my chest starts to burn.

* * *

Her husband returns in a black Mercedes. I watch from behind the bushes lining her front yard. She opens the door and runs to greet him. Open arms. He lifts her off the porch and spins her. He kisses her long and hard.

"I've missed you, baby," he says. "I've fucking missed you."

She meets his gaze, stares deep and wraps her hands around his neck. "I've missed you, too," she says.

My legs cramp from crouching. I collapse to my knees, weak.

I send her more coupons:

Mid-century madness!
Retro deals!
Screaming Eames Bonanza!
Atomic Riot!

She doesn't come back to me.

* * *

I double my usual dose of Ativan before going to bed.

Flipping my book open, I turn to my favourite poem, the one with the mirror, the four-cornered god. My hardness throbs in my right hand, slick with lotion, my palm warm like the inside of her.

Her poetry pleads.

Whatever I see I swallow immediately. . .

The sound of her voice filters in my head, her pain a trigger. I tighten my fingers and beat myself into shame. My eyes squeeze out tears. The book falls from my grasp and I slip back and press my head against the wall. My gaze drifts to the ceiling. Even in the darkness, her face is there. My eruption stains the sheets.

I have looked at it so long I think it is a part of my heart.

* * *

I find her new driver's license in her mail box. She looks rigid in her picture, without her smile. According to the card, her birthday is just a week away. She needs her smile, her real smile, not the fake one she puts on for her husband.

I pick out a present from the antique store. It's a choker of delicate pink pearls. I wrap it in white tissue and put it in a box. I sign my name on the card.

* * *

Her husband leaves on her birthday and she drives straight to the liquor depot for another bottle of vodka. That's when I deliver her present, my footsteps quiet on her doorstep while she pours herself a drink inside.

She comes into the store a day later, the box clutched in her hand. She throws it down on the counter.

"What is this?" she asks.

The necklace slips out of the box, the tissue gone.

"How did you know when my birthday was?"

My throat tightens. "I thought you'd like it. It reminded me of you."

"You can't do this," she says. "What if Ted saw this?"

"He's no good for you," I say.

Her eyes widen, pupils dark. "Please," she says, her grip tightening around her purse strap, "no more of this. I don't want you at my house anymore."

She leaves, her footsteps sounding thunder on the floor. A hot ache fills my lungs and I flatten my palms over the counter and try to breathe normally. My chest heaves.

* * *

The next night, I bring a ladder and climb up to the window. She's with her husband, kissing him. He fondles her. He grabs her hair and pushes her back on the bed. He yells at her, his voice penetrating the glass.

"Tell me you want my fist, slut."

She moans, but he slaps her face until she begs for him. Then he rubs between her legs, inserting his fingers into her, one by one. He shoves his whole hand into her warmth, pumps his arm until she moans. Her body flops around on the bedspread like a fish on a line.

My grasp tightens around the ladder rung. My breaths are hot, heavy. It's like looking at her through a lake. My eyes sting.

Everything gets so blurry.

* * *

My brother comes home with a dark-haired girl clinging to his arm. He throws a grocery bag on the counter. It's filled with packaged fish. There are red discount stickers on the cellophane but the fish already smells of sea rot. They're whole fish, their horrible eyes gaping wide.

"This is Andrea," my brother says.

The girl laughs.

"We're gonna get so blazed tonight," he says. "We're gonna have a mother-fucking fish stick *binge*, bro!"

I've been reading all afternoon, the Ativan swimming through me, the darkness separating her from me, preventing me from sleeping.

"You look like shit," my brother says. "You should fucking join us, man."

I shake my head. The whole room spins, a rotting ocean. My stomach turns and the sickness builds in my throat, wanting to come out.

His gaze drops to the book in my grasp. "You still thinking about that angelfish? I told you, man, you're aiming way too fucking high." He puts his arm around the girl's waist. "Andrea here, she's not quite an angelfish, but she's pretty fucking close."

The girl laughs again. She looks at him instead of me. "I'm a starfish, baby."

"Seriously, man," my brother says, "just get blazed with us. Maybe Andrea will make you feel better. I hear starfish are good at sucking."

I swallow another Ativan instead.

* * *

She goes to the gym. She picks up groceries. She parks in front of the liquor depot and she walks inside. That's when I grab the hammer from the back of the antique store van. That's when I bury a nail into one of her tires.

The air hisses gently from the hole.

I drive circles around the parking lot until she emerges with her bottle of vodka. She bends down, runs her hand over the tire. I pull up beside her.

"Gotta flat?" I ask.

She looks up and jumps, taking a step back when I climb out of the van. "You did this," she says.

"I'm just trying to help."

She digs through her purse and pulls out her phone. I step forward but her eyes go wide. She clutches the vodka to her chest.

"He's only going to hurt you," I say. "I know you. I know you better than he ever will."

"Just leave," she pleads. Her voice shudders, draws attention. "Just leave me alone," she says, repeating herself, making a stanza.

The words claw at my heart.

THE ART OF ANGLING

* * *

I stain my sheets thinking of her.

Faces and darkness separate us over and over.

She says she doesn't want me but one day I'll save her from her dying reflection.

She rewards me with tears and an agitation of hands.

She'll be beautiful again. She'll write a poem about me, and she'll recite it in my ear every night while I'm making love to her, making her whole.

* * *

My brother buys more fish but he spends all his time getting high with Andrea and he forgets to fry them. Every time I open the fridge, the smell of rot gets worse.

* * *

Her husband comes back in his Mercedes, in his slacks, his dark red shirt and his black tie. He's her whole life and he shouldn't be. Every night the light is on in their bedroom. I sit on the veranda, listening to the sound of him gutting her from the inside out. Then he leaves and she buys another bottle of vodka.

At night, all the lights are off.

This time I wander to the back of her house and I wedge a crowbar under the sliding panel of her patio door. The shakes take over my whole body, the darkness a part of me. I jerk the crowbar back and forth. The rotating motion of the panel sounds like fucking. My tendons flex, tight, taught. The lock breaks, feeling like a release inside my chest.

My heart pounds harder than ever.

The inside of the house is like the bottom of a lake. My shadow traces dark undercurrents over the hardwood floor. The staircase creaks, every footstep a throbbing echo in my ears. I reach for her door and tighten my grasp around the cold knob. Inside, there's the silver glow of the mirror in the dark, reflecting her.

I close in. Everything smells like rot.

I kneel on the bed and crawl to her. I climb on top of her and press my lips to her salty skin. Her mouth opens, gasps. My grip tightens over her wrists, but she manages to flop away. She's stupid and she doesn't want me. Women only have a five second memory span. I slap her the way her husband does.

She screams. I cover her mouth, muffling her voice. She only speaks with her gaze, eyes gaping wide.

"He's ruining you," I say.

She squirms and moans, her hot tears streaming against my hand.

"I'm trying to help you," I cry. "I'm trying to save you before you rot away."

Her breath shudders under my palm. I push down because I don't want to hear what she has to say, because her voice in my head is better, the one where she's a young girl drowning, crying for help.

I am not cruel, only truthful. . .

"Please," I beg. "Just let me save you. I'd do anything to save you." I lean over her, my lips against her forehead. Her skin is wet, slippery, salty. She struggles, her palms pressed against my chest. She's shaking, like a dying fish I have to throw back.

She comes and goes.

I cry out her name. I repeat it over and over.

"My name's not Sylvia," she gasps.

SHE COULD BE THE ONE
PHILIP HARRIS

Daniel held the tiny bottle in his hand and smiled as he listened to the chatter from the passengers around him. Closing his eyes, he let their words wash over him, savouring the moment as he always did.

The train eased to a stop as a disembodied female voice declared their arrival at Nanaimo Station. Daniel opened his eyes as the doors slipped apart and a handful of commuters shuffled out onto the near empty platform. The only new passengers boarded further down the train. Daniel watched as they settled down into their seats, steadfastly avoiding sitting next to any of the other passengers. It seemed most people would walk the length of the carriage to avoid the close proximity of another human being.

A dishevelled man boarded the far end of the train and a wave of revulsion flowed down the carriage as the other passengers caught sight of his matted beard and coat of nameless stains. Two carriages away and Daniel could still pick up their disgust as they shifted in their seats, silently willing him to move on past them. The man stayed by the door, standing quietly, forced into feeling ashamed by his fellow travellers. Daniel shook his head lightly and switched his attention back to the conversations of the nearby passengers.

The doors were just closing as she darted onto the train, squeezing her body sideways through the rapidly narrowing gap. Daniel looked up and caught her apologetic look as the doors, having detected her presence, shuddered to a halt then shuddered open again. A businessman clutching a copy of the Globe and Mail glared at her but she was already past him, sinking into the seat opposite Daniel as the train dragged itself away from the platform.

The woman closed her eyes and slowly massaged her temple. Daniel was suddenly relieved she couldn't see him looking at her because he wasn't just looking; he was staring and staring hard.

Daniel glanced towards the businessman and flushed scarlet at the grin on his face. The businessman gave Daniel a look that screamed "You've got no chance," and returned to his newspaper with an amused shake of his head. Daniel gave a quiet little snort. He wasn't exactly Casanova but he'd had his fair share of luck, both good and bad, with women. Beautiful though she was, Daniel couldn't see any reason why he couldn't be as lucky with this woman as any other. After all, she wasn't wearing a ring.

The woman opened her eyes, let out a deep breath and reached down towards her case. For a moment Daniel thought she would pull out the papers; try to snatch a head start on the evening's work and give herself time to sit down with a glass of wine before she headed off to bed. Instead, she ignored the papers and dug around for a few seconds before bringing out a battered paperback.

Daniel glanced away, both to avoid her gaze and give himself time to play his favourite commuter game—Guess the Book.

A moment later he looked back and smiled. The woman had already flicked the book open about a third of the way through and Daniel could see its front cover. It was a crime novel, just as he had guessed, and he recognised the author. She was well known and well respected. He'd never read one of her novels but from comments he had over-heard she had crafted a series of gruesome but intelligent stories about a New Orleans coroner.

The woman looked up as the train pulled into Broadway, catching Daniel's eye for a split second as she looked towards the door. Half of the passengers filed off the train and began to scurry down the platform towards their bus or to transfer to another train at Commercial Drive. They were replaced by a much larger group of commuters and the train was delayed again as two young boys held open the doors for a third.

Reluctantly the new arrivals shuffled down along the train as it moved out of the station. There were still a few individual seats free but again the majority of people pre-ferred to stand and Daniel found his view of the woman blocked by a tall man wearing an eBay security pass. A young Chinese woman sat down next to Daniel, she apologised for something, but he ignored her. The three young boys stayed by the door, chattering in loud voices about the group of girls they'd picked up the night before.

Daniel shifted in his seat and the Chinese woman apologised again, this time he managed a half-smile aimed at reassuring her, but it just seemed to embarrass her fur-ther and she looked away. He peered through Mr eBay's legs. The woman was still reading her book but that was all he could see. He sighed and looked around the car-riage at the near blank faces of his fellow passengers then moved on to an advert for a company offering some sort of team building exercise. Halfway through the advert, as the flea market slipped into view, Daniel spotted a misspelled word and gave up.

Two stations later, as the train dove under the city, the woman slipped her book back into the case, stood up, and slowly eased her way towards the door. Daniel waited until the train began to slow for the station before he stood up himself. She'd stepped straight off the train and was hurrying across the platform before Daniel had managed to squeeze past the three boys to follow her.

When he reached the escalator she was already halfway up, trying to subtly ease her way past a rather bulky tourist who was too busy chatting to his companion to no-tice anyone else. Daniel walked rapidly up the escalator and stopped a few steps behind the woman. By that point she had given up making any progress past the tourist and was waiting patiently behind.

A busker burst into life as they reached the top of the escalator. He was playing some sort of folk song Daniel didn't recognise but the woman paused for a second, smiled at the busker as she dropped a handful of coins into his guitar case then headed through the glass doors towards Granville Street. Daniel followed her but his earlier confidence was already beginning to wane. It didn't feel right. The moment was gone.

As the woman drifted along the walkway, glancing at the rows of chocolate in the newsagent as she passed, Daniel dropped further back. It was too soon. As the woman headed into a nearby shop, Daniel stopped. A man brushed past him, muttering at him to look where he was going. Daniel almost pointed out that he was. He stood for a cou-ple of minutes, the rush of commuters washing around him, then turned and headed back to the SkyTrain; regret already gnawing at his insides.

Two days later he gave in and started looking for the woman again.

The first day he waited on Nanaimo station for five hours. By nine he'd decided that she wasn't going to appear. Maybe she'd worked late or gone out for a post-work drink and taken a taxi home. Or perhaps she'd left early and he'd arrived at the station too late. Maybe he'd just missed her in the groups of people boarding the trains.

The next day he arrived earlier and stayed later but there was still no sign of her. Again he decided she must be working late or partying with friends. It was a Friday after all.

After spending Saturday morning plotting the approach he would take when he finally met up with the woman, Daniel headed to Robson Street and the crime section of Chapters. It didn't take him long to find the book the woman had been reading and, after flinching at the cover price, he bought it.

Outside, the sun was already burning through the clouds and Daniel decided to walk down to Canada Place and get some fresh air before he went home to study the book. The crosswalk outside the store was already flashing and Daniel hurried across; just making it to the other side as the signal urged him to stop and the traffic pulled noisily away behind him. Daniel began to move off towards the waterfront; then stopped. A second later he turned back. The woman was there, back on the other side of the road, walking away from him down Howe. In his rush to cross the road before the signal changed he'd scuttled right past her. He couldn't see her face but she was wearing the same clothes he'd seen her in on the train and he knew it was her.

Daniel searched desperately for a gap in the traffic, cursing at his inattentiveness. A few seconds later the traffic slowed. He spotted a half-gap and darted into the road. The first car had almost stopped and Daniel made it across its front with only a glare from the driver. The second had to brake, hard, and horns blared as it slid to a halt a few inches short of Daniel. He held his hands up in a half-hearted apology as he looked for a way across the rest of the road. Pausing briefly at the centreline, he slipped between the now slow moving cars and reached the other side in one piece.

Daniel dodged round the corner, narrowly avoiding a couple of women consulting a map, and was just in time to see the woman disappear through a doorway. He knew the shop, had been inside once when he'd first moved to Vancouver. They sold furniture, mostly beds and sofas, along with a few miscellaneous ornamental monstrosities only their designer could love. Daniel took a deep breath and began walking down the road. His heart was racing, either from the trip across the road or from seeing the woman again, he wasn't sure which.

He didn't know what he was going to say to the woman when he got there. He couldn't exactly follow through with his other plan. Dozens of cliché laden opening lines rolled through his head as he walked down the road. He dismissed each one in turn, searching for something that was at least passably intelligent; something she wouldn't think was too ridiculous. He still hadn't thought of anything when he reached the shop doorway and he nearly walked straight past in despair. At the last minute he forced himself inside.

The air in the shop was thick with the smell of apple scented candles and Daniel nearly gagged. He paused for a moment, trying to regain some composure. A young woman sighed as she squeezed past him to get into the shop and Daniel shuffled sideways to give her more room. And there she was; at the back of the shop making her way up a couple of steps leading to a raised section packed with candles and candle holders of all shapes and sizes.

Daniel reached the bottom of the steps just as she finished looking at the candles and turned to make her way back to the main floor. He froze as she walked down the steps towards him. He backed away, running a hand through his already tousled hair. As she reached the bottom of the steps she looked at Daniel, a puzzled look at her face. He pulled his hand away from his head, catching his elbow on a display of wrought iron candlesticks in the process.

Daniel whirled round and grabbed at the candlesticks, pushing them further away in the process. Lunging forward he seized all four of the tall metal stalks and clutched them to his chest. His face flushed scarlet and he started apologising to everyone he could see.

The woman stepped past him, her eyebrows raised, a slightly bemused smile on her face. Daniel shuffled the candlesticks until they were upright, then nearly toppled them over again as he let go of them. He stood watching the candlesticks for a moment, hands hovering nearby in case one of them took it into its head to fling itself over again. When it was clear the display was staying put he turned and walked briskly out of the shop, relieved it hadn't been the woman from the train.

By Monday Daniel had read the book three times, using the third to memorise key points, character names and other elements he could use in a discussion about the story should the opportunity arise. He wouldn't even have to lie too much about enjoying it. As always he was disappointed with the ending, in real life, murderers don't always get caught, but the book was well written and well structured; entertaining in its own way.

He reached Nanaimo station just before noon, determined to see her this time, even if she only worked half a day on Mondays. He sat on a bench near the top of the escalator of the westbound platform, the book tucked into his coat pocket. He examined each person as they reached the top of the escalator, dismissing most of them instantly. A handful of times he thought he saw her, then had to force his heart to calm down as he realised their hair or their eyes were wrong or they were too tall or too thin or too fat.

Eventually, around seven, Daniel had to leave the platform. Nature's call proved too strong. As one train left the station he darted down the stairs and round onto the patch of grass next to the station. It was beginning to get dark and he hoped no one could see him standing in the bushes. Behind him, a bus pulled into the stop outside the station and a young woman stepped off. An ice cold wave flooded down his body as Daniel realised who it was. Seconds later he realised he was wrong, she was much too tall and only partly because of the high heels she was tottering along on.

Another train arced into view down the line just as Daniel reached the top of the escalator and he hurried down the length of the platform, checking to see if the woman was already there. He couldn't see her but the train arrived before he could be sure. By eleven, unwilling to concede that the first time he had seen her she might have been on a one off journey, Daniel decided she must have gotten on that train after all; he'd missed her that was all.

By Thursday Daniel was arriving at the platform by eight thirty in the morning, hurriedly switching platforms around lunchtime and not leaving until well past ten. He spent the entire day sitting on the benches at the top of the escalators; a small black bag containing a couple of sandwiches crouched at his feet. Apart from a couple of glasses of water in the evening, he'd almost completely stopped drinking and he was becoming dehydrated despite the cool weather. Each night he left the station a little bit more despondent, certain it was time for him to give up, but each morning he resolved to try again; just one more time.

SHE COULD BE THE ONE

Thursday morning, about five minutes after he arrived at the station his patience paid off.

He'd gotten into the habit of counting the number of people getting off the train at the station while he was waiting and she was the nineteenth arrival. There had been so many false alarms Daniel had started to wonder whether he was misremembering her and she was walking right past him each day without him realising. He needn't have worried. He recognised her the moment she stepped off the train and would have known it was her even without the pounding of his heart.

She had one of the free papers tucked under her arm and was sipping from a large cup from one of the coffee houses that littered downtown Vancouver. He almost leapt up and dashed towards her but stopped himself as he remembered his plan. Instead, he had to watch as she walked past him, trying to calm his rolling stomach and reassure himself that this wasn't his only chance to meet her. He was almost sick when she disappeared out of view down the stairs, subconsciously convinced that he'd missed his chance. Standing quickly he moved to the top of the stairs and watched her as she walked past the slower commuters. Moments later she was gone and he was left alone on the platform as the train pulled away behind him.

As his racing heart began to slow, Daniel weighed his options. He was hungry and thirsty and he'd need his strength to talk to her. Eventually, after considering numerous disastrous possibilities, he decided to make a run for a coffee shop, buy a drink and some extra food to get him through the day then take up his place on the return platform in case she worked part time and went home at lunchtime.

Eight hours and two trips to the restroom at that same coffee shop and Daniel was beginning to think he'd blown it. Then she appeared at the top of the escalator and his heart tried to rip itself out of his chest.

He stood up quickly, then immediately sat back down again as he realised there was no rush, the train hadn't arrived yet. He watched her as she walked past him towards the far end of the train; not even trying to hide his interest in her. She was wearing the same outfit he had seen her in that first time and looked even more stunning than he remembered.

She looked down the track away from Daniel for a while then suddenly turned and began walking slowly towards the bright yellow paving at the edge of the platform. Looking past her, Daniel could see the glare of an approaching train as it rounded the corner towards the station. As the woman approached the edge of the platform Daniel became convinced she was about to throw herself in front of the oncoming train. He was about to dash across the platform to pull her back, making a complete fool of himself in the process, when she stopped just short of the edge and looked towards the train again.

Daniel stood up, his stomach churning as the day's sandwich threatened to make its presence felt. Digging around in the bag at his feet he pulled out his book, checked the bookmark was still poking out from between the middle pages and slowly walked towards the woman. He reached her just as the train pulled to a stop. The woman shifted sideways to make way for a handful of passengers that burst out of the carriage as the doors opened. Daniel stood behind her, giving her just enough room to ensure she would board the train before him, without there being space for anyone else to force their way between them.

The woman waited as the last straggler dawdled off the train then slipped through the doorway. Daniel hurried after her, just managing to get himself in front of a young boy trying to push his way past. It was one of the older style SkyTrains, with bench seats located along the edges of the carriages rather than horizontal bus-style seating. Daniel silently prayed that the woman would sit on an empty bench. She turned left towards the back of the train and sat down in the middle of the left hand row of seats. The seats opposite her were empty but a teenager was heading towards them from the far end of the carriage. Daniel darted across and sat down before anyone else could get there.

Daniel stole a glance at the woman to make sure she wasn't considering moving and then settled down into his seat. He managed to avoid looking at her again until the doors shuddered closed and the train began to nose its way out of the station. She was bent over, rummaging around in her bag. Daniel shifted position, moving his book into his lap. A moment later she sat up, a book in her hand, and he realised what an idiot he'd been.

It was over a week since he'd last seen her and she'd finished the book she'd been reading. The book he was carrying was all wrong. Then the woman opened the book and its cover came into view. She was still reading the same one. True, she'd almost finished it but that just gave them more of the plot to talk about. He waited for a moment then opened his own book, flicking past the bookmark until he only had a couple of chapters left and the murderer had been identified.

Daniel waited, pretending to read the book and hoping the woman would look at him of her own accord but apart from checking which station they had arrived at every time the train stopped, she was engrossed in the story. Daniel bided his time. Finally, as the train pulled into the station at Science World, his patience paid off. She looked past him to check the station name then caught herself as she noticed the book Daniel was holding. Daniel made a show of looking down at the woman's book then laughed.

The woman smiled warmly, her eyes sparkling.

"Are you enjoying it?" Daniel asked. And there it was, welling up inside of him as it always did. The gift of the gab his Ma had called it; his Irish charm. The right words tumbled out of his mouth, sugar coated by his soft accent. His nervousness dissolved and slowly but surely he shifted the conversation past the book and onto more varied topics. Instinctively he knew when to listen, when to talk, when to make her laugh and when to become more serious.

As the train pulled into Granville Station Daniel began to stand up, then had to sit back down again as he realised the woman wasn't getting up. She didn't seem to notice and when the train arrived at Burrard they moved off the train together; chatting as though they'd known each other for years.

When they reached the surface Daniel felt comfortable enough to risk breaking off in a different direction. As he turned, their brief goodbyes completed, she called after him.

"Hey! Do you fancy going for a drink?"

Daniel turned back; his hands in his pockets. He checked the tiny bottle and smiled.

Daniel held the tiny bottle in his hand and smiled as he listened to the chatter from the passengers around him. Closing his eyes he let their words wash over him, savouring the moment as he always did.

"They've found her, dumped in an alley downtown."

SHE COULD BE THE ONE

"I've told my daughter to be careful."

"I hope they catch him soon, it makes me nervous about going out."

Daniel opened his eyes and looked towards the woman that had spoken last. She returned his gaze and he smiled softly at her. Blushing she turned back to her friend.

A few seconds later Daniel noticed her sneaking another look at him and he smiled again. He'd seen her on the train before; perhaps she could be the one.

THE REFRIGERATOR
JONATHAN LAMBERT

Sam Merchant pulled into the parking lot at CENTURY AUDIT and turned off the engine. He turned the radio up full blast so the speaker grills rattled with each beat. He closed his eyes to meditate for a minute. His nerves were getting the better of him. The first day in a new job was always the worst. It had been over a year since he had a paying job. He steeled his mind and cracked the door of his Chevy Cavalier and set his left foot on the asphalt below.

No fuck ups, he thought. Twisting his body to the right, he grabbed his briefcase and Smartphone then stepped out of the car and looked up. A two story brick structure stood a short distance away. His eyes fell upon the obnoxious neon sign flashing CENTURY AUDIT above the door.

Tacky, he thought, *but a job is a job.* He began walking toward the entrance.

The double doors opened as he approached, sensing his weight on the mat. Warm air from inside streamed out like exhaled bad breath as he stepped into the foyer. His eyes settled on the receptionist. She was a nice looking older woman with long white hair.

"Good Morning," she said. "Are you Mr. Merchant?"

"Guilty as charged!"

She smiled at him.

"I'm Clara Teasdale," she said as she extended her hand, "welcome aboard. I can show you to your office, and Mr. Carrion, your boss, has left an envelope for you. Please follow me."

Sam followed behind Clara down the carpeted hallway, noting with bemusement an abnormal number of coffee stains and what appeared to be wads of chewing gum stuck to the floor. As they passed a brightly lit room, Clara paused for a second.

"This is the office kitchen. It's likely you'll be spending a lot of time in here, so I wanted to point that out right away."

"Okay," Sam replied, with surprise on his face as he looked in.

Two employees were quietly talking in the corner. They both turned their heads in his direction. Sam nodded his head as a greeting, but neither responded. They continued to stare as Clara led on.

Clara continued down the hall with Sam in tow until she reached the office earmarked for him. She unlocked the door and placed the key in Sam's hand. In his other hand, she placed a yellow envelope.

"Here we are," she said. "You get yourself settled. I'll be out front if you need me. And again, welcome aboard."

"Thanks!"

Sam stepped into his new office. It was nice and clean, despite the hallway leading to it. He hung up his jacket on the hook behind the door, and sat down at his desk. He shook out the contents of the yellow envelop. A single yellow sticky note fell out. Sam picked it up and read the finely printed text.

Merchant,

THE REFRIGERATOR

This is Mr. Carrion, your new boss. This is the only time a message from me will be hand delivered to you. From today forward, we will communicate only by posted notes on the office kitchen refrigerator. I took the liberty of leaving a message for you there already today. Please check it and also continue to monitor for communications from me every day upon arrival and departure.

Sam was speechless. He read the note again. Then a third time. *Weird* he thought. *How the hell is that going to work?* He got up, feeling stunned, and walked to the door. He headed down the hallway to the kitchen and to the office refrigerator to see just what this first note said.

As he was walking down the hall, Sam saw another employee coming in the opposite direction. The employee looked him over, and then stopped.

"Are you Sam?"

"Yes, Sam Merchant. You are?"

"Stephen Trudeling. My note from Carrion said you have something urgent to tell me, so what is it?"

"Huh?"

"That's what it said!"

"Let me see it."

"I already pitched it," he said. "Just asking you what it meant."

"I have no idea what it means," Sam said. "I just started today. Ten minutes ago actually. I'm still finding my way around here."

"Well, when you figure out what you're supposed to tell me, I'll be in my office. It's two doors down from yours."

Sam felt uneasy as he continued down the hall and entered the office kitchen. More employees were now sitting at the group table eating breakfast. The hushed conversation stopped as soon as Sam entered. Again he nodded to no response, then turned and looked at the refrigerator. It was covered in yellow notes. As he approached it, he felt the eyes of every one of the employees on him. Watching him. He stood in front of the refrigerator and looked at the notes. The first one he looked at was addressed to him. He peeled it off. He had to squint as he read the same finely printed text.

Merchant,

Please inform Stephen Trudeling that he's an asshole and incompetent, and fire him for me.

Regards, Mr. Carrion.

Sam read the note again, not believing what he saw. He had never fired anyone before. He had never even supervised. He plucked the note off the refrigerator and walked back to his office, amazed that Stephen hadn't already seen it. The minute he left the kitchen he heard the conversations resume around the kitchen table. Walking toward his office, he decided to approach Stephen and tell him about it. He stopped at Stephen's door and knocked lightly.

"Figured out what you're supposed to tell me?"

"Kind of . . . take a look at my note."

Sam handed the note to Stephen, and grimaced while waiting for his reaction.

"Is this some kind of joke or what? You know I can't read it."

"What?"

Stephen handed the note back to Sam. The message was there, plain as day.

Merchant,

Please tell Stephen Trudeling that he's an asshole and incompetent, and fire him for me.

Regards, Mr. Carrion.

"It's not blank. Look again." He handed back the note.

"Dude, stop screwing around! It's your message, not mine. To me it's blank. Zip. Nada. You should know that. Let me get back to work. I don't need this crap, I've got a heavy load today."

Mystified, Sam left Stephen's office and walked back to the kitchen. He stood in front of the refrigerator, covered in yellow notes. He pulled one off and looked at it. It *was* blank. He grabbed a second and a third. Both blank.

They were ALL blank.

* * *

That evening, Sam told his wife Megan the whole story. She listened intently as he went over every detail. When he was finished, a silence filled the room until it was broken by Megan.

"God Sam, I don't know what to think."

"I know, me either. This place is crazy. I'm dreading tomorrow."

"Maybe he was using some kind of invisible ink?"

"That reacts with each person? I don't think that's possible."

"Yeah, so what will you do? What will you do about Stephen?"

"Well, I'm not going to fire him. I don't even know if I'm his supervisor. I don't see how I can be held responsible for that at all. If Carrion wants him fired, he'll have to do it. Or leave him a note to the effect."

"Maybe this job was a mistake."

"I need this job, Megan," he said as they climbed into bed. "Badly, as you know."

* * *

As he entered CENTURY AUDIT the following morning, Sam found himself going straight to the office refrigerator. It was plastered with notes. He could tell by the different arrangement that they were all new. He scanned them, again all blank, until he saw one with writing on it. He plucked it off the door and looked at it.

Merchant,

THE REFRIGERATOR

I noticed Trudeling reporting for work today. I thought I was clear. Carry out my instructions immediately. Trudeling does not finish out the day, one way or another.

Regards, Mr. Carrion.

Sam whirled around and walked out of the kitchen and directly to Mr. Carrion's office. As he neared, he noticed that the office was dark. He tried the knob and it was locked. He put his face and hands against the window and tried to peer in through the blinds. It looked like a normal office, but appeared to be unoccupied for quite some time. Nevertheless, he had the distinct feeling that someone was inside and watching him. Sam's skin turned to gooseflesh as he walked back to his office. He grabbed a notepad and a Sharpie and scribbled two words on it.

I REFUSE!

He walked into the kitchen, glaring back at the three employees on their break, slammed his note on the refrigerator door and then went back to his office. He was too angry to work on anything so he sat back and watched the clock as it ticked away the minutes and hours, wondering if Carrion would press the Trudeling issue further. He didn't, and at the end of the day both Sam and Stephen Trudeling left the building at the same time, neither acknowledging the other. Trudeling, Sam thought, DID finish out the day.

* * *

As he reached home, he could see Megan peering out the window, alerted by the sound of his car pulling into the driveway. She ran to the door an opened it as he stepped on the porch.

"So, what happened? Tell me everything."

The corner of Sam's mouth turned into a smile for the first time during the long day as he thought of Megan anxiously waiting to hear what happened.

"Wow," he said with a smile. "I don't think you've ever been this interested in my job before!"

"Shut up," Megan said and punched him in the shoulder.

He told her of his refusal to fire Trudeling, and his certainty that tomorrow was his turn to be fired. Megan's face went from curiosity to outright worry as he went through the details.

"Are you going in tomorrow?"

"Of course. I'm not fired yet."

"There's something else I wanted to talk to you about, Sam. For the last two days I can't shake the feeling that someone is watching me. I feel it most in the kitchen."

"What do you mean *watching you*?"

"I can't explain it really, but it's there. Just a feeling like I'm on a hidden video camera. You know what I mean?"

"Like you're being watched? Sure. I have it too."

"You do?"

"Yep. I feel it at work. It's only been two days but I feel like everyone's looking at me, whispering behind my back. It's like they are waiting for something to happen."

128

"I really wish you'd start looking for something else. I don't like your new job."

"I will, but after a little while. I kind of want to see where this goes. Plus a two day stint doesn't look so good on a resume. Maybe I'll be fired tomorrow anyway. I did refuse to do what he asked."

"I'm sorry to say I hope you are fired," Megan said as she drew close.

Sam hugged Megan and rubbed her back as they sat down for dinner and a quiet but stressful evening at home.

* * *

As Sam arrived the next day, he nodded a good morning to Clara, and then began to walk past her when he noticed something wasn't right. Her eyes were red with tears and her mascara had run. She had obviously been crying.

"Clara? What's wrong?"

"You haven't heard then?" she said.

"Heard what?"

"Stephen Trudeling died last night."

Sam felt his heart lurch forward in his chest. "What? How?" he gasped.

"His wife found him severely beaten and unconscious in their kitchen. He died on the way to the hospital. Apparently all the doors to the house were bolted from the inside, so she thought the killer was still in the house. She ran to the neighbors and called 911."

"Oh my God!"

"Some detectives are supposed to be here this morning to question people; they haven't made any arrests yet as far as I know."

Sam felt the onset of fear as his heart began to race.

"I think I'm in shock," Clara said, but Sam noticed the corner of her mouth trying to suppress what looked like a smile.

"Me too," Sam said as he turned and took a first step toward his office. Then he turned. "Has Carrion said anything?"

"Well, he was the one that told me, via my note. He must have been here before I arrived. I even showed up earlier than I usually do but I didn't beat him in. My note also said to tell the maintenance crew to fly the flag at half-staff. I wish he'd hurry up and leave."

"Leave?" Sam said. "He's leaving?"

"Rumor has it that he's looking for his replacement. He hasn't found anyone around here worthy so far, that's for sure."

"One can hope."

"Hope that he's leaving? Or that you might be worthy? Most employees thought Trudeling was going to get it, but not now for sure."

Sam didn't answer. He continued down the corridor to his office, then reversed his path and headed to the office kitchen.

The kitchen was deserted. Even the normal breakfasters weren't there today, but he still felt as if someone was watching him. He looked at the refrigerator. It was full of notes, except for one spot in the center. *A spot where Trudeling would have plucked off his note,* Sam thought, *if Carrion hadn't killed him.* As soon as he saw the gap in the notes, he was sure it was Carrion. His eyes narrowed as he looked down the right side of the refrigerator for his note. It was there. He plucked it off and looked at it.

Merchant,

Seems you don't have to fire Trudeling at all. Stroke of luck for you. I shall deal with your refusal later. You aren't like the other sheep, are you? For now, see that you promote someone to Trudeling's position. No need to clear it with me. I trust your decision.

Regards, Mr. Carrion.

* * *

Sam sat in his office seething. The detectives were onsite, and he was waiting for them. He was going to tell them everything. He *knew* it was Carrion. He reached in the recycling bin for yesterday's note, the one that said Trudeling wouldn't finish out the day, but the bin was empty. *Damn I should have kept that note,* he thought. Without it, he didn't have anything to place suspicion on Carrion. They would probably think Sam was a disgruntled employee. He was going to tell them anyway, at least to put Carrion on their radar if nothing else. As he was thinking exactly what he would tell them, the phone rang, startling him from his thoughts. The caller ID displayed PRIVATE. Sam grabbed the handset, almost dropping it from nerves as he brought it to his ear.

"Merchant."

"Mr. Merchant, Mr. Carrion would like you to check for updated communications from him, immediately. Just so you are aware, recycling is picked up every evening. Have a good day."

Click. The call was over and the phone disconnected faster than the time it took him to lift it to his ear. *Was that Carrion himself,* he wondered, *and they ARE watching me.* Sam got up, his heart pounding, and looked around. He felt observing eyes all around him as he turned the handle on the door and started down the hall for the kitchen once again. He looked down at his feet as he hurriedly walked the corridor. The kitchen was still empty, and the lights were off. He looked at the door of the refrigerator. Most of the notes were gone, picked off and carried away by the other employees to whom they were addressed. There were only three notes on the door now. Two were blank, so he grabbed the one with writing on it and put it in his pocket. He would read it in his office. He turned and left the kitchen.

Safely behind his closed door, Sam read the note.

Merchant,

Talk to the cops and this time YOU won't finish out the day. You have a decision to make, and one choice has potential for you. Don't forget to promote someone.

Regards, Mr. Carrion.

The phone rang again, startling him for the second time in a few short moments. This time the Caller ID display had *his* name on it.

"Hi Megan."

"Sam, I finished work early today, and it's so creepy here all of a sudden. I can't shake that feeling I told you about, that someone is watching me. I even think I heard whispering in our kitchen. I'm scared!"

"Me too," Sam said. A knock on his door interrupted the call. "I've got to go; the police are here to talk to me about Stephen. Can you go to your sisters?"

"Stephen? What happened to Stephen?"

"He was killed last night."

"Oh my God! Sam, don't worry about me, I'll be okay. I just wanted to talk to you about it. Will you tell them about the note?"

"I plan to."

Sam set the phone down in its cradle, rose and went around his desk to the door. Clara stood there with two men wearing bad ties and jackets. She had a smirk on her face as she led the men into Sam's office and introduced them.

"Sam, these men are detectives. It's about Stephen."

Clara left, closing the door as the men introduced themselves as Detectives Fisk and Johnson from the Fredericksburg Police Department, investigating the homicide of Stephen Trudeling. Sam shook their hands and motioned for them to have a seat.

Johnson was the only one to speak. "How well did you know Mr. Trudeling?"

"I just started here three days ago. I just met him. I didn't really know him at all."

"You say you just started here three days ago?"

"Yes that's right."

"That's surprising. We received a note from the CEO Mr. Carrion since he is unavailable. He told us to talk to you. He gave me the impression you are very senior in the organization."

"No. As I said I just started."

"Well your boss must think very highly of you. Do you have any idea who might have wanted to hurt Trudeling? Did he have any conflict with anyone around here?"

"I really wouldn't know."

Johnson continued his line of questioning for ten minutes, under the watchful eyes of Fisk. Sam remained steady with his answers, denying knowledge of any helpful information, until the detectives were satisfied and performed the obligatory card drop and the request that Sam contact them if any new information or thoughts came to mind. He shook hands and closed the door behind them as they continued through the office. He was sweating, and he was certain Fisk picked up on it. He sat down in his chair and blew out a sigh of relief, then wondered what he had just done, and why.

The day continued on, uneventful but for the ominous feeling of eyes.

* * *

When Sam arrived home later that evening, Megan met him at his car. A sense of unease began to ripple through him when he saw her standing in the driveway. She lifted up her hand, and his heart leapt into his throat as he saw a yellow sticky note stuck to her fingers. He jumped out of the car and ran to her.

"Is that what I think it is?"

"I don't know, Sam. It was stuck to the fridge, and I know it wasn't there when I left this morning. It looks blank to me, but . . ." she said with a tremble in her voice.

"Let me see it," he said.

He peeled the note off her fingers and looked it at with trepidation. Same script. Same handwriting. He felt the contents of his stomach swirling as he read it aloud.

Merchant.

Excellent job today in your 'interview'. You've been promoted to Executive Director of Audit. I look forward to your continued success.

Regards, Mr. Carrion."

Sam's mind was a whirlwind of thought as he contemplated the fact that Carrion had been in his house. *How the hell did he get here before me? Had he come during the day? How did he get past the alarm system?* His initial fear began to give way to a confused sort of rage.

"Sam, I'm scared," Megan said.

"I'm not scared. I'm pissed!"

"What are we going to do?"

"I'm going back there. Right now. I'm going to corner that bastard. I haven't even seen him *once* yet, but he's got to leave sometime. If I miss him tonight, then I'll see him when he arrives tomorrow morning."

"I don't want to stay alone, Sam. Let me come with you."

Sam never even heard her.

* * *

The neon sign was still lit and flashing even more obnoxiously in the night air as Sam raced into the parking lot and came to a screeching stop. He ran up to the building and found that the doors had been locked. His key chain was still in his hand and he tried his internal office door key on the external lock, surprised to find that it fit. Once in, he proceeded directly to Carrion's office. The office was still dark but now the blinds were partly closed. He put his hands around his face again and tried to peek between the slats, but he could see nothing in the shadows behind the glass. He kicked at the door.

"CARRION! ARE YOU IN THERE? CARRION? IF SO YOU'D BETTER OPEN THIS DOOR. WE NEED TO TALK!"

Only silence greeted him. He waited a bit longer and then headed to the office kitchen. It was dark in the kitchen, with only the light from the corridor faintly illuminating the room. Sam stood in front of the refrigerator, clear of notes for the first time since he had started.

"Fucking Nutjob," he muttered under his breath and kicked the refrigerator door. As his foot connected with the bottom of the door it made an audible sound—almost like a low groan. Startled, Sam stepped back from the door. Then, in the faint light, he saw movement directly in the center. A square began to materialize in the door. He squinted and leaned in closer as the square materialized into a yellow note.

"Holy shit!"

His first instinct was to run, and he took a few quick steps toward the corridor before he stopped. It felt as if every nerve was standing on end. He slowly turned back and stared at the yellow note. He could just make out a line of script on it, but not quite. On courage alone he took a tentative step back toward it. Then another, and then another. Slowly and cautiously he crept closer, as if he was expecting it to rear up and attack. He reached a trembling and tense arm out until his fingertips touched the metal of the door just to the side of the note. It felt normal. Then he slid his fingertips to the left, pulled the note off, and retreated back a few steps. He looked down and read what was on the note.

Merchant,

I love the aggression. You've been promoted to CEO. I'm moving on. Good luck. Now OPEN THE DOOR.

Regards, Mr. Carrion.

Sam remained in front of the door for a long time, terrified, frozen where he stood, and unsure what to do next. He read the note several times, trying to understand what it meant while still shocked at how it had materialized from the metal door. He looked at the door. It appeared to be normal. He leaned in again and rapped his fist on it. It was just as solid as it looked. He stared down at the note again.

In for a penny, in for a pound, he thought as he grasped the door handle and pulled. The door resisted opening. Sam inched the heel of his left palm into the groove at the side, and pulled with his right hand on the door as hard as he could. It suddenly yielded with a popping and sucking sound and flew all the way open.

Sam winced as the sudden jerk nearly dislocated his shoulder. His left hand instinctively reached up and began rubbing his right shoulder as he felt himself being pulled to the door by some unseen force.

His hands caught the sides of the open refrigerator as he looked within its depths. It was endless. The shelves and food inside were visible but translucent, like a hologram projected into the rectangular opening. The back was shimmering and he could see behind it as the force increased until every single muscle in his body was engaged in keeping him on the outside. Soon it was just too much. His arms were on the edge of breaking under the force, and he could hold on no longer. He let go. His body traveled straight through the faint images of the shelves and containers and continued straight through the shimmering back wall of the refrigerator.

A few seconds later, Sam was gone. The door remained open, and the light from inside cast shadows in the empty room. A strange silence filled the entire floor of the office, and not even the sound of air conditioner could be heard.

* * *

Jimmy Carter pulled in to the lot of CENTURY AUDIT, both excited and nervous.

THE REFRIGERATOR

First day on the job, he thought. His very first job since graduating. He had no idea what to expect, except maybe the same old Mr. President jokes he'd been enduring all his life. He got out of his car, and looked at the building. *Very respectable,* he thought. A small sign with the name CENTURY AUDIT hung over the door. He grabbed his briefcase, Wal-Mart tags still attached, and walked in. A young woman stood at the receptionist desk, arguing with an older lady.

"You know something, I KNOW YOU DO. And I'm not going to rest until I know what went on here!"

"Please Miss—if you don't leave I'm going to have to call security."

"Until I find out what happened to Sam, this isn't over," the woman said as she stormed past Jimmy out the door.

"You must be Mr. Carter," the older woman said.

"Yes Ma'am!" Jimmy replied.

"Welcome aboard. My name is Clara Teasdale. Let me show you to your office. I have an envelope for you as well from your boss, Mr. Merchant."

"Great! Can't wait to get started!" said Jimmy as he followed Clara down the hall, listening with amusement as she whistled "*Hail to the Chief*".

Megan entered her house, sad and confused. The silence was everywhere without Sam. She knew that CENTURY AUDIT was hiding something, but what? Sam never returned after he went to confront Carrion over a month ago. She called the police and filed a missing persons report, but their routine act disheartened her. She even talked to those two detectives that were investigating Trudeling's death, but they were just as confused as she was.

She walked into the kitchen, still feeling observed, but even that felt different now. It felt warmer somehow. As she looked at the door, she gasped. There was a yellow note there, one that wasn't blank. She plucked it off and looked at it. A calm swept over her as she looked at it . . . it was Sam's familiar script.

Megan.

I had to leave. I don't think I can see you again, I'm sorry. I do love you.

Sam

Megan put her head in her hands and began to cry. Just then the refrigerator door popped open, startling her out of her grief. It was different inside now. The shelves and bottles and leftovers were dim and she could see through them. She could see deeply into it, past the back wall to another place. And then she saw Sam. He stood there, smiling at her. He held out his hand and beckoned her. She moved closer.

"Sam?" she said.

He didn't answer, just continued to beckon her. She put a foot into the fridge, it passed right through the shelves. She reached her hand forward, brushing Sam's fingertips. Then he gently clasped her hand.

"Do you love me?" he asked.

"Oh Sam you know I do," she said.

"Then come."
With a whistling sound, Megan disappeared through the back of refrigerator.

STRANGER CALLS
TYLER MILLER

Marlon Bouman's marriage was over. He knew it. Pat knew it. Hell, everybody knew it. If he was honest with himself, the whole sad, silly affair had lasted longer than he could have expected, and ended just as dirtily. Hadn't they told him this was how it would play out?

Certainly Linda, his ex-wife had said so when she signed the divorce papers. "You chase a younger woman, Marlon, you better be ready for it when she sticks it to you. It'll be a hard, cold knife, and it'll slice."

Boy, hadn't it. He'd be bleeding for many years to come. Bleeding out half his income, the plush high-rise condo in Manhattan, the Porsche. He shook his head sadly at the thought.

Pat Bouman sat in back seat of their Mercedes. As Marlon pulled to the curb outside the Point Loma Best Western, she gave a quick, disapproving glance out the window and let out her patented sigh of displeasure. A little wheeze that somehow encompassed all her hate and all her disgust.

"You're a hopeless fucking romantic, Marlon."

Marlon stopped the car. He took a long, deep breath that did nothing to relax his nerves. "You didn't have to come," he told her.

"And let you what? Run all over San Diego banging cocktail waitresses? You think I don't know what you're like? Or did you forget that I know *exactly* what kind of man you are?"

Marlon's fingers tightened along the wheel. Four years ago Marlon had met Patricia Hurlingston right here on Point Loma. She'd been serving martinis and daiquiris at a little bar called Willy's along the beach. Marlon had been celebrating a long spring vacation with Linda. Linda, however, didn't like the sun. Her sister got melanoma in her thirties, and was in and out of hospitals for years. Marlon had meandered down to the beach on his own, ordered drinks on his own, watched the sunsets on his own. At least until one Patricia Hurlingston, all of twenty-three, decided to join him.

The beginning of the end. And now he'd returned to the beginning. Wasn't that part of a poem? Marlon wondered. Eliot, perhaps.

The valet appeared at the curb. A boy, no more than twenty. He reached out and opened Pat's door.

"Finally," Pat barked. "A real man."

Marlon briefly considered slamming on the gas and yanking away from the curb, leaving Pat Bouman in a squealing drift of burning rubber. Never looking back. The thought flickered in his mind, bringing a lilting smile to his lips. The next thought came was of Pat crying behind a witness box in a courtroom telling how her cruel, insensitive husband had left her without any warning, and the happy fantasy blew out like a candle in a cold wind.

"Can I park the car for you, sir?"

The valet was tapping on the window. Marlon hadn't noticed him.

"Can I park the car for you, sir?"

"Sure. Sure. Why the hell not?"

"And the luggage? I can bring it to the room."

Marlon told him the room number.

"Won't be five minutes, sir."

Marlon gave the boy a nod. The kid slid into the seat, lanky and twitching with the energy of youth. They were all the same down here, Marlon thought. These California boys. All blond and blue eyed and happy, like life was going to deal them a royal flush instead of the old busted variety. Must be something in the water.

The Mercedes pulled away.

"Where the hell's the luggage?"

"He's bringing it to the room."

"My purse is in the backseat."

"I'm sure he'll bring that too."

"After he rifles through it. Jesus, Marlon, you really are a simple old man, aren't you? You just go around trusting everybody."

"I trusted you."

"Look where that got you."

Marlon checked in with the concierge. They took the elevator to the top floor and found the room at the end of the hall. The valet was already waiting. The boy held out Pat's purse.

"You didn't take anything, did you?"

"No, ma'am."

"And you didn't dint the car?"

"No, ma'am."

"Don't *ma'am* me you little pipsqueak. I ain't your grandmother."

The valet, thankfully, remained silent.

* * *

When Marlon first met her at Willy's he called her Patty. She put an end to that.

"I'm not a line in a child's nursery rhyme," she'd told him. She was never Patty, and only rarely Patricia. She was just Pat. Like a man's name. And there was something distinctly masculine about Pat, but not in the way she *looked*. If she'd aged in the last four years, the only effect it had on her was that she had become more voluptuous around her already sculpted hips, her languorous breasts, and the already contoured slope of her petite little ass. But she took things like a man. When she wanted Marlon, she took him. When she wanted Marlon's money, she took it. Now, when she wanted everything, she took that too.

The affair surprised him. Not the why but the *who*. Val Negrete. Not the young, sophisticated type Marlon had expected, but a dull, witless financial advisor even older than Marlon. When he found out he called Linda. He could practically hear her shaking her head through the telephone.

"What the hell did you *think* was going to happen?"

This, their last vacation together, was little more than a pitiful farce. It fooled nobody, not even Marlon, who'd come to accept that he'd done what so many aging men had done before him: embraced the cliché. All he wanted now was a few lazy days at the beach, sipping Mai Tais and watching the waves roll in and the surf drag out.

He'd gone down to the front desk to get a second ice tray. You could never have enough ice. He could have phoned it in, but getting it himself meant getting away from Pat. He took his time. When he came back, he slipped in the door, hoping she was still in the shower.

Pat sat on the edge of the king bed. A bath towel clung loosely around her still dripping body. Wet strands of hair hung along her shoulders like sleeping snakes. Beneath her feet, a soggy puddle spread out from her toes.

"You're making a damn—"

He saw her face.

He thought the streaks on her face were from her head. It took him a moment to realize they were tears. It struck Marlon that he'd never actually seen Pat cry, that he'd never even imagined her crying, that he'd believed, somehow, ridiculously, that she was beyond crying. Seeing tears now startled him, unnerved him. He dropped the ice tray. It landed softly on the carpet.

"What happened? What is it?"

At first she didn't speak. She didn't even see him. Then he moved toward her, and she caught the movement in the corner of her eye. She jerked upright, her eyes still not quite seeing, or maybe seeing but not seeing *him*, Marlon, but something else, something that wasn't her soft, overweight husband in his Tommy Bahamas.

Pat flung herself backward onto the bed. The towel fell loose, tangling between her legs and then flapping to the floor, revealing her in a way Marlon found obscene. Her arms flailed as if warding off an impending attack. She let out a loud screech, a sound Marlon had never heard before, not from Pat, not from anyone. It stopped Marlon in his tracks.

"What the hell is going on?"

She didn't stop until she was all the way on the other side of the bed, legs still kicking, arms still pinwheeling, and then she went right off the other end, tumbling onto the floor. The screech cut off. Marlon heard the loud thump of her head bucking against the far wall.

She's gone fucking mad.

Marlon crossed the room. Pat lay on the floor. When he came around the bed, she saw him, really saw him, and the tension drained out of her lithe little body. He reached down and took her by the shoulders and brought her back onto the bed.

"What is it? Tell me what the fuck is going on."

Her eyes darted back and forth, searching beyond Marlon's shoulders at the edges of the room.

"I was just in the shower," she said, her voice thin and weak. "I didn't even hear it ring."

"What? The telephone? Somebody called? Who called?"

Pat shook her head. "It's him. Jesus Christ it's really *him*. I don't know how he . . . I didn't even hear it *ring*. I just came out and the little light was blinking. You know how it blinks? When you've got a message? It was just blinking, blinking. And I didn't know. I thought *you'd* called. But it wasn't you. Wasn't . . . it wasn't you. It was him."

"Who? Who the hell was it?"

He wanted to shake her. She wouldn't look him in the eye.

"Was it Val? That motherfucker. He's got no fucking right calling you here. I swear to God I'm gonna find that creaky old fuck and . . ." Marlon trailed off, envisaging various methods of torturing the man who'd cuckolded him.

But Pat shook her head. "Not Val," she said. "*Him.*"

It occurred to Marlon then that perhaps Val had not been the only man sleeping with his wife. Had there been others? How many? He pulled away from Pat, trying to read the map of her infidelities in the lines of her face. She put her face in her hands and cried.

Marlon got up and went to the phone. He picked it up and hit the message button.

A voice spoke:

"That you Patty Cakes? I know it's you. You miss me? Thought you was the little birdie that got away, did you? Thought I wouldn't find you? Silly Patty Cakes. Dirty birdies don't get to fly away. Dirty birdies get what they deserve. And you know what you deserve, don't you? You know what I'm gonna give you."

The voice dropped to a sing-song, a creepy, high falsetto that raked across Marlon's ears.

"Patty Cakes, Patty Cakes, baker man. Bake me a bitch just as fast you can. Stick her and stuck her and cut out her little V, put her head in the oven for the baker and me."

Marlon dropped the phone.

The line dangled. The voice on the line chuckled. The phone went dead.

* * *

Marlon emptied five of the mini-liquor bottles from the fridge into her before she settled down. He tucked her under the covers and wiped her head with a damp cloth.

She told him the story.

When Marlon had first met her she'd been hustling tables on Point Loma for a little more than a year. She'd heard the rumors even before she took the job, but she hadn't really believed them. Word was someone was harassing the younger waitresses out on the point, some of the guests in the hotels too. Got their number one way or another, and then the calls began. You never knew when. Late at night. Mid-morning. Sometimes, eerily, right when you went on lunch break. Almost like he was watching you.

"What kind of calls?" Pat had asked, but the other girl's at Willy's only knew what they'd heard.

"Sex stuff," one girl said.

"Worse than that," another girl said. "Frightening stuff."

"What do ya mean, frightening?"

And the girl spoke in a whisper: "Threats, you know, like how he'd like to kill you, how he's gonna do it, like he's already planned it out."

Pat gave the girl a practiced eye roll.

Later, she had the story confirmed by a waitress out on Coronado Island who used to work on Loma but left when she'd gotten the calls herself.

"Who the hell is it?" Pat had asked her.

"Some freak," the waitress told her. "Some sick fuck getting his jollies. And nobody does nothing about it? What can they do, girly? It's harassment, ain't it? Sure, but that's part of the job description. You think you're just writing down what people want for lunch? You're taking shit. That's the job. This is just more shit."

And the tougher girls, the ones like Pat, stuck it out, while the weaker ones found jobs somewhere else.

"And they never caught him?" Marlon asked.

Pat shook her head.

"But they were just phone calls. Nothing more."

And her head shook again.

Two girls went missing. One before Pat was hired at Willy's. Megan, a sixteen-year-old scrubbing tables at Jay Kid Bar & Grille. A runaway to begin with, which was why no one spent much time looking for her when she didn't show up for work one evening. Some said she just blew on out of town, one more restless leaf in the wind, but the girls who knew her said she left things behind, the kind of things a young girl takes with her whether she's blowing out or not. And they knew she'd been getting the calls.

The second was a twenty-five-year-old blonde working a tiki bar on the beach. Worked the point for four years. Got engaged to a bartender on Coronado. Disappeared the week before the wedding.

Pat had also heard the story from the bartender. "She wouldn't have left me. Not like this. We were in love. Amy was her name. She'd gotten calls too."

"And you were getting them then?" Marlon questioned.

Another nod. "Two weeks before you showed up."

"Like this one?"

"It's him, Marlon. I don't know how he found me. Remember I threw away my phone after you went back to New York? You bought me the new one with the private number."

He remembered. She'd told him her phone didn't work anymore, was always cutting out. She didn't want to miss any of his calls. He'd thought she was being cute.

"And then I moved away. I thought that was it. I never even told you about it. It was just a trashy bit of the past, you know, the kind of thing you didn't bring up because it made you feel kind of dirty. It was over. I was never going to hear that awful voice again."

Marlon gave the bedside phone a nasty look, as if the phone itself had committed this wrong. What kind of a world was this where someone could reach out from some distant part of the world and straight into your bedroom and disturb your whole existence? Put fear in your heart. Cause you to sweat and shiver and lie down in a panic.

"Don't worry, dear. I'll take care of it."

* * *

The girl at the front desk looked confused.

"I just don't know how that could happen. If someone calls, they need your name and your room number to ring through. That's the only way we do it, Mr. Bouman."

"*Bow*. Like bow and arrow. Not bough."

"Mr. *Bow*-man. That's the way we do it. Name *and* room number."

"That doesn't make any sense. We don't know this man. We only just arrived here yesterday. We didn't even tell anyone we were coming."

Marlon's voice was rising. His thick, meaty hand clenched atop the counter.

The girl was small and doe-like, with saucer-shaped hazel eyes and fat, pouty lips. She chewed the lower lip and stared at Marlon like he was an oncoming truck she couldn't avoid.

"This couldn't be a prank?" she asked. "A friend with a poor sense of humor?" "I just told you, *no one knows we're here.*"

The girl's eyes widened, and Marlon thought she might break into tears.

"They'd have to know your name and room number," she repeated, using this mantra like a shield. "It's company policy."

"Then someone must have broken company policy."

The girl's eyes jerked even wider, something Marlon frankly thought impossible. She looked like the very mention of rule breaking might induce vomiting.

"Oh no, Mr. Bouman."

"*Bow*-man."

"Mr. *Bow*-man. This is a good company here. Not like some of the other places I've worked. My last job, people didn't obey the rules at all, not even the manager. You wouldn't *believe* what people got away with. But it's not like that here. I've only been here two weeks, but I can already tell you that this is an . . . *upstanding* company."

Marlon frowned. The girl was clearly an idiot.

"You worked around here before? On Point Loma?"

"Waitressing."

Marlon leaned forward and lowered his voice. "You ever get any strange phone calls?" The girl reeled backward. Her widened eyes could bulge no further, but her face sagged limp and ashen.

Marlon left her there at the desk feeling too much like a man who, instead of swerving away, had swung intentionally toward some innocent creature cowering in the headlights.

* * *

They decided to spend the day off Point Loma. They drove to Old Town and ate Mexican food and drank margaritas. Pat was quieter than usual. She picked at her enchiladas and slurped on one margarita after another. Marlon shuffled her from one gaudy tourist attraction to another. On one level he told himself if he just kept her moving he might break the spell that had come over her. On another, deeper, level he silently acknowledged that this was the first time in their marriage she'd ever shut up; he rather liked it.

When they returned to the hotel late in the evening the sun was fading over the horizon. The room was dim with the dying light. In the center of the room beside the bed they saw the blinking red light on the phone indicating they had a message.

Pat lurched back against the wall. Her hand came up to her chest. She shook her head violently, nearly smacking her cheeks against the wall.

"I can't do it, Marlon. I can't hear it. I can't listen to him anymore. I just can't. I *won't.*"

"Settle down," Marlon told her. "I'll answer it. You just take it easy."

Marlon didn't want to hear it either, but he wasn't about to admit to Pat the tingling chill riding down his spine or the vice-tight knot curling in his stomach. He went to the phone. He picked it up and pushed the message button.

There was a click and a pause.

Then a voice.

Marlon listened.

Across the room, Pat began to cry.

Marlon set down the phone.

"It was the restaurant. You left your wallet."

* * *

Pat locked herself in the bathroom with the rest of the mini-liquor bottles and her cell phone. She said she needed to call Jefferson, her life coach.

"The windbag?"

"He's got *training*, Marlon. He's a *counselor*."

"He's a sham."

But Pat already had the phone open and the bathroom door swinging shut.

Marlon lay on the bed and rubbed his temples. Life coach. Jesus. What next? The man wasn't even a real shrink. He had a degree, sure. In outdoor recreation. Marlon had looked up the degree requirements when Pat hired the man. Two classes in psychology, one of them child psych. Not exactly what Marlon considered qualified, although he thought the child psych might go a ways in helping Pat. Two psych classes and you could call yourself a counselor. Marlon dug his thumb into the space below his ear, trying to rub away the headache he knew was coming. The bastard charged more than a real psychologist. How'd you figure that one?

When the scream came from the bathroom, Marlon nearly tumbled off the bed. He hurried to the bathroom door, but it was locked. He pounded on the door. The screaming continued. Marlon turned and butted his shoulder hard against the door. It didn't buck.

Another scream.

"Open the fucking door!"

The sound of sloshing water interrupted the screams. A second later, the door opened. Pat fell out, wet and naked, into Marlon's arms. Marlon whipped her around and stepped into the bathroom, half-expecting to find someone standing there beside the toilet. But the bathroom was empty.

On the floor was Pat's open cell phone.

An icy voice issued from the tiny speaker, one Marlon had already heard before.

"*. . . baker man, gonna cut out your eyes just as fast as I can. Gut you and shuck you all night through, open up your veins to see if they're blue. . .*"

Marlon strode forward and stomped on the phone. It snapped in half, but for the briefest second Marlon thought he heard that cackling voice still coming from the speaker. He stomped on the phone again, and all went quiet.

* * *

They were ready to check out in the morning. There was no reason to stay. Marlon asked for an early wake-up call, and by six he was showered and shaved and dressed. He went down for the continental breakfast and ate a blueberry muffin and a banana while watching the Today Show. Back in New York, the sun was shining, people were smiling, and Al Roker was thinner than ever. It was a pleasant fantasy to wile away the morning with, this happy existence uninterrupted by life's darker elements.

He remembered when he was a kid and the neighbor boy down the street got a new dog. A large lab blacker than coal dust, only its teeth were white. For a time Marlon loved nothing more than he loved that neighbor kid's dog, and he traveled the half-block every day after school to feed the lab whatever morsel Marlon had saved from lunch. He stroked the dog's head, said good dog, even tried teaching the dog to sit and fetch. And he'd thought that was how the world worked. Life was good.

One day Marlon had come after school and the dog wasn't there. He waited in the alley, thinking the neighbor had simply brought the dog inside. Eventually, the neighbor boy came out and told Marlon to go away, the dog was gone.

"What happened?" Marlon had asked.

The neighbor boy crossed his arms. "The dog ain't no more."

"But why? What do you mean?"

And the neighbor boy told him. "My neighbor shot him. He kept shitting in his yard and he told us he wouldn't take no more of the dog's shit and the dog shit there again and the neighbor shot him."

Marlon remembered how he'd gone home and sat in his room and stared at the wall. He'd wanted to cry, but for some reason the tears wouldn't come. And he realized now that that was the first time in his life he really understood that life wasn't what adults told him it was. He'd known then that there'd be days when the sun didn't come out, when people stopped smiling and never did again, when Al Roker would finally put back on all that fucking weight no matter how many fucking salads he ate. Because that was life, and life wasn't always good.

A cell phone rang behind him. Marlon jumped.

He left his dishes on the table and went back to the room. Pat was awake. He laid out her clothes and she got dressed. They picked up their bags and went out.

Marlon took the bags to the street. The valet appeared. The kid immediately took the bags from Pat's hands.

"Let me handle those," the boy said.

"I can take them."

"Not a problem, ma'am. That's what I'm here for."

But Pat was insistent. She snatched the bag back. "I said I can take them. I'm not a fucking invalid, you know."

The boy stood silently.

"Just go around for the car, will you?" Marlon said.

"Right away, sir."

The boy disappeared.

Pat clutched her luggage bag. "Well, I'm *not*. I can take care of myself."

But Marlon heard the waver in her voice.

"I'll check us out."

He went inside to the front desk. The doe-eyed girl was gone, replaced by the concierge. Marlon put the room keys on the counter.

"Checking out so soon, sir?"

"Afraid so."

"Nothing wrong with the service, I hope."

"Nothing at all. Just a change of plans."

The concierge took the keys and typed on his computer. A receipt printed. He handed the receipt to Marlon.

Marlon was halfway to the door when he turned back. The concierge smiled.

"Yes, sir?"

"I'm afraid my wife was a little harsh with your valet. She's . . . under a lot of pressure, but still. It was inappropriate."

The concierge's smile faltered. "Sir, I'm not really . . ."

"No. Here. He's just a boy. He works hard enough without people biting his head off."

"But really, sir . . ."

Marlon waved a hand. He already had the wallet out. He fingered a couple twenties.

"But, sir, if you'll please . . ."

"Look," Marlon huffed. "You're not one of those damn places that doesn't let their people take tips, are you? You want to underpay a hardworking young man and then not let him take any tips when he earns them by the sweat of his brow? This is America, god damnit. Let a man work."

The concierge's smile had entirely disappeared now. Marlon thrust the twenties onto the counter.

"But sir, you don't understand."

"I understand plenty."

"No, you see, we don't employ a valet. That's what I've been trying to tell you."

Marlon blinked. "What's that?"

"We don't have a valet, sir. I'm not sure who you are talking about."

Marlon left the twenties on the counter. He rushed back out the door.

On the street, Pat Bouman and all her luggage were gone.

NJORD'S DAUGHTER
CHRISTINE MORGAN

The longship rests at anchor in the sheltered cove, sail furled, oars stowed. Water laps in gentle wavelets against its hull. Clouds scud across the dark sky, obscuring the moon, smelling of rain. A single oil-lamp flickers with thin light.

The men finish their cold meals of hard bread and herring, then go about the business of preparing to sleep. They wrap themselves in furs and cloaks, bedding down in the spaces beneath or between the oar-benches.

One plucks at a harp. His voice drifts with sweet melody as he sings an old mournful song of Njord the sea-god, and the mountain-giantess Skadi.

He sings of how Skadi went to Asgard seeking compensation for the death of her father . . . how the gods offered her one of their own as a husband, but bade her choose him by only the sight of his feet while the rest was hidden by a drape . . . how Skadi had chosen those she thought must be Baldr's, but they belonged to Njord instead . . .

He sings it well.

And oh, he is lovely, that one, handsome of feature, fine-built of frame. Red hair hangs thick to his shoulders. His beard is lush and full.

How she adores him! How she has adored him since first her gaze fell upon him!

She floats closer.

So close now . . . if she reached up a hand she might almost touch him. . .

* * *

Farald's fingers paused on the harp-strings. The skin at the nape of his neck seemed to crawl.

He looked around but beheld nothing to account for his sudden unease.

The Wind-Chaser had been put in here for the night, along this rocky stretch of coast far from any village or hall. They had encountered no other ships since making trade with a fat little knarr two days ago. The weather was mild and these were friendly lands.

Yet the nape of his neck still did prickle.

An omen? Some foreboding?

The sound of a soft splashing drew his attention down toward the sea. An otter diving, he thought, or the quick leap of a fish. But he saw only a tangle of slick, ropy kelp adrift on the current.

A few of the men, his ship-mates and oar-brothers, glanced over, curious that he had stopped in his song.

Farald smiled, shaking his head as if to shake off the sensation. He resumed singing of how Njord could not stand to forsake his deep realm, while Skadi yearned for her home in the high rocky peaks, dooming their marriage to unhappy uncompromise and they had parted their sad ways.

* * *

145

NJORD'S DAUGHTER

She submerges just in time, hiding her face from his sight. Her large eyes peer up through the floating strands of her hair.

Distorted by sea-water, she still finds his visage handsome.

Yes, how she adores him . . . how she loves and craves him!

He must be hers, *will* be hers!

When he turns away, smiling his beautiful smile, she surfaces again to listen.

It is a story she knows well, and always has known.

But she will never tire of hearing it from this man's lips, her beloved.

To her woe, it is over too soon. He covers the harp with a case of leather and settles into his sleeping-place with his wool cloak pulled snug around his shoulders.

She slips lower, trailing her hands along the hull by where he lies. Only this curved layer of planking separates them.

The thudding of many mens' heartbeats vibrates through the timbers. She ignores the rest, concentrating only on one.

She flattens her body against the ship's underside as if pressing herself to a lover and fancies she can feel the heat of his flesh through that thin wooden shell.

Soon, she'll know the embrace of his arms, the taste of his breath, the touch of his skin. Soon, he will be with her, he will be hers, and they'll be together.

Always.

* * *

The Wind-Chaser made favorable speed to the next settlement, which was large enough to offer good opportunities for trade—reindeer hides and antler for pottery and fleeces— and to replenish their provisions with grain, dried vegetables and cheese.

Most of the men squandered what little money they had on the usual pastimes of drinking, gambling and whoring. Others purchased trinkets or oddities, spices and treats.

Farald bought a necklace of flameworked glass beads of many colors; he saved the rest of his wages to put with his share of the journey's profits. Which was not to say that he went without enjoying himself. He took his harp and sat on a stump near a brewer's hut, where in exchange for his music he was offered barley-ale and seed-cakes.

He soon enough noticed a girl lingering about, a plain creature whose movements were slow and limp-hampered. Though she troubled no one, folk sometimes sneered as they passed her.

She wore a shabby kirtle with no apron-dress over it, the cloth perhaps once dyed green but faded almost to grey. Her face was pale, her hair and eyes darkish, and if he thought anything further of her at all it was just that she must be some unfortunate cripple. He was glad if his harp-playing and singing gave her day a bright spot of joy.

* * *

Her legs ache. Her feet hurt. She is clumsy and she hates it. She was never clumsy before.

The heaviness and weight . . . the tottering for balance . . . the hard pull of the hard earth, waiting for her to fall . . .

Each dragging step is painful. Muscles cramp and clench.

They make it seem so easy, so natural. They are graceful. They stand. They dance. They run.

She forces herself to walk. She has to. She does it for him.

She does not dare yet to approach him, but the pain of being parted from him is a pain greater even than that in her sore legs and feet.

He sings livelier songs, cheerful ones to amuse and entertain the crowds. He sings of Jotunheim's master builder and how Loki took horse-shape to trick the giant into losing a bet. He sings of dwarf-gold and Saxon silver, of battles and kings and bold deeds.

And when, at last, he and the others return to their ship, she follows.

She wades into the surf, dives beneath the waves, and follows.

* * *

They sailed to an inlet where Utwald, whose ship the Wind-Chaser was, had a brother who had a farmstead and hall. There, Utwald assured them, they would have welcome and hospitality for a few days.

Utwald's brother, Utbranni, made good on that promise. His was not a grand hall, but comfortable. His farm thrived. His folk raised pigs and tended fruit trees. The men feasted on boiled pork. They drank their fill of apple-wine.

Then, one evening when he'd had perhaps slightly more than his fill of apple-wine, Farald stepped out of the smoky hall for a breath of fresher air. The night was cool and damp, fog-wreathed.

He felt a prickling on the nape of his neck. He caught a glimpse of furtive movement from the corner of his eye and turned.

A girl stood half-hidden behind a log-pile. Dark eyes stared at him through tangled dark hair.

Farald opened his mouth to speak, but at that moment two of his ship-mates staggered from the hall. They bumped into him, bumped into each other, laughed heartily, and slung companionable arms around his neck.

"Sing with us, oar-brother!" Vafri cried.

Gullaug blinked in the direction of the girl. "What's this? Have we interrupted?"

"Interrupted?" Vafri reeled about, nearly toppling and taking them all down with him. "Oh-ho!"

A tumble of logs spilled from the pile as the girl spun to flee. She ran with an ungainly, lurching stride like the bounding of a maimed frog.

"Did you see her?" Farald asked.

"The girl?" Gullaug hiccuped a gusty belch fragrant of apples and pork. "Bah. You can do better, my friend. You can do much better."

* * *

She runs, and it is agony, it is torment, it is as if her feet are being gashed by the sharp edges of a thousand broken shells. One leg buckles under her, seized by a furious spasm. She goes sprawling in mud and pig-muck.

147

NJORD'S DAUGHTER

Her lungs sob and labor. Her throat burns. She can no longer run but crawls, crab-scuttles, finally forces herself upright.

At the shore she falls again, onto wet sand where she flops and gasps like a fish. She pulls her body to the water. She rolls into it.

Grace returns, but with it comes shame, a fevered shame, shame and rage.

She had been so close then . . . close enough that their eyes met . . . close enough to speak, he'd been about to speak . . . to speak to *her*. . .

* * *

No one at Utbranni's hall recognized her by his description, such as it was. None of them knew any girls with a crippled gait. Gullaug and Vafri were of no help either. In the end, Farald had to wonder if it had been in his head, the apple-wine playing pranks on his mind.

The Wind-Chaser sailed on.

It came next to a fishing camp, where boats from many small islands converged to hold a market fair. There were crabs and mussels, racks of fish being dried or smoked, salt and salt-barrels, hooks, nets, traps, and all manner of other goods. The sky overhead wheeled thick with shrieking gulls.

He saw her again.

Or thought he did.

If it *was* her.

Others did confirm having seen a limping, dark-haired girl in a faded grey-green dress. But nobody knew her. Nobody knew her name, or what settlement she was from.

And it might have been some other, similar-looking girl. Might have been? Must have been! Had to have been! How could it possibly be the same one?

Still, the doubt preyed upon him.

He began to sleep poorly, afflicted often by troublesome dreams. The feeling of being watched, and followed, would not leave him even when the Wind-Chaser was beyond sight of any land.

"You're imagining it," Utwald said to him. "No other ships have been near enough on our course, and it's unlikely any mystery woman could hide herself away among us for long."

* * *

The sea rises and falls in slow, gentle swells. It cradles the longship, rocks it like a babe in the arms of a mother.

Above, stars glimmer, but mist rings the moon and a new storm is coming.

Webbed hands grip the rail. Her body lifts up, hair coursing sleek down her back.

He is still lovely, although he seems to have grown thinner, although worry creases his brow and his eyes twitch with restlessness behind their closed lids.

The temptation is strong to simply take hold and seize him. With her strength, she could pull him over the side, into the water.

But he sleeps in the narrow space beneath the oar-bench. She does not want to hurt him by pulling too roughly.

Nor does she want to wake the other men. They are sailors, yes, traders, not a war-band, but they are still far from helpless. They would attack her. They would not understand that she means her beloved no harm.

She wants only to have him for her own, and forever.

With a briny sigh, she lets go of the rail and slips once more into the silent depths.

* * *

Rain poured down in relentless torrents. The men were drenched, miserable, bickering and foul-tempered.

The weather soon worsened, clouds lightning-split, the skies shaking with thunder. The wind was not in their favor. With all hands at the oars, backs and arms straining, the Wind-Chaser still tossed and bobbed like a child's carved wooden toy.

They put ashore on a desolate pile of rocks and drift-wood. A rough stone outcrop overhang offered some scant shelter where they could at least huddle together, even if they could build no fire for warmth.

Farald, exhausted as any of them, lay nonetheless wakeful. He listened to the sounds of sea and storm, and his ship-mates snoring. It seemed to him that he heard other, stealthier sounds as well . . . the shuffle and slap of limping steps coming ever closer.

A great glaring sheet of Thor's fire lit the night. Farald flinched from it but saw in its stark white flash a shape looming nearby. A hunched female shape, dripping wet, tangled hair streaming—

His shout of alarm was lost in the thunder-crash. He sprang to his feet, rudely jostling the men sleeping beside him.

Another great flash showed him her dark eyes and pale face.

Voices called out with questions or in irritation. Bodies stirred. There followed some moments of disgruntled confusion, and at the next brilliant bolt, Farald saw she was gone.

* * *

The others try to calm him. He struggles with them. They restrain him, holding his arms, keeping him from rushing headlong to where she had been.

She clings to the rocks in the foaming, seething surf.

So close, again, so close! He'd been almost within reach, almost within her very grasp!

The worst of the squall passes. She listens to them argue.

Her beloved insists she was there. The others say they saw nothing. He demands that they be truthful, quit decieving him, he knows what he saw! They say he must have glimpsed a formation of rock or some wave-sculpted tree limb, and that his treacherous mind did the rest on its own.

They reason with him. This island, they tell him, is in the middle of nowhere. There've been no other ships. No one lives here.

They ridicule him. Does this girl that he sees fly on eagle's wings to get from one place to another? Is she a sorceress, perhaps?

He finally succumbs.

At the first brightening of morning, they set sail again. The storms are far from over —the weather-wise among them know it—but they set sail just the same.

* * *

"We make for Hillfort!" Utwald, wrestling with the steering-oar, had to yell to be heard. "Jarl Wulfstan has a hall there!"

The sea heaved and dipped. Waves crested froth-capped. The mast groaned. The timbers creaked. At any moment it seemed that the Wind-Chaser would be smashed to pieces, scattered like breadcrumbs.

Under other circumstances, Utwald's men might have objected. Jarl Wulfstan was a war-lord of fearsome reputation, with half a dozen dragonships under his command. He would, at the best, expect a healthy bribe for his help. At the worst, he'd seize the ship and all it contained, forcing them into his service as bonds-men or slaves.

But Hillfort was the nearest settlement, if they could only reach it.

At that moment, Farald found, he did not care if safety did mean an iron chain around his neck.

Njord did not seem inclined to let them reach Hillfort or safety. Although they'd thrown offerings of ale, meat and silver over the sides, the sea-god whipped the wind and waves ever higher.

Soon, they gave up at rowing and could only hope to ride it out. Some of the men, Farald included, lashed themselves to their oar-benches so as not to be flung overboard and drowned.

Such a death would be by far the most dreadful. To plunge into the salty waters, to feel the chill leaching the heat from their bodies . . . to suck their lungs full of the sea . . . to have their skin slough off white and wrinkled from their blue and bloated flesh . . . to be eaten by fish, picked at by crabs . . . to have their bones tumbled loose with the tides, and sand-polished . . . their skulls with gaping eye-sockets home to tiny sea-creatures. . .

Worst of all, they would know neither golden Valhalla nor even the grey dreariness of Niflheim, Hel's realm. They would go unburied, spirits doomed to wander. They might become draugr, cursed corpses seeking to slaughter the living.

Howling gales snatched the rain this way and that in tattered curtains. The thunder was such that Thor himself must have been battling giants just above the dark clouds.

"There!" Vafri pointed ahead.

Farald craned his neck and squinted to look. Others did likewise.

A jagged crack of lightning showed them what Vafri had seen—a rock bluff with a large hall built atop it, and a harbor protected by a stony breakwater.

Men cheered.

Then a mountainous wave reared up beneath the Wind-Chaser, rolled the ship, and crashed down upon it.

* * *

She is amazed by the power, awestruck at the devastation.

How quickly it happens . . . the flip of a fin, the blink of an eye . . . and the ship is reduced to wreckage . . . splintered planks and barrels . . . all their goods and provisions, their weapons and belongings. . .

Some of the men kick and flounder for the surface. Others cling to floating debris. Still others, knocked senseless or already dead, drift slowly toward the sea bottom with arms and legs loosely trailing.

Those who'd so frantically lashed themselves to their benches now just as frantically try to work themselves loose as the ruined hull begins sinking.

With an undulant flex of her body, she dives. Her gaze darts about, seeking and then finding her beloved's red banner of hair. The redder red of blood mingles with it. He is wounded. Unconscious.

She reaches him in two strong strokes. He is tied to his bench. A quick bite shreds apart the rope and frees him.

At her touch, in her arms, held tight against her, he is safe.

One of the bound men sees her. He'd had the presence of wit to draw a belt-knife and cut at his bonds, but at the sight of her, he strikes out with the blade.

A swipe of her hand sends the weapon spinning from his grasp.

It is fascinating to watch them as they drown. How their eyes bulge with terror and their cheeks with held air. How they fight against nothing . . . tenacious to the bitter end, even after all hope is gone. She watches last breaths burst from their lips, wavering bubbles like malformed pearls and moon-jellies.

She swims to the shallows, then to the shore. She carries her beloved onto a beach of gritty pebbles.

He vomits up sea-water from his lungs, throat and nose. He coughs. He chokes and spits. The blood flows more freely from a gash on his brow. His eyelids flutter.

"Who . . . who are you?" he says.

"Eylig," she tells him.

He seems about to say more, but then his head lolls and he is unconscious again. He is more badly hurt than she thought.

There is a clamor from further up the pebbled beach. Men from the fort, having witnessed the disaster, come running with torches sputtering in the rain. They call back and forth with considerable excitement.

For a moment, she hesitates, torn by indecision.

She has him now . . . has touched and held him, spoken to him, told him her name. He is hers!

But if she takes him to the sea now, he might not survive.

She cannot lose him.

She cannot leave him.

She cannot let him die.

The men and torches are getting closer.

She decides.

* * *

Jarl Wulfstan proved to be far less fearsome than his reputation would have it. He welcomed the survivors into his hall. He had their injuries seen to. He fed them and clothed them. He treated them as guests.

Of the dead, he was no less courteous. Those whose corpses could be found, or that washed ashore in the following days, he had decently buried in a field behind his hall, setting an outline of stones in the shape of a longship to surround their grave.

The war-lord did, of course, claim as his own fair salvage and plunder what goods or provisions were yet of any worth. But he was generous enough to let the Wind-Chaser's men—the living and the dead—keep any small valuables they had on them at the time.

Farald, with a mud-plaster dried and itching on his head, ran the necklace of fire-worked glass beads through his fingers. He'd kept it wrapped in a scrap of cloth, in the belt-purse where he also kept his silver.

It was not much money, and he had been counting on more as his share of the trade-profits. That would not happen now. But it was small price enough to pay for his life. Many of his friends, his ship-mates and oar-brothers, had not been so lucky.

He could not, with much clarity, recall how he had made it to shore.

The storm, yes, the storm he would never forget. The storm and the terrible wave, but, after that it was muddled. He did not know what struck his head, or how he came loose from the oar-bench he'd been lashed to.

The jarl's men discovered him on the beach and brought him to the hall. One of them said he thought he had seen someone else there, rushing toward the surf as if to go back and save another . . . but no one came forward, and no one else knew who it might have been.

When Farald dredged at the silt of his memory, he sometimes half-remembered a face . . . a plain, pale face with dark eyes. . .

"You imagined it, just as Utwald said before," Gullaug told him. "Just as you imagined it that night we sheltered under the outcrop and you woke us with your shouting over nothing at all."

"You saw her," Farald protested. "When we stayed with Utbranni."

"I was drunk," said Gullaug. "I might have seen my own sister and not known any better."

"It was the same girl."

"The same one you say you saw when we traded for fleeces? The same one you say you saw at the fish-camp?"

"Yes. . ."

"You think she follows you, without ship's sail or eagle's wing, and now you think she saved you from drowning?"

"I know how mad it sounds," Farald said.

"More than mad. Impossible. She'd have to be one of Njord's own daughters, a wave-maiden, driving a porpoise-drawn chariot. And if you believe that, Farald, you've been listening to too many sagas and songs."

* * *

Eylig waits.

She must.

She dares not attempt to venture into the hillfort, which is surrounded by an earth-works wall topped with brambles, and defended by a war-band of many fierce armed and

152

armored men.

And she knows that her beloved will not stay there long. He will return to a ship, return to the sea.

In the meantime, she has his harp. She found it in the strew of wreckage. It is un-broken, but whether it is ruined or not, she does not know. Its leather case was water-fast enough against rain and sea-spray, not immersion.

When she plucks at the strings, they make pained dying-animal sounds. This might merely be her lack of skill.

She keeps it for him. Cherishes it. Anticipates the moment she'll return it to him, how delighted he'll be. Even if it does prove ruined, the fact that she's kept and cher-ished it for thought of him cannot help but move his heart by the gesture of her devo-tion.

So, she waits. She watches from afar.

He will return to the sea.

He will.

* * *

A few of his surviving ship-mates decided to accept Jarl Wulfstan's offer and stay on. Farald, however, wanted only to get home. He was promised passage when next the jarl's biggest ship—the Ice-Wolf, a large drakkar—went to bargain for timber.

Farald's time passed uneasily in Hillfort at first. He felt certain that he would catch sudden sight of the pale, plain-faced girl. But he did not.

He dreamed of her sometimes . . . of sensing a presence or hearing a step . . . of opening his eyes to find those dark ones peering down into his . . . of a name he could not, upon waking, remember.

His head ached for a while even after the itchy mud-plaster was removed. The bruise on his forehead went through vivid hues like the north-lights gone sickly. When the last yellowed tinge faded, he was still left with a scar that ran unevenly from hairline to eyebrow.

At last, he agreed that Gullaug must be right. He had seen her, once, and imagined the rest.

The Ice-Wolf set sail on a fair day, the skies stretching blue in all directions to merge with a misty line at the horizon. In the distance, whales breached and spouted, showing again why this was called the whale-road. A lone great petrel glided above, grey-tipped wings extended.

The jarl himself did not sail with them, but came down to see them off. They made sacrifice of a yearling ram, slitting its throat, catching the blood in a bowl, mixing it with mead, pouring an offering to the gods, then giving each man a hearty drink of it. The ram's woolly head, Jarl Wulfstan held aloft by the stubby horns.

"Njord see these men safely on their journey!" he called, hurling it as far as he could. It struck with a splash, bobbed back up, and then sank.

A brisk wind blew to fill the white-and-black-striped sail, ruffling the proud wolf's-tail nailed as a banner to the top of the mast. The narrow hull sliced a clean foam-track in the water.

Hillfort receded with a goodly speed.

NJORD'S DAUGHTER

But, Farald, standing at the ship's prow with his long red hair streaming, was gripped yet again by that unsettling disquiet.

* * *

They are vigilant men.

Alert for enemies and danger? For prey and opportunity?

She does not know. She does not care.

What matters is that they keep guard even by night. They have a dog—a *dog*!—with them, an immense shaggy elk-hound with an absurd curl of tail and a skull-splitting bark.

When darkness and fog swallow the ship so completely that the guards can see no further than an arm-length, and sounds are so strangely muffled they might have had tufts of fleece plugging their ears, she no more than sets a hand on the rail than the wretched beast smells her.

Does it never sleep?

It comes on the run, baying and howling, and these vigilant men are ever quick to respond.

She cannot get to her beloved. She can only follow.

They cross a sea-stretch and sail into a fjord of clear deep-green water. To either side, meadowland rises in gentle slopes toward dense forests. Higher still are snow-peaks and stone spires snagging the clouds.

Soon, there are farmsteads, sheep-fields and cow-pastures. Folk stop in their work to wave greeting. Children run along the fjord's edge, cheering, brandishing sticks as if they too are bold Vikings. The men wave back, and cheer as well.

Ahead is a large settlement of log houses. It is a lumber-camp where tall trees are felled to be shaped into strakes and masts, planks and oars. Other longships and knarrs are being built, repaired or refitted.

The settlement bustles and flourishes with people. Eylig slips ashore. She finds it easy enough to mix with them, just one more among many.

She chooses a place where she can wait and watch from concealment. The harp, in its leather case, she grips in anxious hands.

When he is away from the ship, that is when she'll go to him. She'll hold out the harp-case. How eager she is to see his surprise and delight!

Her beloved says his farewells. He moves through the village.

His gaze seems searching.

He is looking for *her*!

Eylig starts to approach.

"Farald!" cries a voice.

He turns swiftly.

A young woman runs toward him. He also breaks into a run. Those nearby look on, grinning, as the two meet.

Her beloved sweeps the woman up in his arms, her blonde braid flying. Both are laughing and crying and talking all at once, showering each others' faces with kisses. He brings out a strand of fireworked glass beads to affix around her slim throat. They kiss with even more ardor.

154

And Eylig, clutching the leather harp-case tight to her chest, retreats into hiding again.

* * *

Farald set the hatchet to lean against a stump. He wiped sweat from his brow, then studied his palms, his smile rueful.

How it was that a man could pull hard at the oars, and still have parts of his hands left uncallused . . . yet, there they were, red places that might grow into blisters.

Despite doing all manner of ship's labor for long months at sea, he simply was not accustomed to the hewing of wood. Not only his hands felt it, but the muscles of his back, his arm-sinews, and the rest of him as well. But he did not begrudge his body the aches. They were well-earned, and would be well worth it.

He'd hoped to come home with considerable silver. The deaths of Utwald and so many others had left him just glad to come home with his life.

Happily, Asgrina's family felt the same, and consented to their marriage. Her uncle had gifted them with this fine parcel of land, not far from where he had his own modest longhouse.

There was still much work to be done. He needed to dig out the well-spring, setting flat stones around it. The field would have to be readied for the next grain-planting. Once he'd built the byre, they'd buy a good milk-cow.

Until then, they had chickens . . . Asgrina's garden of vegetables and herbs was already sprouting . . . the fish-traps sunk in the fjord kept them provided. . .

Best of all, most important, they had each other.

He smiled again, this one much less rueful. He sang as he made his way back to the house. It was humble, a single long room, not lavishly furnished, but he wouldn't have traded it for a king's hall.

A leather case, worn and battered, leaned against the threshold.

Farald stopped in his tracks. The song died from his lips. He set down the hatchet and bundle of sticks.

The case was still there.

The case was his harp-case!

Which could not be possible. He'd lost it when the Wind-Chaser sank.

He crouched and picked the case up. The weight was familiar. So was the harp within, if wood-warped and water-stained.

On the nape of his neck, the skin began to crawl.

* * *

Her beloved is more beautiful than ever, stripped to the waist and sweat-gleaming, hair pulled back and tied with a cord.

He slowly turns, still crouching. He sees her.

Now is when! Now!

His eyes go very wide.

"You," he says. "Eylig."

The surprise is there, yes, the surprise, absolutely.

155

NJORD'S DAUGHTER

But . . . the delight . . . where is the delight, the welcome, the love?
Why does the color drain from him so that his face goes ashen?
"Farald—"
She's barely uttered his name when he springs to his feet.
"Asgrina!" he shouts.
There is no answer.
"Asgrina!" Again he shouts it, with increasing desperation.
When there is for a second time no reply, he whirls on Eylig again.
"Where is my wife?" he demands.
"Farald, listen to me." She holds out a hand to him, but her beloved ignores it.
He rushes into the house, out of the house, around the house to the garden, past the pen where hens peck, shouting for the woman. He carries the harp in one hand, but it is as if he's forgotten he has it.
Eylig follows him. She moves now with much less of a limp, having gotten more used to this clumsiness of walking.
She tells him how she adores him, how she's come so far and done so much. He continues ignoring her. Then a glint in the grass catches his eye. He stoops and plucks something from the ground. It is a small fireworked glass bead.
He finds another, and another, and a scattered trail of them that lead to the fjord.

* * *

The water was so clear that it seemed Asgrina lay encased in green amber. Her white arms drifted. Her skirt and apron billowed. Her fair hair wavered like a golden cloud around her head.
Farald leaped in and swam down. It was deeper than it looked. A large rock had been set upon her stomach as a weight. He heaved it off. Asgrina's back arched and her arms swept gracefully to either side as she floated upward.
He burst to the surface with her. He struggled onto the bank with a strength he hadn't known he possessed. Gasping with horror as much as for breath, he lowered Asgrina to the grassy earth.
Any illusions of grace, billowing, wavering and clouds were gone. She dragged slack, dripping, motionless. Water ran from her mouth. She was cold. Cold and dead.
"This is how it must be," said the pale, plain-featured girl.
Eylig. It had come back to him as soon as he'd seen her.
He hadn't imagined it. He hadn't imagined any of it.
"What did you do?" he cried. "What do you want?"
"You," she said, as if he should have known. "Now we will be together."
"You killed her. You drowned my wife!"
"She was not the one you belong with."
A quaking rage replaced his horror. "You mad hag!"
The girl blinked, and when she did so, her strange dark eyes somehow changed. They became stranger, and darker. "Farald, I adore you. This grief will pass and you'll know it for the meaningless—"
"I would never be with *you*!"
"Don't say such things!" She stepped closer. He saw that although the shapeless

156

grey-green kirtle was the same, and the dank locks of hair, she moved with less of a hobbling gait. "I brought you your harp—"

"Get away from me!"

Before he entirely knew his own intentions, he'd sprung up, seizing the nearest object at hand. Which was, as it happened, the harp . . . wood-warped and water-stained, unweidly, woefully unsuited as a weapon.

He swung it with all his might just the same.

* * *

The harp smites her a violent blow to the temple. Eylig falls, reeling, feeling thin and salty blood gush down the side of her face.

The physical pain is enormous.

The other pain is far, far worse.

She stares up at him, her beloved, who stands over her now with his handsome face contorted in murderous fury.

He lifts the harp. He means to bludgeon her with it as if it were Thor's own hammer.

She blinks again. A slow blink that leaves her eyes revealed as they truly are . . . glistening black orbs, shark's-eyes. The eyes of the sea.

He falters. "What . . . what are you?"

Eylig's lips drew apart to reveal rows of teeth like ivory needles.

Understanding seeps into him. He speaks in a stunned whisper. "Njord's daughter?"

Njord's daughter, yes, but no alluring wave-maiden from the songs lonely sailors like to sing. . .

"I saved your life," she says, the words hissing through her teeth.

Her beloved lowers the harp. His throat works as he swallows. "Did you kill the others as well?" he asks. "The men of the <u>Wind-Chaser</u>? Was that storm your doing?"

"Forget them. Forget her. You and I—"

"No!"

He attacks her with renewed rage. She almost fails to raise her arm in time. The harp crashes into it instead of her head. She feels and hears the bone snap. The next one, she tries to twist away from. The harp slams into her back with such force that the instrument breaks apart. Her beloved is left with wood fragments, some splintered thick and sharp as spear-points.

Eylig screams. If she'd been underwater, porpoises would have thrashed with agitation in the deep. Up here, it is shrill and piercing enough to make him recoil.

She flings herself into the fjord and swims to safety. Clumsily, with her lamed arm. Painfully, with her head bleeding, her back and ribs throbbing. She has never been clumsy or painful in the water before.

Only when she's far enough from shore does she surface, facing him where he stands on the bank.

"You *are* mine," she tells him, then dives away.

* * *

NJORD'S DAUGHTER

The skalds, sages and wise-women he spoke to all gave the same reply.

If she wanted him, she would follow. Wherever the seas reached, she would follow. She would find him.

If he fought, and managed somehow to kill her, he would surely draw Njord's wrath ... which would also extend wherever the seas reached.

His only chance, his only hope, was to forsake the sea forever. To never again sail the wide grey whale road, to make his home in no coastal settlement, on no fjord, by no river that flowed to the sea.

He knew the tale of Njord and Skadi, did he not? How the sea-god had been unable to abide the mountain peaks, while the giantess refused to dwell in the depths?

Farald did.

And so, he did what he must do.

He packed what possessions he could bear on his back, and went inland.

Inland, ever inland.

And higher, ever higher.

He traveled through thin-aired valleys where no trees grew, and agile goats grazed on moss and white flowers. He traveled across broad frost-covered plains thick with reindeer-herds.

Finally he came to a great mountain range of stark snow-crowned cliff-faces. Glaciers made mantles of ice on their slopes. Black crevasses split jagged cracks into the stone. Fuming gases spewed like dragon's-breath from holes in the earth. Gaping craters bubbled with boiling mud.

Inhospitable as it was, hardy folk did yet dwell there. Hot springs steamed, the water foul-smelling but said to have healing powers. Winter hares abounded, as did fat tufted grouse, hunted by men and foxes and lynx.

Narrow trails and dangerous passes connected one stronghold to another. Farald was making his way along one of these when, without warning the deadly rockslide struck.

He revived, groaning. Every part of him ached. He felt jarred, bruised and battered. Gritty rock-dust caked bloodied scrapes on his body. It caught in his throat and lungs, making him cough.

His legs were pinned, buried, half-crushed beneath boulders. He could not shift them. He could not get free.

Farald tried calling for help, though expected no answer. The chances of some other traveler being near enough to—

Then came the sound of footsteps approaching.

She appeared around the bend, dark eyes filled with satisfaction.

It could *not* be her!

But it was. Oh, it was.

Instead of the old faded wool kirtle, she wore a tattered reindeer-hide, her feet wrapped in scraps of leather. No hint of a limp marred her gait. She moved sure-footed as any mountain goat.

A whimper escaped him, an unmanly mewling sob.

"You knew," Eylig said, smiling, "that I was Njord's daughter. What you did not realize is that I was Skadi's as well."

WATCHER IN THE CITY
DEREK MUK

May 1977

Lidiya rung up the customer at the cash register, bagging their purchases of the latest issues of *Eerie* and *Creepy*. "Thanks. Have a nice day."

It was a warm day and she opened the front door using a door stopper. Then she returned to her stocking duties, inserting various comic books into their respective bins. A couple of people called in sick and she had to hold down the fort today. No problem, she liked working alone anyway. The less distractions the better.

Lidiya was a tall Caucasian woman with a 'thick,' muscular body, having short, jet black dyed hair and a healthy golden tan that could be attributed to her daily jogs and exercise regimen. She wore a tight black tank top that revealed a snake tattoo on her wide tanned back, and had on a short matching black skirt, exposing her giant, muscular thighs and calves. A few guys asked if they could arm wrestle her and Lidiya always accepted the invitation. And *always* won. But she was modest about her victories.

Seconds later, the front door bell chimed, indicating a customer had come in. She turned to see a young, slender man around her age step in, sporting a purple Mohawk and shaved head, dressed in a black leather jacket and torn jeans.

"Hi, Lidiya," the man smiled.

"Hello." She didn't return a grin. And she vaguely remembered his name . . . Ray or Raymond, or something like that. Truth was, he was a regular customer but she paid him no mind these days, not since the numerous times he asked her out. She politely declined his offers. But the guy kept inviting her to this or that. Man, he was persistent! Lidiya told her boss and he considered banning him from the shop but Lidiya told him she could handle it. Actually, Ray or whatever his name was, was honestly a nice, smart guy, but she just wasn't interested in dating him.

Surprisingly, he didn't pester her today and made a straight beeline for the 'Recent Releases' section, flipping through an issue of *The Incredible Hulk*. The store was empty except for the two of them. The radio near the cash register was playing "Dirty Deeds Done Dirt Cheap" by AC/DC.

Lidiya watched him from the corner of her eye as she continued stocking, glad he wasn't bugging her. She observed him moving on to the 'Erotic Comics and Art' section later, an area with a hand written sign that read: *'Adults only! No one under 18 allowed!'*

Lidiya was proud of that sign. She hand crafted it herself using various colored inks. That was the extent of her artistic talents, at least on paper. Now music, that was a different story. Rock and punk music was her passion, and she kept honing her skills as a guitarist and singer nightly with her band.

She went to the cash register when Ray or whatever his name was walked up to the counter with some comics.

He flashed her a friendly grin. "Busy day?"

"Hardly," she replied, gesturing at the empty store with her head. "Everyone must be at the beach."

"Wish you were there, don't you?"

She took some bills he gave her, producing some change for him. "I don't mind working." She didn't look at him as she said it.

"Hey, have you seen that new movie, *Star Wars*? It's awesome."

Lidiya nodded. "I've seen it twice already." She handed him his bag.

Ray paused for a moment, mustering his courage to say something. He looked at her and said: "I hear you like to arm wrestle."

"Who told you that?"

"I just heard." His grin turning faintly mischievous.

She shrugged, not smiling. "Yeah, it's fun."

"Can I arm wrestle you?"

What's this skinny guy thinking?! I'll beat him in seconds! "Uhhh, not now. I'm busy working."

He paused a beat, as if debating whether to chance his luck or not. Then he simply said: "Have a good day," and left.

June 1977

It was ten minutes till seven. Lidiya finished dusting the store's front window display of Mego action figures. There was Batman and Robin duking it out with the Joker, Captain Kirk and Mr. Spock caught in a phaser battle with a Klingon and Spiderman was engaged in a fist fight with the Green Goblin. Another clever concoction of hers.

Ray or whatever his name was, suddenly stepped into the shop and bought some Richard Corben comic books. She noticed his Motorhead shirt.

"Cool shirt," Lidiya commented, handing him some change and his receipt.

He smiled. "Thanks."

After her shift ended at seven she split, shrugging into her black leather jacket with the Motorhead logo on the back of it. As she was walking away from the store, someone behind her said: "Nice jacket."

Lidiya spun around and faced Ray or whatever his name was. He was finishing a cigarette. She forced herself not to break out into a smile. "Thanks."

"Want a cig?"

"I don't smoke."

"That's good! Stay healthy. Me, I've been smoking since I was thirteen so it's hard to quit. Know what I mean?"

"Yeah. Take up some exercise. That'll keep you healthy."

"What kind of exercise do you do?"

"I run and lift weights." She was wearing her tight black tank top again and a short black miniskirt. She noticed Ray checking her out. She looked good! Her thick, muscular thighs and calves turned him on.

"Good for you! Keep it up."

"See you later," she said, and walked off.

"Bye."

* * *

Unbeknownst to Lidiya, Ray followed her on her walk home along San Francisco's Geary Boulevard. He kept a discreet distance behind her, hiding behind garbage cans, cars, or whatever else he could shield himself behind when she looked around. About fifteen minutes later she made a right on Thirty-Fourth Avenue and entered an apartment building.

Ray saw an abandoned warehouse across the street from the apartment building and ran to it. He was able to pick the lock of a side door and snuck in, making his way to a third story office facing Lidiya's building. The office was dusty and full of cobwebs but it would do just fine. After sweeping the window free of cobwebs he looked at the apartment building and saw that a light was on in a unit directly across from where he stood. And luckily, it was Lidiya's apartment.

She didn't see him. She took off her black leather jacket and went into a room where Ray couldn't see her. Minutes later, she came back into view, completely naked! Well, naked except for a pair of leopard skin leg warmers that were around her calves.

Ray's jaw dropped open. Her body was amazing. Nice tan, brawny arms, medium-sized breasts with big, dark nipples, and a big, curvy ass. What caught his eye especially was the dark, hairy thatch of hair covering her pussy.

The show was about to begin! He quickly whipped out his pair of binoculars and watched her do some stretches in the middle of the living room before pumping some iron. She did three sets of squats while carrying a bar with two big plates on each end. He had a great view of her backside, admiring her big butt. His binoculars were so powerful that he was able to see the beads of sweat trickling down her back. Wow!

After the squats, Lidiya sat in a chair of a leg curl machine, using her strong legs to lift some heavy weights. She was facing him this time but still didn't see him. After four sets of this she moved to a leg press machine, added some weights, sat down in it, placing her bare feet on a metal plate raised slightly above her and began lifting. This girl was an animal!

Ray had an enormous erection as he watched. Lidiya lifted some dumbbell weights later on a bench, and she topped off the evening by doing some naked yoga. Ray's eyes bulged out. This was way better than a strip club! He'd do anything to be in her apartment right now. Well, almost anything. He could literally smell the sweat from her body at that very moment.

* * *

The next afternoon, Ray followed Lidiya home again. But this time, instead of holing himself up in the warehouse office, he waited until someone opened the apartment building's front door and snuck in behind them. People did that all the time. Then he scrambled up to Lidiya's unit on the third floor.

Unfortunately, he couldn't pick the deadbolt lock on her door, so he waited around the corner. About twenty five minutes later, she came out of her apartment wearing a black bathrobe, a plastic trash bag in her hand. While she went to dump the garbage, he ran to her door, smiling when the door handle turned.

Her unit smelled of toast. He quickly hid himself in her bedroom closet. Moments later, he heard the apartment door open and close. The sound of bare feet padding on the kitchen linoleum. He sneaked out of the closet and observed her working out naked again through a crack in her bedroom door. Now he was closer to her than ever! He had an erection again.

After replacing some weights, Lidiya knelt down on the carpet and began doing some yoga. Her large butt was inches away from his eager face now. Oh, Lord! A river of sweat ran down one of her butt cheeks. It was warm in the apartment even though the windows were all open.

Seconds passed before she got up and headed for the bedroom. Oh, shoot! Ray didn't have enough time to hide in the closet and she caught him red handed.

Lidiya stared at him, covering herself with her leather jacket. "What the hell?! How did you get in here?"

Ray was just as shocked as she was, backing away. She was so close to him now he could detect the perspiration from the gorgeous body of hers.

"Answer me! What the heck are you doing in here?"

His mouth was a giant O. "Uhhh . . . I . . . I . . . I . . ."

She stood there naked, staring at him, waiting for a reasonable explanation. When he didn't respond, she persisted: "Well? Tell me! Don't just stand there like an idiot! C'mon!"

"Uhhh, I . . . I . . . I . . ."

"Spit it out!"

"I . . . I just wanted to ask you if you wanted to arm wrestle."

She continued staring at him for a moment, and then said: "Well, why didn't you just say so!"

He was surprised. "What?"

"You heard me!" She threw her leather jacket back on the bed. Now her big, dark nipples were right in his face, teasing him, enticing him, seducing him, and doing an erotic dance before him. His underwear was all wet from pre-cum. *And* that big hairy dark bush covering her pussy was right in his face! *God help me!* Well, he got what he wanted. Be careful what you wished for.

Her tall frame towered over him. "C'mon, let's do it then!" She took his arm and led him out to the kitchen, where they placed their elbows on the counter and got ready to arm wrestle.

Can't believe this! he thought. *Wrestling with a naked woman!*

"One, two, three!" Lidiya said, and they started. She knew this was gonna be a piece of cake. No way a skinny guy like him could win! No chance at all!

That's why she was shocked, her mouth gaping in fact, when his little arm over-powered hers and was within inches of slamming it on the counter. The combination of her naked body sweat and salty breath aroused him even more.

No way! she thought. *This isn't happening! This is impossible! How can he be win-ning?!*

With a triumphant grunt, Ray or whatever his name was, slammed her arm down on the kitchen counter. She stared at him in disbelief.

He shot her a proud, cocky grin. "Rematch?"

"Okay."

They set their elbows on the counter again.

"One, two, three!" Lidiya said.

She was astonished when Ray beat her again.

"Hey, I did it!" he said. "C'mon, give me some credit. Or at least a prize."

She regarded him for a moment. "What do you want? A date?"

Ray smiled. "That would be nice . . . but I had something else in mind."

"What is it?"

He got closer to her and slapped her big bare ass and whispered sexily into her ear: "Let's just fuck."

That's when Lidiya went straight to her bedroom and got on her bed, waiting for him.

SHE LIKES SURPRISES
NATHAN ROBINSON

I had hidden myself away in the tight confines of the hallway cupboard, because it was dark in there, and also I could see out through the horizontal slats in the door. I could see out but no one could see in unless they opened the door of course. But I didn't think anyone would do that, no one knew I was there. When she returned, I planned to jump out and give her, her present. She likes surprises; this was to be one of my grandest and most romantic gestures yet.

The problem was I didn't really know what time she would be back from work. She should've been back, but she hadn't arrived. Every ten minutes or so, I would check my watch against the light coming in through the slats of the door. The last time I checked it was nearly six o'clock. I couldn't see much of anything. The sun had gone down on the chilly February day, the fourteenth to be precise, and the streetlights had come on. The street lamps outside the building didn't provide sufficient light to the end of the hall, so I guessed it to be closer to nine o'clock. I don't know why I thought that, I've always been good at guessing the time. Sometimes I'd guess what time it was before looking at my watch. More often than not, I was right, give or take a minute or two.

I should have brought a torch, but quickly dismissed the idea straight away. I had more than enough to carry as it was. I didn't bring my phone. I never took my phone with me. It's too precious to lose.

The wooden box was her present, to be given to her as soon as she returned.

My legs had started to hurt yet again, the pain cycling in spastic waves. They'd started hurting earlier that afternoon, and after the first hour, the cramps in my legs started to tremble. At one point I thought that I would collapse into a pathetic heap on the floor. Deciding an action should be taken to allow me to remain hidden, I placed the present on the shelf next to me. Then I placed my palms on the sturdy shelves either side of me, lifted myself up, bringing my legs up close as I could to my chest. I stretched my legs down, twiddling and flexing my brittle toes. My muscles rejoiced and sang relief at the feeling of movement.

The cupboard was small, but I could stand up without touching any of the sides. It was filled with spare sheets and towels and the like. A row of old ladies shoes sat tidied along the back wall; battered walking boots that had seen better days lay tumbled over each other in one corner and a pair of Wellingtons encrusted with dried mud from some winters walk in the other. Also, my plastic yellow carrier bag with the tin of red paint and brush, sat on the shelf beside me.

I had considered going for a walk through her flat, stretch my legs, and maybe get myself a snack to keep up my energy. But if she were to come back suddenly, I wouldn't know till I heard the key in the lock, and that would ruin everything. All my preparations would be flushed down the toilet.

I had disciplined myself beyond this.

I waited, she was worth it. I thought maybe I could turn the hall light on, just so I could see what time it was on my watch. No, I told myself. I mentally slapped my hand in the process. She had gone to work when it was light, so she had turned all the lights off as she left, and therefore was expecting to come back to a place of darkness. I thought maybe I could just check quickly, pop the light on, see what time it was, then return back to the cupboard unnoticed. The problem was that the switch was at the far end of the hall, next to the main door. What if she were to walk in while I was in the hall? I couldn't risk been noticed until she was well inside.

Behind me, beyond the wall, I could hear the old lady next door with her TV on too loud. Some dumb game show, I assumed. The audience cheered and clapped like automated seals. The walls were cheap and all too thin in the old blocks of crumbling council accommodation. But I didn't care did I? It didn't matter.

I tried to think where she would be; out with friend's maybe? She never stayed out this late, she was usually home by six, seven at the latest.

What if something bad had happened to her? I dreaded the thought, trying to place it to the back of my mind. But horrible scenarios forced their way back to the front.

What if she had been raped or robbed or worse, then the surprise would be ruined, all that preparation pissed down the drain. After all that, some random stranger could just come along and ruin everything. *No not now after everything*, that couldn't happen. My surprise would have been for nothing.

I opened the box and checked the present was still there. I felt for the smooth formed metal with my fingers. I couldn't see it any more, just a dull glow in the darkness. I found it in a pawnshop in an alleyway just off the High street. It called to me from the glass display case amongst all the other pretty shiny things.

It sang. It sang to me.

Even though it was second-hand, that didn't matter, everything bought is second-hand anyway. I wanted to be modest, so I didn't pick the most expensive, or the biggest. "Just something simple," I'd asked the man behind the counter. He picked it up and placed it in a box for safekeeping.

"Beautiful piece of craftsmanship, a treasure I'm sure." He had smiled, placing the box in a paper bag as he sealed the deal.

I thanked him, smiled and then left.

That had been earlier in the morning. I compulsively checked every hour or so to make sure it hadn't slipped from my grasp. It was truly beautiful, a work of art.

I tensed as I heard a muffled voice in the hallway outside the flat. I grabbed the box from the shelf, making any unnecessary noise before she opened the door. A silken sheet of sweat washed over my body. A dirty puddle of slickness formed in the straining curve of my spine.

This is it, I told myself, she was back; the moment of truth. I hoped she liked the present.

A couple of kids passed like a rabble within the hallway and carried on to the premises down the hall. I heard a door open, slam, and then an abrupt, eerie silence which cut through me deeper than any blade ever could.

The racing fear subsided, but the clinging sweat remained, prickling me with a slick sheen of oily salt. I just wanted to get it over and done with. Get the whole thing out the way. Once I had given her the present, I wouldn't be scared anymore. I just had to sit and wait, bide my time.

SHE LIKES SURPRISES

The silence and darkness invited me to a welcome sleep, heavy weights pulled down on my lids. I needed a coffee. The central heating had come on automatically, and I was starting to sweat buckets. My face and hair were sodden. It ran down my back and into the seat of my pant. My T-shirt clung to me like an unwanted second skin. I needed a glass of cold water to settle my core temperature. Maybe even an iced coffee to settle everything down would cure my ills. My beverage fantasies caused my stomach to gurgle, increasing the strain on my bulging bladder.

The heat was also making me tired and jittery. This wasn't like me! Wasn't like me at all. Why I hadn't taken my jacket off, I don't know. I couldn't of exactly hung it up in the hall, as she'd know I was here as soon as she walked in. I wanted to take her completely by surprise. I had gone through all this trouble for her. I had planned it to a tee; it had taken days of preparation. She would open the door, hang her coat up on one of the hooks, like she always did. Then she would say hello to her green Macaw she kept in the cage in the living room, check her answer phone messages then make herself a drink.

But this night, she wouldn't. It was going to be very special for both of us.

She would see the flowers, the message I had painted on her kitchen tiles in foot high letters, daubed in Valentine crimson red paint. The paint had run while I did it. I had to mop the edges down with a kitchen towel to keep the wording, somewhat legible. I had hoped it hadn't run since I had been in the hallway cupboard. That would have been a terrible disappointment. All of that effort wasted.

The heat was becoming too much for me. Dizzy spells circled the fluid in my head like drowsy boozed up sharks, threatening my collapse in the tiny cupboard. My legs ached to run and gallop as the lactic acid burned away at my eager, though waning stance. I needed some air. I realized I was still clutching the box in my hand. I placed the box back on the shelf beside me and removed my jacket in the confines of the cramped closet. It was a good thing I wasn't claustrophobic. I wasn't scared of much, not even death. When it came to it, I guessed I wouldn't be that frightened when the Reaper came a knockin'.

Women. Girls. Ladies.

I had always been afraid of the opposite sex as a kid. Couldn't talk to them. I'd clam up and sweat. I'd get tongue-tied, make my excuses and run off. Not that I couldn't get the ladies nowadays. I wasn't an ugly mutt. I'm quite cute, so I've been told. Just nervous at first. Soon you learn, if you keep at it. You learn stuff. Techniques and the like from books and films. Just drop 'em a line from a movie or paraphrase a poem and soon enough they are putty in my hands.

I dropped my jacket on the floor behind me. Next-door the quiz show had finished, excessive clapping thundered as the credits rolled. At least someone was having fun. The clapping ceased, replaced by the warm dramatic opening theme from a soap opera.

Before I knew it, my hand had pushed the thin wooden door open. The outside of the closet was warm, but not even half as hot as the accumulated conditions caused by my body heat inside the cupboard. The hallway felt like the Antarctic in comparison to what I'd been accustomed to over the last few hours. I took a few breaths of thankful fresher air. I needed to pee so bad it hurt my stomach; a ball of steaming fluid ached to burst its way out of me as the pressure mounted. If I didn't do something I was very likely going to piss my pants right there and then.

166

There was a mop and bucket in the closet. I seriously considered using it to relieve myself. But I thought about the smell. Would I be able to put up with the pong of the phosphorus vapor? I didn't intend to find out and had held it in for as long as I could. They're two ways to the bathroom from where I was stood. I could either go left, turn right into the living room, past the balcony, through the kitchen and then to the bathroom. Or I could turn right from the closet, turn left into the kitchen then straight across into the bathroom on the far wall. The kitchen and living room were both one big room. The other three doors in the hallway aside from the closet were the front door, the master bedroom and the smaller second bedroom, which I guessed she reserved for guests who stayed the night.

I gently shut the closet door behind me, leaving the present and my jacket behind. I wouldn't be long I guessed, no point taking them with me; it was worth the risk if it meant avoiding pissing myself.

I headed right then turned left into the kitchen. It was lighter than in the closet. Light from the city beamed in from the balcony window. It was raining; spots of orange-cast liquid clung to the window in a scattering of random islands of moisture. I could make out the shape of the dozen red roses I had put in a vase on the worktop. The message on the wall remained; I couldn't make out any runs from what I could see. I continued to the toilet. I turned the light on and had a piss. After I finished I leant over the sink and set the cold tap running, lapping up some reviving fluid to cure my parched throat. I hadn't drank or spoken in hours. I splashed some water on my face to refresh and cool myself. I looked in the mirror and hummed, clearing a clog in my throat. The energy efficient light bulb hadn't quite warmed up yet, so my face was bathed in semi-darkness. My eyes became dark and hollow if I leant my head forward, down from the light. Menacing, I thought, my face from the dark could scare the shit out of her. I flushed the toilet and turned off the light, then headed back into the kitchen.

The Macaw was sleeping in the living room. Good.

I leant in closer to the lettering on the kitchen tiles; I began to read my words.

I love you. Would you do me the honor of—I stopped reading. A thin trickle of paint *had* dribbled down from the overhang on the *r* in *honor*. I ripped off a sheet of kitchen towel, wrapped it around my index finger, and then traced the sticky line down to the lettering below. It had settled in the grout in-between the tiles. It would rub off eventually. The message wouldn't stay forever. It could easily be removed with the appropriate cleaning products.

Never mind.

My concentration was suddenly shifted from the dark red lettering in the kitchen, to the sudden sound of metal clicking into metal. The sound of a key into the Yale lock of the front door. I froze for about half a second too long, until the adrenalin started pumping its urgent chemical wares through my veins and vessels. Every aching muscle from my skull to my sphincter contracted, in readiness to flee.

She was back!

With an unsure urgency, I headed into the living room, knocking past the birdcage waking the Macaw to a rude squawk. I jumped behind the sofa and crouched down while the bird let his annoyances be known. A beam of light blazed in as the flat door opened, cutting through the plumes of dust motes I had disturbed.

Giggling voices.

Male *and* female.

The bird squawked. A primeval shriek when a tiger or other similar apex predator stalks beneath the boughs of the tree they call home. *He was talking to me.*

"Relax Johnny Boy, It's only Mummy," she assured the bright green avian.

"You never told me you had a kid," the man asked, his voice tinged with genuine worry that the presence of a child would spoil his night.

She laughed, bright and young and beautiful. I hated it. "Ha! *Your face!* It's only a bird, Johnny is my Macaw."

"Does he talk?" His voice had brightened as well; I could see his broad, toothy smile emerging in my head. I wanted to punch out his teeth already.

"Sometimes, when he can be bothered."

"Enough of that bird, let me concentrate on *this* bird," he announced cheekily, followed by a growl like a primitive beast.

She giggled. A door was clicked and pushed open, the underside swishing over the soft pile of the carpet. The front door closed, encasing me in the safety of darkness once again. The bedroom door closed. I couldn't hear what they were saying, music started to play. A slow thumping bass beat, then more laughter from the girl and him, followed by a high, excited giggle that caused me to physically shudder.

During their conversation I had been crouched down, my eyes wide and fearful, the adrenalin coursing through my body so fast that I could swear that they could hear my heart beating out from the top of my throat. I'd slapped a hand over my mouth so it wouldn't beat out any louder and reveal my hidey place.

This wasn't part of the plan. This wasn't part of the surprise at all. She had found a boyfriend. When the hell did that happen? This Valentines was supposed to be her and *me*, nobody else.

Keep calm and carry on.

The guy laughed out loud, so did she.

I considered leaving, taking my present and my jacket from the cupboard and leave like nothing happened— she would have never known I was here.

Then I remembered the foot high red lettering I had daubed across the kitchen wall.

Crap.

Leave it, I told myself. Cut and run. It made no sense to start trying to take the paint off. With the heating on it would be dried to crimson crust.

Just leave. Just leave, before the situation becomes more dangerous. It was clear I wouldn't be welcome.

I checked my watch. I could see in the dull light that glowed through the balcony window that it was now half-past nine in the evening. I had been standing in the closet since about four o'clock in the afternoon.

What was I, crazy?

I always thought that she'd be worth it, now I was just pissed off.

A faster dance beat emitted from the bedroom, half drowning a passionate moan from the girl. She called out the guy's name. *Dan.* She should've been calling mine, but it wasn't to be.

Cut your losses, get your stuff and just go. What if they heard me? What if the guy turned violent? I wasn't ready for that, not at all. I'm not the fighting sort. I was far too thin; I'd break if he punched me. I decided to make a move, sitting up from my crouching position. I planned my movements to get the tin of paint, my jacket and the present from the cupboard, then make a sharpish exit through the front door. I lifted a leg up over the sofa, the leather squeaking as I moved over it.

A sensual orange glow shone from the bedroom and into the kitchen. "Want a drink while I'm up? Where do you keep the beer?" the guy asked.

"Just a glass of water, I'm beginning to feel that wine," she droned.

I quickly pulled myself back and resumed my position, squatting and hiding like a doomed fearful spider, desperate not to get caught.

The kitchen florescent flickered on, heavy footsteps across the lino; they stuck and squeaked a little as he moved. He went to the toilet, used it, and flushed.

The sound of a cupboard opening; then a glass smashing on the floor.

"What the hell! Baby, did you do this?" A tremor held in his voice after the initial shock.

"Do what?" she called from the bedroom.

I imagined her to be naked, flawless, every inch glistening with lusted sweat. Spoiled by him now. Ruined. Soiled.

"This message on the wall, it's sick!"

"What's it say?" she asked, her voice sweet.

"Come and look for yourself . . . it's weird."

I could hear the beauty peel herself up from the creased bed and walk into the kitchen with dainty footsteps.

"Christ!" I heard her gasp. "Did you do this Dan?"

"Me, hell no, this is the first time I've been to your place, how could I have done it. I've been with you the entire night, remember?" His voice paused, then, "It's still a little bit wet."

Spots of red on his fingertips? Maybe he wiped them on a tea towel, or down the back of his leg. Did he sniff it, taste it? I very much doubt it.

"Who would do such a thing?"

I gulped, hoping to God I wasn't loud enough for them to hear me.

"I'm calling the police." She sounded serious.

I didn't need this. I nodded no, no, no.

"Check around, see if you can find anything else weird. Check the balcony as well. I'll get my phone. I'm freaked." Her footsteps faded as she headed back to the bedroom.

Dan stood in silence as he pondered his next move. If he checked the balcony, I would be discovered. The sofa backed up to the wall adjacent to the balcony door.

His patted footsteps approached, the bird wolf whistled as he passed. He ignored it. A shadow passed above me, then he came into view. He was topless with his back to me. His hand reached for the handle on the balcony door. Pushing it down, he opened it and stepped outside, letting cool air rush in. From here I could see he was completely naked and built like a small, firm bull.

"Can I have the police please," she asked , while I felt the fear creeping over me like a dangerous monster, nibbling away at ticks.

The balcony double backed onto itself, ending at the exterior wall of the bathroom. From my vantage point I could see him peering into the darkness looking for an intruder such as myself cowering in the shadows.

SHE LIKES SURPRISES

He stopped, resting his thick, root like hands on the railing, taking a deep lungful of night air. I could feel the fresh cold as it blew in. Dan didn't seem to mind; he had a rugby player's physique, tall and wide, not an ounce of fat on his marvelous, flawless body. His legs were astride. I guessed his eyes were shut; the weather didn't seem to bother him at all. He seemed to be enjoying it.

"Hello is that the police. . .? I think someone has broken into my home," she told a distant voice. I wanted to be long gone and into the next sun before they got here.

I decided that if I wanted to get out of here in at least one piece, now was the time for action. I took a deep breath to steady myself then edged my body forward cautiously towards the balcony door. I kept myself low. Not wanting to rouse suspicion by casting an unwanted shadow.

I sat crouched, my face inches behind the man's firm, mocking buttocks. Without a word of warning or hesitation, I grasped hold of his ankles and lifted him up, spreading and then dropping his legs onto my shoulders, pushing up with every measure of strength from my own puny legs. He levered over quite easily as his hands were still gripping the rail. Once he was so far up, his own weight carried him over the edge and into the deep pit of the night. I think I remember him crying out a fading "HEY!" as he vanished like a sprawling white star shape into the eating dark below. I didn't hear him land, but I imagined it was messy.

"Dan?" she called from the bedroom. I quickly retreated back from the balcony and into the living room. I hid behind the door. She left the bedroom and into the kitchen. I headed back into the hallway, hiding me from her.

With a voice tinged with worry, she called out Dan's name again as I opened the closet door and took the box from the shelf. Removing the present I felt its weight in my hand. It pleased me. I felt safer with it near me.

It sung. It sung to me.

Careful of not making any noise I placed the box back on the shelf.

She was on the balcony looking over. Her dressing gown billowed in the night wind. I stormed forward, passionately grabbing hold of a healthy chunk of hair and yanked her back throwing her onto the sofa. I advanced, stifling her scream with a gloved hand under her arm and over her mouth. I pushed my knee into her back, my other hand played with the present in front of her.

"It was supposed to be just me and you." I hissed.

She mumbled something I couldn't understand. I didn't care. She stunk of sweat and sex. She was dirty. Tarnished. Used. No good for anything now.

Her perfume remained a little; I think I could just make out the brand. I pushed her into the kitchen, in front of the red message on the tiles.

"I want you to read it!" I eased my hand off of her mouth, glinting the present near her eye then holding it against her throat.

"The police are coming." A whimper, I barely heard her.

"I know they won't make it in time; I'll be gone by then. Besides they take days to turn up, especially in a shit hole part of town such as this. You'll be lucky if they turn up at all." I was probably right. I jarred her head. "Read it!"

"I love you. . ." Again, barely a whisper.

I pressed the metal deeper into her skin, threatening a cut. "Louder." I wanted the neighbors to hear over their stupid TV shows.

"I love you!" More passion this time, a little better, I liked it.

"Go on," I coaxed.

"I . . . I love you. Would you . . . d . . . do me the honor of hurting me in ways I could never dream or fear. Do anything, defile me. . . " Her lips quivered, the tears flowed. "I am your plaything, I promise not to scream."

My words became hers; her vocalizing my schemes excited me. The jagged blood like writing, now showing it's true significance. The idea was that she would come in after work, into the kitchen, and then I would grab her and do whatever the fuck I wanted to her, then kill her. Seeing as she had brought her latest squeeze back and called the cops, that plan had gone tits up. The whore.

So much for a perfect Valentines.

I breathed a sigh of semi-relief. Closed my eyes and uttered a breathy, "Thank you."

It didn't take much, running the delicate blade across her even more delicate neck. I dropped her to the floor. She didn't scream as she promised, just gurgled and whimpered a little bit as she bled her last over the lino while her legs kicked out as she attempted to right herself. Her hands held onto the vein within her jugular as she tried her best to hold in as much blood as she could. I stepped over the body and tossed the knife out of the window. It would land somewhere near Dan's body, his 'prints' would be washed away by the rain, but they'd find trances of her blood in between the handle and blade.

A perfect murder/suicide; maybe even a sex game gone horribly, horribly wrong; It happens more often than you think. I had to disguise my path somehow. I'm sorry that Dan had to be the fall guy on this, but I've got my own integrity to preserve. Back home I got a wife and kids to feed.

I headed back to the closet, took my jacket, the box and the bag with the paint and paintbrush. I left the paint on the kitchen top, beneath the message. I put the brush in the sink and washed it a little. Don't know why. Habit I guess.

Before I left I said goodbye to Johnny the Macaw and thought about giving him some seed or maybe an apple from the fruit bowl that would no doubt go to waste—then I thought against it. The cops would trace her call and Johnny the Macaw would soon be taken into care. He was an innocent in all of this.

I slipped on my jacket and held the small box of tools that I had used to gain entry to the flat beneath my arm. I opened the front door, closing it quietly and considerately behind me. Once in the corridor, I removed my latex gloves that made my hands sweat so badly and put them in my pocket. I left through the central fire escape, as I knew there would be no CCTV cameras this way. I'd already scouted it out. Before I touched anything else I pulled on a pair of less conspicuous grey winter gloves, so I didn't leave any further prints. Can't be too careful nowadays with all the technology they have nowadays.

Once outside I drew my hood up to shelter me from the rain and Big Brother, should he be watching, then I headed home. There were more single woman out there waiting for me. Maybe they'll be lonelier than this one.

I sure hope so. . .

COLD LIKE DEAD
WILLIAM ANDRE SANDERS

Ashes to ashes.
Dust to dust.

The minister closed his bible and brought it against his chest. He looked around at all of the sorrowed faces standing by the graveside. He stayed silent long enough to observe a moment of silence while family and friends of a lost loved one stepped forward and laid roses on top of the black coffin.

Then he looked up at the sky which was overcast with gray clouds potentially gathering enough strength to deliver an expected wintry mix of snow and sleet. Unfortunately, there was at least one and a half to two inches of snow on the ground already. The roads were treacherous up to now. Even the main highway was slick. The gathering in the cemetery on Guinea Mountain was an attempt so difficult that it almost didn't happen. The curvy one-lane gravel road leading up to the cemetery was thinly frozen over. Every car and truck—including the hearse—had slid to either side of the road, nearly rolling down the side of the mountain. Anything more on the ground by the time the funeral ended, no one would be getting off the mountain, as it would prove too dangerous once attempted.

The minister looked back down at all of the tearful eyes in front of him.

And he smiled respectfully. "Sister Tonya was a precious woman; a loving wife, devoted mother. As we stand beneath the wintry strength of Christ, may we celebrate Sister Tonya's passing into the kingdom of eternal holiness. In the name of our Lord and Savior, Jesus Christ, amen."

Cleak! Clack! Cleak!

Everyone began hearing the sleet as it rained down out of the gray sky falling onto the casket lid.

All of a sudden it came down faster— *Clack! Clack! Cleak! Clack!* tapping constantly onto the coffin.

Jak Sharvy squinted his eyes while sleet struck random areas of his face. He had tried not to cry because it was too cold to want to go through having chapped cheeks, but with his wife inside the coffin it was impossible to hold back expressing his true emotions.

Jak and Tonya Sharvy were approaching their twenty-four year wedding anniversary. As a matter of fact, it was only seventeen days away. In just those twenty-four years the couple had built themselves the perfect marriage. A fancy piece of real-estate on the wealthiest stretch of Pembroke, Virginia, about a quarter of a mile outside town limits. Two beautiful daughters, Amber and Lilly. The girls were only two years a part. Now in their twenties, both girls were married with children of their own. Somehow Jak and Tonya had lucked up and were living out a fairytale in the healthiest argument-free relationship that most couples could only dream about having.

Then it happened.

No one—including Tonya herself—was aware that a brain tumor would bring her to meet her maker on such short notice.

Doctors gave her six weeks to live. Unfortunately, she passed away in the middle of the fifth.

Alone, Amber and Lilly stood on either side of their father. They left their husbands' at home to tend to their children, knowing in advance that managing children would be difficult while mourning the loss of their mother. Especially since all of their children were under six-years old.

Amber rubbed her father's back and took his hand after wiping away her tears. "Come on,

Daddy. Let me and Lilly help you to the car."

Jak sighed. He tried to stop crying but couldn't. The pain was too much. His loss so tragic. His voice cracked when he looked at his eldest daughter and said, "Don't show me no pity. I'll be okay. It's gonna take some time, but me staying strong is exactly what your mother would want."

Amber frowned. "We all need each other right now. Sticking together is really what mom would want. You know that she always put family before anything. This is one of those moments when she would bring us all together and remind us what matters most. So you can't use grief to distance yourself from everyone around you. Use it as an opportunity to open your heart and celebrate her memory instead."

Jak shook his head. "I love you girls, and the two of you know I do, but I'm gonna keep to myself for just a while. I have to deal with this my own way. I don't mean to hurt either of your feelings. I just have so much to have to do on my own, and I don't want anyone telling me what I should or shouldn't do. That was your mother's job and ain't nobody gonna try and fill her shoes."

"Oh . . . Daddy," Amber said sadly. "No one is going to try taking her spot. You know better than to think something like that."

Keeping his feet firmly on the ground while leaning his shoulder forward, Jak separated from the comfort in his daughter's touch. Then he mumbled, "I was just saying."

Amber stepped in the direction he had gone and gently brushed across his side. She reached around the bottom of his back and grasped him lightly. With a smooth tug, she playfully banged her hip against his hip.

"Let's go, Dad. Lilly will drive you home. I would come straight over and help you get things organized around the house, but I'm sure the kids have—"

"No! No! No! I don't need Lilly driving me anywhere. And I certainly don't need any help around the house. I'll go through your mother's belongings and make my own decisions."

"Daddy. That's not why we want to help."

Lilly leaned forward on the other side of her father and glanced at her sister. "Just drop it, Amber. This isn't the time or the place to be having this discussion. We'll wait a couple of days. A week. Hell. We need to give dad however much time he needs. Let him figure out what he has to get done, then we'll worry about taking the next steps."

Amber flashed a distasteful bitchy smirk. "Seriously. You better step down, Lilly. It is my responsibility to see what gets done. Besides, I am the over slash manager of a real-estate agency, and so I do believe my experience puts me in the position to properly advise dad of which things may be in his best interests."

Lilly made a wry face. "Excuse me, snotty college grad. As the *other* daughter, I have the born right to agree or disagree with whatever decisions that you supposedly know might be in his best interests. Therefore, you cannot do anything without my approval. Okay."

Amber gritted her teeth.

Although the girls came from the perfect family, as they grew to become their own individual woman they weren't capable of ever reaching any sort of agreement with each other.

"You're a high school dropout. Mom and dad have had to help you with everything. I doubt you have enough skills to even manage fast food," Amber spat.

Lilly went to step in front of her father and he raised his arm, cutting her off from moving any farther.

"Stop this at once, both of you. This is no way to behave after burying your mother," he scolded.

Lilly backed down. Her mournful drooping eyes examined every detail in her father's bitter expression.

"Sorry Daddy," she said quietly.

Amber squinted her eyes resentfully; even so, she refrained from uttering another harsh word. She put up a pretentious smile just to make Lilly even more furious, then she looked up at her father and instantly took on the role of grieving daughter.

"I apologize, Dad. I shouldn't be bringing up Lilly's issues on this day."

Jak hung his head low, almost touching his chin on his chest.

"That's it. I don't want to hear another negative remark from either of you," he said.

Amber placed her hand on his back at the same time that Lilly took his hand and brought it by her side. The girls realized that they were doing more harm to their father than providing any form of comfort. They didn't speak another word to each other while guiding him up the hill to his car.

Jak approached the driver door.

Both girls remained silent, afraid that having a conversation would only lead them into another disagreement.

Amber had already voiced her opinion about Lilly driving. But Lilly seemed reluctant to do so since she walked to the rear passenger door.

Amber looked at Lilly and nudged her head in the direction of the driver door, as peaceful measure of telling her sister to take their father's place behind the wheel.

Lilly only stared at her, wide-eyed and motionless.

Jak glanced across the driver seat and over the passenger side. There was probably room just enough for him to squeeze in the driver seat. Flower arrangements given to him by the funeral home crowded the passenger seat and floorboard. The backseat was also almost entirely taken up by flowers, with sandwich and vegetable platters provided to him by family and friends. He wasn't positive, but there was enough space for Lilly to wedge herself in the only available spot behind the driver seat.

He looked back at her and shrugged his shoulders. "Sorry, hon. You're going have to try and make do in the back."

She didn't hesitate. "It's okay. I can fit."

Amber rolled her eyes when he wasn't looking and with both hands she grabbed the top of the driver door and held it firmly in place.

"Please Dad, you're in no shape to sit behind the wheel. Especially in this type of weather. Let Lilly drive you home. Do this one little favor at least to make me happy."

Jak snapped his head around, scolding her with his eyes.

"Make you happy? Your mother just died and you're worried more about having everyone please you than thinking how you're going to live the rest of your life without her."

Amber put one hand on her chest.

Her mouth dropped open.

Suddenly she choked up, teary-eyed.

Before she could get a word out, Lilly had opened the rear passenger door and jumped in the vehicle.

"No. Absolutely not," Amber said, as she began to cry. "I'm just trying to look out for you. I know how ripped apart you must be feeling inside and I don't think your mind is capable of taking on routine activities. You're devastated. And so you need people to rely on. Lilly should take it upon herself to help in every way she knows how. I shouldn't have to be getting frustrated over thinking for the both of us. That's what it all boils down to."

Jak sighed. He looked toward the heavens beating his face with sleet.

"I do rely on you, Amber," he said compassionately. Even his eyes relaxed and showed whatever softness he'd found inside him. "I rely on both of you girls. The past couple of days have just been so difficult that I don't want to deal with it anyone. I need breathing space. Time to think."

Amber uprooted a much needed smile and touched the side of his face.

"Awww— I know it's rough. I'm dealing with the same issues."

He leaned against her hand sliding down his face. For a moment her touch reminded him of Tonya caressing him before giving him a goodnight kiss.

"I'll give you a few days to be alone, then I'll come over and we'll discuss what you should do about the house," she said.

"What about the house?" Lilly asked curiously, from the back seat.

Jak bowed his head. "Actually, sweetheart, I think I already know what to do with the house, but we'll talk more about it when that time comes."

Amber kissed him on the forehead. "Okay. Fair enough. Don't hesitate to call me if you need anything."

"I won't."

"I love you, Dad."

"Love you too, sweetheart."

Without another word, Amber walked away, leaving Lilly confused about what might be happening to the house her mother loved.

Jak got in the car, shut the door, started the ignition, and turned the heat on high. He put his hands together against his mouth and breathed into them. Then he pulled them away, rubbing his numb fingers together.

"What did Amber mean when she said she'd come over and discuss what you should do about the house?" Lilly asked.

"Not now, Lilly."

She moved forward quickly in the space between the driver and passenger seat. "You and Amber can't push me entirely out of the picture. I have the right to know what she's up to."

Jak glanced at his youngest daughter's face in the rearview mirror. Her narrow eyes studied him intently while she awaited his response. He dropped the gear in *Drive* and the car crept ahead onto the icy gravel road.

"Sweetie, I don't want you to go and take this the wrong way, but the house is filled with memories of your mother. Too many of them. Everywhere I turn there she is. And I can't spend every day for the rest of my life surrounded by haunting reminders."

"What are you getting at?" she asked rather suspiciously.

Approaching the downward slope of the mountain road, Jak pressed the brake and held it on the floor, knowing ahead of time the ride to level ground was going to be treacherous. He glimpsed up at the rearview mirror long enough to notice Lilly still next to him.

"Sit back, honey. You might want to fasten your seat-belt."

"I want to know what the deal is with the house," she said.

Jak was hesitant.

Then he said, "I'm going to sale the house."

"What! No! You can't do that! You can't get rid of the house just because mom isn't there!" she yelled wistfully.

"I don't have a choice."

"Me and Amber should have rights to the house if you're seriously looking to get rid of it!"

"And I don't disagree. But I'm in a bind. I need someplace else to live and I don't have the financial resources to move on. If I am able to sale the house, at least it would provide enough to afford me something else. Something that isn't going to plague my memories—every day—or my emotions, reminding me that she has gone . . ."

"Doesn't Mom have a life insurance policy? Wouldn't it cover a down payment?"

"She does have a policy, but I've decided to divide it amongst the grandchildren by opening up savings accounts for them."

Lilly rolled her eyes, and sighed. "I guess Amber knows about all of this already."

"Yes, actually, she does."

"So what did she have to say about it?"

"She was overwhelmed."

Lilly looked out the window beside her. "Of course she was," she said under her breath. "Whatever Amber wants Amber gets."

The ride from the cemetery to halfway up Big Stony Creek was a long, tense journey. On an ordinary day the drive could be made in fifteen minutes or less, but in a blistery winter mix like the one coming down, it took nearly twice the amount of time.

The two-story yellow house that Lilly grew up in stood high on a hill off the right side of the road. It was beautiful even while surrounded by snow. Four white pillars on the extremely wide porch supported a balcony—the same length as the porch on the second-story. She wasn't able to see it from the road, but behind the left side of the house was a large underground pool. She and Amber spent many summers cooling down in the pool that Jak had built with his own hands.

Jak pulled the car halfway into the circular driveway and parked behind Lilly's Grand Caravan. He looked in the rearview mirror and shut off the ignition.

"I know none of this is what you expected, and I'm sorry it got thrown at you like this, but I truly believe I am making the right decision. I must do what I feel is best for me. And I'm deeply sorry that you are unable to accept these things. I apologize for whatever suffering I might have caused. I just wish you could see it all from my point-of-view. Maybe then you would understand."

"I do understand quite well. You're going to do whatever satisfies Amber. Anything just as long as it suits her. I'm not the idiot she makes me out to be. I know exactly what this boils down to."

"I know you're not stupid, sweetheart."

"You're putting the fate of the house in her hands because she can turn a few quick bucks off it in commission, and then both of you get what you want out of it."

"Young lady, that most certainly is not the—"

"Where does that leave me?" she rudely interrupted.

"Listen to me."

"Dad! How can I listen? I can't even get through to you. My concerns don't seem to matter because you won't stop and think rationally about what Amber has got you talked into doing."

She opened the door and looked at him with long, sad eyes. "I love you, Dad. However, I can't stick around to see you throw away what you and mom worked so hard to call your own."

"Lilly. Wait—"

The door slammed shut.

Then she was gone.

Jak grasped the steering wheel with both hands and pulled himself forward. Suddenly he broke down crying. First was the loss of his beloved wife. Now his youngest of two children was abandoning him during the time when he needed her most. There was no way he'd be able to keep the family together. Not like Tonya was able to do. She was the one woman that always found some way to bring peace between the girls. He didn't know where to begin. Or how to go about beginning it.

He was just a father, clueless to how to stop the ticker inside the time-bomb for a daughter.

He wiped his eyes. Then he cried some more. He wasn't sure what to do, no matter what he eventually might find himself doing, one of the girls would come away unhappy. And this troubled him greatly. It troubled him, for the reason that he most likely would have to continue a parental relationship with only one daughter, while his relationship with the other one existed solely on spur-of-the-moment needs. He wasn't accepting the possibility of having just part-time association. The idea that such a thing might actually happen drove him to aggravation. Acute hostility.

He slapped the steering wheel. "Goddammit!" He watched the rear of the Grand Caravan slowly inch around and out of the driveway. "Why are you doing this to me? Why take the one person I love and turn everyone else against me? What did I do to deserve this? Answer me," he said, crying profusely.

He could no longer keep himself together. His hands trembled and his head began to twitch. He was a nervous wreck, which was the reason he had waited until he was alone to let it all out. He didn't want the girls seeing the extent of damage done to him. It would have only made their emotions twice more difficult for them to handle. He wiped the back of his hand across the top of his mouth, taking away watery snot that trickled down out of both nostrils. "You should have taken me instead of her. This family wouldn't be going through ruins if you had just left Tonya here to handle matters. She had a knack for knowing what to do. She'd have these girls relying on each other for support. I can't get them to be civil with each other for one second!"

All of a sudden he started sniffling and gagging on a wad of agony. "I can't even mourn my loss without worrying about what little family we have left getting torn apart. God. I'm pathetic."

＊ ＊ ＊

By eight in the evening, Jak sat alone on the couch in the eerily silent living-room. Around him were a few boxes filled with Tonya's belongings that he'd began packing shortly after arriving home from the funeral. One box had Amber's name written on it, and another was reserved for Lilly. The large third box had *Go Through* written across it. Of course the *Go Through* box was one the girls would definitely be fighting over. Amber would have to take what she wanted and Lilly the same. Surely, one of them would bitch about whatever the other had taken. Jak tried to be fair by putting less sentimental items inside the *Go Through* box, but he knew this effort was going to turn out a no win situation. Those girls didn't have a rational bone in their bodies.

Sitting upright, with his feet pressing the hardwood floor, Jak blew his nose on an already damp tissue. He looked all around the dim lamplight spread about the room. The maroon walls were bare now, since he'd taken down all of the family portraits and divided them between the three boxes. Besides having the television and cable box, the entertainment center was stripped of Tonya's personal treasures. The dull atmosphere made a perfect companion for what he chillingly deemed the darkest hour of his life.

He pushed back on the couch and laid his head on the top cushion. His eyes fixed on vague light dispersed across the off-white ceiling. Heaven? Not a chance. Such thinking never crossed his mind. Instead he figured how a fifth of liquor might be ideal for a time like this. It would numb the pain and lead him into an eventual blackout, temporarily erasing all memories of his high-school sweetheart turned wife. Unfortunately, there wasn't a drop of alcohol in the house. The Sharvy's weren't keen on drinking things they shouldn't. The last mixed drink he and Tonya consumed was on New Year's Eve two years ago, at Amber's house.

Jak closed his eyes.

Tonya's face leapt forth and took place of the dark.

Pale skin.

Eyes shut.

Lips sealed.

Exactly the way she looked the last time he'd seen her, as the coffin lid was being brought down on top of her slowly.

He opened his eyes again.

Light on the ceiling brightened somehow. At first he didn't think much about it. But then, a tall, lanky, disfigured shadow of a human form flashed across the ceiling and quickly disappeared.

He looked across the room.

White light glowed through the curtains on the bay window in front of him.

Who the hell can that be? He wondered.

Once he approached the window he peeled back one side of the curtain and gazed outside, seeing a vehicle parked in the driveway, its front end facing the house. He couldn't distinguish the make and model because he couldn't see passed the blinding luster getting thrown out of the headlights. Even so he was certain that it wasn't a car, the headlights set too high off the ground.

Knock! KNOCK! Knock!

Someone struck hard on the wooden door.

Jak opened the door.

Surprisingly, there was no one on the other side. No one in sight of the porch. Cautious of the matter, Jak stepped out on the porch slowly; and curious to whose vehicle was parked in front of the house. He went on a blind journey toward the driveway.

"Hey!" he called out to whoever might be inside the vehicle, after raising his hand to his forehead and blocking light from disabling his view completely.

"Who's out here?!"

No one answered.

"I'm talking to you!"

Still, only silence.

Jak approached the driver side but never quite reached the door because he recognized the

vehicle and stopped abruptly.

It was a Grand Caravan.

Dark blue.

He knew just one person with this type of vehicle. And she wasn't in the driver seat. For that matter, she wasn't anywhere near the van.

He spun around and looked at the house.

Where was she? "Lilly!" he yelled, assuming that she might have gone inside the house "Sweetheart! What are you doing here?!"

He barged through the doorway and shot a glance into the living-room. The room was precisely how he had left it when he went outside—vacant of life, void of sound.

He looked around the dining-room.

Empty.

"Are you still upset with me about earlier?! We can work through this! I don't want what family we have left to fall apart and be left divided!"

He thought she would have come forward and confronted him by now. She had a personality that couldn't keep quiet when something troubled her. Never the type to hold anything back, she got right to the point about what mattered most to her. Which was the reason Jak was suddenly feeling uneasy about this peculiarly silent situation.

"Lilly . . . honey! Are you in here?!" Long eerie silence trailed his voice.

He looked beyond the foyer connecting the dining-room and kitchen. Maybe there was something in the kitchen of her mother's that she wanted. At least that was his best guess.

"You need to tell me what you're doing here! Not answering when I talk to you is only starting to make me unhappy!"

A slender shadow rubbed across the wall in the foyer.

"I see you!" he said, watching closely.

The shadow slowly brought the emergence of an actual person. A woman. She was wearing a long black trench coat and white high-heels. Even from where he was standing, he recognized her lips coated over with bright red lipstick. He wasn't really able to see her eyes but he frighteningly predicted them green. He gathered this chilling assumption for the reason that she bore a horrifyingly similar resemblance to his beloved wife. Except her hair wasn't blonde, it was blonde-brown, like Lilly's. Then again, maybe dull lighting made her hair a shade darker than it was naturally. Yet she wore her hair pulled back in a ponytail, which was exactly the same way Tonya had fixed hers daily.

Jak felt everything inside him crumble and drop to the bowels of his existence like rumbling vomit associated with the flu. He had no doubt the woman standing before him was a living replica of Tonya. And she *wasn't* Lilly.

But why was Lilly's Grand Caravan parked outside?

If it was hers.

He didn't know. He thought he did earlier but now he was far less positive. Staying in front of the entrance to the foyer, teary-eyed and confused, he was hoping to hear Tonya's sweet voice come out of her mouth.

He waited.

Waited . . .

She didn't speak.

"Tonya," he said with surprise.

When the woman approached the end of the foyer she raised her right arm in front of her. Jak glimpsed at her hand, however he didn't recognize what was in her grip. Whatever it was it was small and dark. A portion of it jutted just beyond her curved fingers. The longer he looked at it the more it began to remind him of—

BOOM!

Jak screamed.

He fell to the floor onto his back. Light faded gradually. And then he found himself falling deep into a sea of darkness.

He couldn't hear a sound as he sunk into pitch-black obscurity.

* * *

Conscious.

And delirious.

Jak opened and closed his eyes. He was in a dark place. Cold air gnawed goose bumps on his skin. Rough carpet scraped the side of his face as he lay on his stomach. Had he not known that he was on a carpet floor, then he might have imagined someone scrubbing him on a giant scouring pad.

He attempted rolling on his back but realized he was caught in a wedge. On one side he bumped against a hard wall, and on the opposite side he came in contact with something large, soft, and limber. He was able to rock it with a quick nudge; however, it seemed too much for him to push out of the way completely.

He gave up turning over onto his back due to a sharp pain digging inside his shoulder every time he moved. The twisting discomfort was intense, tears withdrew from his eyes. Somewhere near his collarbone the weight of the bullet ached his torn and tender flesh.

Ongoing consciousness made him more alert about his surroundings, and he recognized that whatever he was in, was moving. He also realized his hands were behind his back. He tried moving them and they wouldn't budge. They were bound together.

He pushed with his legs and nudged the large, limber form beside him.

This time it moved a little on its own, then it grunted in distress.

It was alive, and obviously suffering a great deal of pain.

"Hey," Jak whispered.

The living thing groaned quietly.

"Hey," he said once more. "Who are you? And where are we?"

Its only response was another groan.

Jak didn't know when it happened but at some point his transportation came to a halt. He heard what sounded like a door open and close.

Silence surrounded him.

Waiting to find out what may happen next was a slow, agonizing minute. Evidently someone had enough hatred in their blood to harm him, and so that same someone probably had enough passion in their rage to kill him.

Tonya.

She stuck in his mind like the Guardian Angel he wasn't sure ever existed.

He couldn't get over how the blonde-haired stranger shared perfect resemblance with her. She'd given him the regretful feeling that he had attended the funeral of a person he'd never met. Thinking like this disgusted him. He wasn't able to mourn Tonya's death, because in his heart she was *still* very much alive. Thanks to the odd stranger.

Suddenly the hard wall beside him moved out and raised open. Dull light poured inside the small location. He was then able to see the living thing beside him . . . it was Lilly. A severely battered version of his ordinarily beautiful daughter. Her face sustained multiple abrasions, jowls were swollen, her nose broken as it lay almost sideways on her face. Dark bruises circled her eyes, tears roared constantly down her marred, bloody face.

"Oh Christ, Lilly. What happened? Who did this to you?" he asked full of dread.

Lilly opened her mouth.

When she did she groaned and a mouthful of blood rolled out where a row of perfect teeth used to be and spilled on the carpet beneath her head. She closed her mouth—unable to speak one word to her father.

"See what you've caused," a female voice said harshly behind him.

At last the woman had spoken.

Whoever she was she didn't sound anything like Tonya.

Finally Jak was capable of breaking down and crying after confirmation that his wife had actually departed this life.

Yet the voice lingered familiar to him.

"Why are you doing this to us?" he asked.

"Don't give me that. You know exactly what I'm after."

Jak turned his head very slowly, giving himself to the excruciating pounding inside his upper body, like a rampant heartbeat. He looked up at the woman standing outside the rear of the van. He assumed that he was in Lilly's Grand Caravan since she was lying beside him. Now that he was up close to the stranger, he didn't see her having any resemblance to Tonya. Actually, he was beginning to think she looked more—

"Did you think I was going to be stupid and overlook grabbing this once in a lifetime opportunity?" she asked.

Jak swallowed the pulse of his panicky heartbeat throbbing inside his throat.

"Amber. You've gone mad."

"No, Daddy. I'm just taking the smart route."

Grimacing with torment, he shook his head.

"Sure . . . I could have taken a measly commission on the place, but I would fair tremendously from having complete ownership. Take every dollar from the sale and provide a better life for myself and my family. Not to mention how much I would come away with by collecting every bit of value in mom's life insurance policy. And with you out of the way, those numbers will only double my value."

She looked at Lilly, and frowned.

"Poor Lilly. She had to be the sister who couldn't get along. Doesn't matter. I wouldn't have spared her anyway. I'm not in a sharing mood."

"Leave her alone, Amber. For Christ sakes, she's your sister."

"I can't have her in the way. Or I'd have to split everything fifty-fifty. And I'm not about to do that. I'm looking out for *me*. Lilly would do the same selfish thing if she was in my shoes. You know she would."

"You're not going to get away with doing this," Jak said. His voice was beginning to weaken. He gasped. Pain ran down the breath he'd just taken, burning his chest. All he wanted was the pitiless discomfort to go away, and to hear Amber guarantee that nothing awful was going to happen to Lilly. Up to now that hadn't been the case.

He went beyond his suffering and said, "When people notice me missing they'll come pounding your door. It will strike them odd how you lost a father and a sister on the same day. Might even raise suspicions. Eventually everyone is going to figure you out. Then what are you going to do? Money isn't going to matter. You'll be staring at a set of prison bars for the rest of your life."

"Umm . . . I don't think so. I was home when all of this happened. When Lilly was helping you go through mom's things and a burglar spotted the perfect opportunity to strike two defenseless people. Maybe it was someone who knows you. Maybe they knew mom. I'm sure if questioned— *Wha!-Lah!*—I'll have thrown a name out there that will keep the focus off me."

"You're insane. How can you do this to us?"

Amber reached somewhere below his feet and pulled out a crowbar. It was heavy because she could hardly manage it with one hand. She looked at him and smiled sneakily.

"Because I love you," she said.

"Haven't you done enough? I'll give you whatever it is you want. Just . . . please . . . don't do anything you're going to regret. We can somehow find a way to put this behind us. And I'll protect you from anyone finding out about this. Just let us go, Amber. Please."

"I don't want to see you going alone through the motions of life, wishing that it had been you instead of mom. Neither do I want you to shun me and the kids because you feel that she was the most important thing in your life, and without her nothing matters. I'm going to rid you from having suffered those years of depressive lonesomeness because I love you. It's that simple."

"I would never turn my back on you. Or my grandchildren."

She brought her other hand to the crowbar and took full control as she raised it above her head.

"And I'm making sure I never have to worry about the likelihood of that happening."

Wild rage twinkled in her eyes. Jak had never witnessed such insanity overcome the face of his child. She had given herself to hatred and greed and was altered to the embodiment of madness. Even her arms trembled with animosity while holding the crowbar above her head.

"Know that I will always love you, Daddy."

She brought her arms down, guiding the crowbar towards his legs.

Jak screamed.

He conceived the thick metal striking him would shatter bone and fill him with the uppermost grueling pain, but the crowbar didn't hit him. Instead it came down somewhere behind him, in the area Lilly was laying. He wasn't sure if Amber had intended to hit him or Lilly, and he wasn't sure that she had struck her critically. Lilly didn't make a sound. Jak was positive that she would have made some noise if the solid metal rod had come down against her.

Amber dropped the crowbar on the ground. She grabbed her father's legs and strenuously arranged him so that the bottom of his bare toes was scraping rough ground. He didn't bother sitting up to try and get away. His legs were bound together; he couldn't go anywhere if he put his life on the line. Amber reached under Lilly's arms and dragged her out of the van. Lilly wasn't putting up a fight. In fact, she wasn't moving. Or making any sort of sound. Jak couldn't get a look at her face to see if she was awake because her shoulder length blonde-brown hair was draping all around the sides of her head and rubbing the van floor.

Amber moaned and groaned while applying every muscle to tug Lilly's sloppily pliable weight clear of the vehicle. She didn't let go of her sister as she pulled her outside, but did almost lose control when Lilly dropped down and smacked her knees on the ground. She laid her on the ground slowly, and then she grabbed both hands and proceeded to drag Lilly to the side of the vehicle, out of Jak's sight.

He took in a deep breath.

Swallowed discomfort.

And contorted his face momentarily. The tender wound on his shoulder had got more intolerable than when he last breathed heavily.

Amber returned to the vehicle. She swiped her arm across her forehead, taking away cold sweat. "Shoo— one down, one to go. I really don't know if I'm capable of handling you. Lilly was pretty difficult. I'm sure you weigh almost twice as much," she said, nearly out of breath.

"Where is she?" he asked, wincing.

Amber bent down and picked up the crowbar. "You'll find out soon enough."

"What did you do to her?"

She smacked the bar against the palm of her hand.

Again.

And again.

"I had to get her out of my way. Just like I have to make *you* disappear."

"Don't." He groaned. "Amber."

"Stand up."

"I can't."

"Stand up!"

Jak managed in some way to plant his heels on the ground and stand. He was out of the vehicle. Looking around snow and darkness, he realized he was on the bridge between Pembroke and Eggleston. The same bridge he had traveled twice already, to attend and then depart Tonya's burial on Guinea Mountain. He could hear the bitter New River flowing mercilessly far below them. This stretch of the river's path was dangerous; rapids, strong currents, whirlpools—this particular spot under the bridge was known to have claimed many lives.

Jak shivered.

He was freezing.

And he disturbingly sensed that he didn't have to ask again what happened to Lilly.

Amber snarled. "I sincerely wish it had been you instead of mom. She would have given us anything we wanted. It wouldn't have had to come to this."

"I'll let you take whatever it is you want. Just cut me loose and I'll—"

"Sorry, Daddy. But it's a little too late to reconcile our differences."

She grasped the crowbar with both hands and swung at him as quickly as she was able to move. Jak hit the ground immediately. Blood sprayed out of his mouth. The side of his head smacked the cold, wet concrete road and began throbbing beyond the extent of a migraine headache. The instant pain was so ravaging that he couldn't scream or beg for her to stop. Tears poured out of his unfocused eyes. He felt crisp wind burn the saltwater dry on his face. Everything about him ached, which left him lying in a motionlessly dysfunctional state of consciousness.

Then he heard the crowbar hit the ground.

Shortly afterward, he was being dragged on the pedestrian sidewalk next to the edge of the bridge.

Amber grunted constantly.

She sighed out of persistent aggravation, several times.

Jak felt his back press the vertical columns on the guardrail. He was aware straightaway that he was looking at Amber. She was crouched in front of him, slipping her hands into his armpits before attempting to raise him off the ground.

"Dammit, Daddy," she said, gasping. "I never thought you'd be this heavy."

At last she got him on his feet and had to hold him pushed up against the safety rail so that he wouldn't fall back down on the ground.

Jak's head—suddenly and unwillingly—hung low between his shoulders. He lacked energy to keep it up. Besides, he had no desire to offer the slightest attention to his feral child.

Amber thrust against him gently. She touched one hand under his chin and lifted his head slowly. Then she leaned forward and delivered a simple kiss on his anguished forehead.

"All that matters right now is the fact I will always love you," she whispered calmly in his ear.

His only response was a quick cough; probably an indication that he cared very little for what she said.

Amber pulled away from the side of his head and went for his legs. Jak closed his eyes. He fought to ignore about what was going to happen, but he wasn't able to keep the sharp presumption out of his mind. There was nothing he could do to prevent the outcome as it was on the point of passing.

Amber hoisted his feet off the ground and he felt his shoulders lean over the side of the bridge. The river was roaring much louder now. Frigid wind came out of the dark beneath him and chewed around his neck.

"Tell mommy I love her too." She quickly pushed his chest and sent him over the rail.

Winter air ripped through his clothes as he was falling. It shoved so violently against his skin that he almost turned numb.

Then he crashed, head first into the flash-freezing waters of the New River. His whole body jerked involuntarily when he shot beneath the surface. Instant shock numbed him, however, under his skin was the agony of glacial temperatures plowing through every layer of flesh leading to his bones.

Jak had gasped and swallowed a mouthful of filthy river when it consumed him. He continued to hold his mouth open, thinking it be better to drink himself to death rather than suffer cruel winter stiffening him with hypothermia.

He opened his eyes.

The murky water allowed zero visibility.

Nonetheless, he was hopeful light of a distant world would soon invade this below-zero darkness around him, bringing Tonya from the other side to warm him with her tenderness.

Considering his love for her, Jak absorbed mouthfuls of water and persisted to drink more, even though he'd taken the maximum amount the human body was competent to withstand.

He gulped another time.

But he couldn't indulge anymore.

He began vomiting most of the water he'd drunk.

Sinking farther inside the chilled pitch-black, he frantically awaited the moment when Tonya would rise from the dark and embrace him.

Kiss him.

Welcome him home.

DEAR SUSAN
HOLLY DAY

DEAR SUSAN,

Susan can't wait to get home from work so she can fondle herself. Sometimes, she can't even wait that long—she takes her lunch break in the restroom at work and spends her entire lunch break just touching herself. "Some people might say I have a problem," she says, spreading wide for the photographer. "I don't think it's a problem at all."

May

Tom first saw the real Susan in the grocery store about a half-mile from his house, purely by accident. He followed her through the store, pushing his shopping cart, trying to get a good look at her face to make sure she really was "his" Susan. He continued following her outside the store, following her in his car until she finally parked outside a small white house with a friendly but uncomplicated garden.

The next morning, he followed her to work, keeping a good two or three car lengths between them, like they always did in the detective shows.

The casual observer might not suspect that Susan was one of those insatiable types. Tom wouldn't have dreamed it himself if he hadn't seen her picture in the one smutty magazine he allowed himself to get once a month. It came to his mailbox in a brown paper wrapper. Not even the name of the magazine was printed on the wrapper, just the return address. Of course, everyone who saw the plain brown envelope knew what it was. Once or twice a year, a small, unlabeled box containing a DVD would appear along with the magazine. Everyone knew what that was, too. Tom didn't even have a VCR in his apartment, however, so the boxes just piled up in the corner of the living room.

Tom hardly recognized Susan from the picture in the magazine. She dressed simply and conservatively for work, wearing either the same dark blue suit jacket with a long skirt or solid-colored slacks and a blouse. She always wore her straight brown hair up in a tight bun on top of her head, pulled back so severely that the scalp looked taut. She wore no conspicuous jewelry and very little makeup.

In the magazine, however, she wore elbow-length white gloves and a white garter belt with no underwear. Her stockings had dime-sized white lace flowers going up one side, and the material was all sparkly as if it had little pieces of silver woven into the fabric. Her hair hung down her back, the tips caressing the points of her shoulder blades, long, straight and thick like a dark brown curtain. Her green eyes were thickly outlined in black, her lips richly pulsing red back at Tom, who lay quivering and cowering in bed. He could easily imagine Susan alone in the tiny bathroom stall at work, long red fingernails gently scratching the ends of her nipples erect, eyes closed in ecstasy as she leaned back against the wall, legs spread wide over the dark bowl of the toilet, stifling her moans of pleasure with clenched teeth and pursed lips as her fellow employees passed by in the hallway outside the lavatory, oblivious to her orgasm.

HOLLY DAY

June

Susan's office only had a tiny window set in the middle of the wall. It was nearly impossible to see into Susan's office from where Tom sat in his car. She almost never went out for lunch. Every so often, Tom would see her walking briskly from the building to the parking lot, eyes sweeping the lot for her car as if she had forgotten where she had parked, even though she parked in exactly the same place every day. Her flat, sensible shoes made no noise against the black asphalt, quite unlike the slow, sensual echo he imagined the stiletto heels she wore in the magazine would make. She would pull out of the lot carefully, looking both ways before turning out onto the road, returning exactly one-half hour later, often still clutching a partially-eaten hamburger as she dashed back from her car to her office.

Could she actually find time to masturbate *every* day during her lunch break? Tom wondered, dismissing the hamburger. If so, her appetite for orgasm must be truly tremendous—in fact, it must be virtually impossible to satiate her and her voracious sex drive. For some reason, the thought was comforting to him. He would never have to worry about completely satisfying her in bed, because no human being, man or woman, ever really could.

It wasn't long before he was thinking about the two of them sleeping together. He could feel the silk of her soft flesh beneath his callused fingertips, the way the nylon of her sheer pantyhose snagged on the rough bits of skin that outlined his palms. Her thick, red lips smiled back at him in his dreams, eyes half-closed as she watched him move in and out of her. She was the kind of girl who would insist on seeing him put it in her, would watch intently as his swollen penis disappeared inside of her, only to reappear, again and again, wet.

"Dear Editors," he began. It was the first such letter he had penned to the magazine, even though he had been a faithful subscriber for nearly ten years.

"I truly enjoyed this month's spread on "Susan" (pgs. 25-28), and would like to see more of her in the future. Please pass my admiration on to her.

Sincerely, Tom Dunn."

It was not much of a first move, but Tom was a shy man.

The Monday after he posted the letter to the magazine, he made up his mind to meet her. He waited until her car turned the corner into the lot before slowly walking toward his office. He timed it so that as she stepped out of her car, he would be walking right past her. It would all appear to be perfectly accidental.

Susan's matte blue compact sedan pulled into the lot. Tom suddenly felt butterflies tumbling in his gut as he rehearsed how he would say "hello" and smile at her in the most natural and friendliest of ways. Susan parked her car in the same spot she always did and fussed with her seat belt. Tom veered a little from his straightforward path to avoid walking into the fiberglass bumper of her car. Susan opened her door and stepped out of the car, stretching her long legs way out to avoid stepping into a small puddle of rainwater.

"Good morning," she said, smiling at Tom pleasantly.

Tom grinned back, feeling his mouth stretch wide and his head bob idiotically.

DEAD SUSAN

"Good morning," he said, several seconds too late. She had already walked past him and into her office. Tom got into his car and drove straight home, heart beating wildly in his chest. "Good morning," she said, again and again in his head, from her picture in the magazine.

July

Tom received a different kind of package in the mail. Inside it was an eight-by-ten glossy of Susan wearing the same outfit she had been wearing in the magazine. She smiled invitingly at Tom from the photograph, legs spread wide and hanging over the arms of the chair she was sitting on, allowing for a full and close-up view of her private parts peeking out of a pair of white crotchless panties. A smeary lipstick kiss puckered in the bottom right corner of the picture, with "XXXOOO Love, Susan" scrawled next to it in red magic marker. A small handwritten note accompanied the photograph.

Dear Tom,

Thank you for the kind words. It is always nice to hear from my fans.
Write me any time. I promise to write back.

Love, Susan

Tom framed the photograph in the one nice picture frame he had and hung it up in his bedroom. He tried hanging it up in various places about the room, trying to find the one truly right place to display a picture of a naked woman, and finally settled on the wall directly in front of his bed. It was autographed, and to him, it was therefore special enough to be on display and not hidden from prying eyes like the rest of his pornography.

He lay back on the bed and stared at Susan through half-closed eyes. "Good morning," he said aloud, imagining Susan in her simple brown skirt and matching jacket.

Dear Susan,

Thank you for the lovely photograph. I was afraid that you would be like all of the other women in the magazines—aloof, unapproachable—but your quick and personal response to my forwarded letter has proved you to be otherwise. I think you look beautiful both in and out of your underwear.

Love, Tom

August

Susan had been out with a cold or a vacation or *something* for almost a week, and Tom found himself standing like an idiot in the empty space where she parked her car time and again. Finally, one day, he saw her pull into the lot, get out of her car and walk briskly towards her own office. She was radiant in a simple tan blazer and matching pants. Her hair was pulled back in its customary tight brown bun. She dabbed at her slightly-red nose with a white cloth handkerchief as she walked, as if recovering from some sort of sinus problem.

Her hair wasn't really brown, Tom thought to himself as he watched her cross the parking lot. It was actually a sort of reddish chestnutty color, rich and thick like ox-blood or velvet. Her skin darkened to a subtle olive in parts, especially in the crease of her armpits and the dent of her navel. The lips of her vagina were also faintly outlined in gray, almost as if she had applied makeup to the area. Tom knew every nuance of her body, or at least the front of it. He only possessed a small glossy magazine of her bending over and grabbing her ankles, so he knew just a few faint details about her backside.

Sometimes, when he saw Susan across the street coming to and from her car, he didn't see her in her standard conservative office attire at all. He saw her pacing, like a giant caged cat, slowly across the parking lot, naked in six-inch high heels, hair down about her shoulders, thick red lips pouting at him from across the street. And sometimes, staring at Susan's photograph from the comfort of his antique canopied bed, he didn't see her high heels and white gloves at all—instead, he saw her deep, serious eyes studying him over a dull navy suit, lips tucked in a tight, bleary I-don't-want-to-be-at-work-right-now smile, long hair pulled back into a demure and asexual bun.

Dear Tom,

You sound like a nice man. I have received quite a few thoughtful letters regarding the spread I did in last month's issue of S--. I am contemplating doing another series of photographs for the magazine—am thinking of you as I consider and practice poses for future issues.

Love, Susan

Tom had never been into forward women. However, he could forgive as well as expect indiscretion from a woman who claimed to spend her lunch hour masturbating in the company washroom. He was actually surprised that Susan's letters were more like the lines blurted out by the 1-900 girls in the back of the magazines—like "Cum All Over My Melons," and "Watch Me Fuck My Sister," and "I Dare You to Pull My Finger." Susan's correspondences were extremely polite by comparison.

September

The weather grew colder. Susan switched from skirts to dun-colored wool slacks, from thin leather flats to lace-up granny boots. She wore her hair down at the office now, obviously more an attempt to keep her neck warm than to look sexy. Tom liked the change in her. The fact that she grew cold in the fall, just like everyone else did, made her even more human. He managed to walk by her in the morning almost every day now, managed to catch her eye long enough to smile and say "hello" or "good morning." Inside, he was bursting. He wanted desperately to say, "I'm the Tom that's been writing you all the letters," but somehow, the moment never seemed quite right.

Dead Susan

October

Susan answered every single letter he sent her. She enclosed autographed photos of herself in various stages of undress, in provocative poses, close-ups of her snatch. The letters were somewhat reserved, however, with only the occasional references to sex or self-gratification. She mentioned the men in her life a couple of times, although she flat-out stated that all her previous relationships were transitional things, something to occupy her time while she figured out what to do with the rest of her life. Her interests included modeling, going to movies, and snuggling up with a good book. She especially liked to read pornography, and she encouraged Tom to write her nasty letters.

Tom tried to comply with her request, but always felt his letters falling short of what he really wanted to say. Finally, after many tries, he came up with:

Dear Susan,

I wish we could get together in person. There is nothing I would rather do than follow you into the lav at work and watch you play with your cunt. I want to help. I want to help you get yourself off. I want to hear you say how good it feels, how good I feel.

Love, Tom

His hands actually sweat as he wrote. This was what he had meant to say all along. It felt good to say the truth for once, instead of beating around the bush with, "Gee, you're so pretty," and, "I'll bet your hair smells nice." He felt strangely empowered by getting this simple truth off his chest and onto paper. He read his letter over and over to himself before finally signing it and stuffing it into an envelope with a photograph of himself. He had to get this thing out with the mail today, now, before he lost his nerve.

Susan's letter came back faster than he could have expected. Inside the large, flat package was a glossy photograph of Susan sitting with the legs spread wide open over the arms of a chair, wearing only a white garter belt with lace hose and elbow-length gloves. The corner was signed "XXXOOO Love, Susan." It was exactly the same photograph and autograph she had sent him with her very first letter. There was no other correspondence enclosed.

Tom drew the bedroom drapes tightly shut and turned off all the lights. She must have made a mistake. The second eight-by-ten glossy must have been intended for another of Susan's admirers, and the letter that was supposed to go to Tom had been sent to that person by mistake. Surely, if Susan had sent another photograph of herself to Tom, she would have signed it with more than all those "X's" and "O's". Not after all the letters they had already exchanged.

Susan smiled at Tom from across the room, the slick surface of the photo catching and reflecting the barest stream of light coming in through the cracks where the drapes met. Her smile seemed sad today, almost apologetic. Of course it had been a mistake. Tom gathered up with little nerve he had left and picked out some casual clothes to wear. He was going to speak to Susan about this, now, in person, like he should have done in the first place.

It was about noon when he pulled into the parking lot. Susan's car was parked in its usual spot. Tom walked quickly to the door of her building and let himself in. The hallways leading to the private offices were dimly lit and cool. The building was quiet, save for the sound of someone typing in one of the rooms, and the voice of a telephone going faintly unanswered in another.

Tom stood in the lobby and held his breath. He had only a general idea where Susan's office lay. He tiptoed past the nearest office and peeked in. A man's suit jacket hung from the coat rack in the corner. The next office was also empty, but a familiar brown leather purse was slung around the desk chair. Tom closed his eyes and breathed in the faint perfume that still permeated the room, a scent that suited Susan perfectly. He thought he could smell her hair if he breathed in deep enough.

The soft pad of high heels on carpet startled him out of his reverie. He quickly ducked into Susan's office and pressed back against the wall. An older woman in a charcoal business suit walked past the open door, glancing quickly at her watch as she did so. Tom looked at his own watch and realized that this was Susan's customary lunch time. Since she wasn't in her office, and her car was still here, there was only one place she could be.

Tom waited until the woman disappeared outside before braving the outside corridor. Halfway down the hall, he found the women's restroom and let himself in. He closed the door quietly behind him, careful not to let the latch click as the lock slid into place. There was only one pair of shoes in the restroom, peeking out from under the far stall. They were flat, black, and sensible. They were Susan's.

"Hello?" he said, walking toward the stall. "Hello, Susan?"

"What the hell?" called back a voice with a pronounced East Coast accent, "this is the woman's restroom, idjit. Is that Jack? This isn't funny."

"Susan, it's Tom!" The words burst out from between Tom's lips, having been held back for so long. He reached the fall wall and tugged at the door. The cheap latch holding the door closed came off of the frame and clattered loudly to the ground. The door swung wide open, revealing an angry Susan pulling her stockings up and her shirt down.

"Who the hell are you?" she snarled, trying to stay in control of the situation.

"I'm Tom!" Tom said again, smiling. "I wrote you the letters, remember? To the magazine. You sent me your picture. You sent me a bunch of pictures." He grinned wickedly at her. "I see you've been masturbating in the lavatory again. Naughty, naughty."

"You're the guy from the parking lot," said Susan, recognition slowly dawning on her face. "I'm sorry, but I have no idea what you're talking about. My name's not Susan, it's Jennifer." She had managed to get her hose up around her waist. "And I never wrote you any letters or sent any pictures."

"You're lying." Tom spat the words out at her, and then said it again in a much softer voice. "You're lying. I've been watching you for months now, watching you from across the street in my car, reading your letters in bed at night, trying to write back to you and let you know exactly how I feel. I wrote to you from my fucking *heart*, do you understand? I wrote to *you*." He felt it all then, all the passion and terror and love and pain that had been building up inside of him since he first saw Susan's picture in his magazine. Ever since he recognized her as the woman in the grocery store. She was so close now he could smell her, could smell the last traces of urine in the toilet water, the fresh scent of her sweat overpowering the sweeter scent of her signature perfume. She was so close.

"I'm not Susan," Susan said again in a small voice, trying to stand up. She tried to push her way past Tom, out of the little stall. "I'm Jennifer. Jennifer."

"No." Tom took hold of her arm and pulled her back to the toilet, gently at first, then harder. "No."

"Let go of me." Susan opened her mouth and closed her eyes as if preparing to scream, scream, as loud as she could, as loud as they had taught her in those self-defense classes her employer had paid for, the self-defense classes that had never mentioned what you were supposed to do when confronted by a stranger in a cubical too small to move properly in. Tom slammed his open hand across her face to cover her mouth, hard. Susan fell back against the side of the stall and slid to the ground, staring up at him, terrified.

"Oh, shit," whimpered Tom, stepping back. "I didn't mean. . . Please don't scream. I just wanted to keep you from screaming. I don't want t o hurt you. Please don't scream."

Susan pushed herself up with one hand on the toilet and shouted, "Help! Somebody, help!"

Tom caught her across the face with his palm again, stopping the scream again, pushing Susan hard against the side of the stall again. She fell against the flimsy metal frame and slid down to the ground. Her head lolled and smacked the lip of the toilet seat, hard.

"Now look what you've . . . damn it." Tom held his breath, listening for footsteps, someone coming to investigate the noise. Susan lay on the ground with her face in the toilet. Blood pinked the white porcelain and turned the blue toilet water purple. "It's okay. I won't hit you again. Please don't scream anymore, okay?" He pulled her up into a sitting position. Her eyes stared dully at him, stared straight at him, just like they did from the picture in his bedroom. "See? Nothing happened. It's okay. Right?"

Her body seemed much heavier than the 110 pounds she claimed to weigh in the magazine interview. He grunted as he lifted her up and set her down on the toilet. He leaned her far back against the wall, legs spread out wide to brace her from slipping off the seat. "It's going to be okay," he assured her. Her hose came off easily, over her slim ankles and tiny feet. Her skirt was a little more difficult, but he was able to manage it with her body slung and balanced over his right shoulder. He unbuttoned her white silk blouse and pulled it off, one arm at a time. He left on her slim, white cotton bra, although it wasn't as sexy as the bra she wore in the photographs.

"Everything's going to be all right," he kept saying, over and over, not sure if he was reassuring her or himself. Everything seemed bright and shiny, as if extra lights had been turned on in the room. His breath sounded ragged and incredibly loud in the quiet of the empty restroom. He crawled backwards on his knees from the woman and gave her a little smile. "See? It's just how you like it. It's just how you said you liked it."

Susan was stripped down to just her bra and cotton underwear, head leaning back against the wall, eyes closed, as if she was asleep or overcome with ecstasy. Her right hand was buried deep inside her underwear, her left was just inside the bra, cupping her breast. He had pulled her hair down over the part of her face that still dripped blood.

Tom looked at his watch. It was almost twelve thirty. People would be coming in from their lunch breaks soon. He stood up and patted Susan on the head, awkwardly.

"I'll be seeing you around, all right?" he said, smiling again. He had to get out of here before he passed out. The stall had grown so hot and thick he could barely draw a breath without gagging. The hallway was still empty when he crept out of the bathroom.

He drove straight home. Nobody followed him to his apartment building. No one stopped him on the stairs. He slammed the door behind him and stood in his living room, heart pounding, head pounding. It was just a bad dream. It didn't really happen. It couldn't have happened.

The day's mail was piled up on the floor next to his feet. Hidden between Victoria Secrets catalogues and books of money-saving coupons he found another letter from Susan. He opened it with trembling hands, expecting to see a picture of her as he left her, propped up in the bathroom stall, blood running down her face, eyes wide and blank. But no—it was a small one of her wearing a short white skirt and a tiny halter top. He could tell from the photograph that she was wearing no underwear.

Dear Tom, **her letter began.**

It is always lovely to hear from you. Last night I had a dream that I was lying out on the beach with my eyes closed and I felt firm, strong hands all over my body. I didn't open my eyes, but I knew it was you from the way you took control of me so quickly, from the way you said my name over and over as I pretended to still be asleep. Your strong, callused hands gently slipped my bathing suit top off, and I felt soft lips and a wet tongue sliding up between the cleft of my breasts. . .

THE BIGGEST FAN
TAMMY A. BRANOM

Aaron flipped through the stack of mail. "Junk, junk, bill, bill, junk." He stopped at a purple-hued envelope. The sweet scent of women's perfume wafted into his nose. He rubbed his finger over his name that was so eloquently inked on the front. *Aaron Lancaster.* Happiness filled him every time he saw the name. Even better to see it on a letter from a fan. "Hmmm, no return address." Flipping over the envelope, he found the address, but no name. He smiled. It was obviously from a woman. They always approached him "incognito." Turning for the house, he patted the letter under his nose and inhaled deeply. Definitely a woman. He tucked the stack into his robe pocket and continued home. As he strode up the curves of the driveway, he lost himself in the thoughts of another time and place.

At the doorway, a bare leg poised over the threshold. His eyes followed the exposed curves to the bottom of his shirt tail hiding the beauty beneath. "What took you so long?" The young woman twirled her long, wavy, auburn hair around her finger and arched a slender leg and thigh outward. Aaron's eyes glued to the shimmering shadows of rich gold naturally set in her locks.

He smiled at the splendor before him. "Mail." He held the stack out. With a quick snatch, she took them all and threw them casually over her shoulder onto the floor. "No fan mail today," she said. "Besides, I'm your *biggest* fan. Gripping his robe collar, she tugged him inside.

He followed willingly. Oh, how Aaron Lancaster *loved* his fans.

* * *

Aaron blinked awake. The sun's fingers stretched across his bedroom and onto the bare skin of the woman next to him. He slipped from beneath the silk sheets, snagged up his pants, and quietly exited the room. In the hallway, he hopped into his trousers and headed down the grand staircase spreading into his mansion's antechamber. Shivers skipped up his legs as his feet touched the cold marble main floor. Scanning the foyer, Aaron finally spied the mail the woman had tossed aside. Apparently, the maid had gathered it; neatly stacking the envelopes on the table next to the door. He paused at the mirror above the stand and combed his disheveled blonde hair with his fingertips, rotating his head side to side to make certain his primping was complete. His blue eyes sparkled back at him as he raised his chin and smiled at himself. After a moment of self-adoration, his attention returned to the stack of mail.

Sorting the layers of mail, he homed in on the purple letter. Pinching its edge, he tugged it out in a quick jerk like a magician attempting to pull a tablecloth from beneath an assortment of table trimmings. The rest of the mail splayed out in all directions, scraping across the floor. Aaron ignored the mess as he pressed the letter under his nose. The scent still lingered. He closed his eyes and imagined what the woman would be like as he slid his finger under the envelope's top edge. As he split the lavender paper, the perfume drifted heavier on his senses. Beautiful golden calligraphy etched the top center.

194

Ms. Janice Mason
4128 SE Ainsworth Court

Aaron's eyes passed over the rest. He wanted to get to the good parts. He skimmed over her swirling letters and heart-dotted *i's* to what he sought.

I'm a local entrepreneur.
Mid-30s. Athletic.
Meet for dinner and talk.
I'm a big fan.

No shockers with that letter. It seemed quite average, except she was a local business owner. This intrigued him. Without further hesitation, he dug his cell phone from his pants and called the number she eloquently penned beneath her name.

After a couple of rings, her voicemail responded.

He sighed. He had so hoped to hear her true voice, not the cold, empty computer announcement. "Ms. Mason, this is Aaron Lancaster. I received your letter today. I would be most interested to meet with you for dinner. Please contact me at this number. I look forward to spending an evening with you."

A wily smile curled up one side of his lips as he dropped his phone into his pocket.

"Aaron?"

He swung around to find the woman from his bed standing on the staircase behind him. "Yes?"

One long bare leg slowly stretched down to the next stair. "Are you coming back upstairs?" She extended her other bare foot and poised her polished toes over the edge of the stair. Enchantment spilled from her smile as she meticulously placed each footstep down the staircase as if she were royalty.

He swallowed hard as his eyes strolled over her form. At that moment, he drifted to past memories of women. How their eyes would sparkle at the sight of him. How they would gush over him. And how he could make them *scream.* Old desires swelled.

His phone vibrated. The name "Janice Mason" glowed on the screen. He raised his forefinger and turned away from his temptress. "Miss Mason, I'm surprised to hear back from you so quickly."

A soft chuckle answered him. "Bonjour, Mr. Lancaster. I'm very sorry to have missed your call."

Aaron smiled. "That's quite all right." He slipped out the front door to get away from the prying ears of the woman on the stairs. "So, would you like to have dinner tonight? I have a standing table at . . ."

"If you don't mind, I have a particular restaurant in mind. It's to die for."

He faked a laugh. "To die for? I'm not so sure that sounds like a good place to eat."

Janice giggled in return. "Pardon my expression. I simply meant it was absolutely wonderful."

"I understand." Aaron ran his hand through his hair. Normally, he called the shots; he picked the places to go. "What's the name of the restaurant?"

A hush hovered in the airwaves between them.

"Ummm, Ma Soeur."

Aaron's left eyebrow arched. "I haven't heard of that one at all." Lines of concentration grooved his forehead. "The name is French. It means 'my sister.'"

A soft gasp, barely audible, whispered through the phone. Then Janice asked, "Really? What an odd name."

"Honestly," he said amid chuckles, "most of the good eateries have peculiar names."

"True," she agreed. "So, are you game?"

Stroking his jaw, Aaron shrugged. "Sure."

"Can I pick you up around six?"

Now things were getting much too out of balance for Aaron. "Since you are choosing where we eat, I think it only appropriate for me to drive." He wasn't so certain about giving up all the control to a woman he had never met. He hadn't let that happen for a long time.

"No sense of adventure, Mr. Lancaster?" Janice cooed.

Aaron bit his lip. He closed his eyes and greeted the memories of his past. Once upon a time, he liked it when the women took charge . . . until one went too far.

"Well, Mr. Lancaster?"

Janice's voice broke his reminiscing. He sighed in pleasant abandon. "Six will be fine. Do I get to know where we're going?"

"I already told you."

"I mean the address."

"No surprises?"

"I need to let people know where I am. As it turns out, my books made me valuable to some."

Again, she giggled. "I understand. It's at 429 North 52nd Street."

His lips tightened. *52nd, Why did that sound familiar?* Maybe he knew the Ma Soeur after all. "Thanks. So, I'll see you at six?"

"Six. Definitely." She quickly added, "I must say, I'm very excited about spending the evening together, Mr. Lancaster."

"Same here," he replied.

As Aaron ended the call, he slinked back inside his home. On the inside, the young woman stood like a barricade with her arms crossed and foot tapping the marble floor. "Who was that?" she demanded.

He pulled back his shoulders and stuck out his jaw. "Another fan."

The woman's eyes blasted daggers at him. "Is that so?"

Sucking in a deep breath, Aaron spread out his hands and shrugged. He offered no excuses. She should have realized this wasn't a forever thing. He blew out his inhale hard.

"You know I'm your biggest fan." Tears pooled in the bottoms of her eyes. "I don't care what any other bitch says."

Aaron puffed his chest. He owed her nothing. It wasn't as if she was paying him. "Maybe you should go now."

Her hands curling into fists, she turned and scurried up the stairs, into the bedroom, and returned, her clothes heaped in her arms. Her makeup blotted huge black patches below her eyes and streaked all the way down her face creating a mask of sorrow.

Dismayed by her appearance, a faint feeling of nervousness sat in the pit of his stomach. A distant memory knocked at his mind. Reaching out for her, Aaron said, "Wait." Nevertheless, she pushed by him, her hand blocking his arm from wrapping around her.

His eyes followed her. He suddenly realized he didn't even know her name. He gulped down the lump in his throat and clenched his mouth tight. Huffing, he turned and jogged up the stairs. "Oh well," he mumbled to himself. "She'll be back."

* * *

The clock chimed 5:30 p.m. Aaron pulled back his sleeve to glimpse at his watch. He couldn't believe he was actually nervous. Why did he let her decide everything? He'd checked online for the Ma Soeur. It was where Janice said it was. However, there were no reviews, no indications of what to expect.

He peeked at his watch again, and then out the window once more.

He rubbed his forehead. "This is ridiculous," he said aloud. "You're not that guy anymore. You need to let go." For a brief moment, he relaxed. Then he noticed a silver sports car slowly traversing the driveway, and his stomach fluttered again.

He darted through the door to meet her outside.

"You're early," he said as he opened her car door. One lean leg glided out. Aaron's eyes did a long, slow sweep up her leg following the suggestion of sensual curves—over her slim hips to the soft, jutting mounds of her breasts to her delicately carved face. His eyebrows sprang up at the sight of her wavy reddish-brown hair, the strands gleaming in the last light of the day.

"I thought you could show me around your lovely home," she said as she squirmed seductively in her seat.

Aaron absently smiled. "If you would like."

She slipped her leg back inside. "Well, since you're out here now, let's just go on to Ma Soeur's. Perhaps you can show me around later." She started the car. "Get in, handsome." She motioned him to the passenger side as she closed her door.

His blood pounded through his veins, and his heart hammered against his chest. His skin prickled and his palms sweat puddles. "Sure." He found himself lost in past thrills. Exhilaration engorged his flesh. He slid into the passenger seat.

"This will be fun," she said, her gaze as sparkling as her smiling lips.

He leaned over, one hand fingering into her hair, the other sliding along her thigh. "I think you may be right," he said. As their mouths joined, Janice's foot plunged onto the accelerator. The motor roared vibrations through them.

"Are you certain you don't want to come inside first? You seem a bit revved up just now," he said.

She pulled away. "Later," she replied as she inspected herself in the rearview mirror and smoothed her hair. She dropped the vehicle into drive. "In the meantime, we can get to know each other a bit more."

Aaron gave her a sidelong glance and sunk into the seat. "What would you like to know?"

"Well . . ." Janice stole a look in his direction as she drove. "What made you decide to be a romance writer? I mean, that market is mostly dominated by women." She reached across and rested her hand on his thigh. "But, I must say, your books are worth every penny. You make even the most seasoned female romance writer seem sloppy."

Aaron dipped his head and peered out the side window. A blush tinted his cheeks and his lips tightened in a suppressed smile. He loved the admiration. "Let's just say, I was weary of my past."

"Really?" Janice's brow shot up. "What sort of job did you have?"

A smile tipped at the corners of his mouth. "It was draining work," he said.

Janice scrunched her face. "Draining? Are you alluding you were a plumber?"

Aaron threw back his head and laughed. "No, not a plumber."

"Thank the heavens. You are too handsome to be a plumber. Too sexy, as well."

His cheek flushed again. "Thanks."

Road hum filled the car. Awkward silence crept between them.

Janice cast a couple quick sideways peeks toward him. "You're not going to tell me, are you?"

"Tell you what?" He leaned against the car door, cocked his head, and peered at her.

Her eyes rolled back and forth between him and the road. "What you did before you became a writer."

Aaron's eyes narrowed and his mouth dipped to a frown. "No." His response cut sharp. Pinching the corners of his eyes, he shook his head. He hated when they asked.

She centered her attention on the road and huffed. Silence hung again. "I just wondered where you got all your ideas," she finally said. "If you dreamed them up or if they were from experience."

"Does it matter?"

"Well, maybe." She forced a tiny smile.

Aaron winced as his whole body tensed. He needed to divert the conversation. "Perhaps later I can show you." His fingers trailed along her arm to her neck and traced her jaw line.

Her muscles tensed under his touch. "Possibly." Keeping her focus forward on the road, she maneuvered through the streets catching all the green lights as if they were at her command.

Nodding to himself, Aaron settled back into the passenger seat. "So, what do you do?" Aaron turned the question on her.

She volleyed a similar disapproving leer toward him. "If you won't tell me yours, I won't tell you mine. Fair is fair."

He shrugged and turned his attention out the passenger window. "If you insist."

"I do." Finally, a red light forced her to stop. Grinning, she leaned across to him and kissed his cheek. "Maybe you can make me talk later," she cooed. "Or maybe I can make YOU talk."

He spun his body to her, his elbow cracking against the armrest. A barrage of confused thoughts hit him as he gawked at her. Baffled was an understatement. He nodded absently. "You can try."

She crushed her lips against his. "Definitely."

Bright high beams closed in behind them. The lights filled Janice's car as if they were floodlights. The engine revved and the vehicle behind shifted to and fro.

"I think someone wants to race you," Aaron said with a slight, impudent smile.

"Not happening."

The lights lowered behind them. The light went green and Janice turned the corner to North 52nd Street and maneuvered into the parking lot. The vehicle behind them lagged at the light, and then puttered through the intersection and past the lot.

Aaron eyed the car going on through. "Ex-boyfriend?"

Janice cocked her head. "Ex-girlfriend?"

"I don't have ex-girlfriends. Just great fans."

"Really?" she asked, her tone elevating.

Aaron tilted his head sideways in her direction. "If you knew enough about me to find my number to call me, then you obviously know enough about me to know that."

Janice's face burned scarlet. "Yes, I guess I do." She pointed to the building adjacent to the parking lot. "That's Ma Soeur."

Squinting through the dusky evening air, Aaron followed her finger. The back door of Ma Soeur opened and a silhouette darkened the light from inside. The door then slammed shut.

"You have reservations, right?" he asked.

"Of course," Janice answered with a wide smile. "So, let's go." She exited the car with Aaron following suit. Grabbing his hand, she tugged him along in hurried steps through the lot and around the side to the front of the building. Neon lights radiated an eerie pink glow onto the sidewalk. A bell jangled as Janice thrust the door open. Inside, a single table draped with a billowing white cloth sat in the middle of the dining area. A red rose in a slender vase adorned the table. Two pulled back, ornately designed wooden chairs waited for them. Soft, blue lights cast a ghostly hue around the room.

"I take it that's our table?" Aaron said.

She grinned and towed him toward it. "Yes," she said, her voice just above a whisper.

He slid a chair out for her, and then seated himself. "I must say, I'm impressed. All this for me?"

Janice leaned her elbows on the table and rested her chin in her hands. "You don't think you're worth it?"

"Apparently you do," he said smoothly, with no expression on his face. He looked around. "This must have cost quite a bit to reserve an entire restaurant."

Janice relaxed back in the chair. "Not really. The restaurant is not open for business yet."

Aaron stared at her, his face sagging. "I thought you said . . ."

"I said I had a particular restaurant in mind. I said nothing about it being open." She bent toward him again. "Or that it even served food."

Aaron stood, his chair flipping backward and cracking against the wooden floor. His chest heaved as his breaths emptied shallower. "This is NOT humorous if that was your intention."

"Sit down, Mr. Lancaster." She motioned her finger downward.

"I will not. I'm leaving." He strode to the door.

"I don't think so, Mr. Lancaster," she shouted after him.

He twisted the knob. He yanked and pushed, but the door didn't budge. He pummeled his fists against the windowpane. The glass grumbled yet did not break. Fists clenched, he wheeled to Janice. "What is this?"

"Come sit with me, Mr. Lancaster. May I call you Aaron?" She flung her elbow over the back of her chair.

"No!" His nostrils flared. "No to both."

"I see." She tapped her lips with her forefinger. "How about Lance?"

Swallowing hard, Aaron tried to moisten his lips with his cottony tongue. Words stuck in his throat.

"No?" She snapped her fingers. "Maybe you want to be more formal. How about Mr. Wood?" She threw her head back as she exploded in laughter. "Lance Wood! What a name! Where did you dream that one up? Or is that your real name and Aaron Lancaster is your fake name?"

His body stiffened and his face drained. "I . . . I . . . I don't know what you're talking about."

"Don't be coy with me. That is your *other* name, your other persona. I know very well who you are and what you have done."

He sucked a shivering breath. "Then, you have me at a disadvantage."

Janice tapped her fingernails on the table. "I thought you might remember the name. Unlike you, I did not change my name to conceal my identity." She stared at him, waiting for him to acknowledge that yes, he recognized it.

He shook his head. "I have no idea who you are."

"Then let me enlighten you." Janice stood. "There was a young woman who wasn't very pretty. She didn't have many dates. In fact, she went out with only one guy when she was in school, if you want to call it a date. Some freak who asked her out on a dare. She wouldn't spread her legs for him, so he kicked her out his car. Literally. When she hit the ground, a rock cut her face. It left a scar. An indent on her left cheek." She poked her finger on her own face. "Ring any bells yet?"

Aaron's features stilled. He shifted on his feet. "I'm sorry, but no. I don't remember anyone like that," he said flatly.

"You don't remember the scar?"

"No." His voice lowered.

"She said the two of you talked about it. She said you told her it wasn't all that noticeable."

"I don't remember. . ." He shook his head with short, quick pivots.

Janice threw up her hands. "She said you told her she was pretty. You gave her a sexy little red camisole to wear under her clothes for when you two would meet. It had a rose." She poked between her breasts.

Aaron's shoulders drooped.

"Now you remember?"

Rubbing his forehead, he closed his eyes. "I'm not certain."

Her eyes widened. "You don't even remember her name?"

He glared at her. "She could have lied to me, you know. A lot of the women who were my customers gave me fake names."

Teeth clenched, Janice stomped up to him. "You lied to her."

"Of course I lied to her. I lied to them all. They paid me to make them feel good so along with the sex were the lies. Do you think I would fuck most of them if I wasn't getting paid?"

"Even my sister?" She jabbed her hands onto her hips.

"Your sister?" Aaron's eyes widened. "Mason," he said in an exhale. His head fell back and he stared at the ceiling. "Rose Mason. I remember now."

Janice spun and returned to her seat at the table.

"So, why am I here? Why are you doing this? Where is Rose?" he asked.

Folding her hands politely on the table, she gazed straight ahead to his empty chair. "You are here because I asked you here. I am doing this for my sister." At last, she swiveled her head to him. "Because Rose is dead."

His mouth dropped. "Dead?" He rolled his eyes to the ceiling and back to Janice. "Now I remember this place, this address. It was all over the news." Opening his arms, he moved toward Janice to hug her. "I'm so sorry about Rose."

She jerked away from him, the chair tipping onto two legs. "It's your fault."

"My fault? How can it be my fault? I haven't seen her in years."

"Since you stopped being a prostitute?"

His jaw muscles twitched. "Yes."

"She loved you, you know."

Aaron said nothing. Yes, he remembered Rose. All too well, as a matter of fact. He recalled their last meeting; her frenzied crying, her screamed threats of killing herself.

His thoughts redirected to an escape plan. The dim dining area spared no light for him to outline a get away route. There were no other tables and therefore, nowhere to duck for cover should she brandish a weapon. His only chance was to subdue Janice physically.

"She loved you because you treated her so kindly. Then you disappeared."

He inched closer to Janice. "I went to Europe."

"She was devastated. Broken." A tear trailed down her cheek.

"Look, I'm sorry. . ."

"She never married because no one ever "measured up" to you." Out of the blue, she laughed hysterically. "Get it? 'Measured up?'" She clutched her belly and bent over in feverish squeals and howls.

Seizing the opportunity, Aaron reached out to capture her arms. She bolted upright in the chair as if suddenly electrocuted. Her laughter died against the walls as she glared at him. Devious. Deceitful. Her pupils pinpointed to tiny dots that never strayed from his. The look prickled his skin and his hair stood on end.

Aaron stopped. "Why am I here, Janice?"

"My sister was so empty after you left. I bought this place to give her something to do, to give her purpose. We were going to name it Rose's." Her entire body slouched. "One day, I came in and there she was." Janice motioned to the rafter above the table. "She hung herself."

"Oh shit," Aaron muttered, although it was more in concern for himself than for the sight Janice must have witnessed. To tell the truth, Rose's obsession drove him away. Although saddened later by the news she had hung herself, Aaron was not surprised. Actually, he was somewhat relieved. Nevertheless, he credited her with changing his life—for better or worse, whatever the point of view. However, he could never admit that, especially now, to her sister.

His eyes darted around the room again as he desperately hunted for an exit from this woman's apparent madness.

Janice dug her cell phone from her purse. "Rose was so excited to hear your voice." She played back the message. "Ms. Mason, this is Aaron Lancaster. I received your letter today. I would be most interested to meet with you for dinner. Please contact me at this number. I look forward to spending the evening with you."

Aaron moved toward her. "You said Rose is dead."

"I did? Oh, I'm sorry. I meant she *was*."

"Was?" He cocked his head.

"Ohhh, Rose," Janice called out. "Come out, ma soeur. Lance is here."

Aaron twirled side to side.

"Call to her, Lance."

He backed away. "No."

Janice raised her arms to the ceiling and spouted a chant. "Adeo mihi proficiscor vos solvo. Alive undead vos vadum exsisto imbibo. Cruor quod erant fang. Imbibo mihi mote is exsisto."

Clenching his fists, Aaron ranted. "You and your sister want to play games? Find someone else to fuck with." He spun and took a step toward the door. A black shadow figure materialized and undulated along the wall next to the only obvious way out.

"Say her name, Lance."

Muscles tightening, Aaron could not look away from the shape. He inched backward. "No," he said, his voice crackling.

"Say her name, Lance!" commanded Janice. She slapped her hand on the table.

He jumped. His teeth chattered and he closed his eyes. What if he did? Would Rose appear and kill him, or would this all end? He opened his mouth, but nothing came out.

"SAY . . . HER . . . NAME."

He forced his clattering teeth to part. "R-r-r-rose." The name drifted on his quivering breath.

The darkness oozed out onto the floor as the form thickened. As if compelling itself from the wall, a head protruded outward from the thick black with long smoky trails streaming and waving like hair. Discernable eyes, nose, mouth, and chin assembled within the outlined face. The more distinguished the shapes became, the more feminine they looked. Hands, then arms appeared and spread wide, as if to wrap the ghostly limbs around Aaron. Between them, a void as deep as the universe opened.

The entity turned to Aaron little by little. "Laaaancccce." A hushed voice from nowhere, everywhere, rippled the quiet.

Aaron dropped to his knees. "Rose."

A motor raced. Lights tore through the front windows, dissolving the shadow. The front of the building collapsed as the lights crashed through. Just as fast, the lights reversed, leaving a crumpled Aaron on the floor amid dust and rubble. Another figure appeared and grabbed his arm. "Get up!" a woman's voice commanded.

Aaron struggled to his feet as the air billowed into a thick cloud of dirty powder. He peered into the heavy dust cloud. Janice's body lay sprawled on the littered floor. Rubble blanketed her. The rafter from above split in two, presumably upon impact, and the splintered ends pierced the floorboards on either side of Janice's still form.

The grip on his arm tightened. "Get in the car!" The woman tugged him to the passenger side and shoved him in. He watched as the female tossed something into the demolished storefront, then dashed to the car and bounced into the driver's seat.

"Who are you?" he mumbled.

"You don't remember me?" she asked.

"What's your name?" Blood streamed from somewhere above his forehead, dripped off his eyelashes, and plopped onto the front of his shirt.

"You poor thing," she cooed. "Everything will be just fine. I'm here for you."

Aaron drifted into unconsciousness as she dropped the car in reverse and sped away. Within moments, an explosion completed her task at the wrecked building. She peered into the rearview mirror. The firelight glistened red in her eyes.

"Goodbye, *ma soeur*," she said, her farewell consumed in searing bite. "No grand opening for you."

* * *

Aaron blinked awake as a soft, cool cloth swiped his forehead. As his vision cleared, he saw the woman he had told to leave so he could meet with Janice Mason.

"Take it easy," she said. "You're safe now."

He attempted to speak, but his words drifted silently over his parched lips. His mouth and throat burned as if he'd walked through the Sahara Desert.

"Shhh. Don't try to talk." She wiped his face and neck. "I understand you want to know what happened." She dabbed his forehead more as he nodded. "And, I guess I should tell you." Sitting up straight next to him on his bed, the woman folded her hands on her lap, the cloth balled into her palms. "You see, I followed you. I wanted to know who it was that was so important to you that you would toss me, your biggest fan, to the side like you did." She patted his arm. "But, I'm not angry at you." She rolled her eyes. "Well, not anymore. I know you're sorry about telling me to leave."

He wriggled nervously in his bed. His eyes glanced around his bedroom. Although it was the same, something was different. "Where . . . am . . . I?" His voice barely carried the whisper.

"You're home. Don't you recognize it?"

He shook his head.

"Well, I have taken a few decorating liberties, but over all, I left it essentially the same."

Squinting, he saw pictures in the same places, but they were not the paintings he had hung. They were now professional photos of her. He slid his hands to his sides and attempted to scoot himself into a sitting position.

"Relax." She grasped his shoulders. "You should rest some more."

He continued squirming against her grip until he was sitting.

"Fine." Releasing him, she straightened herself. "You should be grateful. I followed you. I watched from the windows. I saw what that crazy witch was doing." Resting her hand on his knee, the woman pursed her lips. Her fingertips dug into his kneecap. "I had to save you. I mean, as a fan, I am obligated to look after you." She hung her head. "Please understand. I had no choice. I was not going to let that bitch hurt you."

Aaron's eyes widened. This woman had killed for him, yet he couldn't find it in him to be pleased or proud about it. In fact, he was scared of her.

"So, here I am." Her face lit up with a broad smile as she waved her hands and arms like a teenager.

Writhing himself more upright, Aaron breathed protests that were as audible as a puff of air. He swung his leg to the side of the bed and she spread her hand on his chest, stopping him. "You're not going anywhere." She lightened her push. "Besides, don't you still want to know my name?"

Muscles quivered in Aaron's jaw as he cocked his head.

The young woman smiled and wiggled where she sat as if she were a giddy child. "I knew you would. So, here it goes." Her grin sagged; her gaze hardened. "Everybody calls me Candy. Daddy would say I was sweet as Candy, so the name stuck." She scratched her head. "Stuck. That's sort of funny, I guess." Her mouth took an unpleasant twist. "I remember his kisses. . ." She closed her eyes and turned her head away. Her hand on Aaron's chest closed to a fist, gathering his shirt along the way. She gritted her teeth and wrenched his shirt. Her clutch pumped in and out, coiling tighter each time as if preparing to pull him in for a punch. "I ran away. I ran from the past, the ugliness, the pain, the humiliation. I ran from a family who would never let me forget."

Aaron held his breath.

"But, I'm back now." She let go and faced him. As she smoothed his shirt, her face parted in her previous broad smile. "See? We're kind of alike. Other names. Other identities."

Aaron still didn't breathe as he lifted an eyebrow.

"We just need to start over." The young woman thrust out her hand for a greeting. When he didn't respond, she clasped his hand with both of hers and shook it hard. His arm bobbled as if made of rubber. The shaking broke loose his breath. "Hello, Mr. Lancaster. My name is Candace." She leaned closer to him and whispered, "That's my real name." Again, her face wilted into vacant melancholy. "Candy. Candace." All of a sudden, she leered up at Aaron, grinning . . . devious, deceitful. "Candace Mason."

TILL MY DEATH DO US PART
ROB M. MILLER

Excitement and apprehension played within John's gut as he thought about all the months of romance about to pay off. At least it hadn't taken long to meet Stephanie, like it had with some of the others.

Thank God for the personals. John glanced at Stephanie, making sure the look was brief, knowing his eyes needed to stay on the gravel road. Still, Stephanie's high cheekbones, ruby lips, blonde hair, and Red Door scent clawed for his attention.

He liked that.

"Don't know if this drive's romantic, or creepy." Stephanie's voice held a seductive edge.

John laughed. "We're out . . . alone, 40-minutes from town, listening to smooth jazz and going to a gorgeous lake. Definitely romantic." John reached over and gave Stephanie's knee a pat before resting his hand. "Plus, we had a superb dinner . . . and Netflixed *The Wedding Planner*." John looked at Stephanie and winked. "Now *that* makes the trip romantic."

"Romantic it is, huh?" Stephanie's left hand rested on top of John's. "All right."

John drove around a bend and into a small lot. Twenty, or so, logs lay in a line, marking the parking spaces for this section of Battle Ground Lake. Pulling in, John killed the engine, and faced Stephanie. "So, what do you think?"

"Well, it's . . . uh, gorgeous, and . . ." Stephanie unbuckled her seat, and with a mischievous grin, looked around the lot and the lake, ". . . it's very, very—*private*." She grinned and pulled John close.

There was no hesitation. His mouth opened and took Stephanie's lips between his, then opened wider as he probed her mouth with his tongue, enjoying the minty taste of her Tic-Tac breath, feeling her tongue circling his. He enjoyed the taste of her . . . the feel, enjoyed the Red Door smell. And even though the music was off, he could still hear the sweet jazz playing away. Finally, after a minute long kiss, Stephanie started to separate.

"Let's get out and see this lake of yours."

"You got it." Faint tinges of guilt crept into John's thoughts, but were quickly dispelled, their appearance more reflex than anything genuine. Long ago, he'd chosen to hold his pride and to bury all feelings of guilt, to bury them as far as they could go.

Stepping out, John quickly noticed Stephanie wasn't doing the same. Taking the hint, he rapidly walked to the other side of the car and opened Stephanie's door. "If you please, why don't you step out and get acquainted with the lake?"

Stephanie smiled, again showing off her bright, high-priced teeth, and held out a hand. "By all means, kind sir."

John took hold of the dainty fingers and helped her out of the car. Electricity still sizzled from her kiss, and again he marveled at how much she looked like his Elizabeth, and yet was so brazen with her sexuality. Still, she was no match for his wife, no replacement for the love they shared, and which *still* flowed through the talisman waiting impatiently in his pocket.

Stephanie breathed in deep and loud.

John could tell she was enjoying the clean, night air. "You like?"

"Hmmm?" She closed the car door.

John pointed to the trunk and started walking to it. "The air here. How do you like it?"

Stephanie followed. "Love it. Clean, like at the Columbia Gorge. But warmer. In fact, for being night-time, I'm kind o' surprised at how warm it is. Clear, too. It's beautiful." Stephanie motioned towards the sky. "Take a look."

"Oh, God, you're right." John popped the trunk, a grin on his face splitting him ear to ear. "You couldn't ask for a clearer sky, or a bluer moon. There's gotta be a trillion stars out."

"Yes, it's perfect." Stephanie reached into the trunk and grabbed two folding chairs. "You getting the cooler?"

"Got it." Yes, it is a perfect night. Too bad it's going to be all too brief. He picked up the red Coleman, filled with wine coolers, cheese cubes, and John's guaranteed weapon, gourmet chocolate truffles. Then he closed the trunk with a downward shrug of a shoulder, and quickly moved to catch up to Stephanie, who was already heading toward a lakeside picnic table.

"'Bout time . . . that too heavy for ya?" Stephanie playfully bumped him, her shoulder against his.

"It ain't heavy, it's my cooler."

"Now that's corny." Stephanie scrunched her nose. "You know—" Stephanie hesitated, her eyes looking around.

"What?"

Stephanie looked at John, then continued her beeline for the table. "The quiet. So nice, so different from the city."

"Different, yes. Quiet-er, certainly. But listen . . . open your ears, and *really* listen."

"It's all right. But yeah, I hear it." She chuckled. "There's some chipmunks over there . . . squirrel's maybe." She motioned toward a stand of Douglas Firs. "The breeze coming in from the lake . . . and there, you hear that?"

"Yes, an owl."

"Let's hope it's spotted." She reached the table she'd picked out. "Could always use more of them."

"I agree," John said. "I mean, they *do* make for some good eating."

"Oh, stop it, that's terrible."

Their table, one of five, was set about 18-feet from the placid lake. John set the cooler down at the end of the table, purposively covering up some illiterate's attempt at memorializing poetry, the first stanza starting out as: There once was a man from Nantucckkitt. John was familiar with all these tables. The lake had been a favorite place for him and Elizabeth.

It was also an extreme dose of pain and pleasure when he came here now, an opiate-laced straight-razor put to his soul each and every time.

"You there, John?" Stephanie stared, the two chairs having been dropped to the ground. "Hey, hello?"

"Yes . . . yeah, I'm here." John sported a sheepish smile. "Lost in thought for a moment. Guess I'm a bit nervous."

"Nervous?" Stephanie walked to John and grabbed his hands. "What's up?"

"I don't kn—" John started to answer, eyes downcast.

"Oh, come on." Stephanie gave John's hands a squeeze. "Don't give me that. You can tell me . . . spit it out."

Eyes up, John stared into Stephanie's face. He could almost melt in her soft gaze. She was wonderful. She was caring, truthful, sexy . . . and *real*. Very real. Just like Elizabeth had been. A knot started to form in his stomach, and with it, a reminder that hardened his resolve. They all had been like Elizabeth. They'd needed to be.

He sighed, returned Stephanie's squeeze with one of his own, and smiled, his face taking on a boyish you-caught-me look.

"The truth is . . ." John started, "I've something to ask."

John's sentence had hardly ended before Stephanie—eyes wide with expectation—said: "Ask. *Ask ask ask.*"

"Not now!" John brought a finger to his mouth. "Maybe later." He opened up the cooler and pulled out a couple of Seagram's.

Looking up, John saw Stephanie standing, arms crossed, body leaning, a look of exaggerated impatience on her face. He felt like an idiot standing there with two bottles in his hand. Smiling, John offered one. "I was just thinking I'd better wait. At least . . . till you're a bit drunk. Or better yet, till *I* am."

"I'm not accepting that bribe." Stephanie motioned to the offered beverage with her chin. Then, with a short whip of her head, she swung some of her hair away and back over a shoulder, a movement John felt was extremely sexy, especially given the way Stephanie did it. She stared at the bottle, then back at him, and with a commanding look about her cheeks and lips, said, "Ask. Dammit all, John. We've been dating for almost six months, now. Pretty heavy. So ask. I've waited, and I've *earned* it. Ask."

John felt his stomach knot again, this time worse than when he'd been driving. So much had been done, and all for this moment. It had to be genuine. *Had* to. Stephanie had to not only say "yes," but it had to be from the heart. He believed she'd say it. But he didn't really *know*. One was just an intellectual belief, based on experience, the other was the proof in the pudding, and that hadn't yet happened yet. What if she says to wait? What if she wants to live together first?

What if, what if, what if?

He could doubt for hours, but now was the time. It tickled that though he looked in his thirties, he was actually closer to 139, and could still feel anxious in the presence of a woman. He also knew the knot in his gut wasn't going away until this was over. So he sucked in a deep breath, reminded himself of who he was, the caliber of person he knew Stephanie to be, and what she was going to help him do. He *needed* this. If he was going to see his wife, if he was going to hold Elizabeth—feel *her* again, then he needed this. Stephanie would *not* give him anything less than a honest answer.

He set the drinks on the table, the look on his face part embarrassment, part shyness, and part hope—and despite the ulterior motives, all genuine. "Stephanie, will you marry me?"

* * *

"John, we need to talk." Elizabeth Seever stood in the middle of the living room, back straight, voice attempting to sound stern. Sunlight, streaming through a window, bathed her in light.

John thought her an angel only playing at being human.

The living room was immaculate. No surprise. But John could tell that Elizabeth had paid even greater attention than usual. The hardwood floors were spotless and shiny. Their Persian rug, clean, fringes perfectly laid out on the floor. Scented candles, French Vanilla, were lit and spreading their pleasant scent about the house. Every piece of furniture had been dusted, the wood polished, and all staged just right. In fact, the whole house, both stories, all four bedrooms, kitchen, dining room, pantry, den, office, as well as their two-and-a-half baths, were all tip-top. John had casually inspected the house earlier, having picked up on the cue that *this* conversation was coming. Their home was consistently clean, easy enough, seeing it housed only the two of them. But Elizabeth, nonetheless, had worked even harder to perfect it. It was one of the quirks John learned of shortly after they'd married, her working even to the point of exhaustion, doing housework to bolster her bravery whenever she needed to "talk." Confrontation had never been one of her strong-suits, especially since she'd discovered some of what he could do.

He'd tried to assure her and then reassure, to convince her she had no reason to be afraid. That no one did—*almost.* He kept too low a profile to have enemies. And for the few he did, they hadn't feared for long. John had made sure of it.

But with Beth, he had felt, *still* felt, true frustration. She *really* had no reason to fear him. Not him.

Ever.

She'd been the first to capture his heart. He loved her purely and irrevocably. There'd never be another. The truth of his feelings came when he discovered he couldn't explain the "because" of his love. Yes, she was beautiful, tall, with long blonde hair, lips—the full kind—that simultaneously made her look intelligent and sensuous, a body firm and shapely, the kind that he knew would age slowly and graciously. Yet, he also knew that if something were to mar her looks, it wouldn't matter. Nothing could ever disfigure the dignity, the goodness, the saturated sensitivity of her spirit. He belonged to her forever, and she to him. Today, though, he knew what she wanted, could even appreciate the bravery she was showing, coming like this.

John looked at Beth from where he was seated in the recliner. He set aside the sketch he'd been working on, placing it on a small folding table beside the chair. The drawing was coming along nicely, its lines and curves almost finished. Only a bit of perfect shading waited for his hand. When completed, John would burn it, and then that partner of his, good ol' embezzling Jeremy Michaels would no longer be a problem. John didn't know the details of how Jeremy would end his own life: razor up the arms, cord from the ceiling around his neck, or his face put into the running underbelly of a lawnmower, but it—Jeremy's suicide—was inevitable. Jeremy wouldn't be able to resist the compulsion.

"John?" Elizabeth said again.

"Listening, hon. What's going on?" John tried to look non-threatening, to be the strong-chinned sensitive man that Elizabeth loved, but he knew what was coming. She wanted a divorce. He also knew she loved him, which made everything all the more painful.

"Here." John pointed at the soft-backed chair to his right, doing his best to make sure the gesture looked like what it was—a request. He loved Elizabeth, and wouldn't command her to do anything. But he needed to re-win her, somehow. He had to, because the one thing he could *not* allow was for her to leave. "C'mon, Beth, take a seat."

"I'd rather stand." Her eyes glanced at the sketchpad John had been working on. She bit her lower lip.

Shit. Why'd I have to be working on this now? "I'm sorry." John flipped the pad upside down. His pencil, bumped, rolled off the table and landed on the floor. John ignored it. Elizabeth did, too. "You can do whatever you want, I was just thinking you might want to—"

"I want to leave," she said, interrupting him, voice trying to be strong, but coming close to cracking.

John felt as if his heart were in a vise, slowly being crushed, an omen, perhaps, that he might soon lose the one good thing in his life. "Beth, look. We can . . . I love you. We can work through this. We c—"

"I want out," she yelled. "Out, out, *OUT.*" Her two hands beat the air in time to the words. "I want THE HELL OUT."

John stood in a flash. Elizabeth had gone into hysterics. It had happened before, and it had been ugly . . . was ugly now, with Elizabeth's screams jabbing into his mind like an ice pick. John remembered his former master's final utterance, just after he'd buried the man's misericorde in his chest. Blood, looking black in the moonlight, had gurgled from the ancient wizard's mouth: "Your love will be your doom."

Grabbing Elizabeth by her shoulders, he gripped her against his chest, oblivious to the fists trying to beat him away, his mouth whispering a calming cant in a tongue known only to a few still walking the earth.

"LET ME GO . . . I WANT OUT." Black mascara rained in pain down the woman's tortured face. "Please, you goddamned devil witch bastard!"

"I can't," John whispered to the air, wishing he could cry. "I just can't. Till I die, you're mine." He hugged her tighter, pinning her arms, overwhelming her small stature with his physical superiority. Resuming the cant, he concentrated on seeing her at rest, asleep and at peace. It was one of the few spells that would work on her, however temporary—their love-bond preventing him from using anything else.

Elizabeth finally fell under control, lost in ensorcelled sleep, floating amidst a sea of energized calm. But for John, her pleas remained with him long into the night.

* * *

Stephanie's eyes seemed to reflect the moon's beams, her cheeks becoming flush in the light of the area's lone lamppost. "YES." She giggled and danced a wild jig. To John, it looked like an excited parody of Jennifer Beals's famous water-scene in *Flashdance.* "Yes, yes Oh God, YES." She ran around the table and quickly grabbed John by the back of the head and pulled him down to kiss her full on the lips of her five-seven frame.

"*Mmmm,*" John moaned, kissing her hungrily, hands reaching down to the small of her back. He separated after a moment and said: "Are you sure you can handle being Mrs. John—"

"Mrs. John E. Seever?" She stepped back a foot, picked up her Seagram's berry cooler and twisted off the top, and held it in a toasting gesture: "The wife of a successful boilermaker? Damn-well-Skippy!" She tipped the bottle and took a long swallow. "Hell, I can't wait."

Boilermaker, ha, John thought, happy with the middle-class cover he'd selected. Rich enough to enjoy some things, but not *too* rich. Elizabeth had been the same way, as well as the others who'd followed. They wouldn't have been attracted to him if they'd known of his true holdings. In the abstract, yes, they would've been excited, but in reality, it would have been too intimidating. And since Elizabeth's death, he hadn't the time or the desire to find women only drawn to the green.

At least the knot had disappeared. Lori, Kay, Michelle . . . all the others, John reminisced, and *now*—Stephanie. How many more for you, sweet Elizabeth? A thousand and then another to hold you once again.

Gladly, my sweet.

John took out the talisman, Elizabeth's wedding ring, the token that *still* maintained the bond between him and his betrothed, the ring that would once again enable John to hold his dear wife.

Stephanie's eyes grew wide at the sight of it, a slender 18ct three-quarter carat Diamond Eternity, its ten stones all channel-set in a band of yellow gold, and she gasped in near-shock. John knew the ring looked modest, its gold and diamond content totaling a worth of only around a thousand-five. But this ring was *priceless,* crafted from the golden haft of his master's misericorde, many decades before. "My, God, John . . . it's beautiful. Absolutely beautiful." She took another quick, but long swallow from her bottle, set it down, and let out one of the most girly screeches John had ever heard.

Taking the ring, she readied herself to put it on, alternating looks between her hand, John, and the ring, all the while her pearly-whites showing in the most sincere of smiles.

John didn't feel the return of any knot, but did recognize the coming on of adrenaline. He had no idea how long Elizabeth would be staying, or what she'd have to say, or *what* she'd remember. Thinking of the last time Elizabeth had been summoned brought shivers to his spine, a waking nightmare whenever he thought of it. A memory he wanted replaced.

He blamed what happened on some hidden defect that must have resided inside of Michelle, some terrible worm that had burrowed deep into her soul, waiting to spring failure to the summoning like some devil's Trojan horse. His reunion with Elizabeth had been bittersweet, minutes only, full of sorrow and regret.

This time he had reason to hope for better. He'd prepared more diligently, had exorcised the portals of Anubis more precisely, and had hungered for his dear love lost with even greater ferocity.

"Hon, here goes." Passion laced her words. "We're gonna make it . . . we're going to be so, *so* happy." She slipped on the ring.

John smiled and continued watching, looking deep into those bluer than blue orbs, and at Stephanie within them. For a moment everything stood still, with John's awareness of everything outside of Stephanie's eyes seeming to vanish: the soft rippling of the lake, the light from the lamppost, the sound of small creatures making their way, even his own breathing.

Stephanie staggered for a moment, eyes locked, and then her face became caught in a rictus of surprise. Her eyelids fluttered for a couple of seconds—shaking, coming close to closing, as if caught in some kind of struggle, and then, *finally,* they blinked, and dark magic transpired—*transferred.* With that briefest of moments, with her lashes coming down and back, again and again, the four lids giving each other the briefest of kisses, John knew . . . *knew* that Stephanie had winked away, and his love had returned to him, once again.

The physical changes started immediately, and John stared, transfixed by the transition. Then, breaking his focused stare with a concentrated act of will, he said: "Elizabeth, my love."

Then he stepped forward to embrace his wife.

* * *

Eyes wide with fear, wrists and ankles involuntarily straining against the ropes that bound them to the oversized wagon wheel, hands opening and closing blood-engorged fingers and thumbs, as if on their own, John lay naked, without a gag, but wishing he had one. Dried tear-tracks marked his face, his 12-year-old mind doing its best to keep the whimpers at bay.

The wheel sat at a 90-degree angle, held up by rusty chains from the barn's ceiling where they were threaded through a couple of old pulleys. Garland had chosen the site well. The barn had been abandoned for years, the sole survivor of a homestead struck by lightning. Outside, roughly a couple hundred yards away, sat the remnants of a stone chimney, and bits and pieces of rotted fencepost. There would be no interruptions at this lonely, dead farm, and despite John's pain, he *didn't* want any. He just wanted to survive this ordeal and to make Garland proud.

"Are you ready?" Garland stepped up. The heat in the barn was hellish, suffocating, the rickety structure acting as a heat-trap, exceeding the 100-degree Arizona-bake taking place outside. Sweat ran freely from Garland's scalp and through his thin gray hair, cut like a halo, encircling his bald pate.

John remembered in conversation, shortly after the man had bought him, Garland calling it a tonsure sunburst.

Looking at his master, he tried his best to show his adamancy, and said "Yes" through gritted teeth. He'd been on the wheel for more than six hours, and for more than twelve the day before, when he'd had the back of his body worked. Now, he felt nearly done in, with his limbs and body wracked with muscle-cramps, and wave after wave of ravenous pain coursing through his nerves.

Garland frowned as he reached into the side of his coarse monk's robe, and, as done the day before, pulled out his misericorde. The slender blade, long golden hilt, and finger-guards made the weapon look like some kind of macabre cross. John feared the blade . . . and loved it. He'd already felt its painful kiss the day before. But during the night, he'd also felt the orgasmic energy it had imbued him with. But now, after completing half the initiation, John knew what the blade really was—a warlock's fang, the physical embodiment of a master wizard's awesome authority. He was now *bound* to Garland, to his blade, and would soon be all but immortal, with only the fang, and very little else, able to take him from this life.

Garland leaned close. "I sense a dangerous weakness in you, boy."

With his new other-vision, John could see the man's heavily wrinkled face, could see each individual line on his forehead, scalp, nose, throat, and cheeks, separately and together—*simultaneously*. Could see them chapped, chaffed, cracked and bleeding. "I don't . . . don't understand."

Garland drew closer, and John had no doubt about his master's claims of being several thousand years old. The man breathed in deep. Then his eyes rolled back till there was only white, and he blew black fetid breath into John's face.

John's body came alive under the power of Garland's terrible demon-laced sigh. He felt his pulse pound in his temples, tasted copper from where he'd bitten his tongue, felt his heart thump as if trying to beat its way out, his fingers, hands, and feet, which should've been painfully numb, instead becoming painfully and vibrantly aware.

Full-blown howls, more powerful than the ones given previously, escaped from John's lips as Garland weaved his blade around and *in* to his body. John could hardly believe the enchantment, the power, the terrible but blessed miracle of what was happening. Hadn't believed it, till Garland had shown him his back, hours after the first ritual, and had proven to him that, truly, what had been carved into his flesh—lines, sworls, glyphs and symbols of power—had been carved into the deepest depths of his soul. Thankfully, he'd been assured, the flesh would mend. His soul, however, would be permanently marked and empowered.

For now the pain was present.

"Let it out." Garland's voice was more soothing than any baby-holding mother's. "Let it out, my dear boy—all the pain, sing it out like a song . . . *all* of it." He continued working, letting the blade dance around the boy's body, his own moving like a maestro in heat commanding hell's own orchestra, drawing craft into the boy's flesh, watching as it transferred itself to something intangible, and far more important, eternal, and precious than mere flesh. "You know you desire love, and *that* is wrong. Let it leave, along with the pain. Let it ride on the waves of your turning. Let the desire go, or you *will* pay."

Garland paused after an indeterminate amount of time, holding his blood-drenched blade over John's heart. *Let your desire for love go, for you . . . and for me.*

John, with eyes clenched, couldn't tell if Garland's words were spoken aloud, or if they were being spiked into his mind. He couldn't tell if his ears were doing the hearing, or if, through the lines now etched into him, he was perceiving Garland's thoughts. He started to believe the latter, when he sensed words from his master's mind, something that shocked, mortified, and warmed him *all* at the same time . . . Garland thinking: *Please, for I am afraid that I am starting to love you, the son I could never have.*

He wanted to somehow communicate to his master that, yes, he could obey, he could, and *would* learn the words of power, the dark wind, and of how to summon the black rains, but that he *could* love him, too, could have a father—could *be* a son.

But no words escaped, and no thoughts from his mind. He was too busy screaming, feeling the cuts on his body, and then feeling them deeper, as deep as deep could be, the wounds feeling like an acid of death and pleasure and pain, *pain, pain, pain.* The cuts drawn on the canvas of his flesh, working in and through him, dark wounds transforming him, bringing to his spirit an epiphany of the darkest sort.

John wanted to relay his feelings to the man whom he had lived with and served these last six years, but his over-taxed nerves wouldn't allow it. They were too busy being ignited by black fire and steel. Too busy being aware of every artistic finesse-filled movement as Garland started to carve an ancient rune over, and into, his still beating heart, a gatekeeper sign that would open up—as promised—the libraries of Hades.

A promise delivered.

Images, chants, thaumaturgic wet-dreams sent by Horus, Set, and Pope Innocent the II, saturated the slim areas of his consciousness not being flooded through with torment. Then they fanned throughout the rest of him, washing through every cell, soon joined by the laws of hand- eye, and finger-magick, the rules of conjuration, and the necessities of placating the furies. John became engorged, the precious red fluid coursing through his veins seeming to collapse into his loins, making him grow, making him ache with desire for fruit, for authority, for women and blood, death and glory. My first erection, John thought. How wonderful.

Garland worked with no misstep, no hesitation, and John's flesh parted with no resistance. Smiling, tears poured down the man's face as he said, "I'm so proud of you."

* * *

John watched as Stephanie's features became that of the woman he loved, the eyes quickly shifting, becoming wider spaced, the nose shrinking, but only the tiniest bit, any changes in height and weight indiscernible, with the two of them—Stephanie *and* Elizabeth—so similar to begin with.

Elizabeth swayed as if relearning how to stand. John hugged her close, again wishing he could cry, regretting that Garland had cut that function from him. Then, feeling her legs were weak, he guided her to the table.

She moaned, her eyes clenched, and her left hand rubbed her forehead as if trying to massage away some horrible headache. Then she looked at John and gave a sorrowful smile.

John's heart sank.

He looked at the sky, needing a reprieve—if only for a moment—from Elizabeth's reproving gaze. But instead of seeing the clear view that had been there moments before, he saw a sky quickly filling with heavy-laden clouds.

This was not supposed to happen. Elizabeth should've come back like the first time. With Lori's sacrifice, Elizabeth had returned initially numb, with no memory of her suicide. She'd stayed with him for thirteen days before falling asleep and dissolving into dust. But then, almost two years later, with Kay, she'd come back traumatized, knowing she'd blown her brains out. He'd managed to calm her down and get her home, where she'd stayed for only three days. Then, the nightmare—Michelle's offering bringing Elizabeth back for only minutes.

A handful of hellish minutes.

"This has got to stop." Elizabeth was on her knees at the lake, drenched from—but oblivious to—the rain pelting like bullets shot from the guns of seraphim.

John also ignored the weather. "I need you." He looked for sympathy in Elizabeth's eyes, and sensed very little, not knowing if what there was, was for him, or for her own cursed return. He sat on the table where he'd proposed years earlier, hands reaching down and caressing her cheeks. "I can't . . . let you go."

Elizabeth stared, tears, perhaps, moving down her cheeks along with the rain. John hoped that was the case, knowing that then it would mean she still had some feelings for him. "You're murdering people, John. Women. And . . . you're doing this for me? FOR ME? Because you love me?" She grabbed John's hands and tore them from her, pointed a stabbing finger and yelled: "You remember? YOU remember, Master Warlock, how I had to escape you?" The finger jabbed to the words, her clear blue eyes penetrating to his core. "You remember," she commanded, "what I was willing to do, and then you wonder? You fucking wonder, you sonofabitch, what I'll be willing to do to escape you again!"

And he remembered. . .

In the beginning, sex hadn't been a problem. In fact, for Elizabeth, sex with him had been thrilling, but later, and not too far into their relationship, she found out his problem.

He couldn't give. He could thrust, flick, lick, tweak, pinch, nibble, kiss, bite, and do all the mechanics, but there was a lack of sensitivity, a void, where there should have been a union, a meeting of their hearts. This tore into John, and butchered Elizabeth's feelings, her self-esteem. Eventually, she came to believe his confession, that it was *his* problem. And that it was a problem he *couldn't* fix.

Elizabeth had also discovered it would be during sex—not lovemaking, never lovemaking—that she could make her break.

From the moment she'd learned what he was, John had her leashed. Financially she was outgunned. He could track her anywhere, could buy anything or anyone to serve and answer his bidding. But more, she knew she was bound to his power, knew he could sense whenever she planned to bolt. Knew he could quiet her, too, with but a whispered word, or a small swirl made in the air with his little finger, quiet her for a time more strongly than any administered bit of Valium.

But not during sex.

Then, with focus turned upon the ravenous need to climax, he'd be blind to everything, and especially to the stirrings within his wife.

They were fucking. Elizabeth hated to think of it like that, but they both understood that's what they did, and over the years they'd learned to make do.

She'd been poured over with Red Door perfume, her nude body ripe for invasion. Her arms were raised, holding the headboard to push herself back on to him, as he, on his knees—spread so far apart he was almost doing the splits—held onto her thighs, and with body straight, pounded her rapidly, a staccato sound of *slap slap slap* echoing throughout the bedroom, his thrustings coming close to moving their king-sized bed.

Elizabeth moaned, her sounds of *ah . . . ah . . . God*, matching the rams against her shaved mound. John could envision her face, the dreamy quality it took when she was getting laid. But he didn't open his eyes to check.

He was too busy concentrating.

. . . *slap slap slap*. . .

"John. *Ah . . . ah, John*." . . . *slap slap slap slap*. . . "John!"

And he opened his eyes and saw—

The gun, a .38 Lady Smith. Surprisingly, not pointed at him, but under Elizabeth's chin.

. . . *slap slap slap*. . .

"I loved you." Her pain was clear. "But I've got to go." She squeezed the trigger, and brains and skull blew against the headboard—an instant hell-spawned Picasso of blood, matter, and fluids—with splatter and Beth-fragments decorating the pillow, the sheets, her body, John's front—his face.

He screamed, "Nooo." And to his everlasting shame, with eyes pleading to cry, he realized his betraying cock had climaxed from his dead wife's still-spasming body.

Bitter cold blowing from the lake jerked John back to the present. He looked at his wife, regret radiating throughout his body. Feelings coursed through him, as well: anger toward his choices, the mother who sold her son for a mere week's worth of opium, at Garland for transforming him, and even at Elizabeth, for never accepting him and enjoying the life he'd tried to provide.

"Honey?"

Elizabeth's face was difficult to read. She looked sad, with signature dimples rising to the surface as she sported a partial frown. "John, you never were one to listen."

He tried to give a compassionate grin. "Not about losing you. Never that." John started to step forward, but Elizabeth halted him with an outstretched palm.

Elizabeth stood. This time there was no mistaking whether or not she had any strength. She stood easily, with an economy of motion and with a grace that even in the simple act of standing, was still beautiful to his eyes.

"You're feeling good?"

"I'm feeling like you, hon." The words cut. "I'm feeling damned."

John did his best to ignore the castigation, his mind too busy searching for something positive to say, but then something caught his attention, sent shivers up his spine. Elizabeth was oblivious to the cold. The sleeveless vest Stephanie had worn showed Elizabeth's arms clearly in the darkening night, and they were smooth. The ten-thousand involuntary signals that a body gives off when in the bite of chill were all absent.

Something was wrong. Terribly wrong.

His scars started to respond to a charge in the air. There was no stopping it. He could feel them moving beyond the layers of his soul, moving outward, surfacing, coming from under his flesh, raising under his ski—

—and then they were visible, looking like brands, welts . . . *scars*. A lotus-hand on his left cheek appearing as a welt, hard and ugly, a pentagram of conjuration on his forehead. The sign of Anubis lay on the right side of his face, its lower parts moving down his neck and under his shirt, hundreds of others covered his body now, many overlapping, some starting to writhe.

Readying John for war.

What the hell? John briefly thought, before his hands shot out at Elizabeth, thumbs and middle-fingers closing on one another, the other three fingers of each hand pointing toward his wife, the gesture automatic, the casting of a ward of protection. His other-vision could see energy forming around his hands, blue and red light starting to arc from finger to finger, hand to hand.

A flash of lightning lanced the sky, the bolt striking and obliterating into black char several tall cedars behind Elizabeth. Quickly following, came the thunder, a booming that sounded like some horrid devil belching from a perch in Pandemonium.

Elizabeth, still standing, but with feet now in the air, several inches off the ground, laughed—long, hard, and raw, a voice not her own, but still vaguely familiar. She lifted a finger . . . her ring-finger, and said in her own voice: "I warned you, John. You bumbling fool. I begged, I *goddamned* pleaded . . . but you *wouldn't* stop."

John felt fear. It wasn't the first time, but it was the first since he'd been a child that he'd feared for his life. He felt his own energies starting to fade before his wife, the blue and red lights that had been arcing about his hands—Ra's Blessing—starting to flicker before disappearing entirely. He'd been rendered naked. He couldn't fathom what had happened. Elizabeth was crafting, *here,* in front of him, *to* him, and he didn't know how, or *if* he could stop her—or if he even wanted to. "I don't understand." He told the truth. "What's going on? What are you doing? I . . . love you. That's all any of this was ever about."

"Really, Warlock?" Elizabeth rose in the air till her vested chest was on-line with John's face.

John suddenly felt weak, first in the legs, but then at the center of his conjuration power, the mark on his forehead, the mark signifying him as a master, the mark that was faltering beneath a simple woman, a dead woman.

Not dead anymore, John lamented. I made sure of that.

What the hell am I going to do?

Elizabeth let out a cackling laugh, one that hit the air in time with another flash of lightning, the bolt this time hitting Elizabeth in the hand.

No, not her hand, John observed, but her ring. He knew the mark of the bolt, and his fear grew. *Necros-Astrape.* "Lightning of Death." She has it, he realized, she has the warlock's fang. Garland's fang . . . in a different form, oh yeah, big-damn-deal, but still his fang.

"Feel your folly," Elizabeth yelled as more lightning poured into the ring.

Suddenly, John felt himself thrust a couple of feet into the air, jerked by invisible fingers from the heavens, but beckoned by something far deeper. Then his back bridged violently and his arms and legs were pulled away from his body, marking him in the air as a living X.

John froze. He stared at Elizabeth, watched as a dark blue light formed into a ball around her left hand, before bleeding up her arm and over the rest of her, in mere moments surrounding her in a witch's aura.

"I haven't been alone, John. Oh, no, lover, not alone at all. I tried to warn you. Garland tried to warn you—"

Garland! John pondered. How the hell did she find out about—?

"—many, many years ago, but you wouldn't heed wisdom."

He remembered Garland's sagacity: "John, if you love something, set it free. If it comes back . . . then it's yours. If it doesn't . . . hunt it down and *kill* it."

"Now we're here, *they're* all here, John—everyone you've murdered, and they're hungry. And I can't stop them . . . not my surrogates, nor any of the others."

John couldn't begin to recall all those he'd put down, but he remembered many, remembered them by name: Elizabeth, surely a victim of his as much as all the rest, Lori, Kay, so many others . . . Michelle, Brian, Hobbsworth, Jeremy, so, so many more—Garland's voice was there, too.

Then he started to feel . . .

. . . an itching over his entire body . . . that became a burning, then a BURNING.

He was on fire. Warlock's Wrath, John knew. It licked away his clothes, turning them to ash, but left his flesh alone, opting to burn deeper, to the searing of his soul. His eyes clenched tight and he screamed.

And he screamed again, even as he felt his throat turn hoarse, raw, then useless, blood flowing down his esophagus from the deep gash his teeth had involuntarily gnawed into his tongue. He tried to protect himself. Words of a darker canting vainly worked to escape from his lips, but they disappeared like mist, his crafting powerless against the fang.

John forced his eyes open, hoping to see Elizabeth.

She was still there, floating, surrounded by witch's light, still dark-blue, but getting darker, turning midnight-black, but still visible—Elizabeth *still* visible.

Crying? John pondered, seeing tears streaking down his beloved's face. He suddenly felt hope for deliverance, even as he involuntarily pulled against the invisible vises holding him in the air.

He tried to beg, but only a raspy "*Beeeth*" came out. Then his body started to go into a spin, a counterclockwise turning that fanned wind into his body, billowing out his cheeks and stretching the skin around his eyes, thrusting his orbs to one side. John briefly wondered if his eyes would soon burst in a splash of oracular fluid, a red-and-white cocktail decorating his face, a tribute to when he'd been sprayed with Elizabeth's own warm blood.

Straining against the spin, the pressure building in his skull, he cried again: "Eliz . . . aaa . . . *beeth.*"

John's mind whirled with his body, bewilderment and terror his only anchors of assurance that all that was happening was real. No dream here no dream here no dream here no fucking dream here, ha ha.

Then he stopped—on a dime, body instantly still, but his sweetbreads, lungs, everything, smashed to one side. The pressure on his wrists and ankles was still there, and getting worse—the invisible clamps slowly crushing bones in their merciless grip.

John tried to see, but couldn't. His eyes had become empty vessels without focus, dizzy spheres in his hammering skull, uncontrollable, and with no allegiance to his brain's commands.

His mind, though, *did* feel. His marks, glyphs, symbols and runes, the blade-etched names of power of Egyptian and Babylonian gods, of European devils and saints, Japanese *oni,* and Native American manitous, began to harden on his body, forming themselves into a grotesque tableau of cicatricial flesh.

Behind John, the lake came alive, an ominous movement he knew bode nothing well. He craned his head over a shoulder, wanting to know the cause of the sound.

His other-vision saw the water was churning, boiling it seemed, a 10-foot wide swath of water running from the bank and off toward the center of the lake, and into darkness.

John saw fish start to float: bass, catfish, and trout—all dead.

"John?" came many-voices-as-one.

He turned back to the front, the movement dipping his nerves in ground glass.

Elizabeth was there, still floating, but closer now, left hand clenched, crackling with dark force.

"I'm sorry." Elizabeth caressed John's cheek. "I truly am."

"Please. Don't do this, let me go. Let me go, and I'll let . . . I'll *let* you go."

"Me go?" Elizabeth's visage started to change, subtly for a few seconds, getting

217

older, with just the slightest signs of newfound crow's-feet around the eyes, and then aging rapidly, her once unchecked beauty becoming that of an old crone. John felt himself moving backward, undoubtedly toward his doom. Elizabeth moved with him. "I'm no longer yours to set free. Another has done that, a price I had to pay. A promise I *had* to make."

With tortured eyes, and an even more tortured understanding of what was happening, John glanced at the water, at the swath of bubbling liquid below. He again took in the boiled fish and wished he, too, were now dead, but understanding he wasn't going to be that blessed.

Then his body stopped, an ever-growing and speeding whirlpool of water forming below, a gaping swirl of bubbling black-in-the-night liquid that led *not* into the depths of the lake, but to a far darker place. He knew who'd promised Elizabeth her final rest.

Garland, John thought. You bastard of a whore-devil's ass.

His body rested in the air, its X shape still held by invisible manacles, waves of pain continuing to pulse through his nervous system from the wrenching of his muscles, the forced activation of his marks of power, the scars of passage that had transcended him from mere mortal, the witch's fire blazing from his wife—Garland's fang.

I'm being pushed aside, John thought. By the god's . . . I'm being pushed aside. The revelation hit with the force of an iron cudgel, incredulity and shame for having been so stupid, *so* manipulated.

Elizabeth now looked like a mummy: clothes rotted, flesh rapidly turning to dust, its particles blowing away in the night's feral wind, her face all but a skull.

"*Goooood*-bye, Joh—"

Listening to Elizabeth's final farewell, John turned as the last of her blew away. He'd not missed the forlorn regret in his wife's parting salutation, nor missed the signification of her words—Beth's recognition of his final damnation.

Then his bones started to mend, and a thousand other wounds began to heal. Again Garland's fang—fitting itself onto his finger—denying him any escape.

"John?"

He heard the voice, but not from without, not now, not with the ring resting on his finger. No. He heard it from within his *own* vessel, the home from which he'd soon be banished. He saw the swirling pool below, the chasm that would lead his spirit to. . . Elizabeth was right, there'd be others waiting—and hungry.

"Garland?"

"Time to go, boy," the old master said, the command filled with dread portent, with each word consecutively different, sounding different, with the first word spoken in Garland's voice, in a tone and with a sound that was as John remembered, but with each word following quite different, more vibrant and alive, y*ounger,* the sentence closing out with the wizard sounding like a young man, a young play-toy apprentice, wannabe, perhaps—the last word coming out as if spoken with John's own tongue—for it was. "You have erred in not following the path. Erred with your love."

He spoke the truth. "Garland, please—"

"You'll dwell in me, now . . . till I die." Garland laughed. "But you'll not be alone. There are those who've gone before, sacrificed themselves, *like* you, despite my warnings. But there are others, too, John. Those that you've struck down, those bound to you, never to be released till your ultimate passion. They will spend eternity eating and shatting you out, their epicurean feast never-ending. If I could stop it, I would. But I will not die for you, and I'm tired of sleeping. Your foolish love awakened me, and now I'm making my new home . . . out of *you.*"

Descending, John, with other-vision fading, looked down. He *knew* what waited at the bottom of his fall, the cackle and *rap-rap-rap* of knuckles and bone banging together, fur being preened, teeth and fang and horn, fetid breath, forms that had once been human, but since malignantly warped by their torment, by their lust for revenge.

Comeuppance into perpetuity.

Yes, he knew Garland's words were true, even as he felt himself slip away, and Garland taking residence, taking the place of his soul and heart within his body, soon to live in *his* home, to sport *his* flesh and muscle, till one day another apprentice turned pseudo-master, made his sacrifice. He *knew* as he floated downward, that he would be eaten and expelled, with no parting, no rest, and no escape, till the day his master, the *true* master, finally died.

He thought of screaming, but laughed at the senselessness.

The wails would start soon enough.